FIFTY-FIRST STATE

FIFTY-FIRST STATE

Hilary Bailey

This first world edition published 2008
in Great Britain and 2009 in the USA by
SEVERN HOUSE PUBLISHERS LTD of
9–15 High Street, Sutton, Surrey, England, SM1 1DF.

British Library Cataloguing in Publication Data

Bailey, Hilary, 1936-
  Fifty-first state
  1. Conservative Party (Great Britain) - Corrupt practices -
  Fiction 2. Terrorism - Great Britain - Fiction 3. Great
  Britain - Social conditions - Fiction 4. Great Britain -
  Politics and government - Fiction 5. Suspense fiction
  I. Title
  823.9'14[F]

  ISBN-13: 978-0-7278-6693-6   (cased)

All Severn House titles are printed on acid-free paper.

Typeset by Palimpsest Book Production Ltd.,
Grangemouth, Stirlingshire, Scotland.
Printed and bound in Great Britain by
MPG Books Ltd., Bodmin, Cornwall.

Thanks to friends at the Crouch End Novelists' Group, especially Margaret D'Armenia, Iris Ansell, Jennie Christian, Dave Cohen, Lawrence Estrey, Frances Kelly and Gail Robinson.

And to Ian Abley.

Part One

One

A woman, Jenny Henderson, sits under an old, twisted-trunk apple tree which is just coming into leaf, in the back garden of a house in north-west London. It is evening. It will be dark in two hours. She faces her house, where, in the dimly lit kitchen, a man's figure is moving to and fro. She sits at a slatted pine garden table, writing in a notebook with a ballpoint pen. She is wearing two sweaters, a thick skirt, thick tights and sturdy brown shoes. Overhead, a noisy blackbird is hectoring its mate. The woman has already written:

> This will be my account of the events leading up to what we are now calling 'The Occupation'. Officially, of course, it's not an occupation. It is 'Assistance'. But with the fighter planes screaming over the country as if to tell us 'We are here', the skies full of surveillance helicopters, and helmeted Marines in military vehicles driving through our cities and villages it certainly feels like an occupation. That's what we call it, anyway, and so do our European neighbours.
>
> My story of some of the events in the two years leading up to this US Occupation is personal. I'm a fairly ordinary woman, a solicitor, in my fifties, living in a London suburb. All I intend to do is record the lives and thoughts of people I knew, or of people they knew, during the cruelly brief period when Britain somehow turned itself from an independent democracy into a US client state. The Fifty-first State, we say. I plan to tell the story as carefully as I can, only embroidering where I think it safe to do so. Some of the people I'll be writing about are important in the world, some are not. All they have in common is that I know them and I've talked to them. Myself, I was and still am a bystander — except when it came to the terrible matter of William Frith and Jemal Al Fasi.

This preamble concluded, Jenny puts down her pen. She is a tall, middle-aged, ordinary-looking woman, round-faced and blue-eyed. As a young woman she was probably pretty, but this is not a face to retain good looks into middle age. Nevertheless, she is pleasant-looking, steady-eyed and clear-skinned. An observer would sum her up as reliable; a woman who could find a fire extinguisher in a crisis, make up an ice pack for a sprain, feed unexpected guests without fuss, a woman to whom a distraught woman would turn, crying, 'Have you seen my little boy?' and expect a sensible response.

Suddenly, still holding her pen, Jenny turns and looks round at the house behind her, a house just like her own. Beyond the garden wall of this house, though, the ground is untended, brambles encroach on a strag-gled lawn, a path and old flower beds are overgrown. Jenny smiles up at the unlit first-floor window. The smile that then illuminates her face somehow belies the imaginary observer's first impressions. It is not a nice smile. It is like that of a girl waving a toy round the corner of a door, showing her brother that though he hid it, she has found it. Or like a man looking at a long-standing business enemy and smiling at him to hint that he now has nearly enough evidence to put his rival into the hands of the Serious Fraud Office. It is a smile in the grey area between 'Gonna get you' and 'Gotcha'. Why would an apparently nice, ordinary woman be smiling malignantly like this at the dark windows of a neighbouring house?

She turns back and writes on:

Inside the house my husband is preparing supper while the power is on. I hope he'll be inventive – we're short of food as well – or it will be bread, cheese and tomatoes, as so often. Meanwhile there are only two hours of daylight left and it's getting chilly. Not that I – and all of us – don't rejoice with the spring. We spent the winter, an unusually cold one, like medieval peasants, though peasants, for the most part, without fireplaces. Because of the oil shortages we had electricity for four, perhaps five hours a day. Two hours in the morning, two in the evening. No warmth, no light, the rest of the time. The only good part was that we had time to get used to it – you do get used to it, up to a point – because the big oil crisis came in August last year, 2016. During the autumn our blood thickened, we detected the draughts and gradually learnt the half-forgotten tricks of keeping warm in winter without oil or electricity.

Hard times, indeed. And we are left asking the age-old questions – how did we get here and will we ever be able to get back to where we were? I don't know whether my story will answer the first question and it certainly won't answer the second. But there's an odd, stubborn part of people that insists on wanting to testify and I suppose I'm doing this because of that stubbornness, the stubbornness of the witness on the stand, who insists on pouring out his story, relevant or irrelevant to the case in hand, heedless of an impatient judge, a sceptical jury and an apathetic courtroom crowd. History, as we're told, is written by the winners — well, I say, not always. I say, here is my truth, not *the* truth, but my truth. And I say — if not now, when? If not me, who?

London. April 4th, 2015. 4 p.m.

Looking from his helicopter window, Lord Gott, a director of a City investment bank and treasurer of the Conservative Party, saw below him the suburban houses of London's outskirts, with their little patches of garden and tiny cars moving down ribbon-like streets. Further on, they were over the crowded inner areas and then, only minutes later, there was the river, and then they were turning sharply just behind the Victorian-ornate Houses of Parliament. One of the ugliest buildings in London, Edward Gott considered, though it was his workplace, or one of them.

They began to follow the river south. He noticed the water was high, slopping over the embankment again. At the start of the century the tide had risen from sixteen to twenty-five feet daily. Now it routinely rose five feet higher. An extra five feet, at spring and autumn tides, was no joke for a city built on a river. Nor was there any guarantee it wouldn't go higher. But tall proud buildings, apparently undaunted, gleamed on both banks of the Thames in the sunshine of late afternoon as Gott's helicopter swept over them. An impressive sight, he thought, if you hadn't studied the projections. It was a huge mess of a city, 500 square miles of it, population over thirteen million now and if large areas had to be evacuated – where would they go? The Thames Gateway project, the plan to expand London eastwards, had been stalled for the last fifteen years, hit by a dragging recession which had reduced public spending and had put contractors out of business, because now the insurance companies had also read the projections and the word 'flood plain' sounded to them like 'plague'. Just another of those situations the government could do nothing about – whichever one was in power.

There had been three elections since May 2010, when Gordon Brown's Labour Party achieved an overall majority of only three seats.

Governing with a majority of three is near impossible. In 2012 the country went back to the polls, Labour hoping to achieve a more workable majority. But with the country in recession, the Conservatives won with a majority of eight over Labour, with the Liberal Democrats holding the balance of power. Less than 40 per cent of the electorate had voted in the 2010 election and a mere 32 per cent turned out in 2012 to elect the new government, headed by Frederick Muldoon, a compromise between one contender (too right wing) and the other (too wet.) After two elections in five years, neither conclusive, the government of Britain was being regarded cynically, at home and abroad.

It couldn't go on, Gott thought. If steps weren't taken to solve the situation it would, inevitably, solve itself, and probably in ways no one wanted. You either sorted it out, or it sorted you out, that was the way, in his experience, it worked with businesses and individuals. There was no reason to think governments were any different. 'So you say, so you say, Edward Gott,' Gott told himself. 'Perhaps one day you'll take your own advice and do something about your own predicament.' But he knew he wouldn't. Not now, not after all this time.

But even that thought did not depress him. He'd flown south after breakfast at his house in Scotland. Nothing there to encourage a man, he thought, remembering the frozen look on his wife's face as he looked out of the helicopter window before leaving – she had never liked the paddock being taken over to serve as a helicopter pad. Nothing much in his later date, either, lunching near Lancaster with his factory's research team and finding them as difficult as ever to deal with. He knew they saw his visits like the arrival of an armed man at Mass in a monastery, clanking down the aisle, causing fear and distraction. They wouldn't let him in at all if he weren't paying their mortgages, as well as for every other damn thing in the building. If his team wanted to be involved in pure research, Gott believed, they should seek employment at a university. As long as he was paying they had to come up with results – and not keep them from him when they did. So far, Gott's day had not been pleasant. But now he stretched, luxuriously. He wondered why, with all these hassles, he felt so good. Fifty-four now, fighting fit and undeterred. How long could he go on like this?

The helicopter thrummed on down the Thames. And then there'd be another treat – Graham Barnsbury. As soon as they landed at Greenwich he'd be off to meet the Party Chairman at the House of Commons. Barnsbury was a big, thickset man whom Gott regarded an overgrown public schoolboy, while Barnsbury, he guessed, thought of him, Gott, as a Lowland Scotsman on the make. But they'd get along, as they had to. The problem was that, as Party Treasurer, Gott would not be bringing Barnsbury good news. He'd not brought him any good news since the previous November, when he had been able to announce a half-million-pound donation from a supporter. Which still left the party broke and in debt, although six months further away from bankruptcy. Since then the party finances had been on life support. Gott still had nothing to tell Barnsbury that Barnsbury wanted to hear and, as on other occasions, Gott would sense that Barnsbury blamed him for the shortage of money. The curse of treasurers everywhere. Telling him that the Conservative Party was in much the same position as the Labour Party and only marginally

worse off than the Liberal Democrats would not help. Nor would it help
to remind Barnsbury that the only salvation lay in the Prime Minister
making an effort to push through a bill to fund political parties from the
public purse. Which the PM would not do, because to achieve it he would
need all-party support; all the parties feared that if the state did take over
party funding their banks might instantly call in their debts. In addition,
the PM feared a public outcry about using taxpayers' money to maintain
the parties of 650 MPs they did not like or trust. And, even if all those
things had not been true, Muldoon was so battered by struggles with the
other parties, whose support he needed to get his votes through, and
so worn down by infighting inside his own party that, Gott thought,
he probably had to call for help to lace up his shoes in the morning.
So, Gott decided, he'd have to put up with Barnsbury and his air of
disappointment again.

The helicopter swung towards Greenwich, where the pier was under
water. The *Ark Royal* was bobbing around like a cork at the end of its
anchor chains. They came down on the landing pad, and Gott climbed
out, thanked the pilot and went to his waiting car. He'd cut Barnsbury
short, he decided, go to his bank in Leadenhall Street and deal with what
had arisen since he'd left London the day before and then treat himself
to supper at Sugden's with his friends and protégées Julia Baskerville and
Joshua Crane. They'd be having their usual meeting there, to discuss their
weekly political programme which would be going out on TV later in
the week. He'd be welcome. Julia and Joshua were fun. He'd end his day
on a good note because, then, by God, he'd deserve it.

Gott greeted his young, tall and thin private secretary-cum-assistant
Jeremy Saunders at his waiting car and entered the opulent eight-seater,
custom-made for him because he owned the company. Gott took the
front passenger seat and Jeremy started up. It was only a second before
suspicion flooded Gott's mind. He swung round to look beyond the parti-
tion to the larger part of the vehicle. The seats were all empty but lying
silently on the floor was Jeremy's intelligent Border collie, Finn. Finn
looked sideways at Gott and away again. Lord Gott did not like dogs in
general and Finn in particular, perhaps because Finn was an individual
with whom Gott had to share Jeremy.

Gott turned back. 'Jeremy – how many times do I have to tell you I
don't want that dog in the car?'

'I had to take him to the vet.'

'Nothing serious, I hope,' Gott said harshly, meaning the opposite.

'I felt a lump in his tail. It turned out to be a piece of shot. Must have
been there for ages. He must have been in the way of a gun.'

Gott had the grace not to say any more, although Jeremy knew what
he was thinking. They were drumming along beside the brimming river,

the Houses of Parliament in sight. Jeremy reflected that Gott and Finn had more in common than Gott suspected. They were both intelligent, energetic, self-interested and quick but shallow thinkers – although, Jeremy thought, Finn was of course infinitely more loyal.

Fox Square, London, SW1. April 5th, 2015. 1.30 a.m.

In five hours it would be dawn. The pale sun of early spring would come up, striking the glass of the tall towers of the City of London from the East, gleaming on to the spires and domes of churches, glancing off the water of the River Thames, hitting the east side of the Mother of Parliaments, and filling the streets slowly with light.

Just off one of the streets close to Parliament, dark at this hour, lit only by the weak gleam of mock-Victorian street lights, lies a little square, Fox Square. At one end is the eighteenth-century church of St Botolph's. On the remaining three sides are three-storey Georgian houses. In the centre of the square is a small island, on which stands an equestrian statue of General Sir Galahad Montmorency Havelock, hero of two Afghan Wars. He is seated on a spirited horse, sword raised, rallying his men to the attack. Carved on the pedestal beneath his feet are his dates. Born in 1828, he died on the North West Frontier in 1879. By a coincidence, his great-great grandson had just been killed there, in the rubble of the Khyber Pass.

On the side of the square facing the church, and sideways on to Sir Galahad, in the middle of a row of ten houses, there is a famous restaurant, Sugden's. The surrounding houses are tenanted, as is shown on the gleaming brass plates outside, by firms of solicitors, charities or organizations connected directly or indirectly with the government of the country. The agents of the ducal landlord of the houses would never allow any but the most respectable of firms as tenants. It's unlikely that if Sugden's – a mere restaurant – applied for a lease now they would get it, but Sugden's is an institution. Sugden's has been in Fox Square since the days when it was a chop house catering for members of Queen Victoria's Parliaments and the scribblers who wrote about it.

The small windows on either side of the door are masked by lace curtains little different from those which had hung there in the days of Empire. On the six inches of lintel above the front door the name 'Sugden's' is picked out in black on white. No larger sign could be allowed, nor could any changes be made to the front of the building, but this lack of advertising was not a disadvantage, perhaps the reverse.

Inside the front door is an oak counter, manned at that time by two elderly sisters, big Miss Bonner and small Miss Bonner. To the left, still, is the restaurant, a large room, which was probably at one time the drawing room and dining room of the house. Most of the back wall is now a large window looking out on to a small walled patio, where at night soft lamps burn and, in summer, tables stand.

On this particular night, only two parties of diners remained. One was a group of six men, sitting at the back of the room. The man at the head of the table for six – two businesslike-looking Chinese men, a Frenchman and three Englishmen – called for his bill. William Frith, a tall, thin man in his early thirties came forward with the bill on a plate and handed it to the host, a former Cabinet Minister, who enquired jovially if anyone would like a last drink before they parted. All, to William Frith's relief, declined. 'All right, then, gentlemen,' said their host. 'But I shall be more insistent when we meet after the contracts are signed. I won't take no for an answer then.'

After he had dealt with the bill and seen the men off, relocking the front door after them, William returned to his post. Only two diners, a man and a woman sitting near the windows, were now left so William took the opportunity of sitting down. He wore a dinner jacket and a black tie, his pale brown hair was still sleek and tidy after a long evening but his long face was pale and there were smudges under his large, pleasant brown eyes. He had spent most of the day painting his bathroom, before going on duty at six.

William loved his job. All he wished now was that the couple by the window, lingering over Armagnacs and black coffee, would go, freeing him to go upstairs, get into his day clothes and take the bus back to his flat in Shepherd's Bush and his wife, Lucy. However the restaurant owner, Jack Prentiss, had a firm policy that Sugden's clients should be allowed to stay almost as long as they liked. A lunch might stretch into dinner, a dinner into the early hours of the morning and still the staff would not cough, yawn, shuffle, look discontented or attack the guests by asking, too often, if they required anything else. Only at three would Jack, who lived upstairs and whose hours of sleep were tailored to the movements of his business, come downstairs and ask his guests to leave.

William's eyes, large, soft and fringed with dark curly lashes, rested on the remaining couple seated by the window. His job was to know who belonged to which party, ministry or newspaper, although he himself had no interest in politics. From childhood on he had tuned them out, the way other people tune out football, high finance or health information. Of course, he knew that the pretty, dark-haired woman in the pale linen jacket was Mrs Julia Baskerville, Labour Member of Parliament for Whitechapel Road and Stepney Green, elected three years earlier by the poor London constituency. That was after her predecessor had blotted his copybook with his leadership and been deselected, to be seen no

more. Before that she'd been — what? — a teacher, a lecturer or something. Julia's good-looking companion, who reminded William vaguely
of Lawrence of Arabia in the classic movie, was Joshua Crane, the
Conservative Member for Frognal and South Hampstead. He'd been in
the House for ten years. Julia and Joshua were partners on *Westminster
Unplugged*, the weekly TV show about Parliament, chaired by the skinny
and sardonic Hugh Patterson, previously editor of two national papers.
Their sharp comments, and the way they flirted with each other and
ragged the presenter like naughty schoolchildren was enjoyed by a small
but devoted audience.

William liked them. He also thought there was nothing more than
friendship between them — something he was also paid to know. From
what he knew Julia was married to a surgeon who worked in Houston,
Texas. They were running a long-distance marriage. There was a little
girl. Joshua Crane was also married. William had never seen his wife.

William suppressed a yawn. Julia and Joshua's companion at the table,
Lord Gott, had disappeared hours earlier and he wished the couple had
gone with him, instead of hanging on and on gossiping and laughing.

'Should we do the National Government on the programme?' Julia
asked Joshua.

'We featured it two months ago,' Joshua pointed out.

'Well — what about the prospect of another election?'

'You're getting tired. We did that then, too. Hugh Patterson wouldn't
let it happen.'

'How can we stop talking about it? It's *the* topic. There's no choice
now. We must have a National Government.'

'You're out of office. You would say that, wouldn't you?' Joshua told
Julia. They both knew that the only way forward was an all-party govern-
ment, with Labour and Liberal Democrats in the Cabinet. But Joshua's
Party Leader, the Prime Minister, would never agree to it. The Liberal
Democrats and Labour, being out of power, were in favour. Frederick
Muldoon, though, was in power and not planning to surrender any of it.

'Come on, Joshua. Everything's been stalled for years. It's like living
in the Weimar Republic. A National Government's the only way and you
know it.'

Joshua, who had to support his PM, whatever he thought privately,
said nothing.

Julia turned and caught William's eye. 'I'm sorry, William,' she called
over. 'Give us the bill and we'll go.' She turned back to Joshua. 'They're
saying the Queen's in favour of it.'

'Right,' Joshua acknowledged without enthusiasm.

The business of the bill worked out nicely. It was Julia's turn to pay
— William took a bit off the bill because he liked her. It was Joshua's turn

to tip, so he gave William nearly double what William might have expected. Everyone was happy. Outside the restaurant, as they waited for their taxis, Julia said, 'That policeman rang me up again.'

Joshua laughed. Julia's suitor was a joke between them. A month earlier the spring tides had brought a foot of water into the House of Commons. The proposed billion-pound barrage in the Thames Estuary had never been built. So the water came up and Julia had fallen off a duckboard leading from the car park to the entrance, into the arms of a waiting policeman, who had twice rung her to ask her out for a drink.

'Has the committee come up with an answer?' said Joshua. Julia's friend Alison was on the committee – known, of course, as the Canute Committee.

'They're talking of allowances for Commons' staff for protective footwear,' Julia told him.

'Wellington boots?' Joshua said.

'That's right.' The first taxi – Julia's – arrived. It was hydrogen powered. Julia insisted on using oil-less, in spite of the problems with reliability the taxi fleets sometimes had. In this eco-friendly vehicle Julia would return to her small terraced house in Whitechapel.

Joshua, getting into his own petrol-fuelled cab, asked the driver to take him to an address in Battersea. But just after they had started up he leaned forward and requested the driver go to Chelsea.

William locked the door, cleared the table at which Joshua and Julia had been sitting, put everything on a trolley, ran it through the swinging baize doors to the kitchen, then hurried upstairs past the private dining rooms on the first floor and up to the top of the house. There was a small room off the landing where hanging racks held the waiters' and waitresses' black suits and dresses. He whipped out of his suit and was just doing up his other trousers when his boss, the owner of Sugden's, came out of his flat, pale as a vampire, in his usual purple smoking jacket. William had heard the sound of a television from behind Jack's front door, but had quite hoped, at this hour, to avoid an encounter. He took his jacket from a hanger.

'Everything all right, William?' asked Jack.

'Pretty good,' William answered. 'Twenty covers, not bad for a weekday, and table six had three bottles of Bollinger. One card was refused so the diner paid cash.'

'Who was that?'

'Edward Jeffreys,' William told him.

Jack nodded. 'There's a divorce pending. Pick up anything about an election?'

William shook his head. Jack said, 'Fine.' It was not the fate of a great nation that concerned the restaurateur. It was that during the course of an election campaign, normally lasting something like six weeks, the restaurant would be largely empty. The clientele would be in their constituencies, campaigning, or burning the midnight oil to produce statistics or publicity. They would be studying graphs, poring over newspaper leaders, monitoring broadcasts, creating smears, awaiting the results of opinion polls, all involved in the short but tough episode that is a British election campaign.

'Good,' Jack said. 'That'll keep the private rooms full.'

A group wanting to dine in private, to plan and conspire, would often take one of Sugden's two upstairs private dining rooms. This was filling Jack Prentiss's bank account. From time to time the cabal from one dining room would bump into members of the group they were conspiring against on the landing separating the two dining rooms. William had once asked Jack why secret meetings were so often held in this less-then-secret restaurant, a stone's throw from Parliament and Whitehall. He said the conspirators could have kept their secrets more secret if they'd met in a Little Chef on the M1.

Jack had told him, 'You've got to remember that when Parliament's in session politicians can't breathe the air more than a mile from Westminster.'

William started downstairs.

'All-night bus?' Jack called after him. William had the impression that Jack sometimes got lonely at night, with only his porcelain collection for company. Sometimes he tried to detain him in conversation, which William, after a long shift and yearning for home, didn't always welcome.

'How's Lucy?'

William looked up at Jack. 'I'm not sure. She's usually in bed when I get back and she's often gone to work when I get up.' He added, 'I think it's her in the bed – but it might be the woman next door, for all I know.'

Jack laughed. William didn't like it. As he left, relocking the door behind him, William reflected that shift work was hard on marriages. His boss's life proved it. Two – or had there been three? – of Jack's marriages had foundered. William had decided his would not. At the first sign of trouble he'd leave and look for another job.

He set off through the darkness to his bus stop in Whitehall. He had joined the governed, rather than the governors now: an old man carrying a black plastic bag wandering down to the river to find somewhere to sleep; a group of cleaners chatting in a foreign language on their way to the tube station. Two bemused teenagers wandered down the wide and empty Whitehall, dwarfed by the sombre height of the government buildings. There was little traffic other than the patrolling armoured police cars. The air was fresh, with a feel of spring about it.

After eight hours in the enclosed atmosphere of Sugden's William felt invigorated. He was content. Of course, he and Lucy didn't have enough time together, with Lucy on shifts beginning at 6 a.m. It was hard to meet friends who worked more normal hours. But they managed, somehow, to make their days off coincide. The mortgage got paid and they were saving to get a bigger flat, with a second bedroom, and a garden. Then they would have a baby, they hoped.

The bus eased round the corner from Parliament Square. William Frith, a happy man who had waited only five minutes for his bus on a spring night and was going home to a wife he loved, climbed on.

Off the bus, heading home, William saw, under the street lights on the other side of Shepherd's Bush Green, about 400 yards away, a group of Auxiliary Police, in their olive green uniforms. They were standing behind two young men who had their arms high up against the bonnet of an old car. The policemen were patting them down, not gently, for weapons. They were shouting, 'Don't move! Don't speak! Bastards — stand still! Bastards!' The voices of men who are aggressive — in charge — afraid. The contents of a gym bag were tipped out into the street. One of the young men, dark-skinned and terrified, turned his head towards the heap of clothing on the ground. One of the Auxiliaries handcuffed the second man. William walked by, on the other side, still hearing the shouts. Just after Christmas, on a Saturday, a suicide bomber had blown himself up in a north London synagogue. Six men had died and thirty others had been injured. Another bomb had been discovered in an underground train at New Malden. It had failed to explode. Raids on houses, chiefly Muslim, had been stepped up. Stop and searches of men who looked Mediterranean or North African increased. The powers of the Auxiliary Police had been augmented. William had no quarrel with this. Obviously the two young men weren't bombers but they might have been. Somebody had to check. He'd been stopped himself on the way home twice in a month, pushed back against a wall, sworn at, searched and let go without apology. Even so, the scene he had just witnessed made him feel uneasy, though he was not sure why. He was trying to recall some old film he must have seen on daytime TV as a boy — a dark street, old-fashioned cars pull up, uniformed men leap out — no, he'd forgotten what it was. He put it out of his mind and went home.

The White House, Washington DC, USA. April 4th, 2015. 10 p.m. (GMT).

Seated on two couches in the Oval Office, the President of the USA sipped mineral water while her Secretary of State, Ray Hollander, drank Scotch and water. Hollander's tie was loosened and the top button of his shirt open. His cheeks and chin were darkening. Had there been any public meeting that evening he would have shaved for the third time that day. His President wore a pale-blue linen suit, a baby colour Hollander associated with his second wife, who had often worn it when about to deliver a sucker punch. The President's hair and make-up were impeccable, as always, but a long day was ending and, like a flower in a vase, though unwilted, she gave the impression wilting was not far away.

'So,' she said. 'Call the Chiefs of Staff, recheck the time of the meeting and then, just late enough to catch them and not so late they think we're playing with them, get that Harvard professor into the meeting on Presidential say-so. I need the input.'

'They're not going to like it,' Hollander said.

'I don't want them to like it. I want them to know I want the truth, not a twenty-page report saying ten different things. I want to know — can we handle Afghanistan and a reinvasion of Iraq, if we need to. And will they back me, really back me, if that is what we need to do?'

'Madam President,' Hollander said. The Army did not have enough men. Already the military was discussing the possibility of a draft, hoping Vietnam was enough of a memory now. Hollander knew the spectre of the draft was for ever rising before the President's eyes. And no one thought she would introduce any form of compulsory recruitment in an election year.

He said, 'So it's really going to be Sheikh Mohammed this time?'

'That would seem to be Allah's will.'

Sheikh Mohammed Al Bactari was a senior Shia cleric, fiercely patriotic and ferociously anti-American.

Hollander looked his President in the eye and said, 'Muldoon.'

She looked straight back and said, 'Ray. Not again.'

He had never understood her distaste for Britain and British politics. It could not have been historical. The President knew no history. If it had been personal he would have known about it. Maybe she disliked the style of the Brits, how they talked, walked and thought about things. He sympathized;

he couldn't take that traditional evasive cunning either. He said, 'If these Iraq elections go bad on us and we have to reinvade, the Brits will have to go with us. The other big Europeans won't. But a lot of the Brits were against the 2002 invasion. They couldn't wait to get out. And Frederick Muldoon has no power in the House of Commons and won't ask for the support of the country because he knows he won't get it. But we have to have them, with China and India on the Security Council accusing us of trying for world domination. Then there are the Russians—'

He read her mounting impatience. She interrupted, 'You've told me the problem. Where's the solution?'

Hollander had no illusions about his President. She was tougher than he was, and more ruthless. If he was tungsten, she was kryptonite.

'There's only one. Muldoon goes and the new PM is one of ours and has a strong majority. He backs us militarily and gets rid of the nests of Islamic vipers in their major cities.'

'Just tell me what we need to do,' she said and stood up. He did the same.

'Goodnight, Madam President,' he said.

'Goodnight, Ray, and thank you.' After the President left the room two men came in, nodded and stood against the door, watching him. He nodded back and stood up. 'Just leaving, guys,' he said. But for a moment he paused, staring up at the portrait of a long-dead politician in knee breeches.

'Subvert the government of Great Britain,' he said to himself. 'Yes, ma'am. OK, ma'am. Anything you say, ma'am'

12 Emscott Drive, Hamscott Common, Kent. April 5th, 2015. 2.30 a.m.

Thirty-year-old Kim Durham woke up, sweating, with a start. She pulled herself up and lay back against the pillows. Oh, no, she thought to herself. No, not again. The dream was back, the one where Jonathan told her when he came in from work that the marriage was over, told her while she stood at the kitchen counter, cutting up peppers ('Only fresh, organic food eaten in our house,' she had boasted then), told her there was someone else, someone he worked with, as she desperately tried to understand what he was saying, while another part of her mind equally desperately hoped that five-year-old Rory would stay where he was, watching TV in the sitting room – that dream was back. It had never gone away, really, but over eighteen months it had come back less and less often, filling her with despair, wrecking the night and the next day as well.

But now it had returned. Night after night, there it was again. She knew why, of course. Because one day soon she would have to tell Rory, asleep with his plastic figure of Grimgraw, probably still muttering to him on the pillow beside him, that on the other side of the world he had a brother – half brother – his father's new son. And until she did that, she'd have no peace. But for now, she could not decide when to do it, or how. She was a teacher. She'd seen often enough the effects of such news on a child. Seen it done badly, seen it done well – she ought to be able to manage this, but she couldn't. You couldn't imagine how it would tear you apart twice – once on your own account, the second time when you looked into the eyes of a bewildered, betrayed child.

There was the scream of a flight of fighter jets overhead, that noise those who had been born and bred at Hamscott Common knew well enough to sleep through. Kim knew she wouldn't sleep tonight, or only for an hour or so, before her alarm went off. She lay down and closed her eyes, though.

Resting's as good as sleeping, she told herself. And, it'll all look better in the morning.

It did look better, a little better, as Kim and Rory drove down the country road to the school they both attended; he as a pupil, she as a teacher. It was a clear, sunny day. Big clouds were blown lazily across a blue sky. The hedgerows on either side were throwing out the first, pale budding leaves.

Rory watched a field of leaping lambs, then looked keenly forward as the car rounded a bend. To one side of the now-unhedged road was a fringe of grass. Behind this an expanse of Hamscott Common, old woodland, gorse and unfurling ferns, spread as far as the sky-line. On the other side of the road the Common stretched away, except for the area, a mile and a quarter square, which had been cleared and flattened over seventy years ago, at the beginning of the Second World War. Then it had been Hamscott Common airfield. The buildings, hastily erected, had housed the RAF squadrons fighting the Battle of Britain. From its short runways Spitfires and Wellington bombers had taken off to fight over the coast of England. A very old man who had been one of the pilots lived in the old folks' home half a mile from the base.

Since the war the airfield had expanded and been rebuilt. A short stretch of grass led to the perimeter fence, where two guards in US uniforms stood outside the high-wire gates. Seventy-five metres inside the outer fence lay a second one, also patrolled by armed soldiers. Behind a second fence was a parade ground and, to the rear of this, administration buildings. To the right was the vast expanse of runways, on which military planes stood, to the left, small homes for service personnel, all identical. Behind all this, against the backdrop of tall trees where Hamscott Common, outside the base, started again, were towers and low buildings, always patrolled. Here some thirty nuclear bombs were stored, readied for mounting on the new, heavy B63 bombers.

Rory's head was turned sharply to look at this much-looked-forward-to part of his daily trip to and from school. Often a fighter plane would scream down the runway and lift off steeply into the air, leaving a trail behind as it disappeared like an arrow into the sky. There might be soldiers drilling on the parade ground. Or sometimes a soldier would have stopped a van, and be searching the back, with two other soldiers, rifles at the ready, standing by. Today, however, from Rory's point of view, there was nothing very exciting to watch. The inside of the airbase might have been deserted. There was no one near the runways, on which fighter planes stood; no one came from or went into the administration building. The houses were quiet. Then a small boy came to the door of one of the houses, carrying a ball. A woman followed him. Her eyes seemed to flick, involuntarily, past the fences and over the narrow road, to where, as ever, there was a group of twenty people, men and women of varying ages, in anoraks. A long banner, supported on poles planted in the ground and sagging slightly, read, 'Close the Hamscott Common Nuclear Base.'

The Hamscott Common permanent vigil consisting of Quakers, left-wingers, CND members and others, had been in place for seven years. Though the personnel changed the number remained much the same. Some were people from the local area, attending on a rota system, others were more permanent and living in roughly constructed huts or tents among the trees of the Common. Occasionally, on a random basis, the police came at night in force, with bright lights and dogs, and knocked down these habitations.

The permanent demonstration had a deal with the almshouses down the road. They kept their Portaloo in the garden in front of the ancient almshouses and were offered bathing facilities by the residents. This had been done on a vote, 13-2, by the elderly residents of the almshouses. The trustees of the institution, established in the seventeenth century by a wealthy wool manufacturer, could probably have overturned this decision by their pensioners. However, the old man who had earned the DFC in 1943 and been shot down soon after, and another resident with a granddaughter on the local paper, had been vociferous. The trustees therefore thought it better to leave well enough alone. Thus, the retirement home supplied water in buckets to the demonstrators, and sneaked them in for showers, while the demonstrators replaced electric light bulbs, shifted furniture and, occasionally, smuggled in bottles of port, Guinness and whisky.

Young Rory, though, had little interest in the shabby group of people on the margin of the road opposite the base. To his mind, they just stood there, doing nothing while, on the base, there were uniformed men moving about with guns, the scream of the planes lifting off, people going in and out of the administration block and other children playing in the small gardens.

A year or so earlier he had asked his mother about the demonstrators and Kim had explained they were people who wanted the base closed down. Rory had expressed incredulity and asked why. 'They're against war,' she had told her son, knowing quite well this was hardly an explanation which would make sense to a seven-year-old. A more complicated answer could be worse. The protesters' basic objection to the base was that nuclear weapons were held there, ready to be deployed. And that might frighten her son. It was an aspect of the base that no one in Hamscott Common wanted to dwell on, rather like people living on the slopes of a not-quite-extinct volcano.

When Kim told her son that the demonstrators were against war he only said, 'You have to have a war if the bad guys attack you.' He was not interested in the philosophy of the protesters, only the daily incidents on the base. He could have spent the day there – sometimes, when a picnic was in the offing, he'd suggested having it there, on the verge of the road outside the airfield. Kim always resisted. The idea made her feel uncomfortable even though the base had been there since her parents, both local, had been born. Her neighbours had jobs there, a fellow teacher at her school had gone to teach the air force children there, and houses in the road where she lived were rented out to US personnel. The base had always been part of Hamscott Common. Three generations of children had grown up with an expertise in weaponry and modern warfare beyond their years. Playground war games featured realistic alarm sounds, jet screams and American drill sergeants.

They were past the airfield now and Rory settled back to the dull part of the journey.

Sugden's, Fox Square, London SW1. June 1st, 2015. 8.15 p.m.

Sugden's was crowded that evening. Downstairs there were no empty tables and upstairs both the private rooms were occupied. The Shadow Foreign Secretary was there with Sir Lionel Frame who ran the Foreign Office Middle East department and Joe Middleton, officially a Trade Secretary at the US Embassy in London but generally understood to be CIA. The head of the Muslim Council of Great Britain was dining with the London editor of Al Jazeera and the deputy editor of *The Times*.

'It's bad,' said Joshua Crane, to himself as much as to his two companions, Lord Gott and Julia Baskerville. That morning the newly elected leader of the majority party in the Iraq Parliament, Sheikh Mohammed Al Bactari, had addressed 20,000 shouting supporters outside the parliament building in Baghdad. He had declared that his first move would be to take over the oil companies now in Western hands, nationalize them and run them on behalf of the Iraqi people.

'We've no one to blame but ourselves,' Gott said. 'We pulled out leaving warring national and religious groups, an imposed constitution that was never going to work because no one wanted it to and post-war reconstruction still half-completed. Look at what Al Bactari gets, promising the country its oil revenues – it could stop the Sunnis trying to wreck the government, at least for a while, keep the Kurds in line, more or less, and offer all the Iraqis some hope of an improved life, a bit of prosperity. You could argue that's about the only thing to save the country.'

'If the US doesn't invade to get the pipelines back,' Joshua said. 'There's Joe Middleton over there trying to get the Labour Party to back the US in a new war in Iraq. And get the FO on side. Al Bactari's is a high-risk strategy, to put it mildly.'

'Britain won't go,' said Julia. 'The President owes the oil companies for funding her election to the tune of fifty million. No politician here is in hock to the oil companies . . .' Gott raised his eyebrows. 'All right,' she said. 'But our little fiddles are just that – little fiddles. An American would laugh. I can't see any British government putting troops into Iraq again. I can't see any other nation doing it, either. Thank God.'

'Your views are coloured by your constituency,' Joshua told her bluntly. 'You spend half your constituency time trying to keep your Islamic constituents calm. OK,' he said, seeing the anger rising in Julia, her mouth opening to protest, 'OK, I know they've got a lot to protest about. But the rest of the country has got problems, too. And fears They're worried about bombs – they're more anxious about getting to work safely on public transport than civil rights. A lot of them would be only too happy to cordon off your constituency and make every man, woman and child in it have to go through a checkpoint in and out. They're frightened. When you see a woman from Sulhet half-mad because they've kicked her door in a second time, and this time they took away her husband and son, my constituents see the police taking terrorists off the street. Perhaps Muldoon couldn't get away with sending the troops back to Iraq. Or maybe, just maybe, half the country's so pissed off with living in fear they'll go for anything to give an Islamic country a kicking. I don't know – and nor do you. Whatever we do or don't do here will the Yanks sit back and take it? As you say, the President owes her job to the oil companies. Then there's the humiliation.'

'They never invaded Cuba,' Julia pointed out. 'Now they're doing business with Juanito Castro.' Burly Juanito Castro had taken over in Cuba five years earlier. Whether he was indeed Fidel's son – and CIA operatives had so far failed to get hold of samples of Juanito's hair, saliva or anything else to prove or disprove the story – Juanito was now allowing US businesses to set up in Cuba. He was rumoured to be in negotiations to join the North Atlantic Trade Agreement, along with Mexico, Canada, Guatemala and Honduras. Which might have explained the delay in securing DNA samples.

'Interesting analysis but what do you *think*?' Lord Gott said sourly to Joshua. 'Will the US reinvade Iraq? You're a TV pundit – what do you think?'

Joshua tried to conceal his shock at Gott's unexpectedly hostile tone. He opened his mouth to speak and closed it again, realizing that whatever he said would cause an argument. Joshua knew the reason for Gott's malice – Joshua was now the sitting member for Gott's old constituency, Frognal and South Hampstead. Gott – no longer Edward Gott, MP, but Lord Gott of Trequair – desperately missed the House of Commons. Like a normally patient invalid who occasionally finds spite against the able-bodied welling up inside him, sometimes Gott couldn't restrain his feelings.

Gott's elevation to the House of Lords had been two years ago, after he had refused to vote with his party against a bill to step up government funding for the alternative energy business section. The Conservative Party had opposed additional state support on the grounds that the businesses should be self-supporting. Gott voted with the other side and the bill was passed.

The day after the vote, a slow news day as it happened, the nation's

(Conservative-supporting) best-selling tabloid came up with a banner headline, HE'S GOTT YOUR MONEY, over a photograph of Edward Gott
MP framed against his factory logo Citycars and quoting from the firm's
promotional brochure advertising the electric vehicles. Frederick Muldoon
took the high moral ground, told Gott his disloyalty had brought the party
into disrepute and kicked him upstairs. The House of Lords was now 45
per cent elected and 45 per cent nominated. The remaining 10 per cent
consisted of hereditary peers elected by other hereditary peers. The compo-
sition of the Upper Chamber had been worked out in the traditional British
way. It was a compromise no one liked. But it gave Gott's Party Leader
the power to put him there. Gott was the treasurer of the Conservative
Party and a man of considerable influence, but he missed the Commons.
And he knew that now he would never be Prime Minister.

Julia Baskerville stepped in. 'I'm tabling a motion asking the government to give an assurance that Britain won't send troops to Iraq.' She
looked tired. A well-cut linen jacket and her hair, not in its usual neat
twist but on her shoulders, did not offset her pallor and the circles under
her eyes.

'Bit premature,' commented Joshua.

'Not when your constituency's one third Muslim. Any way, Edward,'
she said, raising her glass to him, 'are you "The masters now"? Or "Have
you lost control"?'

The first words she quoted were those of Frederick Muldoon as, fist
upraised, he had entered 10 Downing Street after the 2012 election. They
had been that morning's *Independent* headline, along with the triumphalist
photograph, followed by the headlined query, HAS HE LOST CONTROL?
The inside pages detailed, with graphs and statistics, the record of steadily
mounting unemployment and government borrowing and the jobs leaking
from the country – a Welsh call centre relocated to India, a Midlands car
factory closed down, a Yorkshire knitwear factory put out of business by
Chinese competition, an Italian shoe firm taking its work from Nottingham
to the Czech Republic. The crime statistics were up. Only 50 per cent
of the bills the government had presented over the previous two years
had been passed, because it had no working majority. The *Independent*
leader had said emphatically that an all-party government was the only
solution,

'So,' Julia said mischievously, 'In control or not, Gott?'

Gott poured a little more of the excellent wine he had ordered into
Julia's glass and said, 'Of course not. Ask any of these nicely dressed diners
around us – politicians, senior civil servants, respected journalists and broadcasters or whoever they may be. I doubt if half of them would know who
the masters are, or ever have been. Deep in their hearts they all know –
and it is a danger to forget it – that no one is in control, ever.'

Julia knew a smooth, question-dodging generalization when she heard one. She pressed. Yes, Edward. But it's serious when the world knows you're not—'

'Carl Chatterton had a meeting with Muldoon this morning to discuss setting up a National Government,' Gott offered.

'Any result?'

Gott's silence suggested the meeting between the new Prime Minister and Carl Chatterton, Leader of the Opposition, had not been fruitful.

He took a menu from the waiter. 'Pudding – no, I thought not. Julia – no. Well, I can't resist the crème brûlée here. You'll share, won't you?' He ordered and leaned back in his chair. Gott was square-faced, dark-eyed and dark-haired. He was stocky and broad-shouldered, giving the impression of energy although he denied ever denying himself anything and claimed never to take any exercise. He said coolly, 'We all know we need a National Government. The Queen gave Muldoon quite a grilling at the last audience, I hear. Naturally, Muldoon won't do it. He's worked, schemed, planned and back-stabbed towards the premiership since he was in his teens. A coalition government wouldn't just be a humiliation, it might end up with the Lib Dems and Labour putting in their own PM. He's already blocked one Private Members' Bill asking for a vote and he'll block the next.'

Julia said, 'Can't you do something?'

'Why would you want me to?' he responded. 'The present situation's not such a bad thing from your point of view, surely? Muldoon won't be able to pass any bills you don't like. And what persuades you that I can do anything?'

Julia smiled, sceptically, at Gott. She liked him, although theoretically he was everything she despised – an investment banker and a Tory behind-the-scenes fixer. She believed that he thought people not fit to govern themselves. She believed that he thought that even if they were fit, it would be better if they did not. Yet Gott had got her the job on *Westminster Unplugged*. He had approached her one day outside the House and implied that she could appear on the programme if she wanted to. Julia, conscious of the value of being a regular face on TV, agreed and next day the call came. She still didn't really know why Gott had done this, except that, as she knew, such acts were a way of life for him. By supplying her and Joshua to Hugh Patterson, the programme's presenter, he'd put them both under an obligation to him. They had become two more strings in his hands, to tug when he needed them, although his hands were already as full of strings as a man selling balloons in the street.

She said, 'You're not so helpless.'

Gott shook his head, saying, but not expecting to be believed, 'I'm out of the House. You've got more power than I have, with that programme of yours. There'll be a National Government soon enough. After a certain point, events have their own momentum – an issue arises that the status quo just can't handle. It could be Iraq. If not that, something else. Suddenly it'll be imperative to have a functioning government. Then there'll be a scuffle and it'll happen – too late, probably, as usual.'

Julia had to go. Her mother was babysitting and had made it plain that she expected to be back in her own home and watching TV by nine thirty. The men tried to persuade her to stay but she insisted, kissed them and left.

When she had gone, Gott turned to Joshua, 'Nice girl. Tell me . . . is anything?'

'No, Edward. There's not,' Joshua told him. 'Not now and never will be,' he added firmly.

Gott's expression was neutral. 'Never's a long time,' he observed, then suggested they end the evening at his club, which was within walking distance.

Two

10 Downing Street, London SW1. June 2nd, 2015. 7.30 p.m.

Frederick Muldoon and his Home Secretary, Alan Petherbridge, sat in Muldoon's office, by a fireplace filled with a large arrangement of flowers and foliage, creamy roses, bright red gladioli, pink and cream orchids. They had no eyes for the flowers.

'Six people under arrest at Fairford and Hamscott Common occupied by demonstrators – how can that have happened? A few hundred men and women in anoraks take over the RAF bases, block the runways and set up camps. Why?' This was not the first time Muldoon had asked this question, or Petherbridge answered it.

'The base was taken by surprise. The Americans are responsible for base security, Prime Minister. Deplorable as it is, the invaders are the usual suspects – peace activists, CND, nuns, SWP. And of course, our old friend, the Reverend Alec Hutchinson. No demo complete without him.' Petherbridge spoke smoothly, giving no sign he had said all this three times already that morning, the first time an hour ago at the COBRA meeting.

The conference call had scanned into the Cabinet Room the director of COBRA, the head of the Ministry of Defence, Chairman of the Armed Services, and senior intelligence and police officers from Britain and the USA. The fifteen-strong committee met, apparently at Downing Street, but in reality from their office desks, their homes or hotel rooms. Such virtual meetings were indispensable in a world where key men and women were seldom available in the same place at the same time. In theory, a virtual meeting was supposed to work exactly like its real-life counterpart. In practice it did not. Most of the participants were unused to the technology. They were accustomed to sitting in a real room with a real temperature and real outside sounds. In addition, at a virtual meeting it was harder to read faces for the sudden tightening of a pair of lips, a faint twitch of the eyes, a sense of who was working with whom against whom. There was no 'feeling of the meeting' to be read by subtle practitioners. And, these days, the participants were wary. A year earlier, at a virtual meeting in Haifa between the newly elected President of Saudi Arabia, the President of Israel and the US Special Representative, a wrongly placed word had caused an international crisis with riots in Cairo, Damascus and Baghdad. So now when COBRA met, the participants could not be absolutely confident they were off the record.

Frederick Muldoon had called the meeting knowing it might lack spontaneity. He did not want contention. He did not want brilliant thinking. He did not want a firm conclusion. The downside was that Alan Petherbridge, crisp but informal in chinos and an open-necked blue shirt, had performed with skill. He had established the reluctance of the armed services to play any part in retaking the base and the competence and readiness of the Kent and Metropolitan Police to do so. When Muldoon, in an effort to undermine him, had demanded to know why there had been no intelligence about the plan to take over the base, Petherbridge had adroitly laid the blame in several directions – MI5, MI6, US military security – and ended by saying there was a full review in hand. The consensus of the men and women sitting round the virtual table in the virtual Cabinet Room was that the Home Secretary, Alan Petherbridge, was the safe pair of hands for the job.

Muldoon, sweating behind his desk, his heavy, fair-complexioned face pouchy with fatigue, understood that although he had succeeded in his primary objective, to make sure nothing too strong came out of the meeting, he had lost ground where Alan Petherbridge was concerned. Petherbridge had come out of it well. Now, dark, lantern-jawed and, as ever, well-shaven, Petherbridge looked fresh and keen. Apparently relaxed, he sat opposite the Prime Minister, his long legs in immaculately creased trousers crossed. He looked blandly at the Prime Minister as he repeated information he had already given to the meeting an hour before.

'There are nuclear weapons on that base,' said Muldoon.

'The majority of these demonstrators are CND. They're not going to arm a nuclear warhead.' He wondered if the Prime Minister was breaking up. He looked bad this morning. There were rumours he was drinking more. Or had he been woken at two or three in the morning by the White House, famous for not worrying about any time zones but its own? Someone in Washington – Ray Hollander, perhaps – could have called up Muldoon in the middle of the night and given him a hard time. After the results of the Iraq elections and Al Bactari's threat to nationalize his nation's oil, the US President would be in no mood to accept that an ally had allowed its rag-tag-and-bobtail citizenry to disable one of their bases. Maybe that was why he looked so rough. But whether it was early-morning phone calls or too much whisky or perhaps just the consciousness of ebbing power, it did not pay to underestimate Muldoon. He had astonishing recuperative powers, second-to-none survival instincts and, in a pinch, he'd fight like a cornered rat.

Muldoon stood up and pressed a button on his desk. The wall behind it lit up. 'There it is then – a crowd of shaggy demonstrators sitting on the runways, encircled by US troops without orders and the whole thing's on TV.'

Petherbridge took in the scene. The sun was shining, the demonstrators were smiling and holding up banners, the armed US troops were standing, looking on and sweating. 'I see what you see, Prime Minister,' Petherbridge said. 'I don't like it any more than you do. All I can say is that the police will be in there in approximately half an hour restoring order and making arrests. The Met and Kent police are already mustered there, fine-tuning the dispositions of Armed Response and briefing the hostage negotiators. We shouldn't need them, but it's just as well to be prepared. The base commander's quite happy to let us deal with it. He's got plenty of armed men to deploy and the bases are, de facto, US territory as we know, but he's quite ready to accept the policy of not using US troops to deal with British civilians.'

'Particularly since you don't seem to have managed to keep the cameras away.'

'They got there fast,' Petherbridge said. 'The local police weren't quick enough. It won't happen next time.'

'There'd better not be a next time.'

The door opened and a lean figure in chinos and a denim shirt walked in springily.

Muldoon said, 'I've asked Tom here to join us. Fresh input.'

'Yes, Prime Minister,' agreed Petherbridge, who disliked the rough and crudely intelligent head of Downing Street's Press Department. He thought they needed no fresh input and if they did, he doubted if Tom Canning would have anything to contribute. He was there for only one reason – to lend Muldoon moral support.

'Coffee, Tom?' asked the Prime Minister, which was, thought Petherbridge, more than he had himself been offered. Canning refused and sat down in a chair opposite the fireplace.

'When this is resolved, we'll need an inquiry,' Petherbridge said. If anything went wrong – and such situations were unpredictable – he guessed Muldoon would try to make sure he got the blame.

'Better get them out first, before thinking about the inquiry,' Canning said easily, implying for Muldoon's benefit that Alan Petherbridge was always the same, uptight, nit-picking and legalistic.

Edmund Jones was shown in. He was Petherbridge's Permanent Secretary at the Home Office. The Prime Minister had not invited him to the meeting. Petherbridge had. He needed a witness.

The PM did not comment on Jones's intrusion. He did not ask him to sit.

'I was just saying, Ed,' Petherbridge remarked, 'that after this bit of trouble is ended we'll need an inquiry.'

Edmund Jones was a short, fair, angry man who found it hard to conceal his irritation. He had been standing beside Petherbridge and now went to the window and picked up the second gilt chair. He put it down, rather noisily, beside the Home Secretary and sat.

'But when will that be?' wondered Tom Canning, cueing Muldoon.

Petherbridge put on small headphones and listened. He said, 'Half an hour.'

'The retaking of the base has been half an hour away for an hour now,' said Muldoon.

Petherbridge controlled his impatience. 'The Metropolitan and Kent police aren't trained to clear air force bases. Our armed response teams are trained on the basis that their targets will be one, or just a few, armed civilians. I take it we want to clear the bases without causing casualties. It's prudent to take time for proper planning and briefings. And let's not forget the cameras will be on the action.'

Canning threw up his eyes and groaned noisily. 'Softly, softly,' he deplored.

Petherbridge said, 'You and I, Tom, might be only too delighted to see an armed-response team gun down two dissident nuns and the Red Vicar. But it wouldn't look good on TV.' He glanced at the face of the Prime Minister, which suddenly looked to him like the face of an old, angry defiant boy.

'There are nuclear weapons there,' Canning added. 'As an adviser, I ask, why don't we let the British Army sort it? After Northern Ireland they know how to deal with civilians. Send them in – these buggers would soon fold.'

'Thank you for the advice, Tom. That was considered. But,' Petherbridge pointed out, 'problems emerged at this morning's meeting.' Which, Tom Canning, you were not at, he thought. 'One is that a sizeable proportion of the public might resent the British Army being deployed against civilians. Another is that Ian Noakes has quietly sounded out the Army. They told him they'd need precise orders, and that if those orders covered firing on civilians the men could be reluctant.'

'First time I've heard of the Defence Secretary going cap in hand to the Army; first time, for that matter, I've heard of the Army being a democracy. I thought the Secretary for Defence tells the Army what to do, and the Army does it,' Canning said.

He'd gone too far and Muldoon said, 'Well, Tom, there are legalities involved.'

Petherbridge would not have objected to Muldoon ordering out the Army (far more reluctant to be involved than the PM knew) and making a real pig's ear of the whole affair, including later lawsuits against HM Forces for undue force and injuries sustained. He said, though, 'I'm sure you're right, Prime Minister, that a firm but not aggressive stance is indicated.'

'Thank you, Alan. I'll convey all that to Washington,' Muldoon said.

Petherbridge left, knowing that once his restraining presence was gone the PM and his adviser would be boys together, enjoying a reviving conversation about the Yanks, the lads of the British Army versus Petherbridge's softy elite force of coppers, showing who was boss, bloody noses and all the rest. Canning was smart and would be playing along. Petherbridge didn't care what they did. They could get out a bottle of whisky and play poker with their sleeves rolled up if they liked.

As his car went through the Downing Street gates there was a small crowd of 200 demonstrators outside, bearing placards – NO WAR ON IRAQ, END THE WAR IN AFGHANISTAN, END THE CRUSADES.

'I'd like to send the SAS in, just to clear away that mob,' he said.

Edmund Jones, beside Petherbridge in the car, suddenly realized how much proximity to his boss repelled him. He feared him, also. He said, 'I think that, and COBRA, went well enough, Alan.'

Petherbridge said, 'So it seems. But we don't know what Washington is saying to Muldoon. That could change everything. When you get back to your office, will you dictate a detailed memorandum about everything you've seen and heard today? I'll do the same.'

'Right,' said Jones. Little wonder Petherbridge was watching his back. He was after Muldoon's job. Everybody knew it, especially Muldoon.

Hamscott Common, Kent. June 3rd, 2015. 8.15 a.m.

Kim Durham, with Rory strapped in his seat beside her, set out to work on a bright June morning. She and Rory had argued. Outside the house, holding his book bag in one hand a bright blue bird's egg in the other – miraculously almost intact, although a chick had hatched through the broken hole at the top – Rory had urged, as usual, 'Let's go past the base.' And Kim, who had seen pictures of the demonstrators inside the base, said no. She did not want him to see a band of people, grubby and dishev- elled, marching about the base behind the wire with their banners, singing and shouting slogans and watched by the groups of resentful armed soldiers. She did not want to pass the line-up of stationary bombers on the runway or drive directly under the circling helicopters. They might pass just as the demonstrators were struggling with those sent to arrest them. Even more, she did not want to answer Rory's questions about what was happening, and why. All her instincts told her that she should keep her child away from this scene.

Half the children at the school would have seen the morning's news. There would be ferocious playground games involving the invading demonstrators being attacked by soldiers. The situation would revive all the other games – swooping, arms outstretched, across the playground, dropping imaginary bombs.

Outside the house, Kim had argued with Rory. 'I don't want to go past the base,' she'd said. 'We'll probably get held up. Anyway, I don't like it.'

'Why not?' he'd cried. 'Everybody else goes there. Everybody goes.'

He'd thrown his school bag down on the ground in the front garden.

'Don't break your egg,' she'd said. And then Rory had crushed the frail eggshell in his fist and thrown it over the garden fence on to the pavement outside, crying out, 'I don't want a stupid bird's egg! I want to see the soldiers.'

Kim, holding her own heavy bag, stood and looked at him and Rory, defiantly, looked back. His mother knew very well that if Rory, normally a reasonable child, had gone into one of his rare, stubborn rages, it would be hours before he would budge. Shouts and yells, even slaps, would not get him willingly into the car. They would be late, very late, for school and she was supposed, that day, to be taking assembly.

She gave in, saying, 'Come on then. Get in the car and we'll go past the base.'

They drove from the house to the farmland in sulky silence until, as they reached the bend in Templesfield Road which would lead them beside the base, Rory began to brighten. He'd already seen the helicopters circling above and now, spotting police cars and military vehicles on the road ahead, craned to see what other excitements the scene had to offer. Then he looked up and gave a scream of delight so loud that Kim almost lost control of the car.

'What?' she asked in alarm, and risking following her son's eyes upwards saw an extraordinary sight. Floating down over the base, like strange drifting birds, were twenty white parachutes, each with the figure of a soldier attached to it, swaying. Some were low enough down over the base, now, for Kim to able to see faces beneath helmets, camouflage uniforms, boots and heavy weapons. Others were still high up, the soldiers swinging like puppets from their harnesses. She stopped the car.

A red-faced, helmeted young soldier appeared beside her open car window. 'Excuse me, ma'am,' he said. 'Will you turn round and go back?' But as he spoke a truck with a dozen soldiers in the back pulled up short beside her. With that vehicle, which had come from her direction, beside her and the other vehicles ahead, she had no way through. Worse, she could see a car behind her and knew that traffic must be piling up behind. Templesfield Road was heavily used by commuters as a short cut to the ring road. She could not move back or forward. Rory was taking no notice of the standstill. As if seeing a vision, he was taking in the slow descent of the parachutes. The first soldiers were landing in billows of white near the runway.

Kim gestured at the truck. 'I can't turn,' she pointed out. The young soldier beckoned the truck on, yelling at the driver, 'Come forward.' The driver yelled something back, and did not move. 'Come on, buddy! Move!' shouted the soldier beside Kim. She began to feel nervous.

Inside the base the landed soldiers, weapons at the ready, were encircling the demonstrators clustered between the big, stationary jets. The demonstrators were haranguing them.

'They're going to shoot the demonstrators!' Rory cried out.

'Of course they're not,' she replied automatically. Trying for calm she said to the soldier, 'If the truck driver won't move you'll have to let us through.'

The soldier ran to the truck and began to shout at the driver. The driver protested. Kim, seeing more and more troops landing on the base with weapons at the ready, saw a space ahead between an armoured car and a camouflaged truck and thought she could get through if the truck would move further on to the verge of the Common. She put the car in gear and edged forward, followed by the car behind her. As she crept on she saw some of the soldiers running to the perimeter of the camp and taking up positions. Rory wriggled. He said, in a high voice, 'What's going to happen, Mummy?'

A jeep, containing three officers, moved out in front of Kim's car, forcing her to stop. One leapt out and ran angrily towards her. At the same time, to her right, she saw a group of five men, spread out, advancing on the demonstrators from behind. Two men, finding they were about to be penned in between the advancing soldiers and the force on the front perimeter, broke away from the group and zigzagged between the fighter bombers, probably planning to escape to the side, across the area in front of the administration buildings.

What happened after that was never made completely clear. Certainly, the troops to the rear opened fire on the running men. Both fell. And, certainly, a bullet went through Kim Durham's windscreen and into her head, splattering it all over her windscreen, the interior of the car and her son, Rory, still in the seat beside her. There was a shouted order and the firing stopped as Rory, screaming, managed to release his seat belt and wrench open the door of the car. He toppled out of the vehicle, righted himself and ran sobbing, his face, jeans and T-shirt covered in his mother's blood, towards a young, and horrified, US soldier. He fell on his knees, his bloody face turned up into the face of the man. He seemed to be appealing to him. For protection, asking him to undo, somehow, what had taken place? That was the photograph that went instantly round the world – the boy at the feet of Will O'Neill, an ordinary soldier who had never fired a live round at anyone in his life.

After that, there was a terrible silence. Rory was pulled away, stunned, from the soldier and put in the charge of a nurse from the base while marines rounded up the unprotesting and shocked demonstrators and handed them over to the local police. They were herded into vans which had been waiting further down the road. The two demonstrators who had been shot at – one dead, one wounded – were loaded into an ambulance. Paramedics pulled Kim from her car, put her body on a stretcher and took it to a second ambulance.

The retaking of Hamscott Common by the Marines had cost two lives, that of Damon Jepson, aged 25, a student and anti-war protester, and Kim Durham, aged 27, a primary school teacher and the mother of a young son.

10 Downing Street, London SW1. June 3rd, 2015. 9 a.m.

Frederick Muldoon had achieved the highest office in the land. This is not done without a speed and resilience which in another context might be defined as bordering on the psychopathic.

One phone call, from the White House, had got him into this position. 'The President feels,' Ray Hollander had said evenly, 'that this is a US base and therefore something we have to take care of. She asks, "Is that OK with you?"' Muldoon found it easy to agree with his powerful ally even though he knew that by doing so he was completely negating the plan agreed earlier at COBRA and confirmed with his own Home Secretary.

Fifteen seconds after he heard the news of Kim Durham's death he had moved from concern about the messy and needless death of a young woman to acute concern about his own situation. He saw now that he had played into Hollander's hands. He saw that the Marines must have been in the air heading for Hamscott before the call. An innocent woman had died and he, Frederick Muldoon, would be held responsible.

Stalking him like a mugger in an alley were thoughts of Alan Petherbridge, who would pick his time to leak the information that his own plan to retake the base, using the British police, had been safer. All that could save him now was a strong and supportive call from the President of the US, an admission that she had personally backed his decision, her apologies for a tragic mistake, her firm assurance there would be a prompt investigation of the error, and her own words of condolence to the family. He needed it now, and he needed it on screen before the press conference. Importantly, he needed to be able to quote the President's own words of condolence to the family.

Muldoon had been waiting for half an hour for the President of the United States to ring back. His office was handling everything else – no other calls would be put through until he had spoken to the President. An aide had woken Hollander in Washington when Muldoon called. Hollander, his eyes sleep-swollen and his hair sticking up on top of his head, had reacted immediately. 'A terrible accident,' he said. 'The President will speak to the victim's family personally as soon as possible. And there'll be a compensation package, of course.'

Muldoon looked at the man who had, only an hour earlier, asked for his agreement that the Marines should land at Hamscott. Who had gained that agreement from him and promptly gone to bed, to sleep. Who had put him in the appalling position he was in today. He disciplined himself to stay calm. He needed more from Hollander now, much more. He needed to talk to the President. He needed to record that talk on film before 10 a.m., the time of his scheduled weekly encounter with the press. 'Will you talk to the President?' he'd asked. 'I'd like to speak to her personally.' There was a short silence. It was four in the morning in Washington and the head of the most powerful country in the world is not woken lightly. For her, perhaps, the death of Kim Durham and the pictures of Rory at the soldier's feet, already on TV, were not as important as the hundred other important matters she acted on daily.

Muldoon waited. Would Hollander wake the President, giving Muldoon the appearance of a man so concerned by this random death that he had called the President of the USA, and so influential that the President had responded personally, or would he have to face the world's press without that backing? 'Let me make some calls and get back to you,' Hollander said.

'As soon as you can,' Muldoon said. 'I have a press conference in an hour and a half.'

Now, the press conference was only an hour off and there had still been no call to the silent room, reached only by the muffled sound of traffic and the incessant ringing of phones in other rooms. Muldoon, behind his desk, backed by a vast oil painting of the Duke of Wellington on a rearing stallion, was sweating. The only other man in the room, his Press Officer, Tom Canning, was in a chair by the fireplace, with a pen in his hand and a pad on his knee. In fact, there would be nothing to write until the President's call came, if it did. Every few minutes one of Canning's assistants came in with a sheaf of messages and silently handed them to him. The British press and the BBC wanted statements. The European press wanted statements on the statements of their own leaders – the German President had wondered what was the status of the British bases, the French President pointed to that status as anomalous, the Russian President had already sent unnecessary and trouble-making condolences to the family. Everyone wanted the PM to respond, but Frederick Muldoon waited for the presidential call that might not come.

Canning was betting that Hollander would not wake his President and, at the last moment, would produce an uncontentious statement for Muldoon to deliver. Hollander would consider Muldoon's long-term prospects, never good because of the small majority, worse after this death at the base. Because, technically, only one man could have authorized the Marines to invade the base and that was Muldoon. And Hollander would know the British press would write the story of a puppet Prime

Minister allowing foreign troops to gun down an innocent schoolteacher, lone parent of a small boy. It was irresistible. And, Canning thought, also as true as any press story ever got.

Canning's wife, who worked for Sky News, had told him as he drank a hasty espresso that morning, 'If the President doesn't come up with something solid for Muldoon this morning before the press conference, the President will be hanging him out to dry. Goodbye, Muldoon, hello, somebody else. Who will that be?'

Canning hadn't answered the question – he'd been rushing through the door – but the answer was obvious. That somebody else would be Alan Petherbridge, the Home Secretary. He was capable and respected, if not liked. And as far as Hamscott was concerned he had clean hands – he'd advised using British police to clear the base. He'd been backed at 6.30 a.m. by COBRA, so Canning understood, and at seven thirty he'd confirmed the plan with the Prime Minister. Muldoon had then reneged on all that, pretty certainly after a call from Washington. It would not be long before Petherbridge, one way or another, made this known.

This put Canning in a bad situation. He disliked Petherbridge about as much as Petherbridge disliked him. He was a cold, smug, clever-clever bastard, Canning thought, and he hadn't recommended a softly-softly approach at Hamscott because he was a bleeding heart, a supporter of people's right to protest, but only because it was the more intelligent way. Muldoon would be lucky to survive, once Petherbridge let it be known he was the hero of the Hamscott Common affair. Ladbrokes would start offering odds on him as the future Prime Minister. And Canning would be out of a job.

Canning shifted in his chair. He was wasting his time sitting here, in silence, while Muldoon refused to speak even to his own Private Secretary. Or the Defence Secretary. Or the RAF. Or Kim Durham's parents. Or the Europeans. And certainly not to Alan Petherbridge. He was only present so that Muldoon would not be alone, waiting for a call from the President of the United States, the only person who could save him from this wreck. But without that call, it was, Canning estimated, twenty to one that Muldoon, unpopular head of a party with a majority of three, would go.

Frozen in horror, Canning watched Muldoon pick up the phone and call Hollander again. He couldn't wrench the phone from his hand but he knew – everybody knows – that phoning again so soon after the first call reeked of desperation. Listening, he gathered that the Pentagon already had reports from the senior officer at Hamscott Common and the Marine commander in charge of the raid. They were being studied as a matter of urgency. 'Has the President been told?' asked Muldoon. Pointless to ask – of course she hadn't, thought Canning. The President would be informed when the assessments were made, Hollander told him. Within half an hour he would have a statement ready, in time for the press conference.

Canning was astonished that Muldoon put the phone down without even asking for details of the military reports. 'Hollander going to wake the President at any point?' he enquired.

'He didn't say,' Muldoon said, adding, in a low, grumbling tone, 'Ray Hollander's never liked me.' Oh God, Canning groaned to himself, Muldoon's cracking. The phone rang again. Muldoon snatched it up. He steadied. Canning wondered if there'd been a miracle and the President was on the line.

Muldoon composed his face and said, 'Prime Minister speaking, ma'am,' and although, over the next five seconds his face completely drained of colour, he continued to speak steadily. Meanwhile, Canning had picked up the phone on the table in front of him and heard the crystalline tones of the Queen of England asking, 'Can you tell me exactly, Prime Minister, what happened at Hamscott Common?' There was no picture on the screen in front of him – the Queen never used videophone.

Muldoon gave a smooth but inadequate answer. He was instantly picked up on various points and examined more fully. He responded calmly. He was asked more questions by a plainly displeased Queen.

When Muldoon put the phone down he was ashen and sweating, like a man with flu, but the episode reminded Canning of one of the reasons why Muldoon was Prime Minister – his nerve. He wondered if, even after all this, Muldoon would survive.

At that moment Alan Petherbridge, uninvited and immaculate, his long, dark-complexioned face set in stone, came through the door. How he had got through Muldoon's defence system Canning could not tell. But here he was, fresh as paint, taking in the situation at a glance, giving Canning a look indicating, if not sympathy, at least some understanding, and saying, 'Prime Minister, I apologize for the intrusion, but there are matters that can't wait.'

If you had to point to the real beginning of our present crisis, it was not the death of Kim Durham. For that we had to wait another four months, until the election of October 2015. But the image of young Rory Durham at the US soldier's feet still symbolizes what happened – what is still happening. There's always a picture – Jackie Kennedy's pink suit, stained with her husband's blood, the naked girl in Vietnam, running. And then there was, and still is, the photograph of Rory Durham kneeling in the road, clutching at the armed soldier's knees. Strange that this image came so early, long before the corruption began, the country was plunged into cold and darkness, the nights were ripped by the sound of the bombers overhead – and long before Mark Moreno died. Before we learned shame, the shame of those who have allowed their country to be betrayed from within, and the shame of defeat.

That picture of Rory was like a prophecy. From that moment on the poster of Rory at the soldier's feet was used on demonstrations – when demonstrations were allowed – and is still stuck up on bedroom walls and in small committee rooms throughout the land. 'Kim Durham' is no longer just the name of a woman. It is the name of a state of affairs.

Young Rory Durham will be seven years old now. After the bruising encounters with the media and the sordid battles with the diplomats, the advisers and the intelligence services of two National Governments, all attempting to get some 'right' answers and statements from them, Rory and his maternal grandparents sharpened up and managed to disappear. I don't know if anyone helped them or if they ever claimed any of the money shoved at them with both hands by Britain and the USA. They're lost to us now, and to history, or so it seems. But, you never know, Rory Durham, one way or another, may resurface. In real life, as opposed to fiction, there's always another chapter, another act, another reel, just when you thought the story was finished. But for the time being, they're gone. Perhaps they changed their name; perhaps they emigrated. The only people who could easily find them are precisely those who want them out of the way, because of what they represent.

So, wishing Kim Durham's family some peace, temporarily at least, I'll go back to the way the world changed after Kim's death. Muldoon was finished by then. Whatever spin his friends and supporters tried to put on it, he was the man who'd agreed to the Marine landings at Hamscott Common and was held indirectly responsible for the death of an innocent bystander. Not only that, he'd sanctioned foreign soldiers firing on British protesters. There are times when spin is not enough, and this was one of them.

What Muldoon did next helped the plans of those working against us. We think the plans were already laid, but Muldoon, acting purely out of pride, egotism and malice, really sped them up. He could not have done more to help the plotters' cause if they'd been paying him. Of course, it's been rumoured that they were, but serious people don't believe it. Even now, when we know so much more about how a man is turned into a renegade, only conspiracy theorists believe Muldoon acted out of anything other than personal motives. But they were enough.

Hamscott Common, Kent. June 3rd, 2015. 11 a.m.

Rory Durham was taken to the hospital and passively endured washing, and being put into other clothes. As the doctor began to talk to his grandparents, Rory, standing beside his grandmother's knee and holding her hand, began to cry helplessly and insist on going back to his house. This was the last thing Matt and Katherine Arthur wanted, but Rory was unpersuadable. He wept, he demanded to go back to his house; he could not, or would not, explain why. Slender young Dr Mehmet, concerned for the little boy, hesitated and then agreed he would drive them back to Kim Durham's house in his own car. He suggested that, as the press was camped at the front of the hospital, looking for pictures of the bereaved family, they leave by a back entrance. With Rory holding his grandmother's hand and crying, the quartet went out into the reception area outside Dr Mehmet's consulting room to find it empty except for a tall man in American officer's uniform. He stepped forward respectfully and said, 'Mr and Mrs Arthur, please accept my sympathy for your loss. A great tragedy – a terrible accident. Our hearts are with you in your bereavement. Now, I apologize for this and I don't want it to look like I'm rushing you, at this terrible time, but I'd appreciate it if you would let me come back with you to your home. There's a good deal to discuss.'

Matt Arthur looked at him blankly. Kim's mother, tightening her grip on Rory's hand, asked, 'Discuss what?'

'The accident – and, more importantly now, what to do about the media intrusion.'

'We just want to take Rory home,' said Katherine.

'Ma'am,' he said, 'if you think about it, I'm sure you'll see the need for some help in protecting your privacy—'

The door of the waiting room banged open and another man entered. He was tall, tanned and wearing a cream linen suit. Acknowledging the presence of the other man he said, without pleasure, 'Captain Struthers.' He advanced on the little group – the grandparents, trying to contain their grief for the sake of the weeping boy, Rory himself and the doctor. His hand extended as he moved towards them. 'Mr and Mrs Arthur,' he said, 'my deepest condolences. This has been a most terrible event.' As they shook hands he said, 'I know this is a dreadful time for you. What we want to do is minimize the pressure from the media . . .'

'I want to go home!' cried Rory. 'I want to go home! Take me home!' He wrenched his hand out of his grandmother's and ran to the door. Mrs Arthur said, 'All we want to do now is take Rory home.' She went to the door to talk to the boy.

'Mrs Arthur . . .' said the Englishman.

'I'm sorry,' said Rory's grandfather. 'We have to take Rory home. Then we're going to stay with family in Brighton.'

'For your own comfort and protection . . .' said the American, Captain Struthers.

Mr Arthur spoke with an effort, 'No,' he said. 'Thank you for your offer, but you – all of you – have already done enough.' He went to the door and picked up his grandson.

When they got to the small red-brick house where Kim and her son had once lived, but would live no longer, Rory and his grandparents got out of the car. Dr Mehmet, the driver, remained in the vehicle, watching the little group standing on the pavement.

In the car, Rory's crying had stopped. He sat between his grandparents, staring forward. They had not seen any alternative to taking the hysterical child back to his home, but both were afraid that in one part of his mind Rory had not accepted his mother's death and dreaded that he thought, perhaps, he would find her when they got back, as if nothing had happened. They had tried to find out why the boy wanted to go home. 'You won't be able to live there any more,' Mr Arthur had told him.

'I know,' he had responded angrily. Now they stood on the pavement. Kim's mother glanced up at the windows, where their daughter had hung curtains when she moved in with the baby, Rory. Beyond the gate was the little patch of lawn with its round, central bed. The roses Kim had planted were in bloom. Below them, in the ground, were the bulbs she had put in, which had flowered in the spring and would flower again in the following year.

The Arthurs were both looking at Rory, so only Dr Mehmet observed a man walk up the road, duck into the garden opposite the house and start taking photographs. He also noticed a car slide into a parking space down the road. Two men got out, and stood on the pavement looking towards the Arthurs.

Rory ran to the part of the pavement where he had thrown the bird's egg. He knelt down and tried to pick up the small blue fragments, most of which were stuck to the pavement.

'It's my fault,' he shouted. 'I said to go there! I said to go there!' He had three little pieces of bird's egg stuck to his palm now.

'What are you doing, Rory?' asked his grandmother. 'What do you mean?'

Still trying to scrape a piece of egg from the pavement, which broke under the pressure of his nails, he began to cry again. 'I threw my bird's egg away. It's my fault – I threw it away.'

Rory's grandfather did the only thing he could think of. He knelt down and began to lift tiny pieces of crushed eggshell from the pavement with his penknife. The photographer began to approach them from across the road. 'You didn't do anything wrong,' Kim's grandfather told the boy. He dropped a few pieces into an old envelope he had in his inside pocket. 'Mr Arthur!' the photographer called. 'Are you Mr Arthur?'

'We'd better go, Matt,' urged Mrs Arthur.

'Just a minute,' said Matt Arthur. He lifted up another tiny scrap of blue and dropped it in the envelope. 'That's it, I think. Do you think that's all of it, Rory?'

'Yes,' said the boy in a low voice.

'Mr Arthur?' asked the photographer, on the pavement now.

'Go away,' said Matt Arthur. The photographer backed away as Rory and his grandparents advanced towards the car. He bent down, 'Are you Rory Durham?' he asked.

Matt Arthur pushed him. 'Get out of the way.'

'Mr Arthur,' called one of the hurrying men. But the Arthurs' car was moving. Inside, Rory wept over his palm, in which three little pieces of blue eggshell lay. Kim's mother burst into tears herself. A car followed them for a while, then gave up and turned back.

43 Basing Street, London. June 12th, 2015. 4.30 p.m.

Julia Baskerville put a mug of tea in front of the Deputy Leader of her party and said, 'I wouldn't have asked you round if it wasn't important.'

She and Mark Moreno were in the sitting room of her small house in Whitechapel. This room, because of the size of the house, a former workman's cottage, was also the dining room. The dining table stood against the back wall, covered in files and papers. Mark was on the couch, in front of the TV, Julia leaning towards him on a low, buttoned chair. Mark, a very tall, thin and balding forty-year-old, looked weary.

'The point is,' Julia said urgently, 'We all know Muldoon's on his way out unless there's a miracle. And Petherbridge is likely to be the next PM. He's tough and right wing. And who've we got? Carl Chatterton. So I and the usual suspects want to put you up.'

'You always want to put me up, Julia,' Moreno said. 'And I always refuse.'

'It matters, Mark. More than ever——'

'I know. But I don't want to split the party. That matters, too, now, more than ever.'

'The last time I saw Chatterton he couldn't even remember my name.'

'I'm not saying he's got spectacular people skills——'

'He hasn't got any spectacular skills——'

'He's a good number cruncher. He did an excellent job in the Treasury.'

'And then he got promoted above his capacity,' Julia said. 'Mark, we all know what happened. It was between you and Blackwood. Half the Party didn't want Blackwood. The other half didn't want you——'

'That's how it works,' Moreno said.

'That's how it worked. But the party in the House is with you now, ever since Blackwood backed US and British troops landing in the tribal areas in Pakistan, because they thought the Pakistan government hadn't done enough to root out Al Qaeda there. And now they can't find them if they were ever there and casualties are heavy – and that's one good reason why Chatterton and Blackwood are discredited – more and more so, day by day, with every squaddie who dies out there. Come on, Mark – we should challenge now.'

Mark Moreno looked at the thin, animated face opposite him. He smiled. 'Leave it until after the summer recess. Conference time. I'll make my decision then.'

'It could be too late,' she warned.

'No reason to think it will be.'

'I've got a nasty feeling . . .'

Moreno stood up. 'I've got a nasty feeling my wife will be an angry woman if I don't get home now,' he said. 'She's going out for a coffee – first since the twins were born. She's like a kid on the way to Disneyland.'

Julia stood also. She kissed the tall man on the cheek. 'I'm sorry, Mark. I wouldn't have called you if we didn't all think—'

'I won't tell you I haven't been thinking about it. It's not just the Hamscott debate. Of course the Lib Dems will walk all over us. It'll be Amir Siddiqi. They'll walk all over the Tories, too. It won't make any difference. When Petherbridge takes over we'll need a credible leader.'

'Think hard, Mark.'

He nodded and left to make his way back on public transport to Greenford and his screaming twins. Up to now he had never encouraged the left-wingers of his own party to think he'd challenge the leadership. Loyalty or strategy? Both, of course. But perhaps this time Julia was right. Chatterton was increasingly a liability. Petherbridge would be a bigger threat than Muldoon. As usual, timing was everything. Success or failure depended on it. Timing – and luck.

Fox Square, London SW1. June 12th, 2015. 8.30 p.m.

Two figures stood by the base of the statue of General Sir Galahad Montmorency Havelock. Facing the statue with their backs turned to the church they were unlikely to be noticed. Even if they had been observed, an accidental meeting in the Westminster village would not have been too surprising. However, this meeting was no accident.

Two days after Kim Durham's death, Alan Petherbridge leaked the memorandum revealing his plan to retake the base using trained officers from the Metropolitan Police and Kent Constabulary, a plan the Prime Minister had approved. Also leaked was the fact that about an hour later the Prime Minister had agreed to the landing of US Marines at Hamscott. The press leapt on it; there was noisy questioning of the Prime Minister in the House of Commons; a week later a poll showed that 82 per cent of the public blamed the Prime Minister for Kim Durham's death. The effect of the leak was devastating. Only one right-wing newspaper had dared, in an editorial, to suggest that the invasion of a base holding nuclear weapons demanded prompt and forceful action. This was followed by a flood of largely hostile correspondence.

It would have helped Muldoon if there had been one person with Asian or Middle Eastern connections among the arrested base invaders. But there were none. Those who had seized the base were peace activists, CND supporters and members of religious groups. There were a few hard-core left-wingers. There were nuns. And the Red Vicar, the Reverend Alec Hutchinson, who had been injured by a bullet in the calf but was soon back in full voice from his wheelchair. Admittedly, some of the arrested men and women had convictions for minor offences – trespass, criminal damage, attacks on the police – but hard as Canning and his Press Office tried, it was impossible to spin these characters into terrorists. Meanwhile, there was no escaping the pictures of Kim Durham and her son in newspapers, on TV round the world and now on banners carried by the government's opponents.

Two weeks later, a second poll showed that 75 per cent of the public, including 50 per cent of his own supporters, thought that Muldoon should be replaced as Prime Minister. Three weeks further on, the same number said that in the event of another election resulting in another hung Parliament, they would support a National Government.

Two days later, a firestorm was unleashed on Syria. Damascus and Aleppo were hit two nights running by a fleet of bombers. A third of the armada of bombers were launched from British bases, including Hamscott Common. The justification for the attack was, said the American President, that Syria had been harbouring international Muslim terrorists who had infiltrated Iraq over the border, flooding the country with subversive propaganda, agents and money. Syrian complicity had created the results of the Iraqi elections. In America, the public was divided about the attacks. The British public refused to believe the President's arguments. The European Parliament met to condemn the raids. The assault on Syria could not have been timed better if the intention had been deliberately to finish Muldoon as Prime Minister. Some thought that might have been the case.

Predictably, there were demonstrations throughout the country. A suicide bomber, a young man from Harlesden, blew himself up in the gardens of Buckingham Palace. Twelve British oil executives in Nigeria were kidnapped. There were bloody riots in the East End and Southall.

The Conservative Party had changed greatly since the days when a contingent of Tory grandees would visit a Prime Minister they no longer required, and, with the air of men putting down a loaded revolver on a table in front of a disgraced officer, suggest the Prime Minister should take the only way out and resign. There are procedures these days – but at this point the inner group of the Conservative Party knew they had no time for a bruising leadership contest. Muldoon must go, quickly, on grounds of ill health. The chairman of the CBI, Gisela Sutter, and the Party Chairman, Sir Graham Barnsbury, asked for appointments. So did an old lion who had once been in Mrs Thatcher's Cabinet (and had been among those who told her she must go). The Party Leader in the House of Commons tried to arrange a meeting with Muldoon. A gentleman closely connected with Buckingham Palace planned to drop in for tea. And there were others – Lord Haver of Blindon, the twentieth richest man in Great Britain, the Chief Whip, the Chairman of the Bank of England, and several more – all men who could not be put off and would not be. The PM's diary filled with the names of his would-be assassins.

After the first of these meetings, Gisela Sutter, the CBI Chairman, reported to Lord Haver and then, separately, to Lord Gott – the two men disliked each other – that Muldoon was not taking the hint. Graham Barnsbury told Lady Jenner, the Conservative leader in the Lords, that Muldoon had told him he thought it important to stay on, to stand firm and weather out the storm. Anything else would discredit the party and him, personally. Such statements have been made by politicians in the past, just before clearing their desks and booking a holiday but Muldoon was that most formidable of obstacles, a weak, obstinate and cunning man. The assassins met and made another plan.

Meanwhile, Muldoon, who knew his world to be full of enemies, cancelled as many appointments as he could, sent the Deputy PM to the House of Commons for Question Time and went to ground, as far as he was able to. The British Parliament has no fixed sessions but votes itself, each year, a generous four months of holidays. The House was due to go into recess in mid-July this year, and would reconvene in mid-October. No child, waiting for the start of the summer holidays, could have looked forward to them as much as Frederick Muldoon did to the dissolution of Parliament, due in four weeks.

Standing in Fox Square by the podium of Sir Galahad's statue, Petherbridge said to Canning, 'Tom, you and I have had our differences in the past but we need you now. You know why. You're the only man Muldoon will listen to. He's in his bunker, like Hitler, and he won't come out. You're practically the only man he trusts. But he can't survive. You know it, I know it, and at the back of his mind he must know it. Quite frankly you'd be doing him a favour, putting him out of his misery.'

And you a favour too, thought Canning. You want poor old Fred out because you're the next in line. He was not surprised. He had seen this conversation coming from the moment, that morning, when Petherbridge had asked for a quick chat. Up to now Petherbridge had stayed out of the fray, presumably because it never looks good when the heir apparent takes the knife to his own father. It was plain to Canning that with Muldoon clinging like a barnacle to the ship of state, Petherbridge had been persuaded to take a hand.

This was not the first time that Canning had been approached to use his influence with Muldoon. It was not the second, or even the third. Previously, he'd refused, giving loyalty as his reason. This was only part of it, and perhaps not a very big part. Muldoon had been Canning's living for seven years. Where would he go when Muldoon went to the back-benches or perhaps out of Parliament altogether? Back to *The Times*? Would they have him – throwing up a career on a national paper to work for seven years as a Press Secretary is not always much of a recommendation? There were other papers. There was PR. There was consultancy work. But a man who has been a PM's lackey and ends up stabbing his boss in the back is not always welcome on anyone's staff.

'It'd be an act of kindness to him,' Petherbridge said persuasively. 'And I'm sure you'd find many people very grateful if you could spare the PM humiliation and the party an agonizing leadership contest in public.'

Canning was not admitting to himself that at that moment he was afraid of Alan Petherbridge, afraid of those dark eyes of his, eyes which never, whether in light or darkness, seemed to reflect anything back to the person he was talking to. He was afraid of that pale, matt face – his own was sweating, he knew – and the firm line of Petherbridge's mouth.

But he could not deny Petherbridge's intelligence and effectiveness. Like a man held in a marriage to an ailing wife, tempted by a healthy and willing partner, he saw it was time to jump – and he jumped. 'How grateful would these people be, do you think?' he asked. Petherbridge told him. Five years on the board of a state-supported institution, the CEO of which was about to retire in two years, three years as Director, then, in all probability, a peerage. Canning asked about guarantees. Petherbridge stared at him with those hard-to-read eyes. 'I'm your guarantee,' he told Canning. 'Believe me – this is the best you can hope for.'

He added none of the softening phrases that help a man to do what he thinks he should not do. He had offered his deal. It was a good one and Canning, flinching under that steady, determined gaze, had never been more certain that Muldoon was doomed. He had the impression that Petherbridge would be angered by a request for a few days to think the matter over.

He said, 'I agree. Shall we talk tomorrow?' The two men shook hands briefly and parted straight away, leaving Sir Galahad alone in the square, with a pigeon roosting on his head. Tom Canning went home to Clapham Common and hit the local pub and Alan Petherbridge went into Sugden's for dinner with some good friends from Amical, the Anglo-American friendship society.

Petherbridge sat down. William handed him a menu. 'Good day?' enquired his American guest.

'Very satisfactory,' said Alan Petherbridge.

Three

10 Downing Street, London SW1. June 15th, 2015. 8 a.m.

Tom Canning sat down opposite the Prime Minister at his small break-fast table in the upstairs kitchen. Muldoon had eaten his eggs and bacon and had started on the toast. His wife was in the country, planning the annual Conservative Ball.

'So what's today's bad news, Tom?' Muldoon asked, trying to sound as he used to. Canning, deliberately, did not smile. Muldoon looked at him, his expression fading. 'What is it?' he asked.

'It's bad, Prime Minister,' Canning said. 'Somebody's got to tell you and I wish to God it didn't have to be me – but the truth is, you must resign. If you do, you go with dignity. If not, you'll be gone in a few weeks and without any dignity at all.' He went on to tell Muldoon exactly who was against him and how they planned to proceed.

'This is a shock, Tom,' said Muldoon. But his manner, Canning observed, was not like that of a man who has had a shock.

At that moment Canning did not know what to make of Muldoon. Having put down his knife and fork the Prime Minister crossed the room and turned on the coffee machine which stood, fresh coffee in the filter, ready to go. He turned. His face was grave. Canning had been prepared for bitterness, for talk, even, of a possible compromise. Muldoon only said, 'I'll talk to the Leader of the House.'

Grateful that Muldoon seemed to have accepted that he had to go, Canning reminded him, 'You'd better ring the Palace.'

Muldoon shot him a bitter look. 'Yes, Tom. I know,' he said. He added, 'Funny how fast things move when they're really determined to get rid of you.'

'It's a rough old game,' Canning said, in a more sympathetic tone.

'It certainly is,' Muldoon replied. Canning stood up to go. 'I'm only upset that it should be you they sent. I thought better of you, Tom.'

'No one could have been more reluctant,' Canning said. 'Believe me, I never thought it would come to this. I'm deeply upset.'

'Thank you, Tom,' said Muldoon. After the door closed behind Canning Muldoon's expression changed. 'Bastards,' he thought, 'Judases – I'll fuck the lot of you.' And he did.

First, Muldoon asked his attackers if they would allow him see out the session and offer his resignation when Parliament reopened in October.

The men and women who had conspired to get rid of him instinctively mistrusted this plan. It had been hard enough to persuade Muldoon to resign and now he had agreed to go, they wanted it over before he had a chance to wriggle out of it. But the current session of Parliament was due to end in three weeks. There was too little time to go through the procedures involved in electing a new leader before the session ended. If Muldoon declared his resignation immediately there would be three or four months of speculation, plots, plans, rivalries and press leaks before the election in October or November. Three or four months during which something could go wrong. Trapped, the party bigwigs agreed to wait.

Then Muldoon tricked them all. The following week, at Tuesday's Question Time, he stood up in the House of Commons and declared a General Election. After the first moments of shocked disbelief a howl went up. Over the noise, which gradually subsided, the Prime Minister stated that the country was in urgent need of a government with a sound majority and a public mandate to govern. The present situation was untenable – a state close to anarchy prevailed. He could not in conscience continue to lead his party or his country in such circumstances. Consequently, he would be visiting Her Majesty that afternoon to ask for the dissolution of Parliament. He concluded by saying that for health reasons he himself would be unable to lead his party into the election. He spoke calmly, as if making the most mundane of announcements and only those who knew him best detected the bravado, or the malicious pleasure he felt when he concluded his statement and sank down into his seat on the front bench.

The groans of disbelief and disgust, which had begun when it became plain what he was saying and then subsided as he spoke on, swelled again. MPs began to rise in their seats, shouting words that could not be heard over the hubbub. The Speaker's calls for order were ignored. And, finally, the Speaker dismissed the House. The noise ebbed as suddenly as it had risen. MPs, sobered, walked out of the Chamber, talking to each other in small groups.

The senior men and women of all parties convened immediately. But the reality was that they could do nothing to reverse Muldoon's decision. It was unheard of to declare an election without consulting the opposition parties. Muldoon had not even consulted his own. It was unheard of to dissolve Parliament in summer, since an election cannot take place until the autumn. But Muldoon had done it. As Prime Minister he had the power to call an election whenever he chose, subject only to the Queen's consent, and the Queen, though technically able to refuse, cannot really do so. Muldoon had found a loophole in the (unwritten) British constitution and driven a coach, horses and outriders right through it.

Muldoon went to see the Queen, in her late eighties now, and tiring, but still very acute. She, reportedly, was so furious with Muldoon that she kept him standing throughout the interview. The Committee for Constitutional Change – nicknamed the Committee for Constipated Change – had been sitting for two years now. Part of its brief had been to examine the traditional powers accorded to the Prime Minister and discuss whether these powers – among others, unilaterally sending troops to war and unilaterally declaring a General Election – were suitable in a twenty-first-century democracy. The Committee was still sitting. Now a platoon of constitutional lawyers was drafted on to it to close the stable door now that the horse had bolted.

The fact remained. The election had been called and the parties would have to fight it six weeks after Parliament reconvened in late October.

The coming election would be a financial disaster for the three main parties. The third election in five years found them without funds. The Labour Party's bankers were threatening; the Conservative Party had only escaped bankruptcy the previous year when Edward Gott found a wealthy man to bail them out. The Liberal Democrats were only slightly better off.

This would be an election fought on overdrafts, by Parliamentarians who had fought too many elections over the past few years asking for the votes of citizens to whom the word 'election' had the appeal of double maths, lawn-mowing or attic-clearing. Party workers wanted never again to deliver another leaflet or organize a public meeting. And, adding insult to injury, MPs and party staffers would have to return early from their holidays to prepare.

The worst blow Muldoon struck was against his own party. Apart from the other disadvantages the outcome of the election would probably be another hung Parliament. The pressure to form a National Government would become irresistible.

However, politics is war and politicians are fighters. Muldoon might have thrown his party into a battle they did not want but they would fight it to the death. And must fight it under a leader. The Conservative Party could not go into an election in the middle of a messy leadership contest. The natural choice was Alan Petherbridge. Party rules dictated that he could not be confirmed without a list of candidates being opened and a countrywide poll of party members. The list was opened. It was made plain that anyone other than Petherbridge who allowed their name to be put forward would be deselected by their local party before the election took place. There was barely time to put together a leadership list with one name on it – that of Alan Petherbridge – before Parliament broke for the summer.

Muldoon's invitations dried up completely. His club, White's, asked for his resignation. An eerie silence hung over Downing Street as the

parliamentary session came to a close. Muldoon put in a call to Alan
Petherbridge, inviting him to a meeting at Downing Street. Petherbridge
had no choice but to go, though he did not know why Muldoon wanted
him and did not look forward to the visit.

Muldoon and his wife were at that time supervising the removal of
their property. It was six in the evening. In the drawing room, where
several tea chests stood open, Muldoon grabbed Petherbridge by the arm.
'I've got to tell you, Alan, exactly what you're facing if we win – and if
you win.'

Petherbridge, his suspicion that Muldoon was half-drunk confirmed,
looked down at the hand and said, 'Enlighten me.'

'Even if you end up with everybody calling you Prime Minister and
going to tea with the Queen once a week, you've had it. They'll tell you
what to do. You can't resist them.'

'Who do you mean?' asked Petherbridge.

'The Americans – the Yanks – of course. Who the hell do you think I
mean?'

Muldoon's wife came to the open door and looked in. Her face showed
icy fury and her expression said, 'What is the fool doing now?' Muldoon,
under that gaze, took his hand from Petherbridge's arm. Mrs Muldoon
beckoned in two men, who carried out one of the tea chests.

Muldoon threw himself into a chair covered by a dust sheet and looked
up at Petherbridge. 'Do you think I wanted those Marines landing at
Hamscott Common, when that poor girl got killed? Do you think I had
any say in that? That's what I'm trying to tell you. They want to raid
Hamscott Common – they do. They want to bomb Syria from our bases
– they do. And they're going to reinvade Iraq – they'll do that, too. And
you'll go along with it. That's the reality – you'll go along with it. You'd
better believe it. Don't kid yourself, Alan. Look at me. I've ended up
hated and booted out – and I never had any choice.'

'Is this why you invited me here?' Petherbridge said. 'Because I have
a meeting.'

The two removal men came back, hesitated and, at Petherbridge's
signal, collected another tea chest.

Muldoon had closed his eyes. He opened them again and said to
Petherbridge, 'You may think you're very clever. Wait till you find out
you're a puppet on a string.' Then he closed his eyes again and Petherbridge
left. In Whitehall he called a cab. 'The US Embassy,' he ordered.

7 Adam Street, Shepherd's Bush, London W12. August 20th, 2015. 6 p.m.

William and Lucy Frith came back into their flat and put their bags down. 'Nice to be back?' suggested William to his wife. She was tanned, her long dark hair pony-tailed. She smiled and said, 'Not specially.' They had enjoyed their economical fortnight in Cos, visiting the ruins, taking boat trips, sitting outside small restaurants in the evening and now here they were, back in their upstairs flat in the small Edwardian house in their small back street in West London, faced with a resumption of the daily grind.

'Next year,' William told her. In a year's time they might have saved enough to get the two-bedroomed flat, with a garden. Then they would hope for a baby.

Lucy smiled again. 'Next year,' she agreed.

'OK — you load the washing machine and I'll open the wine and put out the cheese and olives—' he began, then the phone rang. The news, William understood as he listened to Lucy's voice, was not good. 'We only just got back, Dad. We didn't take the mobile because it's too expensive abroad. What's the matter? Is it Mum — is she all right?'

William's face was rueful as he unzipped a case and began to take out their clothes. He carried an armful into the kitchen. How long had they been back? Five minutes? Not even that. And already the Sutcliffes were ruining the good effects of Lucy's holiday for her. She'd spent the last fifty weeks of the year as a sister in the orthopaedic ward at Hammersmith Hospital looking after smashed-up motorbike riders, old people with their chalky bones in multiple fractures, skate boarders and women whose husbands had beaten them with tyre levers and baseball bats. She'd had a fortnight in the sun and they were hardly back when bloody Joe Sutcliffe rang up, spoiling everything for her. 'Is it Mum?' Of course it was her mum. It always was. 'Is she all right?' No, of course she wasn't — never was and never, William thought, ever would be, as far as he could see.

Marie Sutcliffe, Lucy's mother, had always suffered with her nerves, as her husband described it. There had never been a more sophisticated diagnosis because Marie resisted any treatment other than that given to her by her sympathetic GP — too sympathetic, William thought. A local doctor, a practitioner trained in the Sutcliffes' ways and only called in when things got particularly bad. Sensible Grace Frith, William's mother, told him she thought that even in this day and age situations like this were more common than anyone would believe. The family accommodates itself to the sufferer – their form of behaviour becomes, for them, the norm – no treatment is sought, or, if it is, without much enthusiasm. This can go on for decades, sometimes for ever, unless something comes along to force change. His mother's opinions brought William little comfort.

Lucy had grown up knowing she must be quiet, obedient and careful and never, in any circumstances bring upsetting news into the house. Her small woes – toothache, nasty school dinners, bullying, homework problems – she confided to her father, who dealt with them as best he could. As a family the Sutcliffes never watched anything difficult on TV. If, for example, Joe misjudged the time and caught the last part of the news before the football results, Marie, entering the room and faced with a street scene following a bomb blast, the debris of an air crash strewn across a field, even an announcer reporting a political crisis, would open her mouth in a silent 'Oh' and have to be led off to bed, given a tranquillizer, and calmed down. The effects of this might last for days as pale, silent and tottery, she went about her household tasks. As a child Lucy had been careful not to get lost, or overstay at a friend's house – for Marie was largely agoraphobic and could not leave the house to come and find her. And believed, more-over, that danger lay outside the house – for herself, her child, even for her husband. Marie could go to the village on errands and to church to take part in church activities, but had not, for example, been able to visit her parents in hospital before they died. Her husband, a policeman, had to avoid overtime and, when offered plain-clothes duties, refused. He became a highly competent bureaucrat, but a man who stayed put in his office, coming and going on time.

At one time Lucy had thought of becoming a doctor. When she mentioned it her mother began to cry, wordlessly and inconsolably and was forced to stay in bed for almost a week, taking heavy sedatives. The training, of course, would have meant Lucy's leaving home for many years to study, perhaps never to return. Lucy, young and still not questioning the family rule that her mother should not be upset at any time, did nursing training at the nearest hospital, some ten miles from where they lived. She was usually driven to and collected from the hospital by Joe and, when this was not possible, she took the bus and neither of them told Marie. But youth is strong and its impulses often irresistible. One day she had been obliged to tell a young doctor who had taken her out that she must, absolutely must, be home by ten, or her mother would be very worried. She had also been obliged to keep the family secret about exactly how worried Marie would be, and what form the worry would take. She knew if she told the whole truth the young doctor might ask searching medical questions and offer solutions. The questions would be hard to answer and all the solutions hopeless.

The following day, after her father dropped nineteen-year-old Lucy at the hospital in her probationer nurse uniform, she simply walked to the railway station and took a train to London. Next day, she had signed on at a London teaching hospital, where she went slightly mad, had an affair with a married, alcoholic heart specialist and, a year after the crash, met a young man who had snapped a tendon playing Sunday football. She and William were married a year later.

During the Friths' married life the Sutcliffes had never visited them in London. Marie believed the city to be noisy, dirty, dangerous and full of untrustworthy foreigners. The Friths always visited the Sutcliffes in Basset, the pretty Yorkshire village where the couple – Joe now retired – lived. William endured the depressing visits, watched his words and expressions and counted the hours until they could get away. He could never understand why some form of treatment for Marie had not been insisted on, years before. He suspected her of having no great desire to change things and was indignant about the constraints that had been put on his wife during her youth.

The phone call, because Marie would have spent the last fortnight worrying about food poisoning and air crashes, was par for the course. All William did was groan inwardly until he came back into the living room with a plate of olives in his hands and heard Lucy saying, 'Dad! You can't come here. There's no room. And how's Mum going to manage . . .?' As she spoke she was staring wide-eyed at William, like a woman in a horror film. William was shaking his head and mouthing, 'No!' at her. He could not believe it. The Sutcliffes never came to London. If they were coming – why? It was out of the question, anyway. The flat was too small. Both he and Lucy worked shifts. Marie feared the city and Joe, whose devotion to, and care of his daughter, William couldn't fault, didn't much like him. William felt much the same about Joe. When the two families – William's and Lucy's – had met at the wedding they only got along by making a considerable effort. William's parents, formerly both teachers, were old school, old Labour, *Guardian*-reading lefties. It was lucky that they had retired to Spain, so the two families rarely met.

Lucy was saying, 'Dad! You know Mum hates London. It'll make her worse.' William watched his wife. Joe was doing all the talking. It couldn't happen, William decided – not Joe and Marie here. He remembered an early visit to Basset, when he and Lucy had broken out of the house to go to the local pub for a drink together. Irritable after thirty-six hours confined to the house, William, half-finishing his pint at one go, had said to his wife, 'You're a nurse, Lucy. Why don't you get your mother some treatment?'

'She doesn't want any,' Lucy replied weakly. 'She gets very upset if it's suggested.'

'So the only treatment she gets is when it all gets out of hand and Dr Feel-good comes round with his tablets, or a nice little injection?'

Lucy nodded. Defensively she said, 'There's nothing wrong with Mum as long as she isn't upset. She manages the house and plays her part in the church activities – cake stalls and the like. Even the doctor had to admit that forcing her into some kind of therapy and, probably, permanent heavy medication might make things worse. This isn't straightforward medicine, William. There are no guarantees. The cure can sometimes be worse than the disease.'

'How would you know? No one's tried,' said William. He added that in his, unqualified, opinion, Marie might be better off now if her father had taken a firm line with his wife earlier on and forced her to face the world.

'You can't just say all she needed was a kick up the behind.'

'I didn't say—' William denied.

'No – but it was what you meant,' said Lucy, silencing him, because it was true. 'Anyway – yes, she was a sensitive child – when Dad met her she was working in the local wool shop. And apparently, my birth triggered an awful episode, post-natal depression I suppose, and after that Dad was afraid it might happen again. So,' Lucy said, rather loudly, 'yes – it's a mess but it's our mess and we deal with it and what about another drink.' Then Joe had came in and stayed for an uneasy drink until it became plain that he had come, at Marie's behest, to fetch them home.

And now he could hear his wife making arrangements for the Sutcliffes' arrival, in a day's time. Shaking his head at Lucy, he got a corkscrew from the kitchen, opened the bottle of wine they'd brought home and as soon as she'd put the phone down, handed her a glass. She sat down heavily on the sofa. Lucy had not shed the habit, ingrained in childhood, of not talking about Marie's condition. She sat staring at him unhappily and William waited.

'So what's all this about?' demanded William, not liking his own tone of voice when he heard it. Lucy looked towards the window. There was a primary school on the other side of the road they lived in and William saw she was already weighing the effect of the pupils' noise on Marie.

'It's the school holidays,' he said.

'I know.' She couldn't mean she thought the Sutcliffes would be staying until the children came back to school in two or three weeks' time. He still couldn't really believe they were coming at all.

Lucy's eye went to the umbrella plant on the floor by the window. It had been a foot high when they bought it, just after they were married and was now a big glossy plant, over five feet high. But Marie disliked plants of any kind in the house. They made her heart sink, she said.

'I'm not getting rid of Charlie,' William said instantly. Lucy sighed. William pressed his point. 'They'll have to go to a B and B.'

'Mum can't go to a B and B,' Lucy responded tonelessly.

'She hasn't left Basset for nearly thirty years but she's going to. So what's going to stop her from staying at a B and B – or a hotel, if you like? We can't do it, Lucy – you're on nights next week. I get in at one or two in the morning. How will we get enough sleep? It won't work, you know it won't.'

All Lucy, normally articulate, said was, 'Mum wants us all to be together.'

'What for? What's wrong?' William asked. He half-expected Lucy to tell him either Joe or Marie was seriously ill and in London for specialist treatment. Instead she said, 'It's RAF Thwaite – you know, about ten miles from the village? Apparently the attacks on Syria used planes from there. So last week a suicide bomber drove a van full of explosives up to the perimeter and charged it. He didn't get in. He was shot and the van exploded. A couple of American airmen were injured by the flying debris. Anyway, yesterday, before Mum had even heard about this she saw two tank loads of soldiers coming past the house. They'd come through the village for some reason. Dad had been shopping and when he came in he found her unconscious on the front room floor. Not unconscious, really, more like catatonic, her eyes were open. You know, these fugue states she goes into. Dad called the doctor. He came and while he was preparing the injection he said something about the disturbing news from Thwaite. Dad had heard about it in the village but he obviously wasn't going to tell Mum – but the doctor, stupidly, did. And she seemed to hear, even in the state she was in, and she began to cry and wail – they had trouble calming her down enough to deliver the injection—' Lucy looked at William and what she saw made her break off. 'Anyway, she's very depressed now.'

'Coming to London,' William said. 'If anything happens, it happens here. Where's the sense in that?'

'She thinks we all ought to die together,' Lucy said flatly.

'Sounds a lot easier than living together,' William couldn't help saying. He picked up the bottle from the table and poured himself more wine. Lucy hadn't touched hers. They were in dangerous territory now, moving into Sutcliffe-land, where common sense did not prevail. He asked hopefully, as if the question might have some meaning, 'Did your dad give you any idea how long they planned to stay in London?'

'It's not the sort of thing you plan,' Lucy replied. 'I know you don't want them here.'

'Nor do you,' William said. He changed tack. 'Look, Lucy, this is hopeless. They can't come here. This dying together stuff is rubbish. You're a nurse. You know perfectly well your mother shouldn't come here. She needs expert help.'

'And you know she won't accept it. The only way to do it would be to have her sectioned. I'm not even sure a doctor would agree to it – and you've never been inside a mental hospital. I have. I wouldn't put my worst enemy in one.'

'Joe could pay privately,' William said. 'They can well afford it.'

They had had this discussion many times. They were drifting away from the point and William sensed Lucy was making this happen.

'Think how often we've stayed with them,' Lucy appealed. William might have pointed out that this was not their decision. He could have added that as far as he was concerned each visit to the Sutcliffes had been a waste of free time which would have been more enjoyably spent elsewhere. But Lucy knew quite well what he thought.

William told her this, adding, 'I wouldn't mind so much if I knew how long they were staying.'

'Yes, you would,' Lucy declared.

'Not as much,' said William, drinking. He knew that after one more glass of wine he would start a row. He didn't care.

'There it is!' cried Lucy. The suicide bombing at Thwaite was old news now but on the TV there was a picture of a wide gate being rebuilt, armed guards and fluttering police tapes. A medalled RAF officer and a man in a suit stood in the wind, discussing the event. Worldwide terror, constant vigilance and full alert were mentioned. The terrorist, blown to fragments, had not been identified. The van had been stolen in Swansea.

William said, 'This business at Thwaite is just an isolated incident. Anyway, they live ten miles away. London's one security alert after another. How's your mother going to feel getting patted down going into the Tube? Oh, I forgot, she won't be going into the Tube.'

'I don't suppose she'll be going anywhere,' Lucy admitted.

'No – we're just going to sit here waiting to die together.'

'Mum's just terribly afraid of being left alone, without Dad,' Lucy said defensively. A thought struck her. 'You won't walk out on me, William, if they come?'

'Don't talk rubbish,' he said. 'If I walk out, it'll be with you. Maybe we should go and stay at the B and B.'

Lucy surprised him when she said, 'I thought about that, but it'd put a dent in our savings.'

'Let's go out to the Venezia tonight to celebrate our last night of freedom.'

'I didn't tell you they were coming tomorrow,' Lucy said.

'You didn't have to,' William said. 'I'm good for a week, Lucy. But after that we'll have to think long and hard. And Charlie stays.'

They went to the restaurant and tried not to talk too much about the imminent arrival of Lucy's parents.

Manderton, Oakdene Avenue, Bromley, Kent. August 25th, 2015. 3.30 p.m.

Joshua Crane was only too pleased, on the afternoon of the day after his return from a month's holiday with his family in Italy, to be rung up by Edward Gott and invited to a last-minute meeting over dinner at Sugden's. Standing in the French windows of their long living room, he told his wife Beth, who was sitting by their pool maintaining her tan, 'I'll have to go to London. The election.' In fact, he was keen to get to Chelsea to discover if his girlfriend was back. She'd told him she would be holidaying with friends, unspecified, in Goa while he was away giving his wife what he thought he owed her – a month in four-star hotels in Italy, with shopping trips to Rome and Milan thrown in. But knowing Saskia, she might just as easily have gone to Cape Cod, Saint Tropez or Thailand. She might have found a new boyfriend or even got married. He'd tried phoning her at midnight from the bottom of the garden the day before, but had only reached her answering machine.

Beth Crane looked up from her magazine and said, 'I can't see why. Your seat's safe. And I don't suppose they're going to ask you to stand for leader.'

This squib, after a month of the same, made Joshua revise his plan to be detained in London overnight and turn it into being detained there for several days. When he was with Saskia he always claimed to be staying in Battersea with his old friend, a fellow MP, Douglas Clare. Douglas, without approving, covered for him. Although Beth was, of course, right that the dinner with Gott could not concern any really important matter. The Party Chairman, Graham Barnsbury, who had been hastily appointed election co-ordinator, had already rung him in Italy and briefly checked he would be supporting Alan Petherbridge for leader.

'Perhaps something's come up,' he muttered to Beth.

She sat up and began to file her nails. 'Try to get back as soon as you can. While the boys are still on holiday.'

She wasn't demonstrating any desire for his company as a husband. No surprise there, thought Joshua, piqued. He sometimes feared that his wife guessed something about the affair with Saskia. In morbid moments he wondered if she knew everything about it. He concealed his mobile phone bills, but she could have obtained copies – she might even have hired a detective.

He had accepted that after twelve years of marriage, during which he and Beth were supposed to have drawn closer, they had only discovered more things about each other they did not like. Beth made no effort to bridge the gap (why should she, if she knew he'd been unfaithful to her since she'd been pregnant with Marcus, their first child?). She repelled Joshua's few remorseful, bumbling efforts to improve matters. Joshua wondered if Beth was patterning her own marriage on her parents', which was distant. Perhaps she just didn't like him. Perhaps she knew or guessed about all his infidelities over the years and believed that if she weakened, and tried to trust – even love – him once more, she would suffer even more when he betrayed her again. But when he considered making a clean breast of it to his wife and offering to start again, his courage failed. He doubted if Beth would forgive; he doubted if he would remain faithful to her even if she did. The marriage had become a marriage of convenience, with Beth enjoying the good standard of living and kudos which went with being an MP's wife and Joshua benefiting from the family he needed for his political career.

His solution was to erect a mental wall between his marriage and the rest of his life. If the wall ever came down and he had to confront the situation directly the results, he guessed, would break his heart – separation, divorce, his wife would take his sons away. His sons, he would think – his sons – and then run and crouch behind the wall again.

'I'm not sure how long I'll be gone – I'll ring, of course,' he said.

'Chambers' party on Saturday,' she reminded him.

Barrington Chambers was Joshua's local Party Chairman. A self-made man, he owned several men's outfitters in Finchley and Frognal. Joshua thought privately that while you couldn't really describe Barry Chambers' political views as being to the right of Adolph Hitler's, Barry and Hitler would certainly have found common ground if they'd ever got together for a chat about immigration, gypsies and gays. He would have disliked Barry more if Barry had not been inconsistent. When one of the asylum seekers, part of a band of builders run by a gang master, fell off Barry's roof and broke a leg, Barry gave him a large sum of money in cash to tide him over until his leg mended. Beth said that if Barry had any real concern for the man, or others like him, he wouldn't have employed a cheap firm that had no regard for the safety of its workers.

'You'll come?' questioned Joshua. It was important not to seem to snub the Chambers.

'Of course,' Beth told him. 'But I don't know who's more unbearable – Barry or his wife. He's too loud and she never speaks – but when she does she's got a voice that could cut metal.'

'Thank you, darling,' Joshua said, and, packing a small bag, then drove to his girlfriend's mews house in Chelsea. He rang the bell. There was no answer. The fuchsias in the baskets hanging on wrought iron hooks beside the front door had withered and died. The bay tree in its earthenware pot beside the door was browning. Joshua borrowed a hose from a man on the other side of the mews, who was washing his car, and gave the plants and the tree a good drenching. Doing this, he wetted his shoes and left, disconsolate. His next stop was Douglas Clare's flat in Battersea, where he left his bag. Then he went back across the river to Sugden's, where Edward Gott was waiting for him.

He wondered what Gott wanted. Probably nothing – or just lunch – he thought. Parliamentary holidays are very long, giving rise to all kinds of behaviour – boredom is the least of an MP's problems. And he knew Gott had many sons, six in all. Three were married, with children of their own, and all were expected by Lady Gott to spend part of their holidays at the family's house in the Borders. Joshua had stayed at Brigstock once. It was a semi-fortified house in a charming wooded place by a loch and had been occupied by Lady Margot's family since Culloden (Edward Gott had married above himself. He had brought the money, Lady Margot the status).

Once seated, each man asked the other about holidays, both claimed to have enjoyed them and neither fully believed the other. Gott did mention that in spite of a converted barn and several cottages Brigstock, at mealtimes, seemed crowded, and that he had begun to understand the old tales and ballads where people eating dinner, often relatives, started quarrels and set on each other with swords. Joshua, in turn, mentioned that shopping in Rome's fashion stores with two restless boys, aged nine and seven, made him feel like wielding a sword himself.

Lord Gott asked the waiter about William, whom he'd not seen. 'He'll be in later,' the waiter said. 'What have we here?' Gott said, studying the wine list critically. He ordered a bottle. Then they turned to the menu. Gott settled on veal and fried potatoes as he was, he said, on a diet at home. Joshua ordered trout. 'So,' Joshua said, when the orders had been taken, 'what's afoot, Edward?'

'Not a lot,' Gott confessed. 'It's still Alan Petherbridge, of course. That little turd Geoffrey Shawcross tried to try it on,' Gott added. 'He began to wonder if an open leadership campaign might not make the party look more democratic, wondered if him standing might help. But we got him behind the bike sheds and persuaded him he was wrong. "The election's the thing – your seat's safe, no trouble there?"'

Joshua thought of the coming election and asked Gott, nervously, 'What does it look like?' His own seat ought to be safe enough, with a majority of 8,000, but elections bring out the high-wire artist in politicians – fear, excitement and dread of the unexpected mingle.

'We'll win, barring accidents. Carl Chatterton's got all the appeal of a wet sock and we've shed Muldoon, who had all the appeal of the other half of the pair. We'll have Petherbridge, a new face no one's had time to get disillusioned about. He's been an efficient and careful Home Secretary, due to good luck and good management he's been able to open three new prisons during his period of office and there's nothing the electorate likes better than seeing shiny, new slammers opening up. And he came well out of the Kim Durham affair. So we'll win. But only a third of the public will vote because they're fed up with elections. And politicians. And they're guessing whoever wins won't have a majority – again. Well, I don't think you or I, privately, would dare disagree with them. The upshot will be that Liberals will hold the balance of power again, as usual. Then comes a National Government. Muldoon has made that inevitable.' He added gloomily, 'We can't afford to fight, of course, but we've got to. So have the others and they've no money, either.'

'Petherbridge won't like a National Government.'

'No PM fancies presiding over a Cabinet full of his opponents.'

'What's he like?' asked Joshua, who knew that, as Party Treasurer, Gott must know more about the man than he did.

'A cross between Cardinal Richelieu and Torquemada,' Gott replied readily. 'He's very brainy, of course. Outwardly he's a civilized man. But he's got hidden depths, where monsters lurk.'

'What monsters?'

Gott evaded the question. 'The highest office in the land,' he said, 'is like an extreme psychological test – like being in the condemned cell or suspended in a sensory deprivation tank, alone and afraid. The problem is that the man being tested, the PM, doesn't realize this and no one around him will tell him. Our problem is that we don't know what the incumbent's weaknesses are until he's tested, and by then it's too late.'

Joshua persisted. 'But you say Petherbridge isn't a stable man. What do you know?'

'Not enough,' said Gott shortly.

'There's a Mrs Petherbridge, isn't there? But she's never around. What's the story there?'

'Annabel Petherbridge is very frail, physically and mentally. As long as she stays where she is, on what I believe is a nice little farm in Gloucestershire, she's all right. Too much exposure to the bright lights – or her husband – and she starts to get a little wobbly. She always turns out for the Party Conference and she'll be there in a hat when Petherbridge kisses the Queen's hand. Alan just has to use her sparingly, that's all.'

'What about other women?' Joshua asked.

'Joshua,' Gott told him, 'we're not all like you.'

Joshua looked at his plate, then raised his head. 'You bastard,' was all he found to say.

Edward Gott raised his glass. 'Well – to victory.'

Joshua, numbly, echoed him.

After lunch Gott had another meeting and Joshua went to a film. When he phoned Saskia again, there was still no reply. He then rang Julia Baskerville, suggesting that if she was free that evening they might sit down and make some plans for the new series of their TV show, *Westminster Unplugged*, which was due to start up again in October. By that time the Tories would have a new leader and they would be nearing the end of the election campaign. 'If we don't tell them what we want, the director and Patterson will make all the decisions,' Joshua told Julia, who agreed and said that as she liked to spend as much time with her small daughter as she could, she hoped Joshua would come to her house for supper.

Julia lived in a small terraced house in the East End. Her front door opening directly on to the pavement. When Joshua came in Julia's daughter Millie was lying on the couch in her nightdress watching a video, while in the connecting kitchen, Julia was cooking. The rooms were not large but the room where Millie lay was redeemed by a small conservatory at the end. Open doors let in a small, evening breeze.

Joshua greeted Millie, who acknowledged him without interest, and then joined Julia, who was at the stove, in a flowery shirt and shorts. 'It's boiling in here,' she said to him. 'Do you want to take a glass of wine out into the yard? There's a little table out there.'

'I'll sweat it out in here with you,' he said. 'Can I have a glass of water? I had lunch, and wine, with Edward Gott earlier and then I went to a movie. Now I feel terrible. It must be old age.'

Julia handed him a glass of water and he leaned against the wall, drinking it. 'Good hols?' he asked.

'Wonderful,' she told him. Julia had spent a month in Cape Cod with her husband and Millie. She was so plainly happy that Joshua found himself, in the hot little kitchen, envying her – or, as he took in the long, tanned legs and tendrils of hair falling over her face, perhaps her husband. He shook himself, mentally.

'Yours?' enquired Julia.

'Italy,' he responded briefly.

'What did Gott want? Or shouldn't I ask?'

'The leadership – the election; underneath, it was probably Gott's desire to get away from Lady Gott and his large family in Scotland.'

'Any new candidates for the leadership?' asked Julia.

'I can't tell you,' Joshua said. 'But no, actually.'

'Pity,' said Julia. 'It would have made a programme.' She whipped a pan of fish out from under the grill. 'Just a couple of trout – potato salad, etc.'

'Great,' said Joshua, who had eaten trout for lunch. She handed him a bowl and some plates. 'Can you carry those into the garden?' she asked. 'It'll be cooler out there and anyway, Millie's going to fall asleep in a minute. I let her stay up, but she ought to be in bed, really. We're going to stay with my aunt in Brighton tomorrow.'

'Nice,' he said, walking past the rapt Millie.

Julia, carrying a tray behind him said, 'Up to a point. My aunt doesn't like me, but she loves Millie. We can't stay long. I've got to get back to see my Party Chairman, as soon as he gets back from Bangladesh.' As Joshua put down the dishes she said, 'You know, Alan Petherbridge has always scared me.' She passed him and put down another dish and some knives and forks. 'Damn – I forgot the wine.'

'What do you mean, scared you?' Joshua enquired.

She said over her shoulder as she went back to the kitchen, 'I don't know why. I know what he is superficially . . .' She ducked into the kitchen and returned with the bottle and glasses. 'How he presents himself. There's just something under the surface I always feel, with Petherbridge. I don't know what makes him tick.'

'It's a clock in his tummy,' murmured sleepy Millie.

'Yes, darling,' said Julia to Millie, and wrestled with the cork of the bottle until Joshua took it from her.

He said, 'Gott said something like that. All I see is that Petherbridge is cleverer than most and probably more ruthless. Pragmatic, but that's safer than a man with his head stuffed with ideology.'

'Pragmatic doesn't mean anything. Well, I know you don't like ideals,' Julia said with a smile.

'Your party, of course, being led by that great idealist, Carl Chatterton. Who has the job because your party's more terrified of ideology than mine is.'

'Not for long,' Julia could not resist saying. Joshua opened his mouth to ask a question but she added quickly, 'The National Government's getting closer. We should concentrate on that. Anything else for the programme? I know Hugh wants us to flirt more but when the show starts up again we'll be in the last weeks of an election. No time for fun and games.'

'It's been ninety years since the last National Government if you don't count the Second World War. What say we get a researcher on it straight away?'

Julia agreed. 'At least we can be sure that with a National Government the US can't drag us into a reinvasion of Iraq. No all-party Cabinet would let that happen.'

'Point worth making,' Joshua said. And, in the darkening garden they went on discussing the programme. Julia found Millie asleep, a red bucket and spade having materialized at her feet while they'd been speaking. She carried her and the bucket and spade upstairs to bed. While she was gone, Joshua's phone rang. It was Saskia, back now and wanting to see him. He leaned back. To one side was the wall of Julia's house and on the other, separated only by walls and short yards, were the backs of the houses in the next street. Overhead, in one of the houses, a man, woman and child sat in the window eating. Down the street someone started up the radio.

He wondered why Julia didn't try to do a little better for herself. A Member of Parliament earned approximately double the average national wage and, if you added on the allowances and expenses, it was more like eight times as much. He almost asked her when she came downstairs but decided not to. She poured each of them more wine, sat down and suppressed a yawn.

'Sorry,' she said. 'I came back to a pile of messages and letters from the constituents.' Joshua knew that in a constituency as poor at Julia's – the tenth poorest in the country, wasn't it? – the elected representative would have plenty to deal with.

'I'll be off,' he said. Julia raised her eyebrows, wryly. Because of some last-minute complications about the filming of *Westminster Unplugged* Joshua had been forced, several months ago, to tell Julia where he was to be found – at Saskia's. Now he felt annoyed. This was the second time today his affair with Saskia had been treated satirically. He didn't like it.

106 St George's Square, London SW1. August 25th, 2015. 11.30 p.m.

After lunch with Joshua – which, as Joshua had guessed, had nothing to do with the election or the party leadership – Edward Gott went to his office at Clough Whitney Credit and Commerce in Leadenhall Street and spent the afternoon on business. He then walked to a planning committee meeting at Freedom House, the Conservative Party's headquarters in a street behind the National Gallery. The party was housed on one vast floor of a circular, green-windowed prize-winning building, largely owned by Lord Haver, and popularly known as the 'Granny Smith'.

In a large boardroom seventeen key party men and women were assembled, including Damian Jefferson, the Deputy PM, though not likely to be so for much longer, Jenny Bennett, Head of the party's PR and Advertising, Graham Barnsbury, the Party Leader, Lady Jenner, who led the party in the House of Lords, the Chancellor of the Exchequer, the Foreign Secretary and Jordan Landsman who was responsible for liaison with the local parties. Also present was Gerry Gordon-Garnett, who, it was known, would become Petherbridge's Principal Private Secretary when he became PM. Petherbridge himself was not present.

At this meeting Edward Gott had all the importance of the man who collects, preserves and advises on the organization's money. He sat solidly beside the Chairman, staring at his agenda paper and knowing there was only one item on his personal agenda, and that was not what he was reading. He had to minimize the expenses in what he saw as a pointless election. As he had expected, the collective mind of the meeting was on more interesting subjects than how the bills would be paid – on a fleet of battle buses to tour the country, public meetings in every city, a leaflet to go through every door in the country. When it was Gott's turn to report he was brief. 'You will see from the document I've prepared that the party has an overdraft of a million a half. Interest is currently running at £150,000 a year. Our revenues do not cover this sum and will not in the foreseeable future. As you all know, we have recently moved our headquarters into this building, at preferential rates. I must therefore advise that the national election campaign should be planned on the basis of ten thousand pounds a week. This is lower than any of us would like, but it is all I can advise. Indeed, it is all we can produce.'

This sobered the meeting, though not for long, and Gott made no

further comments as it continued, except to ask, neutrally, for costings
on each suggestion. These were seldom available. He preserved an expression barely short of gloom. Meanwhile, the temperature in the room
rose, was readjusted and rose again. It was as the Chairman of the Policy
Group was making her report that a secretary entered the room and leant
over his shoulder. She handed him a message from his own secretary at
the bank, asking him to call her. Gott apologized and left the room,
fearing that Mrs Jasmine Dottrell had bad news of his family. Little else
would have caused her to call him in the middle of the meeting.

He was nervous until he saw her face on the monitor. 'Ed-ward,' she
said on her usual, Caribbean rising note, 'Don't worry. It's only some
payments received.' Gott frowned. Surely that was no reason to inter-
rupt him in the middle of a meeting? 'A Mrs Caris Brookes has sent half
a million pounds to the Conservative Party. Lord Haver has set two
million. And Mr Julian Finch-O'Brien has asked for account details as he
wants to contribute a substantial sum. That was what he called it. And
he wished to speak to you personally about the donation.'

Gott had expected Haver to contribute, although less than the two
million he had, apparently, given. The other two names were unknown
to him. He asked Mrs Dottrell, who had been with him for fifteen years,
if she had any information about these donors. She had already checked,
and said she had not.

He went back into the meeting, curious about the sudden good fortune
for the Conservative Party and resolving to say nothing about it until the
details were clearer. He did not want the spendthrifts of the committee
on him like a plague of locusts before he was ready.

The meeting broke up at seven thirty and would reconvene at six the
next day, and every day after that until the voters went to the polls in
October. Graham Barnsbury caught Gott as he left and invited him for
a quick drink.

They sat at the back of a shining steel-floored bar by the river, selected
more because it was convenient than because it was congenial. They faced
a whole-wall screen opposite, where a man and a woman, ten times life
size, were having an argument. It wasn't clear what the actors were saying
– the sound on wall-screens was almost always bad. They ordered.

Barnsbury leaned forward over the shiny steel table and said, 'I just
wanted a quick word, Gott. I appreciate that as the treasurer you have
a duty to ensure the party doesn't overspend – but I couldn't help feeling
you were being too discouraging. In future, as a favour to me, would you
mind saying what can be done, rather than what can't?'

'Point taken, Graham,' Gott said easily. 'It was tactics – better to throw
a bucket of cold water over the big spenders at the outset – and I don't
need to tell you, the party's financial position is very bad. If we were a

company we'd be bankrupt.' He decided it was fair to Barnsbury to tell him about the offers that had just come in. 'There might be some light at the end of the tunnel,' he said and told the Party Chairman what he had heard from Jasmine Dottrell. He watched Barnsbury closely as he spoke, but got no impression the other man knew anything about the donations. Barnsbury seemed as surprised as he had been. On the wall the two giants went into a naked clinch.

'This Mrs Brookes – Caris Brookes – have you ever heard of her?' Barnsbury shook his head. 'Or Finch-O'Brien?' Gott asked. Barnsbury denied knowledge of him either, adding, 'Do you think Petherbridge has been doing some intelligent fund-raising?'

'Could be,' answered Gott. 'Do you know where he is, by the way? I rang this morning to talk about the meeting and his secretary didn't seem to know where he was.'

'I suppose he's entitled to a week or two out of contact,' Barnsbury said vaguely. He was thinking about the money. 'We're out of debt,' he announced. 'We ought to take over the floor above for the election. It's empty.'

'Possibly,' said Gott. After the two men parted he got into a taxi and drove to a north-west London suburb. He wondered where Petherbridge was. He was on the verge of becoming Party Leader, possibly the next Prime Minister, if the party won a General Election only two months off. It was a funny time for an ambitious man to disappear.

He banged on the door of an Edwardian semi in a tree-lined street. There, he ate the leftovers from supper – macaroni cheese and beans, warmed up in the microwave, sat in the kitchen chatting with the couple who lived in the house, called another cab and went back to St George's Square, where he had a first-floor flat. Feet up, he called his assistant, Jeremy Saunders. Jeremy, always thin, his face now looking drawn and weary, was on his way back from Heathrow.

'All right, Jeremy?' Gott asked encouragingly. 'Good holiday?'

'Apart from the diarrhoea and a twelve-hour flight,' Jeremy told him, thinking Gott looked fit, well, healthily tanned and had a surprise in store for him.

'Can you look in?' asked Gott. 'I need you.'

'I'm pretty tired,' said Jeremy. 'And I've got to go to my sister's to pick up Finn.'

Gott was displeased. 'Well, get the dog, have a shower and I'll see you in forty-five minutes.'

'Right, boss,' said Jeremy gloomily.

It was midnight before Jeremy, showered and in his pyjamas, came downstairs from the top-floor flat, where he lived with Gott as his land-lord. He entered with his intelligent dog, who knew better than to wag his tail at Gott and pattered over the polished floor to lie down under the long windows overlooking the square. The long lace curtains hung still above his head. The leaves on the trees outside lay heavy with heat and traffic fumes.

Long, lean Jeremy moved as if drawn by a magnet to the table on which Gott had hospitably placed some packages of wrapped sandwiches. He began to eat. Gott silently placed a weak whisky and water beside him then went across the room to stand near the small grand piano he could not play. He said, 'I want you to go to Yorkshire.'

'What – is it, Rodon?' Jeremy asked. Rodon was Gott's car firm in the North West. The research team was headed by the awkward eccentric genius, Leslie Mundy, who was working on a system to re-power, internally, the Citycar, a short-range electric vehicle. He was a perfectionist. He would seldom let his work out of his hands because he always had further improvements in mind. Five years earlier Gott and Jeremy had gone to Rodon. Gott was desperate. Mundy and his research team had been at work for three years, and as yet not one car worker had come through the factory gates and not one spanner had been lifted on the empty factory floor. Costs were spiralling. On that occasion Gott had bullied Mundy into handing over the research and this had at last resulted in the Citycar going into production. Following this episode, either Gott and Jeremy, or Jeremy alone, paid regular unscheduled visits to Rodon.

The Citycar was now in use by people wanting to make short journeys – its range was only forty-five miles before it required re-powering. Early on it had become a national joke, being seen so often standing uselessly at the roadside because the owners had underestimated how long they would be on the road, because they had handed the keys to teenage children, or because it had been stolen and driven away. Mundy pointed out that he had predicted this when production began. Gott had been forced to set up another company, Citycar Rescue. There were enough people ready to pay the relatively large purchase price to use the low-maintenance, ecologically friendly runabout but it was a small market and Gott wanted to expand. Mundy was working on finding a safe way to re-power the vehicle in transit. That way, though it might still be slow – its maximum speed was 40mph and even that speed drained its power faster – it would be able to cover longer distances. Gott was beginning to suspect Mundy might have solved the problem, but was concealing the result.

'Well – I was going to ask you to look in unexpectedly as usual and see what you can find out. It'll be Saturday morning. With any luck they won't be there.' Gott said. 'But your main task is to go to a Pennine village, Kirkby Rodney, and see what you can find out about the early life of Alan Broderick Petherbridge. He lived there until he was twenty

– away a lot of the time at school and university, but that was his home. His father died when he was very young, so I suppose it would have been him and his mother.'

'I've been to Kirkby Rodney. I used to climb round there before I took up an open-all-hours post with you.'

'We all have to pay the rent,' Gott said unsympathetically as Jeremy demolished the last of the sandwiches. 'That's why they call it work.' He handed him a copy of *Who's Who* open at the page containing Alan Petherbridge's entry. Jeremy scanned it. 'Conventional enough. School, Oxford, Harvard Business, Barclays, Conservative Party research; wife – Annabel; address – Backhurst, Chapping, Gloucester.'

'Go and see her, too, on the way back,' Gott said. 'She's supposed to be potty but someone must know something.'

'I'm not sure what you want.'

'He'll be the Prime Minister soon. I'm concerned.'

'What about?' asked Jeremy.

'That's for you to find out,' Gott told him. He doesn't know, thought Jeremy. 'Usual arrangement. Poppy Burroughs at the *Observer* will vouch for you, if necessary. You're researching for a feature she's writing about Petherbridge. Here's a printout of all the press stories about him.' He pushed a heavy file of paper across the table at Jeremy.

'Right,' said Jeremy, who on two other occasions had gone ferreting for Gott, pretending to be a journalist and covered by Poppy Burroughs, whose parents owed Gott some unspecified, but presumably significant favour.

'I'll need you back in a couple of days,' said Gott. 'Things will start hotting up in early September.'

'Right,' said Jeremy and left, with his dog at his heels.

Gott frowned, stood up and went to bed.

Four

Chervil Cottage, Church Street, Kirkby Rodney, Yorkshire. August 26th, 2015

Jeremy walked wearily up the narrow stairs of the pretty cottage belonging to Mrs Debby Carshaw, who had taken him in for bed and breakfast when he arrived in Kirkby Rodney in the late afternoon. There had been no room at the local pub. Mrs Carshaw, a short, bright-eyed woman in her sixties, as broad as she was long, was the retired head-mistress of the village school.

Jeremy had spent a frustrating late morning at the Rodon works near Preston. He had parked his car in an empty space near the building, a space with MUNDY painted on the concrete, ignored the cry of the security guard at this violation, raced into the lift, noted Mrs Jackie Mundy, secretary and guard dog to Leslie Mundy, at her desk in the outer office, charged past her and ran into Mundy's empty office. Mrs Mundy jumped up with a cry as he passed.

A high, screaming whine penetrated the room. Jeremy was reminded of his two-year-old nephew in the supermarket – of Leo lying on the floor by the checkout sobbing and screeching, snot and tears running down his face, yelling, 'No – no – no – not going – toy – no – no – no.' The noise was much like that inhuman howl. Under the window a small steel engine, which Jeremy recognized as a replica of the Citycar engine, was running. Jeremy noted a black box suspended at the rear of the smooth-running engine. The unpleasant noise was coming from this.

Jeremy crossed the room quickly and whipped up the outer casing of the black box. By this time Jackie Mundy, dyed red hair flying and stilettos clacking, had launched herself into the room, run up to him and cried, 'You can't look at that!'

The black casing held some kind of fuel cell, Jeremy concluded, and it looked possible that it was in some way feeding the Citycar battery. Which might mean that Leslie Mundy had managed to create a fuel cell which would boost the electric battery while the car was in motion, in which case you could rechristen the vehicle the goes-all-over-the-country car and Leslie Mundy would become a billionaire and so, for that matter, would Lord Gott and even, he, Jeremy, would do pretty well out of it. If Mundy could eliminate the noise, he thought.

Mrs Mundy somehow stilled the engine. Then she swiftly threw a large metallic sheet over it and turned to Jeremy, pushing at his chest with both hands. 'You're not allowed in here,' she said. Mr Mundy isn't here. You're not allowed in here while he's out of the office.' She had tossed that sheet of anti-static, dust-repellent sheeting, as used in the space programme and operating theatres, over the engine with a practised hand, Jeremy noted. Presumably this was what she always did when her husband had to meet someone in his office.

'I need all the research notes for that fuel cell, or whatever it is – what it is, how it operates on the motor, how it's mounted. The lot, Mrs Mundy – and now.' Jeremy held out his hand.

'You can't have it. Them. They're in the safe. I don't know the combination,' she told him.

'OK,' said Jeremy. 'Where's Leslie?'

'He's in Aberdeen, at the university. It's about that noise – getting rid of it.'

'It's enough to make the driver kill all the passengers,' Jeremy agreed. 'Still, Mrs M, you'd better tell Leslie, with all due respect, he's an arsehole if he's cracked the problem and elected not to tell Lord Gott. To be honest, when Lord Gott hears this, he'll be furious. Can you blame him? R and D running at two hundred thousand pounds a year here – Lord Gott paying every penny of this without a fuss – and when there's a breakthrough it turns out he's the last to hear. Tell Leslie I sincerely hope he isn't thinking of selling this to anyone else.'

'Oh, no,' she protested. 'He'd never do that.'

Jeremy believed her. Leslie Mundy had faults, but he did not think him dishonest. Something struck him. 'Where's the safe?' he demanded. She gave him a sulky look. 'Mrs Mundy,' he said, 'if Leslie's found a way of boosting the electricity without having to recharge a battery, the research is worth a fortune.'

'Nobody knows,' she said.

'He's got a team of five in that expensive lab – that's not nobody. I need to know where the safe is to put a guard on it. Has he taken the research to Aberdeen?'

Her look answered the question. 'I'll kill him,' he said. 'I know Lord Gott would want me to.' This cowed her.

Not wanting to lose this advantage, which he knew could only be temporary, he stalked out. From his mobile phone in the car park he rang Gott, who said, 'That stupid fucker – I'll call him in Aberdeen and shut him up. I'll make him come straight back. In the meanwhile, get a local security firm in there pronto. Well done, boy. Now, speed up to Kirkby Rodney and get on with the rest of it.'

That evening, early, Jeremy went to the larger and better kept of the two local pubs and tried to start a conversation with the landlady, a heavily made-up forty-year-old, who said she could remember nothing about people who had lived in the village when she was a child. She was busy – the pub was full of tourists, many of them walkers and climbers in heavy boots. But her eyes were hard and alert and Jeremy felt sure there was something she wasn't saying.

He decided not to approach the few local men sitting in a corner and instead headed off down the road, where tidy cottages, front doors with gleaming brass knockers, hanging baskets of flowers and ivy hinted at well-off retired people in residence. He went round the corner into a less prosperous small street, at the end of which was a second pub, set back from the street, with about a dozen motorbikes parked on the concrete outside. He braved the looks of the assembled bikers, bought himself a pint at the bar and went into a corner where two old men, one bald, one cloth-capped, were drinking at a beer-puddled table. He offered a drink to the old men – on closer examination they seemed to be in their fifties – and said he was a journalist, researching for an article on Alan Petherbridge.

'Oh, aye,' said the bald man. 'Him what'll be Prime Minister next time, if the Tories get in. I remember the family, don't you, Don?'

'What?' said the other man.

'Wallaces,' the bald man said loudly. 'Wallaces of Foothunt House.'

'Wallaces?' enquired Jeremy.

'Wallaces,' confirmed the bald man. 'The stepfather. That's two pints,' he reminded Jeremy. Jeremy had to push through the massed bikers at the bar. It took time to get served and as he pushed back with the drink someone nudged him, deliberately, he thought, and some of the beer slopped on to his trousers. He ignored this.

'So,' he said, when he had put down the pints, 'Alan Petherbridge had a stepfather, Mr Wallace? He doesn't mention him.'

'What paper?' asked the bald man.

'Paper?' asked Jeremy. 'Oh – the *Observer*.'

'That right?' said the man in the cap. He looked down at Finn. 'Nice dog,' he remarked.

'He is,' said Jeremy.

'Doesn't seem like a London dog.'

'He was born in the country – Gloucestershire,' Jeremy told him.

'That right?' said the man. The words 'down South' hovered in the air.

'What did Mr Wallace do for a living?' Jeremy asked.

'Not much,' said the man in the cloth cap. 'I think he were retired. They never had much to do with the village. The boy, Alan, went to a public school.'

A silence fell. Jeremy, noticing both men's glasses were almost empty, made his way back to the bar. Music started up, old punk rock. Jeremy, pushing through the leather elbows, was unhappy. A voice behind him said mockingly, 'Excuse me, barman. I wonder if you would make me a cocktail?' Eventually, Jeremy was served and again had to force his way through to get back to the table. This was the last time, he thought. He was not going back to the bar again.

He set the glasses down. 'Can you remember anything else about the Wallaces?'

The bald man said, 'They kept themselves to themselves.'

The capped man said, 'It were a while ago.'

'Funny to think he'll be the Prime Minister,' said the first man.

'I'd not vote for him,' said the second.

'I'd not vote for any of them.'

'Do you remember Mrs Wallace?' Jeremy asked hopelessly.

'Poor woman. She died,' said the capped man.

'Buried her up at St Martin's, didn't they?' said the bald man. 'Near Jessie Comstock.'

'Never – she's right over the other side. Mrs Wallace is by my auntie – Auntie Bee Watts.'

Jeremy gave up. He said goodnight to the two men and made his way through the throng in the pub, feeling eyes on his back. He returned to his lodgings. He had been brought up in a village himself and thought he was unlikely to find out very much about a family who had not lived in Kirkby Rodney for thirty years. There would be few who would remember and those who did might not be prepared to speak. He began to calculate how much Leslie Mundy's discovery might eventually be worth to him – Gott had given him some Rodon shares – and fell asleep.

Next morning, Jeremy much enjoyed Mrs Carshaw's substantial breakfast of eggs, bacon, mushrooms, tomatoes and black pudding, as did Finn, who got a few bits of black pudding under the table. Jeremy told her that he planned to go and take a look at Foothunt House, where the Wallaces had once lived, and then take Finn for a good, long walk. He would return to London that afternoon.

Mrs Carshaw offered to make him a packed lunch. He asked for directions to St Martin's, where the men had told him Mrs Wallace was buried. Mrs Carshaw told him where the church was. 'I'm going to Mrs Wallace's grave,' he told her. 'But I'm not getting much local information.'

'That's Yorkshire for you,' said Mrs Carshaw.

'I suppose so,' said Jeremy.

He went uphill out of the village to Foothunt House, passing stony fields in which sheep grazed, then found a drive beyond two pillars mounted with weather-beaten animals of some kind. There were manicured lawns on either side of the drive, and behind the house, high moors stretched. The house, when he reached it, was not large. The two main floors had small windows. Jeremy calculated there were probably no more than six or seven bedrooms. The front door was narrow, and protected by a portico. Even under bright August sunshine the building seemed gloomy and featureless. Jeremy flinched at the thought of those small rooms and the winds coming off the moors in winter. If the Rodon shares turned out to be worth anything, he wouldn't be planning a move to anywhere like Foothunt House. Then a Rottweiler came round a corner of the house, ran up, stopped quite close to him, crouched down and barked at him. He looked round and noted Finn walking, with dignity, back down the drive away from the Rottweiler. Jeremy followed suit.

He headed for the sunny uplands, walked round the waterfalls and ate lunch in a tree-fringed glade with the sound of the falls in his ears. He concluded he had found out as much about the early life of Alan Petherbridge, the future Prime Minister of Great Britain, as he could, unless he spent another month in Kirkby Rodney. Or perhaps another ten years. If he left early he would be able to get down to Gloucester by early evening and talk to Annabel Petherbridge early next day, a plan which suited him very well.

On the way back he visited the churchyard of St Martin's, a small stone church, four hundred years old, set in hilly fields just outside the village. The churchyard was small and in one corner, near the church wall, he found a mossy headstone on which the name of Annette Wallace was cut. Although many of the headstones of other graves had been cleaned and had flowers and plants growing on them, Annette Wallace's resting-place had been neglected. Below the headstone grew only grass, dry and brown at this time of year.

He returned to his B&B where the smell of baking attracted him. When Mrs Carshaw offered him tea he was sorely tempted to stay but told her that although he would appreciate a cup of tea and a biscuit, he had to start on the next leg of his journey. In Mrs Carshaw's neat front room, which he had not before entered, he noted a *Times* lying on a small table beside her armchair with most of the crossword filled in while in front of the fire was another table where, on a chess board, the positioned pieces suggested an ongoing game. Mrs Carshaw caught his glance at it and explained that she was expecting a neighbour later, for their regular game.

Jeremy looked into Mrs Carshaw's round, unlined face and understood everything. He had several ordinary-looking aunts. One, retired, had been a senior officer at the Foreign Office and another was an expert, or perhaps *the* expert, on Hittite inscriptions. He took his cup of tea, sat down in the well-stuffed chair opposite Mrs Carshaw's and came clean. He told he was not a journalist and worked for Lord Gott, whose career he explained. If Mrs Carshaw was surprised by this information she did not show it. She asked him, 'What does your employer hope to achieve by getting information about Alan Petherbridge?'

'Lord Gott believes in information for its own sake,' he replied. 'He's capable of taking a few scraps and coming up with a whole scenario.'

'Does he get it right?'

'Usually,' he replied.

'Alan Petherbridge is going to be the head of Lord Gott's party. Why would your boss investigate him?'

'I don't know,' Jeremy told her. He felt as if he'd been caught in the drawing room holding a football with the pieces of a vase at his feet.

'Do you like Lord Gott?' asked Mrs Carshaw.

Jeremy thought. 'Yes – I suppose I do.'

'I still don't understand why he would investigate his own leader,' Mrs Carshaw persisted.

'He told me he was concerned – that was the word he used.'

Mrs Carshaw sat quite still, thinking. Evidently she came to a decision. 'This isn't for publication?'

Jeremy felt compelled to be honest. 'No – but I can't guarantee it wouldn't be, at some point.'

'All right,' she said. 'I'll tell you. This has nothing to do with politics, of course. It all goes back over forty years, while I was still at school. The Wallaces must have moved into Foothunt House when I was in my early teens – the boy, Alan, would have been about seven but he didn't go to the village school. He was at a preparatory school somewhere. The Wallaces didn't mix in locally, even less than most incomers to the neighbourhood who buy large houses here. They didn't shop locally, they didn't seem to go out much, they didn't seem to know anybody and obviously didn't want to. Alan, when he was home from school, wasn't allowed to play with the local boys. It must have been a lonely life. The point about the villages in this part of the world, which were once very cut off from the rest of the world, is that people feel threatened when they know nothing about the neighbours.

'In a remote village you used to need to know your neighbours, what they do, who they are and whether you could rely on them or not. And the feeling's still there. And, of course, there's nosiness – the Wallaces didn't mix. They didn't have anyone to help in the house. No one went inside. No wonder everybody thought they had something to hide. Of course, gossip went round and then finally it came out that Wallace beat his wife. That wasn't gossip. That was fact. They'd been in the village about five years by then so Alan would have been about twelve or thirteen. Then Annette Wallace was admitted to hospital – where the postmistress's sister was a ward sister. She'd been badly beaten – concussion and broken ribs – she was unconscious and apparently it took her the best part of a day to come round. In other words, her injuries were so severe her husband had no choice, that time, but to get her to hospital. And there – although she made the usual excuse that she'd fallen downstairs – it was plain that this was a beating, and not the first. There were old bruises and badly mended bones when they looked. They tried to talk to her about it but she denied everything – there was nothing anybody could do. They patched her up and sent her home.'

'Oh,' said Jeremy, shocked. 'What about Alan, did his father – stepfather – beat him, too?'

'Hard to say. Didn't seem so. Anyway, two years after that Annette Wallace was dead of cancer. It was the same thing again – she didn't get to hospital until it was too late to do anything about it. God knows what she went through.'

'I saw her grave,' Jeremy said. 'I didn't realize . . .'

Mrs Carshaw shook her head. 'It was a long time ago.'

'Do you think Alan knew what was happening to his mother?'

'A lot can be hidden from children away at boarding school,' she said.

But Jeremy could not help imagining a boy with intelligent black eyes, in pyjamas, on a landing, seeing his mother being punched about the hall, or perhaps just hearing the accompanying sounds, the thuds and crashes of a woman being savagely beaten. Then there would be the limping figure in the morning, the pallor, sleeves falling back to show bruises on the arms. He said, 'Alan must have been fourteen when his mother died. He must have known something.'

'Probably.'

'I wonder what that does to you?'

'Seemingly it doesn't prevent you from becoming the Prime Minister,' said Mrs Carshaw.

'What happened after that? What happened to Wallace? Did he die?'

'Oh, no,' she said. 'He got crippled with arthritis. He's in a retirement home now.'

Jeremy stared at her. None of this had been in the clippings. 'Where is he?'

'It's called Fairlawns. Near Lancaster. I go to see him every Christmas, as a duty. He's a horrible old man. You can't just go there – you have to ring in advance.'

'I'd better go anyway,' declared Jeremy.

'You can try,' said Mrs Carshaw. 'I hope they let you see him.'

'Who?' he asked.

Mrs Carshaw shook her head. 'I don't suppose Mr Petherbridge trusts his father.'

As Jeremy paid his bill Mrs Carshaw sketched a map on the back of an envelope. Handing it to him she said, 'You won't enjoy it.'

'I don't suppose I will,' said Jeremy, who was still a little shaken by the story she had told him. 'Tell me this, Mrs Carshaw. You've been dealing with children all your life, and you've seen a lot of them grow up – do you think anyone could survive that background?'

She shook her head. 'No – it'll have an effect, but you can't judge what that effect will be.'

'Why did you tell me?' he asked, as he walked away.

She paused, as if she hardly knew the answer herself. 'I'm like your boss – concerned.'

Fairlawns Retirement Home, Judge Beacon Street, Lancaster August 26th, 2015.
4.30 p.m.

Fairlawns Retirement Home was a long, two-storey house, no doubt built by some successful coal owner or merchant during the nineteenth century. A drive ran between two well-kept lawns with trees beyond. Jeremy parked his car and entered the hall, with no idea what to expect. He had phoned Lord Gott from the road outside, half-expecting him to be more or less uninterested in the tale of Petherbridge's background of domestic violence. Instead, Gott had said, 'God Almighty. Get into that home and talk to the old man. Have you got a recorder?' When Jeremy told Gott he hadn't Gott told him, 'Drive into the town and buy one.'

'I may not get in – there seems to be a system,' Jeremy warned.

'Make bloody sure you do.'

Now Jeremy, with the pin-sized recorder under the lapel of his jacket, stood in a wide tiled hall. Against one wall there was a pedestal on which stood a massive arrangement of flowers, and beside it was a wheelchair containing the slumped body of an old lady. There was the sound of loud music and gunshots from a television. After a minute a small, dark woman in a checked uniform came hurrying in from one side of the hall, went to the wheelchair and grasped the handles firmly.

'Excuse me,' said Jeremy. 'I've come to see Mr Wallace, Robert Wallace.'

'Through there,' said the small woman in an accented voice, nodding towards the doorway through which she'd come. 'By himself. By the window,' she added, as she began to push the wheelchair with its unconscious burden briskly towards a door on the opposite side of the hall.

Jeremy, realizing he had evaded whatever security system the home operated, moved swiftly into a long, forty-foot room, previously, no doubt, the drawing room of the house. On the near side was a cluster of some fourteen elderly people, seated in chairs or wheelchairs arranged round a large TV showing an action film. Soldiers moved through a desert; explosions went off. Many of the viewers seemed to be asleep. Jeremy crossed a long stretch of carpet to the window end of the room, where a figure in a wheelchair was gazing out at the lawn in front of the house.

Jeremy went to the side of the wheelchair, looked down at a craggy face and asked, 'Mr Wallace?'

The face, with its prow-like nose, looked up at him. Robert Wallace said, 'Who are you?' His small blue eyes, under overgrown grey eyebrows were sharp and angry.

Jeremy put out his hand and said, 'Jeremy Saunders, from the *Observer*. I wonder if you could spare me some time to talk about your stepson.'

'The shit,' said the old man, as if confirming the identity of the subject.

'Alan Petherbridge,' said Jeremy.

'That's right,' Robert Wallace said.

Wallace's legs were covered by a plaid blanket. His hands, emerging from the sleeves of a crisp blue shirt, were placed on the arms of the wheelchair. The knuckles were huge and the fingers distorted, looking, Jeremy thought irrelevantly, less like human hands than the hands of some alien monster in a film. He got a chair and put it near the window, sideways on to Wallace, who had not yet moved his head. Perhaps, Jeremy thought, any movement was painful. He looked at the long, bony profile, topped with a shock of badly cut grey hair, and reflected that Wallace must have been a good-looking man, in his time. 'I expect you know that your stepson is likely to be the next Prime Minister in the autumn. My paper is collecting some background information—'

'He was a little shit as a boy. He still is,' said Wallace. 'I need to get out of here – look at it – zombies round the TV – zombies in charge. Will he do anything? No, he won't. His wife should be looking after me. But no, he likes me trapped here. I'm surprised you found me.'

Jeremy decided to skirt round this topic and thought that from what he'd seen of the old man so far, in Petherbridge's shoes he might want the old man caged up somewhere far away from him. There was the sound of a shattering explosion from the TV, then swelling music.

'It seems like a good, well-run place,' he said. 'But I suppose—'

'You can tell your paper this future Prime Minister doesn't give a toss for his father,' Wallace declared. He looked down the long drive, battles going on inside his head. 'He goes strong on family values and personal responsibility from what I see when those old crones for once let the news go on. Let's see what people think of him when they see what's happening here.'

'Yes,' Jeremy said, producing, for form's sake, a notepad from his pocket. He wasn't sure how to describe Petherbridge, since Wallace had called him his son. Son? Stepson? What?

He asked, 'What about Alan Petherbridge as a boy?'

'Away at school,' Wallace told him.

'In the holidays,' suggested Jeremy.

'Whining little mother's boy – nose in a book – that's what he was,' declared the old man. 'Take me to the lavatory – toilet, as they call it here.'

Jeremy flinched. 'I'll get a nurse.'

'You won't find one. If you do it won't be a proper nurse. Just a little foreigner who can't speak English. Just wheel me there, will you?'

Jeremy took a deep breath, grasped the handles of the wheelchair and pushed in the direction of Wallace's distorted, pointing hand. He desperately wanted to find a nurse to help him in a task he did not fancy, and at the same time feared that if he did he would be questioned and thrown out. They passed the group of TV watchers, left the room and, Wallace still pointing the way, turned into a small room at the back of the hall. He was relieved to see that the bathroom was large – there was ample room for the wheelchair – and the toilet had been adapted for wheelchair users. He pushed the wheelchair over to the lavatory.

'Pull me up,' commanded Wallace.

'Wouldn't it be easier to sit?' said Jeremy.

'I'm not a girl. Pull me up out of this thing.'

Jeremy was nervous. He felt fairly sure Wallace was not allowed to use the lavatory alone, and for good reasons, and that with a nurse in attendance he would have been made to sit on the toilet to pee. What were the penalties for posing as a journalist in a retirement home and then causing death or injury to a patient? He advanced the wheelchair nearer to the base of the toilet and, standing to one side, pulled Wallace up and out of the wheelchair in what seemed to him to be an impossible manoeuvre. He had been unable to find the brake of the wheelchair so now had to take the whole weight of the man, with one foot wedged behind the rear wheel. With an effort, he got Wallace standing on shaky legs in front of the commode. One distorted hand was on the steel handle beside it. His face contorted with the effort, or perhaps the pain he was in, Wallace grunted, 'Flies,' looking down.

Silently Jeremy implored, 'Oh, God. God help me,' and with his free hand reached across Wallace's body and managed to unzip his flies. Jeremy had calculated, with the rapidity of panic, that Wallace was not a man who would allow another man to fiddle about with his penis. He was right. Wallace clumsily produced his organ and pointed it at the toilet bowl while Jeremy, sweating, supported him. A thin stream of urine went into the bowl. 'That's better,' Wallace said with stagey relief. He put his penis back inside his pants, with a suppressed groan. Jeremy zipped his trouser flies, dreading the moment when, somehow, he would have to ease Wallace down again into the wheelchair.

As he was preparing to do this, Wallace began to speak in the monotonous voice of a solitary man who has spent many painful hours rehearsing his monologue in the dark of night. 'Broke. Not a penny to my name. I'm a dependent relative. Dependent on that little shit, the weakling. I'd have had it, all of it, if that stupid bitch's husband hadn't left his money to her weak son. Probably thought she'd make a mess of it, which she would have done. But she didn't tell me, did she, till the ring was on her finger. Hooked – she hooked me – then she told me: 'I didn't think it mattered' – stupid woman, stupid, stupid woman. Then this arthritis. Now I'm in hell. Hell – a prisoner in torment.'

Jeremy, much shaken and still afraid of losing his balance and allowing Wallace to fall, said, 'Mr Wallace—' and was interrupted by a woman's voice saying angrily, 'What's going on in here?' He turned sufficiently to see in the doorway a large woman in nurse's uniform, not one of the small foreigners so loathed by Wallace but a Yorkshirewoman. He was infinitely relieved. He did not care if she had him arrested later, as long as she helped him now. She advanced, pushed down the brake on the wheelchair, pushed Jeremy aside as she took Wallace under the armpit and snapped at him, 'Let go of that handle.' Wallace released his grip and she deftly got him back in the chair, then turned on Jeremy, 'Who are you? Don't you know what you just did was criminally dangerous?' Then she looked down at Wallace and said, 'As for you, you silly old man – words fail me.'

Jeremy said, 'My name is Jeremy Saunders. I'm a journalist working for—'

'My arse,' Wallace interrupted.

'Keep that filthy tongue in your head, Mr Wallace,' the nurse told him. 'If he's a journalist I'm the Mayor of Scarborough!'

'Did you talk to anybody before you visited Mr Wallace?' she demanded. Jeremy said, 'There wasn't anybody . . .'

'What paper?'

'Paper?' he said. 'The *Observer*.'

'Not too sure about it, is he?' Wallace said malignantly.

'Well – I'm reporting you straight to your editor. Feel lucky I don't take this to the Press Council.'

Bloody hell, thought Jeremy. Gott – you got me into this. You'd better bloody well get me out.

'And now you'll leave,' she said. 'Now. Straight away.' She looked down at Wallace again. 'And as for you, you're going to your room, to bed.' She turned back to Jeremy. 'Are you still standing there? Do you want to wait while I call the police?'

With Wallace back in the chair, Jeremy began to recover his nerve. He said to the nurse, 'Don't be ridiculous. This isn't a police matter.'

'I think you might find it is,' she said. 'Mr Alan Petherbridge, who'll most likely be the Prime Minister of this country shortly, has given strict instructions. Visitors to Mr Wallace here have to go through his office. If you want to take on a former Home Secretary and future Prime Minister, then be my guest. I'd advise you to clear out, fast as you like.'

Jeremy got out. On the road to Gloucestershire, where he knew he would find a friendly bed, at his cousin's, the cousin with whom he was in love, he could still hear Wallace's voice echoing round the car. 'I'm in hell. A prisoner in torment.' He put a CD in the player, then remembered to turn off his recorder.

He played the tape over to Charlotte in her little sitting room above the post office she kept. Charlotte was shaken. 'How awful,' she said. 'That stinks. Let's get a drink and go and lie down under the tree.' They went downstairs to the little cluttered garden behind the post office, Charlotte in her nightdress and Jeremy in a T-shirt and boxers. They lay down under the old gnarled apple tree.

'That poor woman,' said Charlotte.

Jeremy, thinking of the neglected grave in the churchyard at Kirkby Rodney, said, 'Yes. Poor woman.'

Villa Contadini, Tuscany, Italy. August 28th, 2015. 8 p.m.

A man and a woman sat on the immaculate terrace of a Tuscan hillside villa, looking west over the swelling hills, the red roofs and cupolas, the peaceful landscape of houses, fields and groves. Ahead of them the sun was going down, turning the sky from blue to indigo.

'I was so close,' said the President of the United States, 'I thought I'd come on by.' She had just had an audience with the Pope at the Castel Gandolfo.

Security men stood against the sides of the terrace. There would be more in the house and some in the garden below. 'You're very welcome, ma'am,' said Ray Hollander easily. He was dressed in holiday clothes, chinos, an open-necked shirt, loafers worn without socks. The President was still wearing the blue suit in which she'd met the Pontiff.

'I guess I just wanted to make sure we're up to speed with this British election we've been bounced into.'

'Well, that gave us all a shock. But I think we have everything under control. Petherbridge is a very quick and able man and that's helped a lot.'

'I hope this money isn't going to waste,' said the President.

'We all hope that.'

'Because when it's gone, it's gone.'

'That's understood. But our donors are businessmen. Their attitude is pretty much that they've assessed the situation, they're investing because they judge there are good opportunities there and if, for some reason, the investment doesn't pay off then they won't like it but they'll accept it as one of the normal hazards of doing business.'

This explanation did not reassure the President. Ray Hollander had known it would not. Many of the backers he had approached for funds had been the President's election funders and if they lost their money they would be less generous when the President stood again.

'It'll be OK,' he told her. 'Petherbridge has been most cooperative. He's drawing up a list of available sites for development.'

'What about the Transatlantic Trade Agreement?' the President asked sharply.

'That's OK, too. He's worked it out with the Treasury.'

'Can he get it through?'

'He says so.'

'Does he know what will happen to him if he lets us down?'

It was growing darker. The President's questioning, suggesting doubts about how he was handling the business he had undertaken, were beginning to affect him. He shouted for the terrace lights to be turned on. A soft glow illuminated the old stones, the plants in terracotta pots and the face of his President. Her face, over not so many years, had ceased to be conventionally attractive, as it had once been; it was now a face of stone, all planes and hollows. The illumination threw a charming light over everything, but emphasized the darkening of the land below them, and the hillsides all around.

'It's all in place. It will work,' he told her. She expected to hear nothing less but she wouldn't believe it. Nor did he. Not until the results came in. He was conscious of the fact that he had never undertaken such a difficult and risky task. If it failed, if the story came out, he was a ruined man. There would be a Senate investigation, probably a trial. He could face a jail sentence. The President could and would deny knowledge. But if it worked he would be very rich and very powerful – unassailable, too. As if she knew what she had done, the President stood. She banged him between the shoulders with a hand which had recently been in that of the Pope. 'I know you can do it, Ray,' she told him.

'Thank you, ma'am,' he said, standing up.

'We're just doing what Americans do,' she said cheerfully.

'We're just doing what the English did before,' he added, trying to echo her tone.

'Sure – they're the guys that showed us how,' she said, and turning on her heel left the terrace, with her guards following.

When Hollander had seen her off he returned to the terrace and sat down, heavily. Lord Haver of Blindon, the twentieth most wealthy man in Great Britain, who had tactfully moved to a room at the front of the house before the President arrived, now came on to the terrace in his wheelchair, pushed by his sturdy manservant.

'Time for a drink?' he suggested.

'Good idea. Then dinner,' said Ray Hollander.

'Don't worry, Ray,' said Haver. 'I've seen the future and it looks very, very good.'

At Castel Gandolfo, the Italian Pope, a man who had grown up with and was now ever-surrounded by the relics of a mighty empire, which had grown great, then fallen, over two thousand years ago, turned to his chaplain, Monsignor Rossato and said, 'They're finished.'

Sugden's, Fox Square, London SW1. September 6th, 2015. 10 p.m.

Downstairs, the restaurant was half-full and demanding attention and upstairs William Frith, in his dinner jacket, was having a row with his boss. William had just asked three diners – an MP, his wife and their guest, the CEO of an important engineering firm – to leave the restaurant. 'Norton was drunk and offensive,' he was saying. 'He was swearing loudly and disturbing the dining room. He was out of control. What did you expect me to do, Jack? I thought he was working up a head of steam to hit somebody. I had no choice . . .'

'You've handled worse, William,' Jack Prentiss said in an even tone. Jack was on the landing of his flat above the restaurant. He wore a purple jacket and had a well-kept hand on a banister. William shot him an angry look. 'Face it, William,' Prentiss went on. 'You've been off your game for weeks. This isn't the first fuck-up. There was that complaint about slow service from Lady Jethro, that mess about the laundry, and that fight in the kitchen – now you're hustling a drunk, protesting MP out of the dining room in full view.'

'So the fucking chefs get into an argument, a woman whose husband left her for a bloke decides to restore her self-esteem in a restaurant, a drunk MP makes a scene . . . Shit, Jack, how much of this am I supposed to take?'

'That's enough, William,' Jack Prentiss interrupted. 'Let's not turn a drama into a crisis. You know I value you but all the arguments and explanations in the world don't change the fact that things are wobbling. Situations you'd once have nipped in the bud go south. I'm on your side – but it can't go on.'

William, enraged, heard him out, then, wordlessly, turned and went downstairs. He went into the staff toilets and splashed water on his face. He washed his hands. He fumed. All very well for Jack Prentiss to sit upstairs at Sugden's, only leaving to attend some auction of old china or an early music concert at a church in Piccadilly. All very well never to soil your lily-white hands, while downstairs the staff fought and the customers drank; then, the minute there was a problem, call him up to the flat like a naughty schoolboy. Jack was a bastard: providing shit pay and lousy hours – for two pins he'd walk straight out. He forced himself to take a few deep breaths and leaned against the wall. Restaurants were closing, because, he understood, the price of oil was so high now. Other jobs were few and far between. He couldn't walk out now and stick Lucy with the bills and the mortgage.

He pushed his hands through his hair, straightened his bow tie and went back into the restaurant. He took up his normal position near the door, watching the waiters and waitresses, letting an unobtrusive eye run over the tables and the diners. He put out extra-sensory feelers into the kitchen, gauging what was occurring in there. He gestured at a napkin which had fallen under a table, at a wine bottle that was empty, and couldn't wait for his day to finish. But he had to realize that when it did he wouldn't want to go home. To get to his bedroom he'd have to cross the living room, where his in-laws would be asleep on the sofa bed. However quietly he entered, Marie Sutcliffe would wake. He believed that even if he were capable of dematerializing and going through the front door without opening it, then wafting across the room a foot above the floor, Marie Sutcliffe would still wake up. Once awake, whatever the time, she'd speak to him instantly, lifting her grey perm from the pillow to look him in the eye. She might say anything. 'Lucy's looking peaky – these late shifts are wearing her out.' 'Mrs Rogers upstairs has sprained her ankle on these stairs.' 'I've made a sponge cake. It's in the kitchen. Do you want some before you go to bed?' If he answered, she would reply and Joe would wake up. If he answered only perfunctorily, 'I'd better get to bed, Marie,' she'd give a heavy sigh and let her head fall, thud, back on the pillow. The night before he'd ignored her completely and stealing towards the bedroom door he'd heard her murmur, as if to herself, 'I'm a burden. If only you knew how often I've prayed God to take me.' He went into the bedroom, closed the door and threw a punch at it, stopping short before he actually hit it and muttered, 'Not as often as I have, believe me.' Then he'd turned to his empty bed – Lucy was working a 10 p.m. to 6 a.m. shift – sat down heavily and pulled off his shoes.

The mornings were little better. Lucy would have got into bed at seven, and William at two in the morning. But the Sutcliffes were comparatively early risers and by eight they would be up, trying to be quiet and cooking breakfast so that if the noise of two people in a small flat did not wake William, the smell of bacon did. Lucy, exhausted, would sleep on. William frequently, could not.

When the last diners left, William went upstairs to change into his outdoor clothes. There was no sound from behind the closed door of Jack's flat and William changed and went down without talking to him, which was a relief in view of their last conversation. Walking tiredly to the bus stop – he felt tired all the time now – he reflected that over the thirteen days the Sutcliffes had spent at the flat he had made love to his wife exactly once. That was when Joe and Marie had gone off on Sunday morning to a nearby Anglican church. Marie did not like Shepherd's Bush. It was crowded and, as she said, 'full of foreigners'. But the experiment had not been successful because the foreigners also went to church. On that occasion, as if they both knew what they had to do, they'd scuttled upstairs like teenagers when they heard the front door open, a memory which annoyed William in retrospect. And it looked as if even that was over, unless the Sutcliffes could find an Anglican church in the middle of London attended only by white, lower-middle-class people.

William stood at the bus stop and thought gloomily that he would not, in the foreseeable future, be making love to his wife again. And he remembered when, a bare fortnight ago, he used to go home feeling a bit tired perhaps, but calm, cheered, on top of his job and looking forward to seeing his wife, either when he got in or whenever she came in from work. Before, on the bus, he'd have been working out how close they were to the new flat, and the baby, or perhaps planning what to do in their next bit of free time together. Now look at him – a row with the boss, Marie and Joe in the front room – it was a nightmare.

A week after the Sutcliffes' arrival, after supper, when they were all round the table, William had raised the subject of the visit. Under Lucy's doubtful eyes – he had not discussed the matter with her – Joe's steady gaze, which must have rattled many a bus stop vandal and car thief in his working days and Marie's timid, fearful look, he had proceeded determinedly with his prepared speech. His and Lucy's working hours. The size of the flat. The conclusion, some phrase of his father's about good fences making good neighbours. When he finished, Lucy was looking at the tablecloth, Joe was still staring steadily at him as if he were incriminating himself and Marie was on the verge of tears, saying, 'Of course, if you don't want us here, we'll go back home.' Lucy said, 'Don't be silly, Mum. We'll manage,' and Marie had begun to weep uncontrollably. Lucy had sent William out with Joe and put her mother to bed – in their bed. 'Let's go to the pub,' he'd suggested to Joe. He wasn't going to apologize. 'Good thinking,' Joe said easily, as if nothing much had happened.

With a pint in his hand, William's father-in-law said, 'Don't think I don't understand how difficult this is or that we're not grateful. It's Marie,' he continued and then told William again how upset his wife had been about the suicide attack at Thwaite airbase and the spectacle of military vehicles full of armed men rolling down their village street. William listened in silence, waiting. He had heard all this before and assumed that, the story retold, Joe would move on to the practicalities, a suggestion about making life easier, a mention, perhaps, of how long he thought it would be before he and his wife could go home. But he did not do this. William had to recognize that Marie's state of mind had become the centre of the Sutcliffes' marriage; it controlled almost all their actions and decisions. In some ways, neither of them was normal. He felt very discouraged. They walked back to the flat in silence.

When they got in Marie and her mother were watching a video of *The Lion King*. Marie could stand very little in the way of entertainment. The news was out, of course, and most documentaries, also films containing violence, sex, bad language or conflict between the characters. This ruled out most films, TV, newspapers, books and magazines, leaving only afternoon TV, Disney films and magazines showing the homes and lives of the rich and famous. Marie lived in the only world she could endure, her own. William, unwilling to sit with three adults watching a children's film, had gone to bed.

As he got on the bus he accepted reluctantly that the row with the drunken MP at the restaurant, ending in the eviction of the whole party, might have been his fault. It was his job to deal with the guests, however out of control they became. Jack Prentiss had as good as told him he was losing his grip. And he probably was. And Lucy was tired and growing paler and thinner – if she made a mistake it would not just be a matter of a few people in a restaurant having their dinners disturbed. The bus arrived, William got on – and he decided to act. This cheered him.

Getting out at Shepherd's Bush, he noticed the Auxiliary Police were on the Green again, clustered round their camouflaged vehicles. It looked as if they'd set up a permanent base there. Why? he wondered. He'd accepted the idea that in these times of terrorism and the threat of terrorism the police needed all the help they could get. But the stories he heard were always about the Auxiliaries being idle and thuggish at the same time. They had a lot of power and were undertrained. People feared them.

As soon as he came in, Marie, who must have been waiting for him, lifted her head from the pillow and said, 'Lucy's period's late. Do you think we could be expecting a grandchild?'

William responded jovially, 'It can't have been me. I haven't touched her for weeks. It must be that rotten Bob from downstairs.' He marched into the bedroom and banged the door. Later, he sat on the bed grinning and dropped his shoes heavily on the floor as if he were drunk. He'd enjoyed that – it was almost the first thing he'd enjoyed for weeks. Marie would have disliked the reference to sex between her daughter and her husband, and the suggestion of adultery even more. Nominating Bob Archer, the Friths' downstairs neighbour, who was black, as the guilty man, made it all the better.

He'd pay – of course he'd pay. Through the door he could hear Marie lightly sobbing. That would wake Joe. Next morning, they'd both be tired. Joe's face would be as long as a fiddle, Marie's eyes would be red and as soon as Lucy got up there'd be a post-mortem into William's drinking habits and general behaviour as a husband. He didn't care. He wouldn't be in the flat anyway. He put his head on the pillow and went straight to sleep. Lucy did not escape so easily. He half-heard her talking to Marie when she came in. When she got into bed he pretended to be more deeply asleep than he was.

When he got up the Sutcliffes were eating breakfast in the kitchen. Marie looked very worn and pale and had an untouched plate in front of her. 'Morning,' said William, pouring himself a cup of tea.

'Can I get you any breakfast, William?' Marie asked with forbearance.

'No. I've got to go out straight away,' he said.

'Why don't you have this?' she asked, indicating her own plate. 'It's still hot but I don't seem to feel like anything this morning.'

'I've got to go and see someone,' said William, putting down his cup and heading for the door. 'Are you feeling all right, William?' Joe called after him.

'Fine. Fine,' said William and left. He went to the café where he thought his friend Mo Al Fasi might be taking a break. Mo would have been up before six to get fruit and vegetables for his father's shop and left one of his brothers in charge while he went for a cup of coffee. He found Mo sitting with a group of Moroccan men at the back of the café and went up to him. 'How's it going, Will?' asked Mo.

'Horrible,' said William. 'Can I have a word? I need to find a flat.' Mo glanced at the other men. His father and uncles had come from Morocco forty years earlier, responding to job advertisements by British companies. They'd worked, brought their families over and, scraping money together, had managed to buy a house in the then downmarket area of Shepherd's Bush. They now owned two shops and several houses.

Nevertheless, the situation was delicate. However, William calculated, Mo owed him a favour, ever since fifteen-year-old William had alibied fifteen-year-old Mo when he'd got into trouble. The offence – a small drugs deal – would have brought little in the way of a penalty but the court appearance would have shamed Mo's father and badly upset his mother. At the time the only person who had known about this was Mo's father. However, fifteen years had passed and perhaps, now, others knew. Which would make it easier for Mo to help William out. That was the way things were. A signal between Mo and the other man evidently passed and Mo said, 'Might have a place.'

They left the café and went to a pub in a quiet street. William had a pint and ordered a tall glass of orange juice, which he fortified with vodka, though he was not sure whether marriage, business and fatherhood had made Mo more conservative. Mo, however, took a swig and did not make any comment about the contents of his glass. Mo was tall, thin and rapid in his movements. As a boy, with his large brown eyes and long curling lashes he'd looked like a Renaissance angel. Now he was married, with three small children and a business. His long face was tired and there were shadows under his eyes. He asked, 'Who's the flat for?'

William outlined the situation with the Sutcliffes and Mo, no stranger to the demands of the extended family, nodded. 'There might be somewhere – Dad's got a flat – one room, kitchen and bathroom, in one of his houses. It's nice,' he said. 'Lucy wouldn't mind it. The last bloke who had it was a BBC producer, commuting from Norwich every week. But he's moved on.'

'What about the rent?'

'Couple of hundred a week. One fifty if Dad's in a good mood.' Seeing William's expression he said, 'I know. I know. But that's the going rate round here.'

'Still got to pay the mortgage, that's the problem,' William said.

Mo finished his drink and put his glass down. 'It'd be better if your wife's parents went home,' he said.

William looked at him hopelessly. 'How's your own family?'

Mo's face closed. 'Don't ask,' he replied. They agreed to meet that afternoon, at the shop, when Mo would have spoken to his father about the flat.

William stopped for breakfast, bought a couple of CDs he would look forward to playing in the new place and went home, relieved. Admittedly, he hadn't seen whatever accommodation Mo's father was renting yet. Nevertheless, he felt confident, a mood which altered when he entered the flat. Marie sat limply on the sofa, Lucy in a chair. Lucy's face was even paler and there were darker shadows under her eyes. She'd had, William calculated, about five hours' sleep. He suspected that Marie had found a way of waking her up early, in order to discuss what he'd said last night.

He went to Lucy and whispered, 'Sorry, love. It was just a joke.' She nodded, wearily. He turned to Marie. 'I'm sorry about last night,' he said. 'I'm afraid I'd had a bit too much to drink.' Marie made no reply to this unapologetic apology but Joe turned stiffly from the window and said, 'All right, William. These things happen.'

'Luce,' William said. 'You look tired. Why don't you go back to bed?'

'I'm all right here,' she said.

William said crossly, 'Well, I'm going to get some sleep,' and went into the bedroom. He lay down on the bed and closed his eyes. He didn't know why Marie, because she'd been upset, had to have her husband and exhausted daughter in the room with her, but he knew this was the case. Then the TV went on, so that if he had been trying to sleep, he would have been disturbed.

This is insane, he thought. We're all living with an insane woman and we're all going mad ourselves. He realized that if Mo's father's flat were a concrete room in a windowless basement, he'd still take it.

Lucy came in, with a cup of tea in each hand. She gave him one and sat down on the bed. It would have been made with loose tea leaves, which William disliked, but he took it anyway. 'Mum was really upset by what you said last night,' she said. 'And that you were drunk.'

'I wasn't. You're not pregnant, are you?'

'No,' she said wearily and lay down beside him. 'I'm so tired.'

'That's what I wanted to talk to you about,' he said. And told her what he'd arranged with Mo. 'I'm making mistakes at work,' he added. 'Jack's annoyed.'

'I nearly gave one patient another patient's drugs from the trolley last night,' she said. 'I was lucky – the patient pointed it out to me.'

'Poor old Luce,' William said compassionately. She began to cry and he consoled her. William had thought he might have to argue Lucy into moving out but he was wrong. This was the Lucy who had got on a train in her probationer nurse's uniform and gone to London one morning. She dried her eyes and blew her nose. 'How'll I tell them?' she asked.

'I'll tell them,' William said.

'Let's just go and look at the outside of the house,' suggested Lucy. 'If we can't see inside until later.'

William hesitated. He didn't want to start putting pressure on Mo, when all kinds of complicated family discussions might be taking place. 'We can go and talk to him,' he offered.

Before they left William told his in-laws they were going to the building society to talk about the mortgage. He didn't want them to forget that he and Lucy were paying it.

At the shop, a supermarket covering the bottom of two houses in a busy street, Mo's brother Jemal was sitting behind the till with his head in a book written in Arabic.

'Hi, Jemal,' William said.

'Oh – William,' Jemal said, barely recognizing him.

'Did you hear about me and Lucy maybe moving into a flat your father's got?' asked William.

'Something about it,' agreed Jemal.

'Well, I don't want to push, but we were wondering if we could go and take a look – just at the outside—'

'I think they went round there – Mo and his wife and Mum – to check it out.'

'Do you think they're going to rent it to us?' asked Lucy.

'I think it's OK,' Jemal said to William.

'Where is it?' asked William.

'Oakham Street. 47 or 49.'

'Thanks, Jemal,' said William. Jemal muttered something and went back to his book.

'Don't get your hopes up,' William told Lucy. 'Jemal's not exactly spot on. I was surprised to find him in charge of the shop. Mo doesn't usually let that happen. Jemal's clever – he got eight or nine GCSEs – but he's hopeless. He went a bit vague and religious at school.'

'Oh, William. I hope it works out.' Lucy sighed.

'Well, if it does,' said William, 'I hope you've got something in your little black bag for when you tell your mum.' He thought Lucy might round on him and call him heartless but instead she said, as they rounded the corner into tree-lined Oakham Street, 'I spoke to a doctor at the hospital and got a prescription for her.'

That was when William realized how hard on Lucy the past weeks had been, harder perhaps than for him. Lucy added, 'She needs professional help.' William carefully said nothing. 'Oh, look!' Lucy said delightedly.

47 Oakham Street was a nice little house with a well-tended front garden, in which some late roses bloomed. The front door was open and William saw Mo up a ladder in the hall.

Mo got down, a light bulb in his hand. 'Come on in,' he said. 'It's small.'

The room at the back of the house was, indeed, small and seemed smaller when Mo, William and Lucy joined Mo's mother and sister, who were already in there. Mo's mother looked very old in her hijab and long Moroccan dress and Mo's sister very young, for a busy solicitor, in her black business suit. But if small, the room was light, looking out on to a small patio. The bed, couch and table looked new and there was a small separate kitchen. Lucy, in the doorway, looked excited. Then she took in Mrs Al Fasi and asked, 'Mr Al Fasi – badly fractured wrist. Is that right?' Mo's mother agreed.

'One seven five, OK?' Mo asked.

'Excellent,' William replied.

'Month in advance?' Mo said.

'I'll bring it round to the shop before I go to work.'

'Cash would be appreciated.'

William saw that there would be no lease but did not care. They had the place, and Lucy liked it. Nothing else mattered.

When they had gone, Lucy went and jumped up and down on the bed. She stopped and said, 'You can shower, cook breakfast and watch TV all at the same time. Brilliant. Only one snag, though – no washing machine.'

'We'll take our laundry round to that flat we're paying the mortgage on and put it in the washing machine we paid for,' William remarked sourly.

'Oh, William. Don't start talking about money.'

'I wasn't going to – I love rent, and mortgages – bring 'em on. I'll pay them all. I'd pay your parents', if they hadn't already paid theirs off.'

Lucy laughed. It was, William realized, the first time he'd heard her laugh for some time.

Five

Sugden's, Fox Square, London SW1. October 29th, 2015. 1 a.m.

The restaurant was almost empty. British elections are held on Thursdays because it had been decided, during the reign of Queen Victoria, that the best way to persuade the British working man, paid on Friday or Saturday, to go the polling stations and vote, was to hold elections on Thursdays, when his beer-money would have run out. The short but intense weeks running up to election day in Britain had passed and the Thursday polling day came. Voting had ended at nine and now most of the MPs who had spent six weeks in their constituencies, asking for the votes of their 70,000 constituents, were still there, watching the votes being counted or at victory or defeat parties. The journalists who had been covering the election were at their papers; party staff were assembled at headquarters.

Only a few senior civil servants were dining, and planning the future. And two renegade MPs who already knew they were still MPs, had taken advantage of an early result to sneak off from their victory parties to work out what they would be saying the next day, on *Westminster Unplugged*.

Julia had nearly finished her wine, although the food had not yet arrived. Joshua refilled it. She shot him a beady glance and asked the question which was already on some lips, and which would, over the coming weeks, be on many more. 'How did Petherbridge do it?'

Joshua shook his head, 'Our policies appealed more, our campaign was better and so was our advertising. Petherbridge had everything under control. *Safety, Stability and Security*.'

Julia stared at him. She did not think Joshua was lying to her, but he was certainly not telling the whole truth.

Joshua Crane had kept his seat in the constituency of Finchley and West Hampstead with an increased majority. Julia Baskerville had held Whitechapel Road and Stepney Green with a reduced majority. But there had been little doubt before the election that both seats were safe for their respective parties.

The exit polls had indicated a strong swing to the Conservatives. Early results were showing the same. Two key marginal constituencies had already gone decisively to the Conservative Party. 'Not quite a landslide, certainly a big mudslide,' said the BBC. There had been exit polls, post-exit polls and computer predictions. All the signs suggested the Labour Party should send back the champagne and the Conservatives send out for more.

Julia was tired. She had walked the streets of her constituency for six weeks and spent almost every evening in strategy meetings. She had seen her daughter only in the early mornings and for whatever time off she could spare on Sundays. Now her party had been beaten again and this time, it seemed, the Conservative Party might even have a comfortable majority, the first straight majority one party had had over its rivals for five years. There had been eleven Labour seats lost already, two being those of close friends.

Already she saw Hugh Carter, who would probably be the new Foreign Secretary, and Rod Field, the editor of the most popular broadsheet newspaper in Britain, drinking champagne at another table with Sukie Bond, the TV presenter. Julia felt sick. She also smelt a rat.

She persisted, 'Come on, Joshua. The results of this election aren't due to more popular policies. Face it, there was hardly any difference.'

Joshua felt uncomfortable. His back had been playing him up for weeks and he'd been living on painkillers. Victory is sweet but pain has a way of souring it. He was depressed too, because his election campaign had emphasized what he knew about his marriage. Beth had been with him, when she needed to be, had smiled and shaken hands and acted in every way as a candidate's wife ought to, but she and Joshua had barely exchanged an unnecessary word during the six weeks of closer-than-usual companionship. The campaign had highlighted the fact that his marriage was little more than a business arrangement. He suspected this was probably his own fault, which did not make the knowledge easier to bear. Nevertheless, bad back and cold marriage or not, he was in. He was safe, and his party was in government.

But he was not comfortable about Julia's question. He had been helped in his own campaign by the knowledge that Barrington Chambers seemed to have money to burn. When he asked questions Barrington had tapped a finger against his nose and said only, 'Ask no questions and you'll hear no lies. That's orders from on high.' He'd been annoyed, and also puzzled, when the party jetted in a young campaign adviser with long dark hair and a CV showing she had spent ten months as a Democratic Party aide. He put this down to Alan Petherbridge's mistrust of him as a member of the awkward squad. Until he heard the stories from fellow MPs.

He said to Julia, 'We had more money.'

'A lot more money,' Julia said. 'Where did it come from?'

That, of course, was the question. Before the election forty million pounds had been donated to the Conservative Party, more than they could ever have expected. No one understood why the donations from supporters had been so generous. A constituency party can legally spend no more than £6000 on its campaign. This covers posters, leaflets and other expenses. However, the law does not regulate the cost of headquarters staff or advertising campaigns. And the Conservatives, taking advantage of their sudden, unexpected wealth, had employed a headquarters worker in each constituency and paid for a vast advertising campaign. All over the country posters went up, simple, polished and effective, concentrating on those two constants – fear of crime and desire for gain. Though, legally, they could not buy more TV advertising space, their party political broadcasts had been much more effective. The other cash-strapped parties could not compete.

Joshua could not tell Julia where the party donations had come from. He did not know. He said, 'Donors thought they wanted a Conservative government under Petherbridge. A party with a workable majority. The country's on the skids. We have 10 per cent unemployment. The donors were backing the party which supports business to get business moving again. The list of donors will be published.' He added, 'God's always on the side of the big battalions, Julia. We had the cash. Our party political broadcasts were attractive – yours and the Lib Dems had the viewers brushing the dog and putting the kettle on in their millions.'

'And what about the transport?'

Joshua suppressed a flinch and kept his face straight. He liked Julia. They worked together. But she was on the other side and he wouldn't tell her what he really thought. Douglas Clare, his friend – and occasional alibi – represented a marginal South Coast constituency. Half his constituents were wealthy commuters or low-paid middle class and the remaining 50 per cent were semi-skilled or unskilled workers, men and women either unemployed or often out of work. The situation of the last group had worsened over the past few years – jobs had been lost when tourism crashed as a result of terror threats and escalating oil prices. Two large local employers had gone bust. At the last election Douglas had only had a 1,000 majority. The Lib Dems had come second but Labour had not been far behind. The constituency was volatile. Douglas Clare was a worried man.

And then, as he told Joshua, not long after he had begun campaigning, the Transport Plan, all two pages of it, had been handed to him by his newly appointed Campaign Officer, a sharp young man sent down by Head Office. The remainder of the plan had been conveyed verbally to Douglas and his Party Chairman, operating at that point as his election agent, in the Chairman's front room, after the sharp young man had swept it for bugs (none were found).

Joshua had rung Douglas that day, at ten, an hour after the polls closed. He was jubilant. 'It was just like the Dunkirk evacuation!' he'd exclaimed. Douglas was a simple patriot who knew about war and heroism. Perhaps uncertain of his analogy he then added. 'Well, maybe like the Dunkirk evacuation crossed with a pilgrimage to Lourdes. Anyway, it was a real

military operation — buses, taxis — the lot.' He returned to his military
comparisons. 'The polling stations looked like field dressing stations in
the First World War — the voters were coming in on crutches, walkers,
practically on stretchers, practically singing "Tipperary". There were quite
a lot with guide dogs, and plenty with their carers. It was all down to
that smart-arse they sent from Party Headquarters. Brilliant, really. And
it's been happening all over. It makes sense. Our voters have always had
a higher average age than the supporters of other parties — it is still fifty-
five. And they tend to live in the country or in leafy suburbs, miles from
the nearest polling station. And think of my constituency, full of old
people's homes. Today, we had a fleet of luxury buses, with toilets. That
got the vote out. A nice ride to the polling station and back — unless they
wanted to stop off at a supermarket or for a nice cup of tea on the way
back. My majority looks as if it's gone up 100 per cent,' Douglas crowed.
'And what that bloke did with the postal votes you'd never believe. Visit
them, ask if they want one. Visit them and help them with the forms. Go
back again, if you have to. Think how grateful they are, for the attention
as well as anything else. So who are they going to vote for? Me. That
alone must have pulled in another four hundred votes. And then the mobilizing of the old and infirm — sheer genius.' Joshua had to admit he found
his friend's attitude objectionable, but he reasoned it was not the place
of a man in a safe seat to cast the first stone at one who had faced elect-
oral defeat and an uncertain future. He'd benefited himself after all.

'What do you mean — transport?' he asked Julia.

'You know perfectly well. Cars, coaches and taxis. All over the country.
They even had ambulances in Dorking, I've heard. What the hell was
going on?'

'People are entitled to apply for free travel in certain circumstances.
There was a social security ruling—'

'Leave out the ambulances. What about the fleets of taxis?'

'We looked after a disadvantaged group of voters — people unable to
get to the polling stations. Effectively disenfranchised by their health.'

'It's illegal to pay for transport. It has to be done by volunteers.'

'Who says the transport was paid for?' asked Joshua.

'Carl Chatterton's already hinting. And you'll have heard the rumours
flying about. You got your votes out by collecting the voters and providing
free transport. It's a scam.'

'Chatterton'll have to prove all this, won't he? Tricky — it's all a grey
area. Were the drivers volunteers? Were the passengers incapacitated and
to what extent? He'd either be in court for years, with appeal after appeal.
Or they'll set up a committee—'

'And Petherbridge will pack it with his own men.'

Joshua shrugged. 'To the victors the spoils.'

'It's that American func-raiser he got in, isn't it?' Julia said. 'That's who planned all this – the election campaign, the transport scam – and what else, I wonder?'

'You're in a bit of a sour mood,' he said. 'I can understand that, in the circumstances. Don't get bitter, Julia.'

Julia stood up and said, in no friendly tone, 'We'd better get back to where we're supposed to be.'

He stood up briskly, she wearily. Victory – and losing – affects the body as well as the mind.

May 2017

Jenny Henderson writes:

That was the start of it really, that autumn 2015 election. It's hard to believe that was only eighteen months ago.

Edward Gott came round last night. He brought food, some lamb chops and a whole Camembert. My husband looked down on to the bloody greaseproof paper where the chops lay and said, 'My God. How did you come by these?'

'I've got friends at the French Embassy,' said Edward.

Sam said, 'Will they help you get out, if you have to?'

'It's been mentioned,' Edward said.

For me this exchange was yet another shock. I was quicker to take in information and its implications, however horrible, when I was younger and in a job which demanded I do so. Plainly it was not just Edward Gott, who lived in the corridors – the lobbies, the drawing rooms, the throne rooms – of power, who saw big trouble looming for himself, to the point where he'd have to disappear fast. It was my husband Sam, an ordinary London GP.

'It's come to that?' I said, staring at Edward. I noticed that suddenly his face had changed. He'd always had a big, square face, not handsome, but energetic and usually cheerful. And now I saw before me a man with lines drawn down from his mouth and a tightness about the eyes. His whole expression was controlled. He might have been the subject of a sixteenth-century portrait of a man of affairs, dressed in a black robe, with one ringed hand, perhaps, on a great book on the table in front of him, a candle burning beside it to signify, perhaps, the fact that his days were numbered – as they would have been in those days, for a man of fifty-six, even without arbitrary arrest, the executioner's blade or assassin's dagger-thrust.

'It's a possibility,' he said. 'Are those spooks in the house behind yours still there?'

'I think so,' I said. 'It's still not occupied in a normal way and the lights still go on and off at odd times. It's been a year now. And there's been nothing to see.' An idea struck me. These revelations are like suddenly realizing you're ill. 'I suppose they're looking at you,' I said to Edward.

'Could be,' he said.

'Jesus Christ,' said Sam, disgusted. He spent his days handing out vitamins the National Health wouldn't pay for, dealing with illness often exacerbated by cold and near-malnutrition and once a week he sat on a committee attempting to block the local Health Authority from closing down all the GP practices in the area. They would, he said, reopen them under a different set of rules. He suspected that Rule One would be that treatment must be paid for.

I cooked the chops. We all sat round the kitchen table, with the door of the lit oven door open for warmth, because the central heating was off.

We'd usually eaten there, anyway, when Edward came in for a pot-luck supper. I got used to his short-notice phone calls, often from his car when he was already on the Harrow Road past Paddington and following the signs to Kilburn or Willesden. I often wondered if Sam objected to these sudden descents but he never had. When I asked him he'd say, 'He's an interesting man. A good talker. He makes a change from bunions and mysterious rashes.' They were like-minded in some ways, both more conservative with a small c than I was. Am? Does the distinction matter any more? They'd make little jokes about my supposed bleeding-heart attitudes. I thought it was because they were worried that I might be cleverer than they were. Not true, but they still worried.

In those days Edward didn't bring food, of course.

I felt, after the grim conversation about the spies overlooking my house from the back, that I ought to try and strike a happier note. But I realized the shadows hanging over us were too heavy. What could I do? Suggest a sing-song? So all I said was, 'Do you remember when you came here after Petherbridge's election? You were starting to look at the accounts.'

'You came with a crate of wine and a bottle of brandy, I seem to recall,' Sam said.

'I needed it,' Edward said. 'That was the day of the Opening of Parliament. Queen's Speech. And after I'd had my little chat with the new PM.'

'Which you didn't actually tell us about,' I said. I still felt annoyed about that. It had been stupid of Edward – but then, although intelligent in many ways, there were some areas where he was no brighter than the average man in the street. In fact, to say that is to insult the man in the street, who might have shown more wisdom than Edward Gott.

'I was shocked,' he told me. 'I needed to think.' He added, 'Even now I wonder if I could have done more to prevent all this.' As if to emphasize what he said, the lights went out. I went to get the emergency lights and lit a couple of candles for the table.

'I'll open the brandy,' said Sam.

'I don't think you could have done anything, Edward,' I said. 'It was planned. We were all deceived.'

Edward took his glass from Sam. 'We were fools,' he said.

10 Downing Street, London SW1. November 12th, 2015. 6.30 p.m.

My Government will extend the provisions of the Anti-terrorism Crime and Security Act to include British subjects under its provisions.

My Government will introduce the Sale of Ministry of Defence Lands Sale Bill to enable the Government of the United States to assume full ownership of and responsibility for specified air force bases in Great Britain.

There were other provisions in the speech, of course, including, among others, the setting up of a committee to review the performance and financing of the National Health Service and another to look at the progress (or lack of it) of the Thames Gateway project. These anodyne proposals were ignored in the furore over the proposed extension of the government's powers to arrest and detain its own citizens. The old Anti-terrorism Crime and Security Act of 2001 provided powers to seize and imprison, without trial and for as long as it saw fit, any foreign national suspected of terrorist activities. This had been censured in the European courts and questioned by civil liberties organizations in Britain. The proposed extension would apply to anyone, British or not, whom the government suspected of being involved in terrorist activities. There would be an outcry from MPs and civil liberties groups about this new provision, which amounted to a licence to seize and imprison anyone at all.

More controversial still was the proposal to hand over airbases to the USA. These had, effectively, become USAF bases after the Second World War, during the Cold War. Now the plan was that Lakenheath, Mildenhall, Hamscott Common, Feltwell, Fairford, Alcolnbury, Thwaite and Molesworth, in all more than fifteen miles of bombers, weaponry and detection and communication systems, would be directly in the hands of the Pentagon.

There had, of course, been no disturbance as the Queen, seated on her throne and wearing her glittering crown and spectacles, read out from the parchment the speech written for her by Petherbridge's government.

But as the Queen was escorted from the Chamber a group including

Edward Gott surrounded the Lord Chancellor, cutting off his stately progress. As the Queen walked out, apparently unaware, or unwilling to acknowledge the hubbub behind her, a Conservative peer held the Chancellor by the shoulder of his robe and asked, 'Was that the Queen of England inviting foreign troops on to British soil?'

'Was she giving the bases to them? Are they Embassies?' shouted someone else.

The group round the Chancellor was getting bigger, pushing and shoving. Alarmed security men and police pushed their way through the mob to reach the beleaguered Chancellor, whose wig had fallen sideways, and hustle him out of the Chamber.

'Bastard!' yelled one of the noble Lords as he was hurried out.

'Fuck me,' said Lord James of Norwich, turning to Lord Gott, 'I've never seen anything like that before.'

Gott refused invitations to join others to discuss the matter. He had to return to his office at Clough Whitney Credit and Commerce. Large oil deposits had been found in the Pacific, north-east of the Barrier Reef. Gott had word that Vladimir Kutuzov, the feared Russian energy baron, was buying in ahead of exact predictions about how big the field was. The world was starving for fuels. Gott had to decide immediately whether to follow Kutuzov on behalf of his clients, or hang back, wait for certainty and then, if the reports were favourable, get trampled in the rush to buy. He was standing looking out of his window on to Leadenhall Street, waiting for his trusted secretary, Jasmine Dottrell, to bring him in some pages of figures when his private phone rang. He was surprised to see on the display screen the Prime Minister's Principal Private Secretary, Gerry Gordon-Garnett, blond and smiling, and even more surprised to be invited to a meeting at Downing Street at six. Gott accepted – he could hardly refuse – but he could not understand why Alan Petherbridge, who had just, via his sovereign, issued his dictats, some likely to upset his own party just as much as the opposition, whose phone must be ringing off the hook, and who had a nest of political hornets buzzing round his head, wanted to see him now. At least having to get to Downing Street prompted a decision on the oil finds. When Jasmine brought in the pages, he handed them to back to her and said. 'Put all this Pacific oil information away, Jasmine. I won't be needing it. Just make sure I can find it if I want it later.'

Sitting opposite Alan Petherbridge in the Prime Minister's office, Gott still wondered why he was there. What had possessed Petherbridge to invite him here on the day of the opening of Parliament when he must have much more important business to deal with, not least the uproar inside his own party about the proposal to hand over the bases? Why him? Why now? On the way to Downing Street he had felt a little surge of hope, of ambition left over from the old days. Was Petherbridge going to offer him a job, he wondered, a place in the Cabinet? He pushed the thought away. Those days had gone. The subject had to be money – party money. But what about it?

He sipped his whisky while Petherbridge drank a glass of water. He waited.

'Well, Gott,' Petherbridge said with some satisfaction. 'Here we are. That's really it, isn't it? Queen's Speech over – time to get on with the business of government. I was sorry to see you in that fracas round the Lord Chancellor.'

'Things got out of hand,' said Gott.

'That was a pity,' Petherbridge said, no mercy in his tone.

Gott was impassive. No one had ever referred to Alan Petherbridge as a charmer, he thought. No one he knew had reminisced about pleasant hours spent in his company. He was never going to be top of anyone's party list. But Gott knew now what Jeremy had discovered about the PM's background. That sort of upbringing was not likely to make a man easy in his skin. In fact, Gott reflected, you had to feel a certain amount of pity for the poor bastard, however unpleasant he was. Gott had a spasm of self-congratulation. '*Tout comprendre, c'est tout pardonner,*' he said to himself. This charitable mood was destined to last about a minute longer.

'What did you think of the Queen's Speech?' Petherbridge asked.

'Controversial,' Gott told him. 'There'll be trouble with the back-benchers. I don't need to tell you that. They aren t going to find it easy to support ordinary British men and women being picked up and banged up so easily—'

'You know the system,' Petherbridge said easily. 'Ask for twice what you want and settle for half.'

So – if Petherbridge had not asked him here for his views on the Queen's Speech, and tactics to get his measures through, why, Gott asked himself again, was he here?

He tried again. 'The same rules apply, I suppose, to the bill about handing over the airbases to the US?'

Petherbridge sat back in his chair. His face was very still and his tone icy when he replied. 'Oh, no, Edward. There'll be no compromises there.' He continued, in the same cold way, saying, 'I haven't had the opportunity to thank you for your letter of congratulation. It was one of the better expressed. It's astonishing how the most capable and intelligent men seem to fall to pieces when the moment comes to write a simple letter.'

The way to deal with power is the same as the way to deal with drunks, madmen and angry tigers – carefully. Gott was careful. 'I was educated in Scotland,' he said.

'So you were – so you were – MacCallum Academy, I believe.'

He was somehow not surprised that Alan Petherbridge had taken the trouble to discover and remember the name of his relatively obscure Ayrshire school.

'You've had an impressive career,' the Prime Minister said. 'You came from an ordinary family – as I did myself. I think your father was a manager at Robinson and Weber. Wool merchants, I believe.'

'That's so,' Gott told him, thinking that his family had, thank God, been considerably more ordinary than Petherbridge's. His own father had not driven his mother to her grave. He had not put his old man under house arrest in an old folk's home. He disguised his wariness as Petherbridge continued to speak in the same flat tone.

'Then Cambridge, then Harvard, then the Chicago Credit Bank, then Clough Whitney where you're a director – a career not unlike my own.' These were not friendly enquiries. They were to warn him that he was under scrutiny. Again – why?

Gott thought, years ago, when he was still in the House, that this would have been a heart-stopping conversation. By now he'd have been looking at a Ministry, asking himself where – Health, Foreign Office, Education – or the wastes of Foreign Aid?

The Prime Minister continued easily, 'I thought you should know Derek Vigo's trying for parole. He's offering to give a fuller explanation of the Kirkham affair, hoping his candour will influence the parole board in his favour.'

Petherbridge had not signalled the change of subject from Gott's past career to this. Gott's stomach lurched. He managed, he hoped, to disguise his concern and said casually, 'Really?'

A man who has been busy in politics and banking for twenty-five years is almost sure to have the odd skeleton in his cupboard. Derek Vigo was one of Gott's.

Three years earlier, Derek Vigo and Edward Gott had been two of the five directors of Clough Whitney Credit and Commerce. Vigo had brought some of his clients, many of them extremely wealthy, some famous, into a conglomerate specializing in health centres and hotels, Kirkham. It was not widely known that Vigo's son-in-law was a major shareholder and CEO of the company. It emerged later that Kirkham was failing when Vigo recommended the bank's clients to buy in. And a year later, it failed. The indignant shareholders mounted an investigation and discovered Vigo's family connection to the firm and the evidence that, at the time when Vigo had recommended it to his clients, Kirkham was already in trouble. It was enough to get Vigo a three-year jail sentence.

Lord Gott's problem was this. According to Clough Whitney's banking procedures, sales of shares above a certain level had to be passed by two directors. In this instance, Gott was the second. Vigo had produced information about Kirkham for his scrutiny. Gott saw instantly that the accounts had been doctored. And Vigo told Gott about the son-in-law, the vulnerable daughter, the autistic grandson and said, persuasively, 'Come on, Edward. Temporary difficulties. It's all being put right. Health centres and hotels. How can they fail?' But the trouble was that oil and gas prices rose, as did inflation, as did interest rates. And six months after Gott, suppressing his doubts, had signed off on the deal, a plane from Atlanta, coming in to land at Heathrow, crashed. It was never proved to be the result of a terrorist bomb. It was never proved not to be, either. The rising costs and reduced tourism finished Kirkham. It collapsed. Vigo went to jail. The bank investigated the deal, and the sign-off. Gott was exonerated and found guilty only of incompetence, not dishonesty. Derek Vigo never implicated his co-director. Two years later, in a rationalization, Gott, who had redeemed himself, merged Vigo's former job with his own.

Gott guessed, somehow, from somewhere, that Petherbridge had discovered his part in the Kirkham affair. And was now threatening to encourage Vigo to tell the full story, including Gott's own complicity in the crash, in exchange for early release.

The Prime Minister feigned doubt. 'I'm not sure,' he said, 'Letting Vigo out early could give the wrong signal. Then again, perhaps he deserves some leniency.'

Gott saw clearly now that he was being blackmailed. But what did Petherbridge want? Whatever it was, he was controlling the conversation now and all Gott could do was sit tight and react as little as possible.

Petherbridge glanced, apologetically, at his watch. 'I just thought I'd let you know about your former colleague's situation. What I really wanted to tell you is how much the party has appreciated your support during the election and to hope we can continue to count on it. Oh – and though it may be premature to mention it, it may be that Graham Barnsbury will be retiring as Party Chairman soon. His wife's unwell. Very sad – but I wondered if you might think, if he does go, of letting your name be mentioned. Nothing set in stone at this point, obviously.'

The prospect of occupying the enormously powerful position of Party Chairman, with access to everything and everybody and a loud voice in all discussions was intoxicating to Gott. The last time the job fell vacant he had missed it because he was in the middle of the battle with Muldoon which had ended with him being thrown upstairs to the Lords. He'd desperately wanted the Party Chairmanship then. He still did. Here was the carrot Petherbridge was offering. The stick was the possibility of Vigo implicating him in the Kirkham affair. You had to hand it to Petherbridge – he was good at this – not so subtle the victim couldn't understand the threat or the bribe and not so blunt the bought or intimidated victim would lose face. And now he had only to nod and offer a few words of thanks and the threat would go away and the job he coveted would be his.

And that was the point when Lord Gott, sitting in his chair at Downing Street, opposite the Prime Minister, had one of those flashes, like a dream, which seem to come from some very primitive part of the brain, take a mass of information, process it and in a microsecond tell us a whole, coherent story. Often an alarming one. Later, of course, he wondered how he could have been slow enough not to see it all before – but at that moment, he was staggered by the revelation.

It had been in August that he had discovered the future Prime Minister had gone AWOL, leaving no contact details with his office, his wife in Gloucestershire or his housekeeper in Kensington. Petherbridge had resurfaced ten days later, offering no explanation. Three weeks before the election Gott had been talking to a bank client, who was on the board of a major oil and natural gas company. It was another tale of toughness and endurance from a battle-hardened executive. 'To get this Kazakhstan deal up and running I had to meet Greg Koslowski and the President of the USA at Camp David in August. Arrived by jet in time for lunch and left at three – deal done. Not bad – eh?'

'Not bad at all,' Gott had agreed.

'There's a pretty fast turnover of people out there, high days and holidays included. Fly in the Canadian timber guys one day, the Venezuelan president the next, then as the President greets the Venezuelan on the tarmac, the Canadians are being loaded for the return flight – hail and farewell – fast turnaround.

'This time, believe it or not, who did I see being routed out, just as I'd got out of the plane, but our possible new PM, Petherbridge. I'm arriving – he's leaving. My seat must still have been warm.' Gott had made no comment at the time, guessing that Petherbridge's trip to the USA must have been during the time he was off the radar in August. He concluded the meeting must have gone badly so that Petherbridge, who had not told anyone he was going, had decided not to refer to it later. But, as he sat in Downing Street, Gott, in a flash, was mentally unscrolling the list of donors to the party during the run-up to the election. Petherbridge had been talking to the President in mid-August. The first heavy donations came in on the twenty-fifth. Followed by more millions in September and October. Arthur Pelman of Pelman Building and Construction, Daniel Oakes of BG Light Engineering, James Bentley of Star Casinos, Haver, of course. Twenty major donors in all. Well, now at least he knew why he was being simultaneously threatened and bribed.

As he said later, that might not have been enough to prevent him from going along with the Prime Minister, until he heard, as if through a fog, the Prime Minister saying, 'We don't see enough of you, Edward. Surely you can persuade your wife down from Scotland occasionally to dine? With some of your sons, perhaps. Or, then, you have daughter, haven't you? Chloe? Why not bring her? These official functions can be very dull without some women present.'

If Gott's revelation about the sources of the party funding had been the nature of an earthquake, this was a bad aftershock. Petherbridge had gone through his life with a toothcomb. The investigation must have taken months, had probably begun as far back as September, when he had calculated that Gott was a loose end which would need to be tied up. The Vigo threat, the Chairmanship promise and now the we-know-where-you-live threat.

Having said what he had planned to say, Petherbridge half-rose in his chair. Gott had just enough control to rise fully and say, 'Thank you, Prime Minister. You've given me a great deal to think about.' If there was anything unusual in his tone, Petherbridge did not seem to notice.

Petherbridge, standing, put out his hand. Gott took it. 'Don't think for too long,' Petherbridge said.

Outside on the murky pavement of Whitehall, with the lights of traffic crawling past in the gloom, Gott stood for a moment, fists clenched at his sides. He knew now that Petherbridge had been months ahead of him. Petherbridge had known from the beginning that sooner or later Gott would work out the real source of the election funds. Gott, as treasurer, was the man who could start credible rumours about the money, or credibly deny them. There was only one reason for the meeting he'd just had, and that was to silence him.

But although Gott was too angry at that point to think clearly, later he realized that Petherbridge's mistake was that however much digging he'd done into Gott's life, he hadn't been similarly energetic when digging into his mind. He had struck Gott in the area of his family relationships. He must have seen Gott's guilty secret as just another means of controlling him but, without realizing it, he had found Gott's sticking point, the area where he was not prepared to concede or negotiate. That last barb he had planted in Gott's hide, instead of making him more docile had maddened him.

Gott marched off towards Trafalgar Square, fists still clenched. As he went he thought, I'll get you for this, Petherbridge. You don't know it, but you're a dead man.

The Garrick Club, Garrick Street, London WC2. November 15th, 2015. 6.30 p.m.

Gott had been at work for two days. Jeremy had gone for almost forty-eight hours without sleep following paper trails from London to Washington to Tokyo to the Caymans through the Channel Islands and on to Hong Kong. He was at last asleep when Gott met Joshua Crane at the Garrick Club.

The bar at the Garrick was full of men in suits, publishers, theatre managers, actors and broadcasters. There was the quick-drink-before-dinner brigade, and there were others who, eminent Shakespearian actors or famous broadcasters though they may have been, had the faces of steady topers everywhere. Crane thought it was somehow typical of Gott to belong to the raffish Garrick Club as well as the gentlemanly White's. Useful, too, for here they were less likely to be spotted by other politicians.

'Let's go and sit down,' suggested Gott. Once they were at a brown table on brown chairs in the brown room he bent forward and said, 'It's like this, Joshua – I'm taking some soundings and you, with your exposure on *Westminster Unplugged*, could be useful.'

'Yes, Edward,' Joshua said attentively. After all, it had been Gott who had pulled some strings (probably here at the Garrick) inducing someone else to pull some strings, who had in turn tugged a few more, to get him the *Westminster Unplugged* spot. Joshua had never regretted it. He enjoyed it; he and Julia hit it off and the programme raised his profile and helped to protect his seat in Parliament from any sudden strike by an angry PM.

'What did you think of the speech?' Gott asked him.

'If the new Anti-terrorism goes through we could all end up in jail. It defies European law and the civil liberties groups are going to be up in arms—'

'It's not easy for the liberal-minded among us,' Gott said.

Joshua Crane had never thought of Lord Gott as a libertarian. 'It isn't,' he agreed cautiously.

'I'm beginning to think Petherbridge must be stopped,' Gott said.

Joshua was amazed. He knew Gott to be a man who liked power and knew that most often power was the gift of the powerful. And Petherbridge was the recently elected Prime Minister of Gott's party. Joshua's too, but he had long been among the dissidents. The Chief Whip had once been overheard saying angrily, 'The usual suspects? Crane, Clare, Whittington,

Harrington, Miss Pym, Mrs Appleby, Treadwell, Seymour and all the wankers? I'll have to go round and tell them their duty – I'd rather go round, stick them up against a wall and shoot them.' He was part of the awkward squad. Gott was not, or never had been up to now.

'Why?' he asked. 'Why now?'

'The bases,' Gott said.

'Petherbridge won't get that one through. He can't – half of us are against him and what do you think Labour will do – they're bound to go against it. And the Liberals. It's suicidal to start your career as PM with a massive defeat.' He paused and looked closely at Gott. 'Do you know why he's proposing it?'

'He'll get it through because he must and yes, I do know why he's proposing it. You'd better have another drink.'

He told Joshua everything he and Jeremy had found out in the two days following his meeting with Petherbridge. Gott and Jeremy had investigated in detail the pre-election donors to the Conservative Party.

From November 2012 up to the announcement of the upcoming election, donations to the party had amounted to a meagre £34,000, part of which had had to go to service a million pound overdraft, the rest not enough to cover anything like the cost of running the party. Then in August had come a two million pound contribution from Lord Haver, a very rich man and descendant of a long line of Conservative politicians, including a Victorian Prime Minister – and, incidentally, a man who had known and disliked Gott for fifteen years. And half a million from Mrs Caris Brookes. The mysterious Mr Finch-O'Brien had given £750,000. Two days later Sheikh Mohammed Khali came up with a million and a half. Lady Davina McCleod gave a million. As September opened the astonished Gott received a flood of donations – half a million pounds from Arthur Pelman of Pelman Building and Construction, a million from Perry Briggs-Anderson of MGA Light Engineering and another from Daniel Silverman of Opal Entertainment. And so it went on. Bewley Aeronautics, Fargo Records, Star Casinos, Mr Daniel Oakes, Mrs Maria Hughes, Halliwell Small Arms, Lord Greaves, Mr Jay Stanton, Jago Prefabricated Buildings – adding up, in all, to a little under thirty million pounds and all delivered when the election campaign was most in need of funds.

The corporate donors were largely entertainment companies, building firms, arms and plane manufacturers and oil companies When Gott had rung the private donors to express thanks, what had they told him? Haver had said, 'Must get the country on an even keel – try for a working majority.' Mrs Brookes, who was a middle-aged lady with a small estate in Wiltshire had said, 'Now is the time for all good men – and women, too – to come to the aid of the party.' Dan Oakes – 'Must break the stalemate.' The business donors had told Gott much the same as Oakes – the new government must be a government which supported business and must have a working majority. The stasis over legislation was harming them. The stories were all much the same. Suspiciously so, thought Gott – the same tale over and over, and stiffly told. They might have been scripted. Now, after his lightning revelation at Downing Street, Gott thought they probably had been. So what was the pattern, if any? Arms, planes, oil and building (the reconstruction) spelt war, one way or another. Haver, he knew, had enormous holdings in oil and gas, much of the money in the States.

Jeremy went to work, following the money from bank accounts to offshore accounts and onwards. He looked into births, marriages and deaths, talked to people who knew people who knew other people. He called the USA, he called Switzerland, he called China, India and Japan. Mrs Caris Brookes of the Old Manor in a Wiltshire village, for example, turned out to be an oft-divorced lady, one of her ex-husbands being Harold Hambro, now a personal adviser to the US President. Mrs Maria Hughes was, in her public life, the Hughes of Hughes Hudson Hatt, PR consultants in New York and London. Pelman already had big building contracts in Iraq; Briggs-Anderson was in the arms trade and would be pleased to get any contracts he could from the US military; Opal Entertainments was partner in a big US entertainments consortium and, if the world were in ruins, there would still be TV networks set up.

The final giveaway was Jay Stanton, born in the USA, though a naturalized Briton, and living in yet another manor house in the British countryside. Jeremy found out that he was a retired CIA man. Though by that stage gaunt and very weary, he couldn't help laughing about that one.

Strings had been pulled by US businesses and, pushed or bribed by US politicians, Petherbridge had got the money. Petherbridge had used it to buy a British election. Gott wondered why he hadn't made the connection earlier. And Jeremy told him, 'Because it's so extreme.'

'Oh – James Bentley, Star Casinos,' Gott told Joshua in conclusion. 'Mustn't forget him. You'll love this. Bentley owns several casinos and would like to get permission for more. But the British government is balky about casinos – they love them and they fear them. Bentley has good friends in Las Vegas and Atlantic City who would love to get into business with him here, if the government could be persuaded to give licences for another fifteen or twenty casinos. What do you think the deal is there?'

Joshua, believing but not believing, shook his head. 'Petherbridge guarantees the permission and the friends in Vegas give the money to Bentley to give to the Conservative Party.'

'When Jeremy worked that one out he panicked. He's afraid of finding his dog's head in his bed one night.'

Joshua had listened to the story silently. He still did not quite believe it. He had believed Gott, up to now, to be one of the sanest men he knew. Yet a sane man can turn into a monomaniac. A sane man in the grip of a conspiracy theory can still find all the evidence he needs to back the theory. But then there was the money – that cartload of money donated in the few short months before the election. His colleagues, the opposition, the political journalists had all been astonished by it.

Joshua was shaken. He said, 'Edward – are you quite sure?'

'Sure as death and taxes,' Gott told him.

A well-known actor came up and asked for a light for a cigar. He gazed deep into Joshua's eyes and saw something there he did not like. When he had gone, Joshua, still wrestling with his doubts, asked, 'So where does this bill to sell the air force bases come in?'

'The first payment on the debt,' Gott said. 'Petherbridge has had the money. Like all creditors, unless he has to pay up from the off, he'll relax and forget. So here it is, written into the Queen's Speech, bloody hard to get through the House, but he has to do it.'

'So why not just go to the press? One article in a respectable paper and the whole can of worms opens.'

'Petherbridge had me in and threatened me,' Gott told him. 'Bribed me, too – the Party Chairmanship when Barnsbury goes, as he may do soon. His wife's sick. Petherbridge needs me to deny everything and maybe cook the books when some clever bastard works it out.'

'What did he threaten you with?'

'An old misdemeanour – and something to do with my family. I'm pretty sure I can manage the misdemeanour. Jeremy's starting on it tomorrow, when he pulls himself together.' Jeremy would be at Ford Open Prison first thing in the morning, suggesting to Derek Vigo that he might prefer becoming the proprietor of a thriving bar and restaurant in Toronto, which Gott had taken in payment for a bad debt, to early parole based on telling the story of Gott's involvement in the financial scandal. Gott reasoned that serving his sentence in full and coming out of jail to emigrate and make a new life would appeal more to Vigo than early release, conversations with the Fraud Squad, the granny flat at his son's house presided over by a resentful daughter-in-law. 'I don't like the threat concerning my personal life – but if Petherbridge follows through on it, I'll take the consequences, if I have to. I've thought it all over, Joshua. It's difficult. For one thing, it would be very hard for me to pull down the party I've worked for and supported all my life. If there's another way, I'll take it.'

'Start by stopping the bill?'

'As the first move to get rid of Petherbridge.'

Joshua drew in a deep breath. 'Oh, shit,' he said.

'Not easy, as I said. I've let Petherbridge think I've taken the bait about the Chairmanship. That buys a little time. But we need to be quick because I think Petherbridge has to push the first reading through by Christmas. I'm guessing the US wants everything in place before the Iraqis nationalize their own oil. Those bases will be crucial, and so will Petherbridge's sense that he has to go along with the American reinvasion.'

'I'll start talking to people,' Joshua said. 'Shall I drop a few hints on *Westminster Unplugged*? Nothing obvious.'

Gott shook his head. 'Not at the moment, I think.'

Joshua, alarmed, looked at his watch. 'I'm sorry. I have an engagement.'

'And I have to get back to my office,' Gott said.

They both stood. Joshua again realized the enormity of what Gott had told him and asked, 'Why do it?'

'Power?' suggested Gott. 'That's the usual story.'

But Joshua thought Gott knew more than he was willing to say. 'I meant,' he said, 'why are they doing it?'

'The US economy is poor. They feel threatened. Like all countries they have a national myth about themselves which doesn't always tally with what observers from outside see. Their narrative is to do with expanding – go west young man – new horizons. When times get hard you saddle up and head for a new place. It's not that stupid.'

Joshua headed west to a dinner party. 'What have I let myself in for?' said the voice in his head. 'Oh my God – what am I doing?'

He found it hard to keep his attention on his hostess, a political hostess of a kind still to be found in London, and his host, the editor of a tabloid newspaper. There were six guests round the well-appointed table in a high dining room. Joshua had brought Saskia, who had not wanted to come and sat, saying little, throughout the meal. There were tiny portions on exquisite old plates, served by a couple from the Philippines.

Gott wanted Joshua to play a prominent part in the rebellion against his own government's bill. Instinctively, Joshua was against it – the Little Englander in him, no doubt. He was shocked by what Gott had told him about the campaign contributions. But he sensed that if he joined this particular dissident section of his own party, this time there would be no turning back. Whether they won or lost, while he was still PM, Petherbridge, energetic, efficient and determined, would seek to destroy him. He'd show no mercy. He'd make sure smears were published, he'd starve him of work and influence and, finally, make sure he would be deselected by his own constituency party.

What could Joshua do if he were no longer in Parliament? He'd started by abandoning a job as a lecturer at LSE to become a research economist with the party but there was little chance the LSE would want to take him back. Farewell to the fleshpots, no more invitations from the knowledgable and influential. He'd be out. His wife would hate him for it. He flinched at the idea of telling her. He put his knife and fork together on the plate, unconscious of having eaten anything.

They might succeed, that was the point. They might win. And he, Joshua Crane would be at the front of the victory parade. He was still a young man – at that moment Joshua saw the premiership, like a holy vision, right before his eyes. What should he do now? To start with – no more high-maintenance Saskia. For the time being, while the campaign was running, he and she would have to keep their heads down. While he was looking at her, she stood up and left the table. Joshua realized he had half-noticed his old school friend, James, get up and go out of the room only moments earlier. Oh shit, Joshua thought, just as the pudding was coming round, they couldn't sodding well wait. Never mind, he told himself, this is a big moment. Make the wrong decision and you're fucked. Make the right one and you could go to the top, the real top, top of the world. And who could he talk to? Julia, he decided. Julia would understand all the issues and she wouldn't tell anyone. He'd ring her next day.

After the guests went home, his hostess said to her husband, 'I'd no idea Joshua Crane would be so dull. Terribly bad value.'

'Not a word to say for himself,' her husband agreed. 'Don't ask him again.'

Six

The Rose and Crown was one of two pubs in the short village street at Hamscott Common. It lay opposite a pretty row of 200-year-old cottages. Its interior, beamed and with a bright fire burning in a large grate at one side of the bar room, seemed to tell its customers that it reflected and preserved the values of the old, rural Hamscott Common.

The landlord, Geoff Armstrong, was a short, sturdy fifty-year-old ex-serviceman. On the pub door was a painted sign reading, 'No travellers. No work clothes. No demonstrators.' Travellers, men in working clothes and demonstrators took their trade to the other pub in the village, the Goat.

That evening, the Rose and Crown was not crowded. At the bar, in their usual positions, were the regulars: Tom, the postman, Warren, the former market garden owner and John, a local handyman. At a table beside the bar was a group of mid-to-late twenties and, at another table nearer the windows, another older quartet in sensible clothing, the men in corduroys and plaid shirts, the women in tweed skirts and sweaters. 'I still say, it's not good enough selling the base off. It's no less than putting a foreign army in our midst,' said one of the men, Julian Simms, to his friend, Harry Wainwright. Julian was an early-retired civil servant and Harry still employed at the Ministry of Health. Harry, with the responsible air of the still-employed, answered, 'I'd say it was a lot less than that. It's a rational solution. It only acknowledges a fact, after all. And there's bound to be a cost benefit.'

'Sell it off and the British government loses all control. They can fill the place with as many Yanks as they see fit – what's that but a foreign army based on British soil?' asked Julian.

At the second table Kevin Staithe, a young local estate agent, said to his girlfriend, Rosie Allen, 'It's disgusting – Hamscott Common becomes American territory – what the bloody hell's all that about? What happens when one of their airmen rapes a local girl? We won't see him in court, you can bet on that.'

Art Newcombe said, 'Cool it. Hamscott's been the Yanks' since the Second World War. Own schools, own shop and if a serviceman fucks up, they cover for him – look at what happened when that barn of Joe Bridges' went up in flames. No arrests, no trial and compensation paid. What difference will it make?'

Rosie, who had been at school with the dead teacher, Kim Durham and was her son's godmother said loudly, 'They've already killed Kim – and you want them to own the base! I'll tell you the difference – we'll never be able to kick them out. That's the difference. They'll take over more and more land. They'll walk the streets as if they owned them. And next time they kill someone they'll hardly need to apologize.'

Harry Wainwright's wife, Wendy, glanced at Rosie, as perhaps pub etiquette suggested she shouldn't. Her gaze was thoughtful. Geoff Armstrong leaned over the bar and looked towards Rosie. 'A word of advice. No politics in my pub, young lady,' he said. Geoff Armstrong would not hear criticism of the base or its occupants. He had been a serviceman himself and he benefited from the trade. He had created two rooms upstairs, with four-poster beds, for the relatives of the officers on the base who wanted to visit a traditional British inn.

'Thanks for the advice,' declared Rosie. 'I hope you'll still think the same when someone else gets killed. Or somebody bombs the base and all your windows blow out. This'll make us more of a target than we already are.' Rosie had said the unsayable. The Hamscott Common base provided many local people with work. She had broken the taboo against speaking about the possible dangers of living near the base.

'That's enough, young lady,' said Geoff. 'US personnel come in here, you know.'

'Well, then,' said Rosie standing up. 'I don't want to upset any of your well-paid customers. I think I'll just take myself down to the Goat.' She eased out from behind the table and began to walk out.

'I hope you'll enjoy the company of the smelly demonstrators there,' Geoff called out to her back. 'Because I don't want you in here again. You're barred.'

Rosie walked out and Kevin, out of loyalty, followed. 'You, too,' Geoff called after him. 'You're barred, too.'

'I see the police have blocked off Templesfield Road,' observed the postman, Tom.

'It's a liberty,' said Warren, 'cutting the village off like that.' Without access by the road running past the airbase, many potential customers of the Rose and Crown would be forced to use the bypass and, once on it, might decide to carry on to the next town.

The landlord of the local pub in a two-pub village has enormous power over his regulars. If he bars them where can they go, every night, for a drink? In Warren and Tom's case, only to the Goat, with its loud music and undesirable clientele. Because the inn, the centre of their lives, was controlled by Armstrong, they didn't mind goading him a little.

Armstrong reacted with force, 'The council's seeing to that – getting rid of all these demonstrators and their bloody nonsense. And they're putting pressure on the trustees of the almshouses to stop those daft old gits aiding and abetting them. Don't worry. It's all in hand.' But he was rattled, and the regulars knew it.

With Rosie and Kevin gone, Art and his girlfriend drank their drinks in silence until they agreed quietly to follow their friends down to the Goat. Armstrong watched them leave, his face expressionless.

At their table the middle-aged couples, who had watched this scene, were silent. Julian said, 'This bill is going to cause a lot of trouble. I've never seen so many demonstrators. Quite frankly, I'd defend to the death their right to say what they like, but not to pee on my roses like the one I caught today. But if this bill goes through certain elements are going to be very unhappy.'

Another silence fell. Harry said, 'I'm beginning to worry about Wendy being by herself here, while I'm in London.'

'I'm sure that's not necessary,' said his wife.

Julian said, 'Quite frankly, I've been wondering whether now's the time to go back to London. I'm worried if this bill goes through Hamscott Common could become a terrorist target.'

'I suppose we all are,' said Harry. 'But let's not jump the gun. It may not happen. There's a lot of opposition to the bill. I'll step up and get us all another drink.'

After Harry had gone to the bar Beth said to her husband, 'We came here because you grew up here and wanted a garden.'

'I know. But if the US gets hold of the base the air traffic overhead will intensify and there's no point in blinking at facts, darling. If they start loading arms and troops for Iraq there's danger of an attack, on land or from the air. What can you do about people who don't care if they live or die?'

As Harry came to the table with two pints, followed by the landlord with the women's drinks Wendy Wainwright burst out. 'Why are they doing this? Why not leave things as they are?'

No one replied. No one knew what to say.

Sugden's, Fox Square, London SW1. November 30th, 2015. 8 p.m.

Edward Gott, his secretary Jeremy Saunders and Joshua Crane were all dining at Sugden's.

'There they are again,' Leslie Smith-Dickinson, PPS to the Minister of Education remarked to the three others at his table. 'Gott and his boyfriend. They don't look happy.'

'Lover's quarrel,' suggested another man at the table.

It was not that, and they knew it. That evening, the Ministry of Defence Lands Sale Bill had been passed at its first reading. Those in favour, 540; against, 83. There were dissidents from both parties: forty on the Labour side, ten among the Tories. Joshua Crane had been one.

It had not helped the government that two days earlier US bombing raids on Syria had been intensified. News reports and pictures were coming in of a hospital in flames, mosques destroyed, people fleeing wildly through the streets, a trail of men, women and children under bombardment, trying to escape from a Damascus in flames. A day earlier, two American oil executives had been kidnapped in Iraq. The raids on Syria were, the President said, to stop them from giving aid, comfort, training, weapons and money to Iranian terrorists.

From Petherbridge's point of view the timing of the raids, many originating from British bases, was disastrous. Earlier in the day, standing in the rain outside the House of Commons, Joshua had asked Gott, 'Why would the US make it harder for Petherbridge to put through legislation they want passed?'

'It makes the job he's doing for them harder. Increase the hours, increase the quotas, grind the faces of the workers, let them know who's holding the whip . . .'

'Even if it means not passing the bill?'

'It'll be passed,' said Gott. 'Petherbridge has moved too quickly for us. The party won't want to break ranks so soon after a victory. And Chatterton's backing the bill. He's persuaded his inner circle and the NEC not to oppose it and do you know why? Because even if Petherbridge has got a thumping majority Chatterton still thinks he's in with a chance, one day, of becoming Prime Minister. He's fed up with seeing his own supporters in the streets, crying out against US actions in the Middle East, backed by Britain. First it was Iraq – twice – then the Lebanon,

now Syria. Every time the US uses those bases to pursue what is basically its foreign policy, not ours, the public gets angrier and the Prime
Minister takes the blame for the actions of a powerful ally he can't control.
If Chatterton got his wish and became PM, his own supporters would be
up in arms against him, asking for his removal. So he's keen to see the
bases in US hands. That way, whatever happens isn't the PM's fault.'

'Mark Moreno wanted to fight,' Joshua said.

'Mark Moreno will be the next Labour leader,' Gott said with certainty.
'But he isn't now.'

'We're fucked anyway,' said Joshua, thinking unhappily about voting
in direct defiance of his Party Leader. 'Shall we get in out of the rain?'

The debate, in a standing-room-only House of Commons, began with
the Secretary to the Minister of Defence, speaking slowly and dully, saying
that over the past seventy years the defence of Britain had depended on
its US ally, that though the enemy had changed over those years, it was
still true that Britain needed their help. The additional advantage would
be the seven billion pounds the US had offered to the British government
for a hundred-year lease, which would go straight to the British taxpayer.
When he sat down there was a single cry from the Opposition benches,
'Kim Durham!' and a roar of attack and defence from both side, which
the Speaker had difficulty in quelling.

The Labour Shadow Defence Secretary's position obliged him to make
a weak speech, more questions than declarations. Would the land on which
the air force bases stood be legally US territory? Where US servicemen
committed a crime against a civilian, off the base, under whose jurisdic-
tion would they come? Was handing over the bases tantamount to handing
over British foreign policy to the USA? Did the suggestion embodied in
the bill come under the heading of the basing of foreign troops on British
soil? Would the Government examine the constitutional implications of
the bill?

When he sat down the same backbencher called out again, 'Kim
Durham!' This time he was followed by Mark Moreno, sitting directly
behind Chatterton, who in turn yelled, 'Kim Durham!' This was Moreno's
challenge, the first time he had publicly defied his leader, an announcement to party and country that he was no longer prepared to be loyal to
Carl Chatterton. The intervention was followed by uproar.

This local excitement detracted from what was agreed later to be the
best speech of the debate. Amir Siddiqi for the Liberal Democrats spoke
calmly, but with an underlying passion. The bill was dangerous, ill thought-
out and possibly treasonable. He would ask bluntly the questions the
Shadow Defence Secretary had asked politely, almost as if uninterested
in the answers. Was it safe to hand over eight air force bases to a foreign,
nuclear power, however friendly? Would the presence of the bases and

their use for US foreign policy bring down on Britain the wrath of the US's enemies? Was the handover not just further proof that Britain was nothing more than a US client state? How would this abnegation of responsibility be seen by European partners? Would the handover not compromise Britain's position in NATO? If the Tory party had been paid by the US they could not have done worse for their own nation. That he spoke not just for his party but for the country as a whole.

This finale, the matter of the money, caused many heads on the Conservative benches to bow. The debate had exposed rocks below the water. When Mark Moreno shouted the name of the woman killed by US troops on a British airbase, he was challenging his party boss's leadership. Amir Siddiqi was, as many in the House knew, referring to the growing speculation about the source of the party's pre-election donations.

Public demonstrations, newspaper leaders, the head-shakings and leaked warnings from other European leaders had made no difference – the vote on the first reading of the Ministry of Defence Lands Sale Bill was won.

Gott called William over and asked for another bottle of wine. 'It's not the end,' he assured Joshua. 'It's not even the beginning of the end. Anyway, you've got the tiger by the tail now, Joshua. If you don't get Petherbridge, now you've voted against him, he'll certainly get you.'

'You don't need to tell me,' said Joshua, tight-lipped.

Sugden's, Fox Square, London SW1. December 17th, 2015. 10 p.m.

Only a fortnight later they were back at the same table. Arriving where Joshua Crane and Jeremy Saunders were already sitting, Edward Gott eased himself into his chair, sighing theatrically. 'Interesting times,' he said as he beckoned over the wine waiter. There were black marks under his eyes and his normally ruddy skin was sallow. With the first reading of the Ministry of Defence Lands Sale Bill passed, the next stage of the fight was on. Gott was canvassing support; meetings up and down the country were being arranged.

That morning the new Iraqi leader, Mohammed Al Bactari, had asked the National Assembly to back him over nationalizing the Iraq oilfields. There had been no opposition. Already there was fierce fighting between Iraqi troops and the US-employed pipeline guards.

The five-year-old New Arab League had issued a warning to the US that more military activity in the Middle East would lead to reprisals. The League, small, factional and not inclusive, led by the unpopular Ahmed Al Saud, was not considered to be a serious threat, yet the announcement had sounded more than usually determined and many of the League states were heavily armed. There had always been a fear that the Arab states would forge an effective alliance – this might be the time.

Parliament was in recess, but already Alan Petherbridge was fielding questions about what Britain's answer would be if the US requested British troops for an invasion of Iraq. He was saying only that no request for military support in any area had been made by the US. This answer was no answer, as the newspapers made clear. It did not help that two officers and nine men from a Midlands regiment had just been killed in an ambush in one of the semi-autonomous tribal areas separating Afghanistan from Pakistan. It had not been Petherbridge's government that had committed multinational troops to the area – but the eleven deaths reinforced the public's opinion that the British Army should not involve itself in any more foreign wars.

At four that afternoon a Muslim man, a Polish IT student – had blown himself up on a bus outside Selfridges in Oxford Street, killing three passengers and wounding seven more. Because it was thought that this might be the start of a series of bomb attacks all traffic in inner London had been halted. A protest about the coming war in Iraq. Sir John Smythe,

the Metropolitan Police Commissioner, said he feared this might be the first of many such incidents. MI5 and MI6 were in conference. Police were on standby. In Edgware Road, outside Paddington Green police station, destination for terrorists suspects, the road was blocked by armed police and traffic only filtered through after checks on the drivers.

When the wine waiter came to the table, he turned out to be the restaurant's manager, William Frith. The real wine waiter had rung earlier, saying he was flying back to Lyons immediately. When Gott asked him why he was taking orders for drinks, William told him about the disappearing French waiter. Gott frowned. 'Well, I hope you're going to stay,' he said. 'People are panicking,' said William. 'And I suppose if it's a real threat my wife and I ought to go to my parents in Spain.' He moved off. It was a busy night. Upstairs, the threat of reprisals from the Middle East or of terrorists at home weren't worrying Jack Prentiss. He was delighted, foreseeing an ongoing political crisis which would fill his restaurant and the rooms upstairs for the foreseeable future.

'Seems a bit premature to start running for it,' Jeremy said. 'We're not in this war. We don't even know if there's going to be one.'

'But some people seem to think so,' Joshua said glumly. He saw the panic beginning in his own life. That afternoon, Beth had asked him if he thought she should retreat with their sons to her parents' small estate in West Yorkshire. They were due to spend Christmas there, anyway. Did he think she should stay on after they went back to school? Would they be in more danger there, near Fylingdales, or in London? Would he feel she was disloyal if she retreated with the children? Joshua, surprised by what he thought was overreaction, did not know whether his family would be in danger in London or Yorkshire. He said, 'I think it's too early to start thinking like that.' Beth replied, sarcastically, 'Well, you're in the government. You ought to know.'

He had gone straight from home to Saskia's flat, hoping to take her to bed. Instead, when he let himself in, although she always heard his key in the lock and the sound of the front door opening, she was bent over the coffee table, expertly snorting up a line of cocaine through a silver straw. Plainly she had decided to abandon any pretence that she never touched drugs. When he had protested, 'Saskia!' she'd lifted her head and said only, 'There's going to be a war in Iraq. And terrorists all over the place. How do you think I'm going to get through a party where everybody's scared? And talking about leaving?'

He told her he thought people were overreacting. She mentioned the explosion outside Selfridges. When Joshua said he could be badly compromised if found in a flat where drugs were in use, she responded, 'You'd better go then.' And so Joshua had gone. It ought to have been a relief – he knew he should have ended the affair weeks before. But these two episodes, with his wife and his mistress, had depressed him. And now Sugden's' wine waiter had left.

'We've got to kill this bill at the second reading,' Gott said firmly. 'It's scheduled two months from now.' He looked Joshua in the eye and waited.

'It may die the death in committee. There are many constitutional questions. And protest mobilizing.'

'Petherbridge will rush it,' Gott predicted.

Joshua nodded. 'Right.' The nationalization of Iraqi oil had ratcheted the situation up several notches. He felt events moving faster, perhaps spinning out of control. He was thinking about his own career. If they could see off the MoD Land Sales Bill Petherbridge might go. He, Joshua, would have been one of the architects of the Prime Minister's downfall, and therefore a favourite with the new PM. Who did Gott, the king-maker, see in the job? he wondered. He, Joshua, would get a ministerial post. He was young enough to rise from there, perhaps to the top, young enough to grab the fairy from the top of the Christmas tree. But if they lost – or even if they won and Petherbridge stayed in office – the conse-quences would be awful – deselection, back to teaching, a lower income and a furious wife.

Gott was saying to the waiter at his elbow, 'I'll just take some quails' eggs. No appetite,' he said to the others. Joshua, after Beth going, and Saskia snorting, and knowing that whatever personal problems he had he was close to the heart of a political storm, also lacked appetite. He ordered a plate of whitebait and Jeremy, whatever his inclinations really were, the same.

'I think we can do it,' said Gott. 'Now there's pressure on Petherbridge to help the USA reinvade Iraq he'll be under continual scrutiny. The public don't want it. At least half the House of Commons don't want it. Overturning that bill will be seen as telling the US we won't go along with the war.'

'The word's out. There was a deathly hush on our own benches when Amir Siddiqi talked about the Tory Party as being bought – wouldn't it help if you leaked the information about where the pre-election donations came from?'

'You're not the only person asking. Everyone is. I'm working on getting rock-solid proof—' Jeremy snorted. 'All right,' said Gott, 'Jeremy is. Meanwhile I'm saying the details of the donations are public and the party accounts are still being worked on.'

'What about Petherbridge's threats?'

'One's dealt with. The other is a threat to my personal life. I made a mistake many years ago. I compounded it. Now it's caught up with me. Simple as that.'

Joshua would have liked to ask for details. He glanced at Jeremy who gave him a warning glance and shook his head a centimetre in Joshua's direction, warning him to say no more.

Joshua speculated. Gott found in bed with a dead boy? Gott with millions of his bank's money stashed in the Cayman Islands? He had to believe Gott was not stupid enough to proceed if Fetherbridge had some truly damning bit of information to use against him. But supposing he had? They'd all be in the soup, tainted by association.

The starters arrived and Gott looked at them, then called the waiter back. 'Do you know what? My appetite's come back. I see they've got that good hare stew on the menu. Fancy some? I bet you do. Hollow legs – Jeremy,' he informed Joshua. 'Fancy some yourself?'

'I suppose so,' Joshua said numbly.

'Eat up,' said Gott. 'It all hangs on what the US President says when she addresses the nation tonight. But I expect she ll only threaten. She won't declare war before Christmas. She'll have a struggle to get consent.'

A former leader of the Conservative Party, one of those revolving-door leaders of the nineties and noughties, came over and murmured in Gott's ear. Then he clapped Joshua on the back and left.

'Well,' said Gott, smiling, 'that man's thinking ahead. He wants to be my friend.'

That was it, thought Joshua. If they overturned the sale of the bases Gott would be an important man. Edward Gott, kingmaker, he thought.

72 Whitechapel Road, London E1. January 14th, 2016. 10.30 a.m.

Julia Baskerville had spent Christmas in Houston with her husband and daughter and now, back in London, was conferring with her local Party Chairman, Mr Zulfeikar Zulani, a local businessman who owned three butchers' shops in East London. He had told her that three young men had been taken away over Christmas by the police. Their families did not know where they were. Two homes in the constituency had been raided and searched, although nothing had been found and the police had left the residents standing in the confusion caused by the search, without apology.

Julia told him, 'I'll talk to DS Spring about it and see what I can do. But he'll tell me what he usually says, that the police were acting on confidential information and the young men will be investigated and released if nothing is found against them. You know it's happening all over the country. I'm sure you suspect the police are under orders to create disturbance and anxiety to frighten the community. It started after the Victoria Station bombing and got worse after the Selfridges bomb. So when I talk to DS Spring he'll know he has orders from on high to do exactly what he's doing.'

Zulfeikar Zulani looked tired. They had been political friends for many years although they still respectfully addressed each other as Mr and Mrs. But in spite of the formality they knew each other fairly well – Julia knew about Zulfeikar's increasing prosperity, that he had fixed his brother's passport, that young Aziz was disappointing his father by being lazy at college and hanging out with the wrong friends. In turn Zulfeikar knew of the difficulties Julia experienced while being, effectively, a single parent to her daughter – and secretly deplored her family arrangements. But neither mentioned, to each other or anyone else, what they knew of each other's lives.

'I'll do all I can,' Julia told him. 'But for all our sakes, I'm afraid of another bombing. It's not just that the police will come down harder – the government will change the law to allow for indefinite detention. This new government is ready to get very harsh.'

'If the US invades Iraq and Britain joins them there will be more bombings,' he said, with certainty.

'I know. I'm due to ask for assurances that won't happen.'

'I wish you success,' he said, without hope. 'It's being said that this government is being paid by the USA,' Mr Zulani said. 'They're saying the election was bought with dollars.'

Julia had heard the rumours but thought they were just the result of tea-room gossip. But whether they were or not, the story had reached Whitechapel.

'Who's saying?' she asked. She noted that Mr Zulani had been studying her face, as if to see what she knew or did not know.

'Al Jazeera television,' he told her.

'I've heard whispers,' she said. 'But I thought it was fiction. Have they any evidence?'

'They haven't given any.'

Gott, Julia thought. Gott would know if there was any substance to the story. But even if he did, would he tell?

Mr Zulani said, 'Even if the story is untrue, it will be dangerous if it is believed.'

Julia only nodded. She was still thinking about Lord Gott. Zulani went on, 'Two young men, probably from the National Front, attacked two Asian boys on Boxing Day. One is still in hospital, and likely to lose an eye.' He added, 'You should know there is a group in the constituency called The Jihad. The leaders are from the Middle East. They are calling on the young men to resist. They are saying the US President will soon declare war on Iraq. And that Britain will follow.'

Julia looked steadily at the man who had been her Party Chairman since she had been elected, and her predecessor's Chairman also. He had hesitated before telling her this bad news.

'If the police think there is a network of terrorists here, they will come down harder. But if I do not speak, I am guilty.'

'I won't mention it,' she said. 'Not unless something serious comes to my attention.'

'Our world is becoming a more dangerous place,' he said.

Hamscott Common Airbase. January 14th, 2016. 3.30 p.m.

The Prime Minister of Britain shook hands with the President of the United States while, behind them, the presidential jet screamed. The President leaned towards him.

'I'll be counting on you, Alan,' she said.

The Prime Minister nodded. 'I hope you will.' The President turned, surrounded by her guards, and walked lithely towards the plane. It was very cold on the tarmac and Petherbridge tried not to shiver as the aircraft taxied. The perimeter of Hamscott Common was two-deep in armed soldiers. Two helicopters rattled overhead. The permanent vigil, which consisted of five cold and obstinate peace demonstrators, had been arrested and their benders in the trees dismantled three days ago, before the President landed. The road to London had been cleared of all traffic for the cavalcade.

During her whole visit, the President had moved inside a half-mile wide cordon of empty streets and buildings. The ostensible reason for this was fear of terrorism, but the Prime Minister also knew that he could not allow the President to see the huge public demonstrations against her. Not that she was unaware of them. Petherbridge had hurried to re-assure her. 'The people who matter are with you. The rest will follow.'

'You will back us?' said the President.

'Of course,' said Alan Petherbridge.

The Silent Duck, Shepherd's Bush Green, London W12. January 14th, 2016. 3.30 p.m.

William Frith waited for Mo Al Fasi at the pub in the side street where they'd met in September. Mo had rung and asked to see him. William didn't know why. His own flat was still occupied by the Sutcliffes.

William and Lucy had spent Christmas in Spain with William's parents. They had both found the situation difficult to explain. On a walk through pines, the sun bright above and a light sprinkling of snow on the ground William's mother had cried, '*Why?* Why, William? It makes no sense.'

'Things are getting worse,' William had replied, vaguely. 'All these worries about another war and all these demonstrations . . .'

In spite of his job, or perhaps because of it, William was not interested in politics. His mother, however, was. 'The European Parliament's more and more concerned about the American military having bases in Britain, without any checks at all. There'll be trouble with Europe if Britain goes to war with Iraq. But why do the Sutcliffes think they're safer in Shepherd's Bush? It's not rational.'

'Marie isn't rational, Mum. You know that. I told you, she wants us all to die together.'

'I'm surprised that with her head-in-the-sand attitude she even knows what's happening,' William's mother said tartly. 'That woman needs urgent professional treatment. Anyway, the situation's ridiculous. Do you want us to come over and give you an excuse to say you need the room so they'll have to leave . . .?'

'Not for the moment, Mum. We're all right for now. Joe's talking about making a move. And Marie's seeing a counsellor. Let's see how it goes.'

But William's mother remained unconvinced.

William was unhappy about what Mo might say. Did he want the flat back? Joe was paying towards the mortgage now and the family had settled into a bearable routine, eating together four or five times a week and spending most of the remaining time apart. But life was still hard, worse than William had been prepared to tell his mother. Marie was, as he had said, seeing a counsellor, but this was not the first, nor the second counsellor she had seen since she arrived in London. In fact, Mrs Wilmot was the fourth, Marie having seen off the first three by suddenly taking a turn for the worse during therapy – when they began to get too close to making recommendations, said Lucy.

As to the Sutcliffes' move – William had not exactly lied to his mother about it but had not told the truth either. Just before leaving for Spain William had taken the bull by the horns and asked Joe what his plans were. He made the point that if Joe and Marie ever wanted to see a grandchild the situation could not go on as it was. Joe had countered by saying that he and Marie had been discussing selling up and moving to London. He suggested that because, however hard they saved, William and Lucy alone would only be able to get a slightly larger flat with a bigger mortgage, William and Lucy should also sell up, then both couples could pool their funds and buy a much bigger house in a nicer area. It was obvious to William that Joe had been thinking about this, checking the prices and doing the sums. And that Marie agreed with the plan, or, when it had been broached, had at least not burst into tears and collapsed, which was, effectively, agreement.

William saw this was no time for tact and diplomacy. Joe had to be told, now, that his plan was off. There was no room for compromise or manoeuvre. He told Joe that he and Lucy liked the area they lived in and wanted to stay there. He added, ruthlessly, that he was not sure that it was a good idea for two – three, counting the baby – generations to live together. Hearing this Joe had looked at his son-in-law in an unfriendly way and remarked that, if that was how William felt, then there was no more to be said about it.

The Silent Duck was empty except for a couple of old geezers, at a table with their pints. Mo rushed in, dressed in a well-cut suit and a very white shirt. 'Sorry, mate,' he said. 'Accident on the M2 on the way back from the accountants.'

'Got you some orange,' William told him, pushing one of the glasses in front of Mo, who sat down. Mo took a swig. 'Thanks,' he said. 'I need it.'

'So how's it going?'

Mo looked at him ruefully, 'That's it,' he said. 'Going's the word.'

'Ah,' said William. 'Going where?'

'Morocco,' Mo said. 'All of us. The whole family.'

'All of you?'

'Yep,' said Mo. 'Me and my wife and the kids, Jemal, Faisal and his wife and kids, my sisters, their husbands and kids, my dad, my uncle, probably – all of us.'

William's heart sank. 'That's a bit of an upheaval. The kids are at school – isn't your niece just starting medical school? – what brought it on?'

'Well, there's been constant harassment of Muslims, you'll know that. There's going to be a war with Iraq – what do you think that'll do to us?

Raics, arrests, imprisonments. The President of the US is pulling Petherbridge's strings. When she insists Britain is a nest of terrorists and spies Petherbridge will go along. Life won't be worth living. What's he getting out of it, Petherbridge? He must have been paid. Now he's giving more power to the Specials. We know what that means. Remember Bob Harris?'

William was shaken by the certainty and ferocity of Mo's diatribe and couldn't work out where Bob Harris came in. Bob and his mates had hung about the school bullying smaller boys and taking their money, phones and watches. They carried knives. William had been one of their victims until he got big and well-connected enough. It was known, but never proved, that Harris and his gang were responsible for the suicide of a boy.

'I thought he went into youth detention,' William said.

'May have done,' Mo said, 'but he's Auxiliary Police now. That's who the Auxilaries are recruiting thugs. They got my cousin Hamed two months ago. He's sixteen. We didn't know where he was until he turned up two weeks later, crying. It's happening all the time. And these Auxilaries follow the girls about and try to get them in corners and pull their headscarves off – it's like they're fair game.'

William felt a twinge of guilt. He remembered the night when, coming home from work in the early hours of the morning he'd witnessed the heavy-handed stop-and-search on Shepherd's Bush Green. Should he have done anything? What could he have done? He'd thought the guy was probably holding drugs anyway.

Mo continued. 'Just before Christmas the cops kicked in Faisal J's door – remember him? The kid who never did his homework and then got ten GCSEs?'

'Oh – yes,' William remembered.

'He's got his own computer repair firm now. So they kick in his door in Ealing, terrify his pregnant wife, the kids wake up, everyone's screaming and crying – they run right round the house flinging open doors and throwing everything on the floor. Then, without a word, they leave.'

William, trying to find some justification for this, asked, 'What did they want?'

'They said he'd been facilitating terrorist groups. He's got business contacts with Saudi and Iran. They must have been bugging his emails. Anyway, they took his computer and three bin bags of papers. Luckily, FJ had most of it backed up at work or his business would have gone down the drain. He's not involved in anything – when would he find the time? He hardly goes near the mosque. You can see what I'm telling you, William. Faisal J yesterday, me tomorrow – what am I supposed to think? My dad's been here forty years; I was born here; my kids were born here

– but there's nothing for us now, with all this. It'll only get worse. We're afraid of how much worse. We're not the only ones leaving.'

'Jesus,' said William, shocked.

'Whoever,' said Mo. 'My uncle's even helping people out with money if they want to go back to Morocco even though they can't afford it.'

'Do you want to go?'

'Not really. The women are crying, the kids are slamming doors – but what choice have I got?'

'I suppose you're selling everything up?'

'That's the point. We're keeping a house here, just in case things change. But everything else has already gone – that's why I was at the account-ant's. So, basically, your flat has already been sold. I'm sorry, I wouldn't have done it, but—'

'You've got to put your family first,' William told him. 'How long have we got?'

'A couple of weeks. The new owner understands the situation. He won't put any pressure on you.'

'We'll go at the end of the week,' William said.

'Thanks, William. Sorry I couldn't tell you earlier. It was complicated.'

'Oh, well,' said William. 'It's back to the in-laws.'

Mo, who lived with his wife, his three children, his Moroccan mother-in-law and a young cousin, looked at him flatly. William suspected he saw the Western family's habit of living apart, in small self-contained units, as both a luxury and an evasion of duty. William had married for love, Mo for a combination of reasons, love not being top of the list. He had been unlucky. His wife annoyed him and she, in turn, thought too often of the young Moroccan she might have married. In contrast William's parents were in Spain, his twice-divorced doctor brother was in Canada and he seldom saw his sister, a busy lawyer. William and Lucy lived alone, or had done.

'You going to live in the new house?' William enquired. The family had been building a house in Morocco, brick by brick, tile by tile, over all the years of Mo's boyhood. He'd seen it once, on holiday, two storeys high and still roofless standing under a blue sky on a piece of land over-looking the sea.

'In a lot of ways, we'll be better off,' Mo said.

'That's right,' agreed William, but he knew Mo didn't mean it.

'I'm really sorry you're going,' said William, remembering the joints they'd smoked behind the council flat garages, or in Noddy Watkins' house while his mother was at work, the stupid teenage parties, the stupid dangerous exploits.

The two men embraced awkwardly, banging each other on the back.

'Keep in touch,' Mo said.

Right,' said William. But he thought they probably would not. He went back to the little room where he and Lucy had been happy and looked gloomily at the umbrella plant, Charlie, which had grown a foot during the autumn it had spent out on the patio and, now glossy and repotted, stood by the window. Even Charlie would not be so happy in future, he thought, shoved back on the bedroom floor again. Now he'd have to tell Lucy. He didn't know what she'd say. They couldn't go trudging round the letting agencies, looking at awful flats. If Lucy said she wanted to she could go alone. William was prepared to do only one thing – confront his in-laws and ask them, firmly, to leave.

Lucy came in blithely with some shopping, announced the menu for the evening and suggested renting a DVD. When she observed William's downcast face, asked him what the matter was and heard they would have to give up the flat, she crashed – it had been a long, hard day – and she burst into tears. After a cup of tea she declared, 'We'll have to go back to the flat. It's too expensive to rent round here. At least we can save more money.'

William shook his head. 'Lucy,' he said, an appeal to reason, a call to action.

There was a long pause. 'I'll ask Dad and Mum to go tomorrow.'

'It's the only way,' William agreed, concealing his delight.

'Eat here – eat out?' Lucy asked.

'Out,' he said.

As they sat down at the Venezia, they ordered and stared at each other, thinking of the ordeal to come. Then there was a loud, reverberating bang, which shook the windows. The floor under their feet trembled. This, in a city, means only one thing.

There was a dead silence in the restaurant. The waiter, who had reached their table with the starters, put the plates down gently on the table and then put a hand on it, to steady himself. 'Scusi,' he said. They waited for a second detonation, which did not come. Another waiter got up off the floor, looking embarrassed, and brushed himself down.

'A bomb,' said Lucy. She got out her mobile phone saying, 'I'd better ring the hospital.' The sister in charge of her ward had heard nothing about the bomb, but as they were speaking her internal phone rang. Lucy waited

Then she said, 'All right, then.' She said to William, 'They're calling in the off-duty staff.'

'I'll come with you,' said William.

They never got to the hospital. First, they smelt smoke and burning rubber. Then, round the cordoned off TV Centre was a disco-night of flashing lights from the emergency services. White-suited, masked figures stood by white vehicles. From the street they could see, under the arc lamps, the shattered window of the foyer and, just inside, an old van, surrounded by twenty men and women, some in police uniform, some in civilian clothes and some in white protective suits. Inside the reception centre of the building paramedics under emergency lighting were bending over bodies inside. As they watched, a woman with blood streaming down her face came staggering out between two green-over-alled men. Firemen were trying to prise open a lift door. There was a smell of fire. As they stood outside the cordon, taking in the scene, a man wandered past them, dazed, his white T-shirt streaked with black.

A young policeman came up to them. 'You can't stay here,' he said. 'You might be at risk.' William, already feeling sick, noted that the policeman was afraid, and trying not to show it.

'I'm a nurse,' said Lucy. 'You'd better let me through.'

The policeman did not protest as she took off her coat, handed it to William, kissed him on the cheek and ducked under the cordon. William watched his wife walk steadily through the flashing lights, the uniformed police, the firemen, and the men in white protective clothing towards the building. He stood with the smell of smoke in his nostrils looking at the lights, through which particles of dust from the explosion were still drifting. His instinct was to go on standing there, as if by being there he could prevent a second explosion, the one which might kill his wife. He waited, seeing paramedics carrying a figure on a stretcher towards an ambulance, a policeman supporting a woman with one leg dragging uselessly behind her, towards the same vehicle. He fixed his eyes on the van but could not see Lucy.

The same young policeman came up to him, 'You'll have to leave. We have to keep the scene clear,' he said.

And William went back to the flat to tell Joe. As soon as he got there he wished he'd gone anywhere but there. The TV was on, showing the devastation at the TV Centre and in the middle of the room Joe Sutcliffe was holding his wife, who was writhing and sobbing in his arms. Joe looked over his wife's head. 'Where's Lucy?'

'She stayed to help,' he told his father-in-law.

43 Basing Street, London E1. January 15th, 2016. 8 30 a.m.

'I can't, Millie. I can't,' Julia Baskerville was saying to her crying seven-year-old. 'Nothing will happen to me. I promise.' She spoke over the ringing of her unattended phone, which, like the scene between mother and daughter had been going for an hour. 'Honestly, Millie. I'm going to be all right. There's nothing to worry about.'

In response, Millie wrenched herself from her mother's arms, marched across the room in her MonsterMoo pyjamas and turned on the TV, which Julia had turned off an hour earlier. It had been her fault that, upstairs checking her handbag and briefcase, she had not detected Millie getting up and going downstairs to turn on the TV. Millie, in search of cartoons, had found the news. Now, for a second time, the scenes of carnage at the TV Centre, the flashing lights of the emergency vehicles, the woman reeling from the doors with blood streaming down her head, the paramedics easing a boy on to a stretcher, were playing in Basing Street, as they were all over the country. Millie, old enough to understand that her mother led her life in a place which might be targeted by bombers, did not want her to leave for the House of Commons. She did not want to go to school. She wanted them to stay at home, together, or, she suggested, buy tickets and go to join Daddy in America.

Julia had tried to reassure her daughter but could not, truthfully, pretend that if there were to be other bombings, the House of Commons was not a likely target. She could not deny that they might both be safer in Houston.

'I have to go, Millie. It's my job. I can't run away,' she said, as a spokesman for the Home Office rallied the nation in familiar phrases, condemning senseless violence, stating that there was a relentless hunt for the perpetrators, urging the traditional British virtues of courage and determination in the face of tragedy, and saying that all our hearts were with the dead and injured and their families. Julia switched the set off. 'You *can* run away. You *can*,' Millie said.

Julia had told her daughter often enough how to behave when approached by someone she mistrusted: 'Scream and run away.' Now Millie cried out, 'Run away, Mummy! Or you might die!'

Julia's mother, who had just arrived to take Millie to school, arrived at this moment and said unhelpfully, 'Well, Millie, I can see why you're worried.' She then told a stream of anecdotes about her great-uncle Bernie's Mickey Mouse gas mask and hiding under tables during air raids and Millie, perhaps persuaded by the fact that great-uncle Bernie was still alive and perhaps more by Julia's agreeing to stay at home doing constituency work that day, got dressed, bolted down a bowl of cereal and set out for school. Julia, in fact, had felt she might be more useful in the constituency. She knew many of the neglected phone calls involved her Muslim constituents, who had been lifted in the middle of the night. With her daughter's cries still ringing in her ears, she rang her Chairman, Zulfeikar Zulani.

Seven

Downing Street, London SW1 January 15th, 2016. 9 a.m.

There were now ten men and women round the long table, each with one, some with two, advisors and bag-carriers behind them, and security men at the door and windows. Police Commissioner Sir John Smythe had been present at the same table the evening before, two hours after the TV Centre bombing. He now reported to the meeting that a witness had seen a white van containing two men in ski masks driving into the TV Centre. A child, now in hospital with cuts and bruises, had been inside the TV Centre and seen the men in masks jumping out and running past her before the bomb went off. A householder had discovered two ski masks in a dustbin a quarter of a mile from the TV Centre. These were being typed for DNA and would be compared with samples on the extensive police database, which now contained DNA samples from a quarter of the population. Questioning of almost 200 people now in custody had produced no serious intelligence.

The rest of the reports were even less informative. Geoff Costello, ginger-headed and weaselly Head of Counter-intelligence, ran through his list of possibles, matching known aims and methods to known terrorist groups. It became plain he had no suspects. The report was more lecture than information. At that point Petherbridge, whose manner was less abrasive than it had been the previous night, cut him short. 'Geoff, I think you're telling us you don't know who did it.'

'It's a matter of time now, Prime Minister. If these men claim responsibility we'll get closer to them. If the interrogations produce some hard information we'll get them. We, together with the other agencies, are putting informants under pressure.'

'There are already complaints that the men in custody are being questioned about matters unrelated to the bombings,' said Petherbridge.

'I don't see how these critics can have any information at all about the questioning,' Costello told him.

'I don't propose to let this meeting be sidetracked by civil liberties issues, whatever they may be, said the Prime Minister. He called on Dame Maria Sutton to report and she did. However, most of the men and women present understood that there was more than one agenda for the meeting. There was the official agenda – the business of reports and action proposals concerning the bombing – and the unwritten one, the problem of what

the Prime Minister was going to announce at his ten o'clock press conference and to the House of Commons at three. People were panicking.
People were grieving for Douglas Wellington, the animal man, who had
died in the explosion. The child in hospital still had his hand, but perhaps
not for much longer.

The invaluable Dame Maria came to his rescue. 'We have a fairly firm
lead concerning a small extremist group in Ealing, pledged to what might
roughly be called anarchist principles – hitting non-specific targets to
cause fear and alarm. Sheikh Ibrahim of the Muslim Council is ready to
pronounce against them.'

'Thank you, Dame Maria. Brief me on that after the meeting, if you
will,' said Petherbridge.

Geoff Costello looked at Dame Maria with mingled respect and
caution. He was certain he had told Dame Maria about the Ealing group
six months earlier. As Co-ordinator of Intelligence she had to be informed
of everything by all intelligence agencies. Since his briefing the group
consisting of eight or nine young Muslim men had done nothing but
meet and talk. Costello believed they would never act. Should they ever
show signs of doing so, Costello, who knew the two group leaders were
lovers, would be able to fracture the group instantly. It could be that
Petherbridge didn't believe the group to be responsible either but needed
to do so. He'd need more than that, though, when the US President got
the Senate to ratify the attack on Iraq, which she surely would, after the
beheading of the two American oil executives kidnapped in November.
And the rolling of their heads into a police station in Baghdad. For him
another war meant public order problems, more extremist splinter groups
and further attacks. As for Petherbridge, he would be trying to get the
press, Parliament and the public, probably in that order, to agree to stand
beside our old allies in their hour of need, as they had stood by us so
long ago. So long ago that people had forgotten; it was something in
black and white on TV.

Sir John Smythe heard Dame Maria's statement and glanced quickly
at Costello, whose face was expressionless. If there was something
about the Ealing group Costello ought to have known, and had not,
his expression, however carefully guarded, would reveal this to Sir
John's experienced eye. But the lack of reaction told him that Costello
already had the information. He, too, admired Dame Maria for her
ready intervention. They had to give Petherbridge something positive
to announce.

Smythe suppressed a sigh and looked at the others round the table. At
least that bit of the business was over. Now everyone would report. In
his estimation the chances of anything worth hearing were small. It was
almost always true that the bigger the meeting the less useful it would

be. He needed to get back to work. There were 200 suspects in custody undergoing questioning.

In the Prime Minister's own office his personal aide Gerry Gordon-Garnett poured himself a cup of coffee and sat down in an easy chair. 'You've got to lighten up.'

'My point, Gerry,' Alan Petherbridge said 'is that I don't lighten up. I'm not Carl Chatterton, who looks like the headmaster of a successful City College and I'm not Amir Siddiqi, who looks like a building society manager. It's being a straightforward upper-class Englishman that got me elected. With the help of Madam President, who also finds my manner and behaviour convincing. Lighten up? The Met Commissioner had two policemen on duty outside the TV Centre, when it's an obvious target. There was nothing to stop the van from being driven straight in, because there were no precautions against it. We're floundering and the public will spot it. Where am I now? Press at ten a.m., visit to the victims in hospital at noon, European Commissioner to lunch. I'll ring the White House before the House at three. Get hold of Jones, would you, Gerry. I need him to brief me on these threatening noises coming out of Europe and decide on a response.'

Gerry Gordon-Garnett set off for the Private Secretary's office and, as he took the stairs, thought his boss was like a robot; he never stopped. Never stopped, never flagged or failed, never forgot. But if he had to drag a reluctant country into war, how could he cope? Maybe he was the kind of man who broke because he would not bend. Strange that when a man became PM, sometimes his strengths turned out to be weaknesses.

Manderton, Oakdene Avenue, Bromley, Kent. January 21st, 2016. 9.00 a.m.

I shall tomorrow put it to the Senate and the country that the American government and the American people must act, promptly and with resolution, against the terrorist government of Iraq to ensure the security of the USA, to regain American property, and to maintain peace and stability in the Middle East

US President
November 30th, 2015

Any attack on the elected government of Iraq will be taken with the utmost seriousness by the nations of the Arab League.
Ahmed Al Saud, President of the New Arab League.
December 3rd, 2015

While deploring the illegal seizure of Iraqi oilfields by the government of Iraq we would regard with grave alarm the prospect of an attack on the government of Iraq by the USA and its allies. We would regard with displeasure any nation of the EU associating itself with such an attack.
Lajos Zilhaly, President of the European Union.
January 20th, 2016

Joshua Crane stood in his now-empty house in Bromley thinking, yet again, that he ought to drain the pool, which gleamed blue outside the big plate glass windows of the living room. He'd have to organize it himself. There was no chance of Beth returning to London, not after the TV Centre bombing.

It had been six weeks since the vast car, heavily laden with clothing, battery lamps, a camping cooker, tins and packets of food and gallons of bottled water, had pulled out of the drive. Beth was going to her parents in a seven-bedroom house but Beth was taking no chances. If a power station blew up or poison was introduced into the local water supply, she and her family would be safe. Beth brought their boys back from school to take part in the move. It was a firm principle with her that a woman needed a man with her to help and, if she could not have a man, the boys would do. 'You can't expect me to do all this alone,' she had told Joshua.

During the constrained family Christmas in Yorkshire, Beth had raised the question of returning to London when the boys' holidays ended and Joshua had agreed this was a good idea. However, he'd been unable to resist pointing out that he had told his wife when she left that there was no big crisis, adding that many who had left were now creeping back, looking shamefaced and often blaming the anxieties of others – wives, children, elderly parents – for their departure.

He'd been irritable. He disliked staying with his in-laws. And he had noticed the regular presence in the house of a tall local widower, an early-retired Oxford lecturer, described by his mother-in-law as 'an old friend of the family' and noted, too, that the man seemed to be putting a lot of effort into getting along with his sons. It hadn't taken the man long to start moving in on the situation, he reflected. And there wasn't much effort to stop him, either. Over Christmas he'd poo-poohed Beth's retreat but, with the TV Centre bombing, it now looked as if she might have been right to run.

If they went to war again in Iraq, there'd be further bombings. The US Senate was sitting and would vote, within days, on the issue of the war. While Iran was, reports suggested, halfway to developing a nuclear bomb. Joshua decided he could not ask Beth to return while everything was so uncertain – and unless he asked, she would not come.

There was still an abandoned Mickey Mouse beanbag in a corner of the room. His elder boy, Marcus, had always resisted any attempt to throw away the beanbag he'd had since he was five. He must have hauled it downstairs before the move. It must have been jettisoned to make room for another three gallons of water.

And then there was the Sale of Lands Bill. Petherbridge was already beginning to muster support for railroading the bill through its third and final reading a month from now. He could no longer count on the Labour leader's support – Carl Chatterton was faced with too much opposition within his own ranks to commit himself. If Chatterton baled out on the bill Petherbridge would need every Conservative vote he could muster from his own ranks; he would need to put pressure on the constituencies of the known dissidents in his own party, Joshua being one of the foremost. His local Party Chairman, Barrington Chambers, had rung him three times in two days, asking for a meeting. Joshua suspected Barrington had already been got at by Head Office. He had engagements up and down the country, a diary crammed with meetings and no desire at all for a get-together with Barrington, at which Barrington would be forced to tell him that if he wouldn't vote with his party on the sale of airbases, deselection was on the agenda. And to top it all there was the call he hadn't screened – Saskia's.

Joshua had spent a lot of time with Douglas Clare in Battersea since his wife had left and he had split with Saskia. Against his better judgement, he had called Saskia twice since Christmas, to find messages on her machine saying that she was filming. Perhaps she was. Saskia normally left messages on her answering machine saying she was unavailable for interesting reasons when the reason might be that she felt she looked unattractive. She had a second phone she would answer to special people, Joshua included. That one had the vision off. When she didn't answer on that phone either he felt a mixture of regret and relief.

When, at eight that morning, he had heard Saskia's pleading voice, 'Joshua – Josh – help me, please,' he answered. The hour alone rang alarm bells. Saskia was not an early riser unless she was actually filming. Her voice was high-pitched and rapid.

'What's the matter?' he asked her.

'These bastards – bastards – are all leaving. And there's no room for me. No room at the chateau, Cape Cod, the place in Scotland, the house in Ibiza. They're all running and they won't take me with them. Where can I go, Josh?'

Joshua reflected. One of the exciting aspects of Saskia's world – fashion, the fringes of the film business – was that she moved with a lot of people richer, more famous or more aristocratic than she was. But if they were leaving the UK because of the bombings and the possible attack on Iraq, it would be a case of *sauve qui peut* – those lucky enough to have somewhere to run to, would run there, but they might not be thinking of inviting beautiful, amusing Saskia Wilkins. They would be making arrangements for their own safety, for the nanny, the Leonardo drawing, the silver cutlery and the bank accounts, not Saskia. As if the house had caught fire, they would be concentrating on priorities.

Joshua had seen his wife go north with his children. He had heard story after story of the same kind – wives being sent off to places of safety, friends off in all directions, pictures taken off the walls and moved elsewhere, jewellery banked. And here was Saskia, with her 'Where can I go, Josh?' What could he say? Telling her not to worry probably would not help. He did it anyway and she replied by shouting, 'You don't care!'

'What are you afraid of?'

'Getting bloody bombed, you fool!' she shouted. 'Look at the TV Centre. They're saying we're going to attack Iraq and the Arabs are saying they're going to bomb us back. They might have nuclear weapons! Justin Soames has taken Cordelia to Turin, the Eastmans are in Long Island, Harriet Schwemmer's in Austria, Brang's in Goa, the Fainlights are in the Loire, Fanny and Bick have gone to Sydney. There's no room for me on the boat, in the plane, in the house – how do you think I feel? Like shit, that's what.'

'I think they're panicking, Saskia,' Joshua said.

'Can't we go away?' she pleaded. 'We could go to Barbados or somewhere. Please, Josh – please.'

'Saskia, I'm a Member of Parliament. In fact, I'm trying to stop a bill to hand over British bases to the US. This would tell the Yanks we won't go to war about Iraq again—'

'You think you're going to *win*? You must be crazy. Fred Carter's gone, with Consuela. They're in Brazil. And he's in the Cabinet,' Saskia told him.

'Shadow Cabinet,' Joshua corrected. 'Family illness, I heard.'

'Family bollocks!' declared Saskia. She had a point, thought Joshua.

'Can't you get some kind of a fact-finding mission?'

'No, Saskia. No.'

'Your wife's not in London,' Saskia accused. 'Well, she's not, is she? She's safe, isn't she? And your children – away at school, out of danger. Well, what about me? What about me, Josh?' She began to cry. Joshua knew that Saskia cried, as children do, to get her own way or from rage. But nevertheless he hated hearing it. He hated his own voice, too, as he said, 'What do you expect me to do? I can't get away, Saskia. I really can't. And I haven't got a bloody chateau or a flat in New York – I haven't got a beach hut in Whitstable, Saskia, and you know it.'

'You know people. What about that man, Lord Gott. He could help.'

'No, Saskia. No.'

'You're a bastard, Josh. You don't care about anybody but yourself. I suppose when they drop a nuclear bomb on London you'll be tucked away underground eating caviar. I hate you, Josh. I hate you. I never want to speak to you again.'

After that, Joshua sat for a long time with his head in his hands. Saskia was resourceful. If she really wanted to get away, she would, probably. But the conversation had worried and depressed him. His wife was in Yorkshire and where would his girlfriend be when he needed her? he thought self-pityingly. On the Barrier Reef, in the Windward Islands – somewhere else.

Haver House, Great Finton, Berkshire. January 25th, 2016. 10.00 a.m.

A heavy mist clouded the great windows of Lord Haver's long drawing room, partly obscuring the lawn and the lake beyond, and wreathing the bare branches of the trees behind the lake.

The small group in the green, cream and gold room barely did justice to the splendour of the setting: the Corot above the marble and gilt wall table, the expanse of intricately woven carpet. Edward Gott thought sourly there was too much gold and too many twiddles on the furniture. If half the stuff had been reproduction and found in a front room in Willesden it would have been considered tasteless. Here, it was authentic but it still looked overdone, a signal of wealth, not loved or liked, only displayed.

Graham Barnsbury, the Party Chairman, sat in a slightly rumpled suit opposite Haver. He looked older and tired. Beside Gott, Lady Jenner, who was spearheading the anti-Ministry of Defence Lands Sale Bill group in the Lords, sat in a tent-like purple dress.

Gott himself was exhausted. He had been rung at nine the previous evening by Haver, who had said, 'I so thoroughly support your campaign. I should be very happy to discuss tactics and funding with you as soon as possible.' He told Gott he was inclined to back the opposition to the bill and would appreciate discussing the matter with Gott and some others of his supporters. He would also appreciate it if, because of his health, they would come to him at Haver House.

It did not trouble Gott that Haver had made a donation of two million pounds to Petherbridge's election fund, because he knew Haver would support any side that would make him richer and more powerful. Haver had already been paid for his earlier support, securing a US defence contract, awarded two months after the election to the light engineering firm in which Haver had a 60 per cent interest. If he were now thinking the bill's defeat would be of advantage to him, then this time he would be prepared to put another million, or more, into sinking Petherbridge. Maybe, Gott speculated, Haver had been paid, but not enough. His support, if he gave it, would be invaluable to the campaign.

He had phoned several of his heavy-hitters. He had persuaded Barnsbury, a latecomer, and a serious acquisition to his campaign – perhaps in the light of his wife's illness he no longer cared for his career, or for Alan Petherbridge – and Lady Jenner, an eloquent member of the Lords

as well as a distinguished physicist, to cancel their appointments and join
him at Haver House. Graham Barnsbury was enthusiastic. Lady Jenner, a
Liberal and no friend to Lord Haver and his ilk nevertheless agreed to
come, for the sake of the campaign.

However, once at Haver House, Gott had begun to suspect something
was wrong. Neither Haver nor his wife had greeted them at the door.
Ushered straight into the drawing room, where Haver was sitting in his
wheelchair with a plaid rug over his legs, there had been no hospitable
offer of tea or coffee or, jovially, perhaps something stronger after the
journey. Gott had put the case for opposing the bill to Haver as force-
fully as he could, but throughout his explanations Haver had sat quite still
in his wheelchair, expressionless and staring hard at him with small, angry
blue eyes.

Lady Jenner, who headed the party in the House of Lords, just studied
Lord Haver's face as he said to Gott, 'Edward, I'm gratified that you –
that you've all – chosen to come here, that you think I can help. I'm
interested in what you have to say. My difficulty is that I believe in loyalty,
loyalty first and last. And however disturbing this state of affairs may be,
I cannot really find it in my heart to back this attempt to unseat a Prime
Minister. It would be demoralizing, to say the least, for the party at large.
The overall result would probably mean a Labour victory at the next election. And, of course, now, at this juncture, loyalty is paramount.'

A few days earlier, the US Senate, after vigorous debate and by a
perilously narrow majority, had agreed to back the invasion of Iraq. Critics
said the Senate had lost the vote and the oil companies and the arms and
aircraft manufacturers had won it. And now the pressure would be on
Petherbridge to put the British forces in beside the Americans, although
the country was 80 per cent against it. Haver's pieties about loyalty
and the rest were nonsense, Gott thought. Haver had reneged – he was
in the business of war and had probably been promised a slice of this one.
Meanwhile, he and two other busy people had cancelled their appointments to come here. Gott was furious.

Graham Barnsbury jumped in. 'I think Edward's made it very clear
that that is not the intention. This opposition to the bill is not a political
manoeuvre. There's no intention to unseat Alan Petherbridge.' Gott glanced
at Lady Jenner's inscrutable face and imagined she knew, as he did, that
if they won the vote Petherbridge would be much undermined and would,
perhaps, have to go.

'Whatever your intentions are, that is likely to be the effect,' Lord
Haver told Barnsbury. 'It will be divisive and dangerous. The implication
of this bill being overturned is that we're prepared to oppose our natural
allies, the US, and give way to terrorists.'

'Not at all,' Barnsbury protested. 'That is not the case and I do not believe it would be seen that way.' Gott glanced again at Lady Jenner and was fairly certain she knew, as he did, that Barnsbury was labouring in vain.

His eyes drifted to the windows and over to the bare, misty trees in the distance. He reflected that, surrounded by his own 600 acres, Lord Haver had less reason than most to worry about terrorists.

Haver said, 'I'd differ with you about that. But the important thing is that I myself feel this is a time to stand firm, with the US, whatever it takes, and to stand firm with the party which will achieve that.'

As Gott looked steadily into the small, inflamed eyes and wondered if he should relieve the struggling Barnsbury in some way, Lady Jenner heaved herself to her feet. 'Lord Haver, it's plain we came here under a misapprehension. I don't propose to take up any more of your time, or my own.'

'Thank you all, so much, for coming to me and putting the arguments,' Haver said. 'I do hope you won't go ahead with your plans.'

Gott was pleased Lady Jenner had made her abrupt move. He also rose. 'Harry,' he said, 'nothing you've said today squares with what you said to me last night. But I assume you have your reasons for changing your mind, although I would have been happier if you'd let me know earlier, and spared me the journey.'

'My understanding was that you were coming to lobby me,' Haver said.

'Well, I'll have to check the recording,' Gott said briskly. 'Good morning.' And he left the room.

He waited outside the house with Lady Jenner, in dank mist. He said, 'Frances – I apologize,' but she said only, 'Don't worry, Edward. Not your fault, I'm sure.' When Graham Barnsbury joined them he apologized again. Barnsbury had at last understood what had happened. 'No apologies needed,' he said briskly. 'Harry's always had a malicious streak, worse since his accident. Obviously, he's made another deal.'

There was more to be said, and it would be, but for the time being they parted by common consent to salvage what was left of their day.

Gott was furious for the first fifteen minutes of his drive back to London, even more aggravated because he suspected that the fields, the village and the woods he was passing all belonged to Lord Haver. By the time he was on the motorway he calmed down and began to assess what had happened. In all probability, after ringing him, Haver had called Petherbridge and Petherbridge had promised him something – defence contracts, post-war building contracts, oil, perhaps. Or even good, old-fashioned cash. There would be a war chest of dollars somewhere to cover a contingency such as this – a direct challenge to Petherbridge, and to the US government who had paid for his election. The banker in Gott wondered who had the keys to the chest. It would be offshore, that was certain.

Gott felt offended there'd been no effort to buy him off. Petherbridge had offered him Barnsbury's job and threatened him with Vigo's revelations about the Kirkham affair. He'd even threatened to expose Gott's private affairs. But there'd been no offer of hard cash, often the quickest way to a man's heart. Perhaps Petherbridge didn't dare to be so blatant. Perhaps he thought Gott would refuse and speak out. But if he wasn't on the payroll, he wondered who else was? How strong were the forces against him? He already had the sick feeling of a man who has made a mistake – causing busy people to come 150 miles for nothing. He started to worry. If he lost the campaign against the vote, he'd lose his influence, his position as the party treasurer, half his life. And he would be dragging a lot of others down with him. The rebels would be demoted, discredited and deselected as soon as Petherbridge could manage it. Was his judgement – was his luck – equal to the task?

He disguised his doubts later when he answered Joshua's phone call. 'Sugden's, private room, six thirty,' he said crisply.

Sugden's, Fox Square, London SW1. January 25th, 2016. 7.00 p.m.

William, supervising the new waitress carrying food upstairs to the Green Room, said over his shoulder to Jack Prentiss, who was, unusually, taking an active hand in the running of his restaurant, 'They want six bottles of Bollinger.'

Jack went to the wine waiter and gave the order. He and William then walked into the restaurant and scanned the busy room.

'All well, William?' Jack asked.

'We've got another ten dozen oysters on their way in a cab,' William reported.

Jack nodded, unsurprised. He knew the nation's legislators' unappeasable appetite for oysters at times of national crisis.

'I meant you, actually, William. You're looking tired,' he said.

'Terrific,' William answered. 'My mother-in-law's been in the psychiatric ward at St Mary's for ten days. Life is sweet.'

'Well, keep up the good work,' said Jack vaguely. 'Sorry to hear about your mother-in-law.' He turned to greet two guests who had just come in. William's buzzer went and he moved into the hall to find out from one of the two Miss Bonners – small Miss Bonner this time – what the message was from upstairs. He told a waiter to take up six bottles of Evian to the Green Room and added, 'Open a window. It must be getting warm in there.'

The 24 hours after the TV Centre bombing had been long and hard for William, though harder for Lucy, who was on duty at the hospital all night. That evening, after Joe had rung the doctor, Marie Sutcliffe had emerged from her comatose condition and instantly started crying out for Lucy, and shouting at William, 'You've killed her. You shouldn't be living here at all. Why couldn't you bring her home? Get Lucy! Bring me Lucy!'

As Joe ineffectually tried to calm and reassure his wife, William looked up the number and started to ring the GP again, which was when Marie, suddenly realizing what he was doing, wrenched the phone from his hand. William snatched it back. 'You silly woman,' he shouted. 'There's just been a bombing – people are hurt – some of them are probably dead. Your daughter's trying to help. Don't be so selfish.'

Although William had only said half, or even a quarter of what he was thinking and feeling, Marie was shocked at being spoken to in this way. She burst into tears. Joe looked at William angrily, then put his arm round his wife and led her to the couch. William, grimly, got through to the GP's office again and left a further, urgent message.

'Don't let them take me away. Don't let them take me away,' Marie implored Joe, through her tears. The phone rang and William's mother asked if he and Lucy were all right.

'Lucy's gone to the hospital,' he told her.

'Oh, right,' said Grace Frith.

Behind William, as he spoke, Marie's voice came, 'I'm all right. I don't need a doctor.' She began to wail. 'I'm all right. I'm all right. Please don't let them take me away.'

'What's going on?' Grace asked.

'Marie's upset,' William said. 'I've called a doctor.'

'Good,' said Grace.

'She's in a bad way,' William mumbled. Tears were rolling down Marie's face. Her mouth was slack. Her round face seemed to have lost all form, as if it had melted.

As soon as William put the phone down Joe said, 'Do you know – I don't think we need the doctor any more, William. Marie's out of the fugue state – that's the dangerous thing – why don't I ring back and cancel him. I'll ring Lucy and ask her—'

'For Christ's sake, Joe, are you mad?' William exclaimed. 'She's in the middle of an emergency. There are injured people everywhere!'

The habit of keeping his wife safe from grim reality was so ingrained in Joe that he began to shake his head at William, indicating that he should watch his words.

William cried desperately, 'Joe – I'm still worried about Lucy. You'd think she was safe enough as a nurse, in a hospital, but how do we know? There are nutters out there. Suppose they picked up one of the bombers with the other casualties. Suppose there's someone in that hospital with a bomb strapped to them. I want to go there and grab Lucy and bring her out, if you really want to know. This is a fucking crisis, Joe, and Marie needs an injection so don't go near the fucking phone or I won't answer for myself.'

When the phone rang again it was Jack Prentiss. 'William, I hate to ask you, but can you come in? There's no sign of Paul, his phone's not answering, and Jean-Pierre's just called to say he's not coming to work, the city's too dangerous. I've got Sally waiting at table and I'm sous-chefing myself.' But William refused. He was too anxious about Lucy. And he knew that if he left Joe would immediately ring and cancel the doctor's visit. Joe did ring Lucy and William did not try to stop him.

When she finally came to the phone what she said plainly disconcerted her father. He put the phone down, glanced at Marie, sobbing quietly on the sofa, at William sitting on a hard chair in the kitchen doorway as if to be as far from the scene as possible, and went back to sit with his wife.

There was complete silence for half an hour, broken only by the distant wail of emergency vehicles. Joe said, 'Lucy says, when the doctor comes, can you ring her? She'll get here, if she can.'

William, on his chair, found it an effort to stay awake. He'd been close to a bombing, he'd seen the injured and the dazed, his wife was at the hospital and he was stuck, impotently, in a silent flat with a madwoman and her husband who had become almost as mad as she was over the years. His mind had gone on strike.

An hour later, the doorbell rang and the doctor came in. William caught Lucy on a break and she said she had a police car lined up to bring her home. The doctor, a tired Sri Lankan, talked to Marie, who had spoken ramblingly of her childhood, her desire for the world to be a better place and her efforts to look after her husband and child as they should be looked after. 'The world is so lovely,' she had said. 'The world is like heaven. And my Joe and my Lucy are like angels.' The doctor was trying to get a history of Marie's mental illness from Joe when Lucy came in, still in uniform, with a bloodstain down the front of her apron. To William this indicated that Lucy meant business. Ordinarily she would rather have appeared naked than shown her mother a patient's blood on her clothes.

She took the doctor into the bedroom for a conversation. When they came out the doctor spoke to Marie, now hunched on the sofa like a punished child, 'Mrs Sutcliffe. I think it would help you to enter a hospital for assessment, and a little rest. Your daughter agrees.' And to William's astonishment Marie said meekly, 'If you and Lucy think it's best, doctor.'

Lucy went back to her own hospital, while William and Joe took the docile Marie to St Mary's with her bag.

The internal phone rang again at the reception desk and small Miss Bonner told the weary William, 'Coffee, a bottle of gin, and tonic water for the Green Room.'

There were nine people squashed in the Green Room, some sitting round a table in the middle, others in easy chairs. Tired lace curtains hung at the window and, beside them but not drawn, tired green and red brocade curtains. There were lamps with cream parchment shades burning in corners of the room. A dim light filtered in from Fox Square. Joshua, leaning on the table, was reminded of having to help his mother clear out her Uncle Charlie's house in the faded West End mews house he had lived in. Not for the first time he pondered about how comfortable the powerful of Britain appeared to be in surroundings redolent of the past – old houses, old colleges like those at Oxford and Cambridge, shabby old furniture, anything somehow linking them with the past. Beside him sat his friend, Douglas Clare, and beside Douglas at the table were two other dissident Conservative MPs members of the awkward squad, the Usual Suspects – old Jacob Whittington and the younger, fatter Emma Pym who had the air, as someone had said, of a magistrate about to order you to be transported for twenty years to Van Diemen's land. The other leaders of Gott's cadre of dissidents, Jenny Appleby and Victor Treadwell, were away holding meetings. Lord Gott, Graham Barnsbury and Lady Jenner were also there. The seven politicians were, effectively, the hosts.

The guests, and the reason for the meeting, were Rod Field, editor of the country's most-read broadsheet, and Amelia Strange, Head of BBC news. Gott, after his dark night of the soul on the road back from Berkshire, had decided not just to rally his troops at Sugden's, but to go public. It was a risky strategy. Amelia Strange was coldly brainy and Rod Field was, it was generally held, a nasty wicked man, exceeded only in nasty wickedness by his employer, the owner of the paper, Helmut Niemeyer. But, as Gott had said, with the Prime Minister under pressure from Washington to join in the invasion of Iraq, and the British public against it, now was the time to press home the opposition to the Ministry of Defence Lands Sale Bill, which would hand the airbases over to the US government.

Gott and Barnsbury sat at the head of the table. Lady Jenner and Amelia Strange were in easy chairs, facing the table. Gott stood up, banged a fork on his glass, and, when he had silence, immediately sat down again. 'I've no need to introduce most of you to Joshua Crane, a young – youngish – MP, a promising man with a big public profile and a reputation for honesty and straight speaking. Nor do I need to say very much about Jacob Whittington and Emma Pym, nor about Jenny Appleby and Victor Treadwell, who unfortunately can't be here tonight. They're MPs, they're honest, they're attractive, they have high public profiles and they're spearheading the opposition to the third reading of the Ministry of Defence Lands Sale Bill, scheduled, I've just heard, for February the eleventh. Unseemly haste – are we surprised? I can tell you we have promises of seventy votes in opposition and I think there may be more from those who don't want to declare themselves but will in the end vote against or at least abstain. There will be a public debate at Westminster Hall a week hence in the name of the coalition against the bill. We have, of course, the support of the Liberal Democrats. I, the distinguished Lady Jenner, the effective Graham Barnsbury and everyone else here, will answer any questions you have to put.'

'Edward,' said Amelia Strange, leaning forward in her chair, 'are you sure the third reading has been scheduled?'

'Quite sure,' said Gott.

Rod Field, who was sitting on a hard chair beside the window, looking as if he was going to get up and go away at any moment, said, 'The important question is what Carl Chatterton's going to do. You have the Lib Dems, you have your well-organized dissidents, Lord Gott, but unless the Labour Party votes with you, and there's no sign they will, all you might have done is stir up a revolt in your own party. Chaos for nothing. So what will Labour do?'

'I don't know any more than you do – or Carl Chatterton does,' Gott told him staunchly. 'I believe the pressure from the Labour voters in the country will make Chatterton oppose the bill.' Field raised his pointed eyebrows. 'Yes?' he said.

'The latest MORI poll says that seventy-five per cent of Labour supporters are against the sell-off,' Joshua said. 'It'll be published the day after tomorrow.'

'You don't need to tell me,' said Field.

'Then you'll see Chatterton has every reason to vote against the bill.'

'At worst he'll allow a free vote,' Amelia Strange said confidently. 'Actually, Edward, I wondered if, as the party treasurer, you have any comment to make about the increasingly loud rumours about the party funding for the last election.'

'I'll be making a statement about that closer to the time,' Gott said.

'What do you mean?' Field asked.

'What I say – I'll make a statement within weeks.'

'Come on,' demanded Field.

Amelia Strange's phone rang. She would not have been interrupted except in an emergency. Everyone in the room listened. 'My God,' she said. Then Field's phone rang, and Douglas Clare's. And then Gott's.

They all had the same news. A gang of unidentified, armed men had taken over the base at Hamscott Common. A US serviceman had been killed and another injured. The base was in darkness.

Amelia Strange and Rod Field left immediately. The caucus remained.

Gott broke the silence. 'Well – that's our story on radio and in the press fucked.'

He was only saying what everyone else in the room was thinking.

19 Claremont Road, Whitechapel, London E1. January 25th, 2016. 8 p.m.

Julia accepted another cup of tea from Mrs Suleima Zulani, who then retreated to the kitchen, where she was sitting with her sister. Julia and her local Party Chairman sat in easy chairs, part of a comfortable suite, in the Zulanis' immaculate living room. At the back of the room, visible to Julia from her chair, young Aziz sat at the table, looking at a page of the textbook in front of him, and following the conversation while pretending not to. Intermittently he shot an unfriendly glance at Julia. Opposite him at the table his sister, a science student, was working at her books.

Six men and a woman, all Muslims, had been taken during the massive sweep following the TV Centre bombing. And Julia had only discovered the whereabouts of one of the three young detainees arrested at Christmas. Nine of her constituents were missing and she, their elected representative, could not find them. The police, under the new provisions of the Civil Contingency Act, had no obligation to give her or their families any information. She had a civil rights lawyer involved, and a second lawyer who specialized in European law. But all civil liberties organizations were working at full stretch now and lawyers for the disappeared were being blocked, obviously as a result of orders from high up in the chain of command.

'I and several others have asked for a personal meeting with the Home Secretary. He'll see us on the first of February,' she reported. 'A lot of questions have been put down—'

Zulfeikar's face told her that he had little hope of a good outcome from the meeting, or the Parliamentary questions. 'These actions are legal,' he told her. 'The only questions will be about whether the powers are being used rightly. And while that goes on these men will be in custody, with the US authorities using pressure to get them extradited to the US. It is the law that is wrong. The law of the land. The law I have obeyed all my life. There is not even any evidence that this bombing was carried out by Muslims. Those who did it have not been found. What can we do, Mrs Baskerville? These young men who see their friends and their brothers pulled off the street in police round-ups will not stay quiet for ever.'

'I understand, Mr Zulani. You know I do. I will keep on working. And I hope we can overturn this bill about selling the bases to the Americans.

That would send a signal to everybody that we aren't passive about US policy.'

'I agree,' said Zulfeikar, 'but what are we going to do about what's happening on our streets?'

'Keep on trying,' Julia said. It was all she could say but in her heart she knew both she and Zulfeikar Zulani were likely to be turned out by a local party unable to bear the slow, shaky and often ineffective operation of the system any longer. The appeals not heard, the peaceful demonstrations ignored, the admonishments from Europe overlooked and mocked.

'One law is bigger than ours now,' said Mr Zulani. 'American law. That is what we all must obey.'

'What are people thinking?'

'Some of us want to go home. Some are going. Some want separate communities – schools, hospital, everything.'

'Ghettoes,' Julia said.

'A name means nothing.'

'And illegal action?' she prompted.

'Of course,' said Zulfeikar. Then his phone rang. His son answered it. There was a long conversation to which Zulfeikar listened. His wife opened the kitchen door and she and her sister came into the room and stood in the doorway, the beginnings of alarm on their faces. Aziz was talking in a torrent, Zulfeikar himself had risen and was putting out his hand for the phone, which his son would not relinquish.

Finally he shouted something angry and at that point the young man slammed the phone back in its cradle, stood up and began to talk aggressively at his father. His aunt let out a soft cry, his mother put her hand to her mouth. Zulfeikar's daughter remained perfectly still, watching. Julia, believing there might be some serious family issue involved, stood up to leave. Zulfeikar did not try to prevent her.

He said coldly, 'You should know. A group of men has invaded the Hamscott Common base. They have taken the soldiers at the base prisoner.'

'Who are they? Do they want something – what is it?' she asked.

'That is not clear,' said Zulfeikar. Julia thought, judging by young Aziz's reaction, more was clear than her Party Chairman was ready to tell her.

Leaving the house she said to Zulfeikar, 'This is very bad news. If there are Muslims involved it won't help us here.'

He replied, 'Julia – I don't know what will help us.'

16 Hamscott Crescent, Hamscott Common, Kent. January 25th, 2016. 8 p.m.

When the phone rang in the Allens' house at Hamscott Common, Rob Allen was watching floodlit football from Prague while his wife, flowered cotton pooling round her feet, pushed material through her whizzing sewing machine. 'Answer it, Lilian,' said Rob. His wife, concentrating on a seam, muttered, 'Rosie?' Rosie, who had protested in the pub a few months before, was at the dining room table, painting the corner of her slightly misshapen thumbnail a lighter colour, to disguise the flaw and replied, 'Can't somebody else?' But no one moved and the phone in the hall went on ringing so Rosie got up and walked slowly from the room, waving her hand about to dry her nail varnish.

'Hello,' she said without enthusiasm, knowing that it would not be her boyfriend, Kevin.

'Rosie – it's Uncle Don,' came an urgent voice. 'Get your father, will you? It's important.'

'He's watching the football, Uncle Don,' she told him.

'Never mind the football. This can't wait,' he said.

Rosie went back into the living room and said to her father, 'Uncle Don. He says it can't wait.'

Her father groaned and rose reluctantly from the chair. The match went on. Lilian Allen's sewing machine continued to whirr and Rosie uncapped the nail varnish again; both women heard Rob's voice rising. Lilian pulled the fabric from the sewing machine and turned it off. Rosie put the cap back on the bottle of nail varnish. By the time they reached the hall Rob had put the phone down.

'Some nutters have taken over the base,' he told them. 'Apparently they've taken the troops there hostage. They're armed.'

Lilian, who had paled, said, 'They have nuclear weapons there.'

'Don's piling the whole family in the car and going to his brother's in Dorset,' her father reported.

'He's what?' said Rosie. Uncle Don was not her uncle, just an old friend of her parents, whom she had known all her life. Don never did anything on impulse. It could take him a month to decide on a family holiday in exactly the same place they'd visited for the past three years.

Her mother was less taken aback. 'It's because of the nuclear weapons,' she said clearly, then put her back to the wall and slid down, slowly, to the carpet.

This, and the sound of police cars suddenly screaming past the house, made Rosie understand, suddenly, that something very frightening was taking place. Her father went quickly to his wife and pulled her to her feet. 'Come and sit down, love. Rosie, put the kettle on and make your mum a cup of tea.'

Standing in the kitchen, Rosie waited for the kettle to boil. She heard the sound of a helicopter overhead. A beam raked the garden, as if looking for something on the lawn, or, perhaps, behind the garden shed. What was going on at the base – the base she had secretly detested since Kim had died?

If a nuclear weapon went off at the base, would they live? Probably not. And what about Kevin? And why, for God's sake, was she standing here, making tea? Leaving the kettle to itself she ran upstairs quietly and got her mobile phone. Back in the kitchen she pressed Kevin's number.

'Tea!' her father called as she listened to the phone ringing. Rosie put some tea bags in the cups and waited for Kevin to answer.

When he did, he looked anxious. He tried to sound normal. 'It's probably nothing – probably all over by now. All I know is what's on the radio and they don't seem to know much either. If they did they'd probably be stopped from telling. The story is, a gang of about twenty men took over the base a couple of hours ago. Some of them may be ex-army. They've killed a Yank and wounded another one. They put them down by the gates and opened up for them to get taken away. How the fuck could they do that – that place is guarded up to the back teeth. And guess what – my mum's hysterical. She wants me to pick her up and take her to London. She's already packed.'

'Are you going?' asked Rosie.

'Not without you, Rosie. What do you take me for? Anyway, I'm literally at a standstill here – oh, shit. Just a minute Rosie – roadblock.' He had a shouted conversation through his car window, then said hurriedly, 'Rosie – there's soldiers here checking everybody's ID. I'll ring you back.'

'Where's that tea?' called Rosie's father.

She put the mugs on a tray and went into the sitting room, looking only at the TV. There were views taken from a helicopter, showing the darkened base encircled by soldiers and military vehicles. Inside the ring there were floodlit ambulances and police vehicles. Figures reminding Rosie of her cousin's old Star Wars figures stood about in white protective suits and helmets. Then the picture changed and there were three men in the studio discussing the implications of the base seizure.

'The ring road's got a roadblock. Soldiers are looking at all the drivers' ID,' Rosie reported.

'I wouldn't have thought anybody outside the base was worth worrying about,' said Rob Allen. 'They sent a note out on the dead Yank. They're a group who doesn't want the bases handed over to Americans. It was signed by a gang called the Jihad, and some British blokes, with their old regiment's name. The Prime Minister's calling them terrorists trying to hold the government to ransom. They might send the Army in.'

'That's obvious,' said Rosie's mother, and ignoring her tea left the room. They heard her going upstairs. From the bottom of the staircase Rosie called out, 'What are you doing, Mum?'

'Shutting the curtains, in case the windows get broken,' called Lilian.

'I think I'll get the cat in for the night,' Rob said. Rosie sat still on the couch, watching the flickering TV and holding her mobile phone. In the distance she heard the howl of emergency vehicles; from the garden she heard her father calling the cat, over the sound of circling helicopters.

Eight

The War Rooms, The Mall, London SW1. January 25th, 2016. 9.30 p.m.

The Emergency Council met in the extensive underground bunkers stretching from Admiralty Arch, under the Mall, to Buckingham Palace. The installation contained bedrooms, computer rooms, dining rooms, a radio station – even an operating theatre in case of need. Twenty men and women sat round the polished table, waiting for the Prime Minister.

John Stafford leaned forward and in a low voice asked Field Marshall Roger Burns, 'Orders?'

Burns said to his trusty lieutenant, 'General, in fact no change. Two regiments ready to deploy. No orders.'

General Stafford frowned.

Burns dropped his voice even lower and said, 'Sorry about Carter and Reid, John.' Bob Carter and Splash Reid had served under the young Lieutenant Stafford long ago, at the start of his career, in the Falklands War. Afterwards, Stafford had said that Carter had saved his life; Carter had countered by saying that Stafford saved his. A soldier's joke. Fifteen years later, with Lieutenant Stafford now a colonel, Carter and Reid, their time up, had left and taken themselves off to a security firm specializing in sending hand-picked military advisers – or, in old-fashioned language, mercenaries – to anyone, anywhere, who wanted them and was prepared to pay. Now they'd signed the note sent out from Hamscott Common on the body of a US sergeant. Burns muttered, 'Why'd they get mixed up in something like this?'

'Money, probably,' said Stafford. 'They're terrorists now. It's official.'

'I have word they've broken open the silo containing the nuclear weapons,' Burns said steadily, in a low voice.

Stafford breathed out, hard, then put his hand to his brow and did not realize he had done so. 'Satellite surveillance?' he asked. Burns nodded. 'The question's still, how did they get through the perimeter?'

'From the back, where the perimeter fences run hard up against the woods. Apparently it's been a hot topic for years – the proximity of the rear of the base to Hamscott Common. But they had motion sensors in the ground, closed-circuit camera surveillance, a patrol. They can't work out how they disabled the patrol. And not one motion sensor was disturbed, setting off all the bells and whistles—'

'Swung through the trees,' Stafford said glumly. 'Dropped down on the patrol then swung back up again.'

Burns looked at him sharply. 'Your guys?'

Stafford lowered his voice further, 'The first ones over rig a rope to bring the others across. I saw Reid do it in Armagh, before he parted company with the army.' Burns' gaze went to Ian Noakes, the Minister of Defence, sitting opposite with two of his staff behind him. Noakes' bespectacled eyes met his, then moved away 'Reid looked like a giant ape,' Stafford reported.

'I spoke to the Chief of General Staff before this meeting,' said Burns. 'He wasn't a happy man. He'd had a word with our friend Noakes earlier. All Noakes said was, "It's up to the PM; wait for the results of the meeting."'

'I think we're all beginning to see where we're going with this one,' Stafford said.

'Sky high, if we don't do something.'

They were now two hours into an episode involving twenty fighter planes and an as-yet-unspecified number of nuclear warheads designed to be carried and dropped by those planes. They still had no plan of action.

The Chief of General Staff, Sir Hugo Lake, had seen the PM immediately after the taking of the base and urged him to use the emergency plan formulated to cover such a contingency. It was crude enough. Special forces would be put into the area by land or air, or both, while the perimeter of the battleground was secured by regular troops. It was a strategy that might fail for any number of reasons but it had the merit of speed. The plan had been designed to take the occupying force by surprise.

However, the PM had refused to authorize a counter-attack, calling it overhasty and risky. He and the Defence Minister had, he told Lake, decided that the strategy stood little chance of success and could endanger the lives of the civilian and military hostages. Lake had argued; Petherbridge had been immovable. Now, it seemed, the invaders had accessed the nuclear warheads. Whether the occupiers were capable of arming them, mounting them in planes and then flying the planes was uncertain. What was certain was that, if they could arm and fly the weapons, nowhere within a 3,000 mile radius from Hamscott was safe from nuclear attack.

Twenty men and women waited for Alan Petherbridge, who was now five minutes late. Which, Burns thought, meant that he was probably on the phone to the White House or the Pentagon, or on his knees, praying.

The silence in the room was profound, as if everyone there was waiting for the *boom* and tremble of a massive above-ground explosion. The missile ore a three kiloton, a seventh of the size of the bomb which struck

Hiroshima, was capable of killing 30,000 people immediately and 50,000 later. Dropped in a city, there would be more immediate casualties at ground zero, tens of thousands, perhaps. Wherever the missile detonated, though, there would be the residual casualties caused by fallout. In a city area it would be easier to muster radiation suits and decontamination units and to provide hospital space, but harder to control a fleeing population blocking the roads. In a country area there would be fewer casualties but it would take longer to bring in help. Judith Woodward, the Health Minister, quantified what she could quantify, organized her own statement, her own arguments, and then, being human, thought of the loss of her career when the provisional plans for such an event went wrong. And then of her impending divorce and her son and daughter, who were living temporarily with her parents in St Albans. After that, like everyone else in the room, she wondered – where was the Prime Minister?

Adam Simcox, from the British Nuclear Agency, mechanically answered a question from a senior civil servant at the Department of Defence. In return he asked if the military were being held back from making an assault on the base and was told they were not. He looked at Field Marshal Burns and at Sir Hugo Lake, and wondered if he was hearing the truth.

Sir John Smythe, the Met Commissioner, gave a note to the officer behind him. His mood was grim. It had been Petherbridge who had tried to persuade the then Prime Minister, Muldoon, not to use the Army to clear the base when it had been harmlessly occupied by demonstrators in June. On that occasion the PM had allowed, or yielded to pressure to allow, the landing by US marines and that had resulted in the death of Kim Durham, in front of her seven-year-old son. On that occasion, Petherbridge, then Home Secretary, had shown restraint and sanity. But now, only six months later, Petherbridge was Prime Minister and the base occupied by more aggressive forces. Smythe already knew that the military plan in place to deal with events like this had been rejected. For himself, he had never been a big supporter of the plan, which, he thought, basically involved no more than sending in the Special Forces fast and hoping they'd pull it off. A gamble, but not taking it meant that the terrorists had now opened the nuclear silo. It looked as if it might have been wiser to send in the commandos. It was too late now. But Petherbridge had refused to use the British Army, just as his predecessor had apparently refused to involve the British police force. So what, or who, were they waiting for? There could not have been a man or woman in the room who did not suspect they were waiting for US Special Forces, US Marines, the 101st Airborne.

So, Smythe thought, they were all sitting here now waiting for the

Seventh Cavalry or for the kamikaze buggers on the base to let off a nuclear device and blow themselves, the cops, the army, the firemen the paramedics and half the county of Kent into kingdom come.

The PM's PPS, was sitting there like a stuffed dummy at the head of the table, standing in for his master and disguising his discomfort about the delay almost well enough, when, thank God, Sir Hugo Lake, six foot four and with a chest solid with medals, got to his feet and asked him, 'Mr Gordon-Garnett – might I ask how long the PM is to be delayed? If the delay is to be a long one, perhaps we could continue with our work while we wait?'

'The PM apologizes. He has been conferring with the President and the US military. I have word now that he is on his way.'

There was a stir round the table at this confirmation of the majority's suspicions. A few eyes shifted towards Field Marshall Burns, to see how he was reacting. But Burns was gazing straight ahead of him, as if his face had turned to stone. Lake, too, was imperturbable. 'Thank you, Mr Gordon-Garnett,' he said, and sat down. He turned to John Stafford. 'That's it – we're out of the picture.'

'Looks like it,' Stafford said. He leaned towards Burns and said into his ear, 'Let me go down to Hamscott.' Burns had expected the request, sooner or later, and now it was plain the tactics were being directed from Washington, he nodded. 'Don't do anything stupid,' he advised. He thought, as Stafford got to his feet, that he himself had probably just done something stupid. Authorizing a general under his command to go down to Hamscott as an amateur hostage negotiator was unwise, to put it mildly. Exactly how unwise it would be deemed, at a possible inquiry, would depend on results. If Stafford succeeded there would be cheers all round. If he failed, and Burns was not optimistic about his chances of success, they would both end up standing on the parade ground having their buttons torn off and their swords snapped across the RSM's knee.

As Stafford left the room he exchanged a glance with Sir Hugo Lake, who looked at him impassively. He just had time to get out of the room before the Prime Minister entered the room.

16 Hamscott Crescent, Hamscott Common, Kent. January 25th, 2016. 10 p.m.

The Allens and Kevin Staithe sat in the unnatural silence of an evening when no cars but emergency vehicles passed the house and no one in the neighbourhood was venturing out. There had been more phone calls that evening – from friends, neighbours and relatives – than there would normally have been for a week. Constantly repeating to callers from outside the area that they could not leave Hamscott Common, that they were, effectively trapped, had been sobering.

Kevin had arrived earlier on foot, the roads blocked. Rosie's Uncle Don had called and revealed that his escape to Dorset had been foiled on the ring road outside Hamscott Common. The Army had blocked off the road and were allowing no vehicles through.

'We're sitting ducks,' Kevin had said.

Rob Allen said, 'No call to be defeatist,' and his wife said nothing.

All they could do was sit and watch TV pictures of the area less than a mile from where they sat – the cordon of troops, the inner ring of men and women in protective clothing, the emergency vehicles, the massed police and the darkened outline of the base. They'd heard the newscasts against the sound of the helicopters circling their house and their passivity had made them more afraid. Rob turned off the TV saying, 'They should have put the SAS in first thing.'

Kevin said, 'All right if we go up in Rosie's room to listen to music, Mrs Allen?'

Rosie's father might once have demurred. He was old-fashioned. He knew what 'listening to music' in a young woman's bedroom was likely to mean and he did not want to condone it under his own roof. But this time he just said, 'All right, Kevin.' But Rosie and Kevin never reached the bedroom because Rob switched the TV on again immediately and a reporter, swathed in a coat and scarf, was saying, 'We understand that General John Stafford has entered the base.'

'First good news I've heard since this began,' said Rob Allen.

Hamscott Common, Kent. January 25th, 2016. 10 p.m.

On the way down to Hamscott Common at an average ninety miles an hour John Stafford had checked the reports on his screen. The earliest had been conveyed by the base communications centre before it was taken over by the invaders. At 7 p.m. on January 25th 2016 a force of between twenty and twenty-five men had entered Hamscott base from two sides, from the rear – the north-east side – and from the east. The small force had, it was assumed, disabled the electric fencing and the patrolling guards. As the communication was made, shots were heard. By 7.15 p.m. the invaders were apparently in charge of the base. Then all communication ended. Later reports from outside the base recorded that all lights had been turned off. A wounded servicemen who had been thrown outside the base at 7.20 p.m., when the first emergency vehicles arrived, had said that approximately fifty service personnel, seven civilian staff, fifteen women, wives of the serving men, and seven children were being held captive. The second man thrown out, a US Army sergeant, was dead. The message in his pocket stating that the base at Hamscott had been taken over by the Jihad group as a protest against the base being handed over to the US, the indiscriminate and unjustified bombing of Syria and the threats to overthrow the legally elected government of Iraq. It was signed by three men: Robert Carter, Raymond Reid and Ibrahim Al Maktoum. Carter and Reid were former soldiers from the Queen's Light Infantry, now operatives for Draycott Security, and Ibrahim Al Maktoum was a British doctor.

Just before they got to the Hamscott ring road checkpoint Stafford's phone rang. Burns told him, in a low voice, 'Do you know where Petherbridge was while we were all sitting waiting for him? Grosvenor Square. Talking to the Yanks before he talked with us.'

'Democracy in action,' Stafford said. 'Any decisions yet?'

'They've already been made without us. This meeting is just window dressing. I'm in the gents. I'd better get back inside. For God's sake be careful, John.'

As they started up after going through the checkpoint Stafford's driver turned round in his seat. 'Think you can talk them out of it, General?'

'What makes you think I'm here for that? Better keep your ideas to yourself, Corporal,' Stafford said. If I can't talk them out, no one can, he thought.

Now he stood under bright lights, surrounded by emergency vehicles, uniformed soldiers and RAF officers, ghostly men and women in white protective suits and helmets, Army and RAF officers in uniform, policemen and men and women in civilian clothing. There were some two hundred people inside the inner ring of Army soldiers and the outer ring of police. Stafford thought it looked like a village, gathered to celebrate some strange religious ceremony.

All attention was on the perimeter of the base, where two protective wire fences, fifty metres apart, defended the base. Beyond the wire was darkness. The parade ground and administration block were empty and silent. The dark outlines of fighter-bombers were visible on the runways. Use of radios and mobile phones was being kept to a minimum. Stafford knew there must be a thousand men and women and 150 vehicles behind him on the site, while inside the base there were approximately two hundred captive men, women and children. And yet it was very quiet. Suddenly he heard a nightingale begin to sing.

He said to Geoff Cunningham, his RAF opposite number, 'I know Reid and Carter.'

Cunningham said, 'They're not talking so far.' The Deputy Chief Constable of Kent could be heard, much amplified, calling 'Reid – Carter – Al Maktoum – please talk to us. Pick up the phone. You are surrounded. Pick up the phone and talk to us.'

'See what I mean,' said Cunningham. 'The advice is, they'll break down and start talking.' His face was pinched under a heavily braided cap. He had been on the site, in temperatures only just above freezing, for three hours now.

'Reid and Carter are tough. The men they're with may be tougher. They've got everything they need,' Stafford said.

'We're thinking of cutting off the water,' said George Medlicott, coming up. Medlicott was the Superintendent of Kent Police. The three men, by the nature of their training, were opposed in their views. Medlicott, a policeman, saw the situation on the base as a siege involving hostages. His training and ethic was to negotiate. As a soldier, John Stafford saw the base as territory taken over by hostile forces and needing to be regained. While the RAF man, Cunningham, who had been furious when the bill to hand over the bases into exclusively US control was proposed, stood between the two, leaning more towards Stafford's military thinking, but fearful of the consequences of an attack. He said, 'Even a leak from a two-kiloton rocket bomb stored there could kill thousands. These people are fanatics. They don't care who dies, including themselves.'

'I can't speak for the others, but Carter and Reid aren't fanatics and they're far from suicidal,' Stafford said. 'No clue about what they want?'

Medlicott answered. 'Nothing beyond the note saying they're protesting.

Reid and Carter – the men who served with you – would you think them likely to take up a cause?'

'The only cause they know is their own. Before that it was them and the regiment. They're in it for the money,' Stafford said. 'What are your orders?'

'Wait for the results of the discussions in London. Then there'll be a decision.'

Stafford turned his back to the centre of the ring of light, where, among the vehicles, there was a black car containing men he thought were American observers. He muttered to Medlicott, 'I expect those buggers can hear us. Turn away so they can't see your lips moving – they've probably got lip-reading equipment.' Medlicott nodded. Stafford said, 'I'm the only person Carter and Reid will talk to. I want to try to go in.'

Medlicott shook his head and muttered, 'Fuck it, no. I can't authorize that.'

'It's the only way we're going to find out what they want. And you know we're waiting for orders from Washington. How long have we got till the Marines come in, ready or not – ten minutes, half an hour? We'll get orders to secure the perimeter, but because the timing'll be kept secret we'll be caught on the hop. We'll be falling over each other outside while the Marines inside the base shoot up the town. Casualties on both sides and a good chance some of the bad guys will escape in the confusion. And that's the best scenario. Because if they've got the skills to arm a plane with a nuclear warhead, then we're really fucked.'

'You haven't got orders,' Cunningham objected.

'Keep your voice down,' warned Stafford, glancing towards the men standing around the black car. 'And turn your back because the Yanks are waiting for someone to go in and, when they do, they'll have orders to shoot.'

Cunningham said, 'I'm the officer in charge of the base and I can't sanction you entering.'

'There's no official chain of command,' Stafford pointed out. 'I believe I have my superior officers' support, which they can't openly give me. Cunningham, we know the Yanks are in charge. But they're not here – yet. And we are. This is our last chance to settle this ourselves. If not, we all know what's going to happen next.'

Cunningham did not like Stafford very much but knew he was right. A base the Americans saw as their own had been taken over by a handful of terrorists. One American soldier had been killed, one wounded and a number captured, along with American women and children. A humiliation, made worse by the fact that it was going round the world on TV, to the sound of cheers in the cafés of the Lebanon, celebratory rifle fire in Iraq and in the federally administered tribal areas of Pakistan and Afghanistan and, probably, the laughter of Palestinian children. The US would have to react, go in and win.

Stafford said to Medlicott and Cunningham, 'You can't sanction my entering the base, but you can't order me not to, because this is a mess and no one's in overall command. No bad thing, really.' To cover them in case of a future inquiry he said rapidly, 'You have both advised me not to enter the base in order to make contact with Carter and Reid. I am ignoring that advice.' He added, 'I haven't got long. A little bird will have told the Yanks I'm here by now. For Christ's sake don't let anybody open fire.'

Neither man made any move to stop him as he walked over to one of the police cars and took the mike from the hand of the officer who held it. 'Switch on,' he said. A PC will not easily question the orders of a General he has just seen talking to the Chief Constable. Stafford took the mike and walked towards the gates of the base saying, his voice amplified all over the area, 'Carter – Reid. This is John Stafford. I know you can see me. I want to come in and talk to you. I'm unarmed. This isn't a trick. We need to talk.'

He was now standing alone with the great gates in front of him. Three men took off from the group of men and vehicles and began to run, fast, towards him. There was a dead silence in the brightly lit space behind Stafford and what seemed to him to be an even deeper silence inside the darkened area of the base. Walking towards the wire perimeter, now fifty metres from him, he called again, his voice echoing over the base and into the close-packed trees beyond, 'Carter – Reid – it's John Stafford. Let me in. I want to talk to you.'

The three men from the black car had pulled up sharp some three metres from him. 'General Stafford!' one called, 'you have no authority—'

Stafford drowned them out with his loudspeaker. 'Reid – Carter. Open the gates. I'm alone.' There was no point in telling Reid and Carter that they were surrounded, with no chance of escape. They were mercenaries, not martyrs, and wouldn't have gone in without a plan, however risky, to get out safely. Ahead of him, in the vast aircraft hangar 500 metres to his right, he thought he could see a dim light from under a hangar door. Behind him the American shouted, 'General Stafford. Be warned. Get back or we are going to arrest you.'

This angered Stafford, who shouted, 'Bob – Splash – the Marines are coming. Let me in. I want to talk.' He ran to the high wire gates and shook them, then saw inside, flat on the ground, a completely black figure crawling towards him from the direction of the hangar. Could the three men behind him see the crawling figure? Stafford wondered.

'General John Stafford. You are under arrest,' called the American.

'Turn around.' The figure reached the gate, raised itself and opened it just as the voice behind Stafford called, 'General Stafford. Turn around or I will open fire.' Stafford pushed the gate – it opened and he ran, zigzagging into the darkness toward the aircraft hangar. Behind him he heard the clang of the closing gates. He heard shots. One hit the concrete in front of him. Seconds later, the black-clad figure was overtaking him, running ahead. When he reached the hangar door it was already pulled back.

He pulled in his breath and advanced. He heard a volley of shots clanging on the metal of the closed hangar door. Inside the vast space of the large, cold hangar a group of fifty American servicemen and women were sitting on the floor with their hands on their heads, guarded by ten men in black carrying automatic weapons. About half this team seemed to Stafford to be European, the other half North African or Middle Eastern. Not that this told you much, he thought. But that was the background. His attention was focused on the middle of the hangar where Bob Carter sat on a chair, one leg of his trousers rolled up and bandaged. Beside him Splash Reid and three other, younger, taller men in black stood motionless and silent as Stafford approached. He asked Carter, a stocky man in his forties with a big round, entirely bald head, 'Wounded?' Carter told him, 'Bullet in the calf. The base nurse patched me up.'

'Still haven't lost your power over women.' Stafford said. 'So – what's this all about?' He nodded towards the captive US servicemen.

'Just a little patriotic demonstration,' Reid said. Stafford had respected Splash Reid as a soldier, but he had never trusted him as a man. Bob Carter, a Liverpudlian, was relatively straight, but Reid came from a family of minor South London criminals. His mail sometimes came from one of HM's prisons.

He said, 'Fed up with being pawns in the game. General. Fed up with being the fifty-first state. Handing over these bases, sir. Foreign troops on British soil.' The phrases came out too glibly for Stafford's liking.

'I'm Ibrahim Al Maktoum,' said the tallest and thinnest of the black-clad men. He was in his late twenties. He had a long, intelligent face.

'I don't understand, Dr Al Maktoum. You've taken this base, very successfully, I must admit. Quite a military feat. But what's your objective? You're surrounded. You'll get killed or caught. Are you planning to use a nuclear missile?'

He waited in some suspense for an answer. Al Maktoum told him, 'That is not our strategy, General Stafford.'

'I'm relieved,' said Stafford, not completely reassured by the cool reply, which made him wonder if there was another strategy which he did not understand.

'What the fuck is happening?' came a cry from one of the captive soldiers. 'What's going on?' Then there was a cry of pain.

'Who were they firing at outside?' Bob Carter asked.

'Me,' Stafford told him. 'It was the Yanks. First they tried to arrest me, then they tried to bring me down.'

'That's my point, sir,' Reid said. 'Fifty-first state.'

Stafford, standing in front of Reid, Carter and Al Maktoum and feeling like an ambassador at a tyrannical court, said, 'Write to your MP about that, Splash. I'm here to tell you it's pretty much certain that at some point, Marines will be landed inside the base. I don't know when but it could be soon. What you need to do is surrender now, or get out fast if you have an escape plan. Otherwise there'll be deaths and casualties. Where are the civilian women and children?'

'In the hospital block. We don't attack women and children. Unlike you,' said Al Maktoum. He added, 'General Stafford. You're a brave man but you're not needed here. I'm going to have to put you under guard.'

The door to the hangar burst open and a small, black-clad man came up. He spoke to Al Maktoum in Arabic and Al Maktoum called over to Carter, 'They're moving the emergency services back.'

'The assault's on,' Stafford said to Carter, but already there was movement in the area where the captive soldiers were being guarded. Stafford, horrified, saw men begin to strap black boxes to the American servicemen. 'Jesus Christ!' Stafford yelled at the seated Carter. 'What the fuck are you trying to do?' His phone rang. He ignored it.

A serviceman who stood up and started trying to fight, although his hands were bound, was struck with a rifle across the side of the head and collapsed in a heap. Five bombs were strapped to five servicemen as the sound of incoming helicopters became louder and louder.

Stafford shouted at Reid and Carter. 'We can still stop all this.'

Carter stood and hobbled fast for the back doors of the hangar, followed by Reid. Carter shouted, 'General Stafford – sir – it's each man for himself.' And he disappeared. As did all the men in the hangar, running through the great doors with their weapons held high. With the helicopters overhead Stafford shouted into his phone. 'Stop the attack! Five personnel have bombs strapped to them. Do you hear me – stop the attack!' But he thought it was probably too late. While some of the formerly captive soldiers ran to the door of the hangar, others remained, their eyes on the five men who sat, motionless, with the bombs strapped to them. A tall, dark soldier went up to one of the seated men, knelt beside him and began to try to release him.

Stafford went up to a tall red-headed soldier with a face so pale he looked bleached. He knelt down and looked at the bomb. 'Don't move,' he said. The soldier said through frozen lips. 'No? I feel like dancing.'

'I'm going to try to cut through the strapping.'

There were shouts and the sound of gunfire from outside the hangar. The doors opened and light flooded through the open doors. The side of the hangar was an ant heap of men struggling free and scurrying for the doors. Stafford began to cut, carefully, through the strapping of the bomb. To one side another terrified soldier was doing the same. The red-headed soldier rose, very carefully and stepped, slowly, away from the black box on the floor. Stafford, desperate, began to work to release another man.

'Better run, buddy,' said a voice from the floor. 'They could be remote-controlled.'

A voice from the doorway called, 'Status report on bombs.'

A voice called back. 'One man still to be freed. Bombs on the floor.'

Stafford laid the bomb carefully on the ground and got to his feet. Then he and the red-headed man ran towards the open door. Halfway there a blast of automatic weapon fire raked both Stafford and the redhead. They fell at exactly the same moment.

7 Adam Street, Shepherd's Bush, London W12. February 1st, 2016. 10.30 p.m.

Because neither of them had to work that night and Joe was visiting Marie in hospital, William and Lucy had spent the early part of the evening quietly cooking a meal together. William had braised chicken breasts in lemon, with just a dash of Tabasco while Lucy had prepared a salad and made her special dressing. Listening to a new CD by Ghost Town they ate their meal together in peace. A good evening for both of them and made better by the prospect of more to come. While Marie was in hospital Joe Sutcliffe had agreed that as soon as Marie, her condition stabilized with medication, was discharged, the Sutcliffes would return immediately to Basset. Joe had talked to Marie, more balanced now but still very afraid of London bombs. Marie had welcomed the move home. Joe had told William, 'We've been here nearly five months and I know it hasn't been easy. You've been a hero, Will, and I appreciate it.' He seemed a different man since his wife had been officially diagnosed as being in need of treatment, and had begun to receive it. Even Marie appeared to accept the need for a return to Yorkshire, using the coded language of the Sutcliffes – she said she had been worrying about the garden and the possibility of squatters moving in.

When the phone rang William answered it calmly, fearing no harm. But the caller was Joe, from the hospital, who said, abruptly, 'Marie's in a state. We're coming back.'

'What!' cried William. 'The thing is,' Joe said awkwardly, 'since this terrible business at Hamscott Common, Marie's been getting anxious again. She's convinced it will happen again at the base near us, at Thwaite. I didn't like to tell you.' The old Joe, protector of Marie, had resurfaced. 'She's panicking. She's gone downhill. She's nearly as bad as she was before.'

'Right,' William said dully. He felt sick, and knew his stomach was telling him something his head was unready to accept. 'You're talking about coming here? Has she seen a doctor yet?'

'The duty doctor hasn't come. She's desperate to come back to the flat.'

'Joe,' William said. But Joe had gone. William suddenly had a clear vision of himself sitting on his parents' terrace on a clear, blue morning. Lucy wasn't with him.

'What is it? Will — what is it?' Lucy cried.

William looked at her, hating her, for a moment, for being her own parents' daughter. Lucy stared at him.

'Joe and Marie are coming back here — to stay,' he said. 'It's something about the Hamscott Common Airbase,' and went over to the TV. In silence they stood looking at the screen.

CNN was showing the Prime Minister at 10 Downing Street. He sat at a desk, crisp and cool as ever. 'Each and every one of you can be sure that we will spare no efforts in hunting down the perpetrators of this atrocity. As we do this, you, too, can play your part. You can deprive these evil men of what they want, to alarm and disturb, by continuing with your normal lives. This is not the first challenge the people of Britain have faced in their long history and they have never yet failed in courage and determination. God bless you all.'

William spun round to face his wife. 'No! No! No!' cried William. 'No! It's impossible!'

'That was the Prime Minister, the Rt Hon. Alan Petherbridge,' said the presenter over the strains of the National Anthem. William threw a plate at the wall. It shattered. 'Fuck them!' shouted William. 'Fuck the fuckers! Why can't they leave us alone?'

Lucy was frightened. 'Oh, William — what are we going to do?'

The Garrick Club, Garrick Street, London W1. February 2nd, 2016. 7.30 p.m.

Graham Barnsbury and Lord Gott were together again at the Garrick Club – the buzz concerning the US election contributions had become so loud that Gott, though still unwilling to divulge his suspicions publicly, had, to give an impression of financial candour, put in place a system of handing over to the Chairman, each month, the breakdown of the party's monthly accounts. It was a chore for both of them but the party had acted, and that was the point.

Graham Barnsbury had never been keen on the Garrick. He found the atmosphere was too Bohemian. However, that evening Gott had to preside over a dinner at the club for a distinguished ninety-eight-year-old author, a former friend of Winston Churchill, who had served his country, undercover, with immense bravery in Greece and Yugoslavia during the Second World War. 'Sorry, Graham,' he said. 'I have to commemorate an aged hero regarded by many, including his own biographer, as a not-so-crypto fascist. But in these dark moments, I take comfort from the thought that a man has to eat somewhere every night.'

'True,' said Barnsbury, but Gott knew he must be thinking about his own home and his desire to be there with his dying wife.

When they first arrived at the Garrick it was to find that the club's surly porter had been supplanted by two large security men. The surly porter stood to one side, watching, while Lord Gott of Weathersted and Graham Barnsbury, the Chairman of the Conservative Party, were patted down by ex-policeman like a couple of miscreants pulled up by the Auxiliaries in the street. The battle at Hamscott Common airbase a week earlier had altered everything. Armed police surrounded all public buildings, the Houses of Parliament were ringed with tanks, as were all airports, docks and railway stations.

Gott gave their orders to the waiter. 'Any news about the ten missing terrorists?' he asked. Barnsbury shook his head. 'They escaped through a gap at the back.'

'Didn't the satellite pick it up and track them onwards?'

'They're saying there was low cloud,' Barnsbury reported flatly. 'Billions and billions spent, defeated by low cloud. Unbelievable. Well, I don't think I believe it. But why lie?'

'Habit,' said Gott. He handed over the folder containing the accounts. Barnsbury did not look at them.

'General Stafford's had his operation. It was successful, up to a point.' Barnsbury sipped from his brandy glass then put it down firmly on the table. 'I might as well tell you – it won't be a secret by tomorrow. Well, to the public, obviously, one hopes – but with the Internet and the Arabic media . . .' He paused and Gott waited, looking attentively at his colleague's worn face. 'I spoke to Ian Noakes this morning. He had me in. It seems there's a missile gone from Hamscott. A tactical nuclear weapon. One megaton, about ten per cent of the bomb they dropped on Hiroshima.'

'A nuclear missile!' Gott said. It was barely a question. 'How did they get it out, under all that scrutiny? Oh, I see, they took it out earlier, before the pressure was on. Then they constructed the siege to mask it.'

Barnsbury said without enthusiasm, 'Quick of you to work it out like that.'

'There were a couple of physicists among the Arabs they caught—'

Barnsbury nodded, 'They won't say anything. They're very tough.'

'They'll need to be,' said Gott grimly. There were rumours about the questioning of the Hamscott Common captives.

'Ibrahim Al Maktoum is dead,' Barnsbury mentioned. 'Wounded in the fighting, apparently. Died of his wounds.' His voice was neutral.

'Well,' Gott said briskly, 'no one's ever accused the British of being afraid of using torture. It's always been a question of who, when, why and how much. As with adultery,' he added. They had settled with each other that neither was going to drop to his knees crying, 'I can't stand it! What about my wife, my children?' Now he asked, 'Can they set it off?'

'Apparently it's a bomb designed to trigger when it's dropped from a plane, tough casing, unsophisticated firing mechanism. It'd take a bit of adapting, then a launcher, even then it might fail. On the other hand, armed, it could detonate by accident, on impact, in something like a road accident.' He added, 'If it's still in the country.'

'I suppose if they had the brains to get it out of Hamscott, they could get it out of the country,' said Gott. He looked at Barnsbury, and signalled to the waiter. Barnsbury said half-reluctantly, 'Well, just one more drink. It's a little strange, Gott. Ever since I heard all this it's been difficult to see things in the same light.'

Barnsbury had never been a thoughtful or imaginative man. That had been his usefulness. And Gott did not want to ask him what his thoughts were. He only said, 'Light of eternity shining over all of us now, I suppose.'

'The Yanks are furious. They've been wanting to clear a quarter of a mile of trees and scrub away from the back of the base for years but they've had the lawyers and the environmentalists and all the local groups against them. The thing's dragged on. You can imagine what they're saying now.' He paused, 'Edward – there's something else.' This use of his first name alerted Gott. 'They're putting pressure on you not to oppose the Lands Sale Bill any more. I'm supposed to persuade you.'

'Consider you've delivered the message,' said Gott.

'The powers that be weren't pleased I came with you to see Haver but they've convinced me to abandon my opposition to the group. I agreed – given my personal circumstances – and they seemed to think I could talk you round. I told them it wouldn't work.'

Gott sagged, momentarily. It was not surprising that in the present climate of fear of terrorism and the news about the missing nuclear weapon, Barnsbury had succumbed to Government pressure. His dying wife was plainly occupying most of his thoughts. He had no strength left for the battle.

Gott asked, 'Is Petherbridge afraid if we knock out this bill we'll go further and attack the whole basis of the ownership of the bases, perhaps start to kick out the Americans?'

'It's hard to know, if the news about this stolen missile gets out, what the public response will be. Petherbridge plans to say that this only stresses our need for US military and other assistance. But there'll be loud voices saying we should get them, and the weaponry, off our turf. There'll be panic and no one can guess which way the cat will jump. That's why he wants unity in the party.' He looked hard at Gott, who shook his head.

'Thought not,' said Barnsbury. He finished his drink and stood up. He nodded at his glass, 'Thank you, Edward.' He had more to say, Gott saw. He waited. Barnsbury said awkwardly, 'There's something else I've been requested to tell you. There's talk of a certain situation in your private life. If you don't back off, that situation will be private no longer.'

Gott knew this speech was costing Barnsbury a lot. 'Don't worry. The threat has already been made. I'll deal with it.' He put out his hand, Barnsbury shook it and walked away. Gott looked after him, thinking that the man had managed, in half an hour, to give him two ugly messages.

Gott stood in the lavatory and straightened his white tie. He looked at himself in the glass, noting the bags under his eyes; he ought to have shaved before he left the office. His beard was coming in grey these days. Now he had to do something he should have done thirty years ago and which had become more and more impossible as the years went by. He'd been a coward, but if Petherbridge was on the verge of smearing him publicly, he must act now. There were things, as the Collect had it, that he had done which he ought not to have done and other things he ought to have done, which he had not done. Perhaps it was the knowledge of a nuclear weapon in circulation that was making him brood, he thought. Or just the prospect facing him in Scotland.

A political journalist came in and said bonhomously, 'Hi, Edward. How are you? How's it all going?'

'Never better,' said Edward Gott. He straightened his shoulders and went off to hail the seventy-plus-year-old achievements in the Balkans of the almost-100-year-old veteran.

106 St George's Square, London SW1. February 3rd, 2016. 12.30 a.m.

Edward Gott, who had a directors' meeting at his bank next morning at nine, had walked home from the celebration of the Second World War warrior at the Garrick. He was trying to clear his head.

Barnsbury's story about the missing warhead had shaken him badly. He wanted to warn two of his sons, one who worked in the City and lived in Bow, the other living and working in the West End of London, to grab their families and leave the city quickly. His youngest son was safe enough in the USA, at MIT, his eldest farmed in Cumbria, Joe was on what seemed to be a permanent holiday in Thailand and Richard was in South Africa. Which left Robin and Jamie in London, possibly in danger. Except – who knew where the bomb was? If it was armed, on a plane, ready for take-off? And, if so, to where? You could run, but who could tell if where you ran to might not be more dangerous than where you'd come from?

If the news got out, there'd be a flight to the country, because people would think it was safer there. If the news got out, if the roads got jammed, even blocked off by the Army to prevent flight, his sons would be angry he hadn't told them sooner, when they and their families could have escaped.

He shivered inside his heavy coat and walked more briskly. He had never known a time when events had moved so fast, shaking, whirring, banging, spitting out unintended consequences, unpredictable as a rocket nailed crookedly to a fence on Guy Fawkes Night.

There was frost on the bushes surrounding the square when he reached home; the bare branches of the trees sparkled with it. He opened the heavy front door and went upstairs to his flat. He needed to think and knew, from experience, that he was on the brink of making the mistakes of a busy and energetic man – mistakes stemming from having too much to do and too little time to think.

He still had a campaign to run, a meeting at the bank tomorrow, his answering service would ring in ten minutes and Jeremy would have left a stack of notes and letters on his desk for him. And – his heart sank at the thought – he had to fly to Scotland and talk to his wife. As he threw his overcoat on the small concert piano only ever played by his daughter, the doorbell rang. He looked out of his window at the empty streets and the bare trees of the square opposite. Outside his door was a large black car and, under a street light and looking up at his window two faces he knew, one Tobias Kerr, his wife's nephew and second-in-command to the Prime Minister's Private Secretary, the other, Gerry Gordon-Garnett. Serious business then, in the early hours of the morning. They must have been driving around waiting for his lights to go on.

Once in the flat, Gordon-Garnett refused a drink and Kerr accepted one. The Kerrs had a weakness in that direction. Gott invited them to sit down and they took two chairs, one on either side of fireplace. Gott himself remained standing. 'Any news of the base invaders?' he asked, thinking that if they wanted something, as they surely did, they owed him some information in return. 'Strange bedfellows,' he said. 'Ex-servicemen and extremists. I suppose the security firm guys were paid.'

'Saudi money,' said Gordon-Garnett shortly. 'But that's not what we're here to talk about.'

Gott looked at the clock on his mantelpiece and said, 'I didn't think so.'

'I don't want to keep you up, Lord Gott,' Gordon-Garnett said. 'But Alan wants you to think about this opposition to the third reading of the MoD Lands Sale Bill. In the light of these disastrous events at Hamscott Common. I don't need to tell you that at a time of national emergency, with the hunt for terrorists going on, we ought to pull together, not divide the party.' He leaned forward earnestly, 'That's what the PM's thinking and he hopes very much you agree.'

'I already had that message from Graham Barnsbury,' Gott said. 'I'm thinking the matter over. I'm asking myself what is in the best interests of the country, as well as the party.'

'You think you're qualified to make that kind of decision?'

Gott went on the offensive. 'At least I don't owe my job to a foreign power.'

While Gott's nephew shot him a look of impatient dislike, Gordon-Garnett did not acknowledge the remark. He said, 'So you don't plan to withdraw your opposition to the bill?'

'I'm considering my position,' Gott told him.

'Alan will be very disappointed to hear that. Very disappointed.'

'I imagine he will be,' said Gott. 'But there's nothing else I can tell you.'

'He asked me to remind you that if you show yourself to be so thoroughly anti-American there's a strong possibility Clough Whitney Credit and Commerce may lose a lot of American clients. They constitute about twenty-five per cent of your cash-flow, I'm told.'

Gott nodded, knowing he had not thought far enough ahead.

Petherbridge, who had been able to command dollars for his election, heavily assisted by the State Department, would certainly be able to put pressure on American investors. On the other hand, he thought, as they say, money's serious – that's why they call it money. The US Government, the CIA, the British Government, whoever was in charge of the operation, could put pressure on the investors to move their accounts, but the investors would still act in what they saw as their own best interests. To succeed they might have to bribe them – how far would they be prepared to go to persuade the bank's clients to alter their banking arrangements? How much would they be prepared to give? Would the pay-off be enough? That might depend on what form it took. If he refused to comply, Gott knew he would be putting himself and his bank at risk. He could be losing his bank a quarter of its funds. But he was already facing the loss of the Treasurership of the party and exile from the corridors of power. He said, 'That would be a misfortune for the bank.'

'Edward,' said his nephew. 'The PM's asked me to appeal to you on grounds of loyalty. You cannot split the party now.'

'This wouldn't be happening if Petherbridge hadn't introduced the bill in the first place,' Gott said bluntly. 'I believe that it, and the threatened reinvasion of Iraq involving British forces, triggered this whole Hamscott Common affair. Now you ask for loyalty. And I can't answer you. I need to think.'

'If you did, and agreed to drop your opposition, Alan would be very grateful,' said Gordon-Garnett.

Gott knew Petherbridge would be grateful and show his gratitude in many ways. Whatever it was, it would be a lot – all the kingdoms of the earth, he thought, having had a churchgoing childhood. Then he pulled himself up short. He had had a long day. He said, 'I will think it over. Thank you for coming to see me. But I have an early meeting tomorrow, so I hope . . .' The two men got to their feet, apologized again for calling so late and bade him goodnight. But in the doorway, when Tobias Kerr was already halfway down the stairs, Gerry Gordon-Garnett turned to him and said, 'If you don't toe the line, Gott, you'll regret it. You'll be made very sorry indeed.' His expression was nakedly malevolent as he turned away and went downstairs after Tobias.

After they had gone, Gott sat down heavily asking himself what he was doing. What was he walking into? Why didn't he just cave in, acquiesce? He'd done it before, a hundred times. What public man, what man of business, hadn't?

What was he worrying about – his immortal soul? He didn't believe he had one. His integrity – what the hell was that? An answer came back to him, as clear as a bell, as obvious as looking through a pane of glass,

'I'm not standing out against Petherbridge because Petherbridge's plan is morally, strategically, politically wrong. I'm standing out against it because it won't work.'

He stood up and said aloud, 'Won't work.'

106 St George's Square, London SW1. February 3rd, 2016. 6.30 p.m.

The TV was on in Lord Gott's car as he was driven home.

'Fourteen terrorists out of a group of approximately thirty men who illegally invaded the Hamscott Common airbase were captured immediately. Seven of the men who illegally entered the base were killed.

'Five US soldiers were also killed and one was severely wounded. General John Stafford, who serves with the Army Chief of Staff and who entered the base, it is believed, as a negotiator, was also caught up in the action and is seriously wounded. He is undergoing medical treatment.

'There is still no answer to many questions. What was the motive of the men involved? What was the nature of the alliance between, as it seems, British and foreign Muslims and former members of the British Army? What was the intended role of General John Stafford? A number of terrorists, possibly as many as ten, escaped and are still at large. I have with me in the studio . . .'

'A lot of people talking balls,' Lord Gott said over the voice. 'Nothing new then, or nothing anyone's telling.'

'John Stafford's being operated on again tomorrow. They've found more bullet fragments close to his spine,' said Graham Barnsbury. 'They've already taken out his spleen.'

'Poor bugger,' said Gott. 'Anything about the CIA trying to kill him before he even got in?'

'No. But if it leaks they'll say he was mistaken for another terrorist, trying to get on to the base.'

'That's a career ended.'

'It probably has anyway. They say he may not walk again.'

The car drew up at Victoria Station. Barnsbury got out, saying, 'Thanks for the lift.' He walked away, a hunched figure in the rain soon lost in the crowd of hurrying commuters.

Barnsbury was taking his wife's terminal illness hard, thought Gott. He'd already told him he was thinking of resigning the chairmanship. Gott hadn't mentioned that Alan Petherbridge had already offered him the job, although he'd suggested to Petherbridge he would accept it. Not that he would. Not that Petherbridge would now give it to him, since he was still mustering opposition to the Ministry of Defence Lands Sale Bill.

They were outside Gott's house now. There was a figure in the gloom on the steps of the building.

'Thanks, Jeremy,' Gott said.

'Who's that on the steps?' Jeremy asked, peering.

'It's a man I called in. I've had your flat swept. I hope you don't mind,' said Gott as he left the car. Jeremy, just starting up to find a parking space said, 'Swept? For bugs?'

'That's right. I think he found something. He's looking pleased with himself.'

'Thanks, Mr Throckmorton,' said Edward Gott, in a discouraged tone.

'Sorry, guv,' said Throckmorton. 'You want my guess – it's British security.'

'That'd be mine, too,' said Gott.

Inside the flat, the security man, a wizened figure with two missing front teeth, held out on his palm ten little red dots. 'All over the place,' he reported. 'All your phones, obviously, in the TV, under your bed, in the shower, even inside that nice piano. And something special for the computer. Want them?' he asked, with the air of a dentist offering a patient the teeth he has just extracted. 'Keep them,' said Gott.

Jeremy appeared in the open doorway. 'Find anything upstairs?' he asked keenly.

'Even in your toilet,' said Throckmorton.

'No!'

''Fraid so,' he said. 'Do you want them?' and he again held out the red dots.

'Do you know, I don't think I do,' Jeremy said.

Money changed hands.

'Right-ho, guv,' said Throckmorton to Gott. 'We'll be back tomorrow to put your infrared beams in. They won't do this again.'

'The toilet, though,' said Jeremy, still shocked.

Gott said. 'I'd pretty much expected it. Here am I, spearheading this attempt to overthrow the bill to sell the British airbases to the US military. There's Petherbridge, knowing that if the bill's defeated it will weaken him here, and his paymasters at the White House will lose faith in him. They won't forgive – they'll do all they can to get him out and get somebody more effective in. Small wonder Petherbridge got his security minions to bug my house. Well, tomorrow they'll put in infrared rays across doors and windows and various other tricky bits and pieces. We'll be able to plot the Queen's assassination in here after that, and no one will know.' He was staring unthinkingly at the small grand piano, on which a vase of roses stood. Only one person ever played it – the person he supposed he loved best of all, if you could weigh these things. It'll be fun, Jeremy,' he said. 'The system will start screaming when a cat walks on a sill or a pigeon lands. It'll scream when the cleaning lady comes in, probably when we do. Come back here with your girlfriend and before you've kissed, the cops will appear. It all adds to the gaiety. Doesn't bother me.'

He sat down on the piano stool and stared at the grim-faced portrait of his grandfather above the fireplace. 'Petherbridge can sit in Downing Street watching me pee as much as he likes. You saw his stepfather – you went to his mistreated mother's grave. His wife's a nervous wreck. And he's a traitor. Do you know what my son Jamie's wife says – she's a child psychiatrist? "He picked sides and allied himself with the powerful man, his father, who was beating his mother, but he would have felt that as a betrayal, seen himself as the betrayer." Not that you need qualifications to guess that.'

But whatever he said, Gott thought of his piano and his daughter who played it and knew he hated Petherbridge as much as he despised him.

Clough Whitney Credit and Commerce, Leadenhall Street, EC1. February 5th, 2016. 11.30 p.m.

Edward Gott took off his black jacket, loosened his black tie and undid the top button of his starched shirt. He got coffee from the kitchenette attached to his office and sat down at the computer. The day had been a long one. The previous one had been even longer.

That was when Gott had flown to his house in Scotland – which was actually his wife's house – landing in the early evening in foggy weather. Perhaps it was the landing that had caused Gott's queasiness. Or, perhaps, the slight nausea was caused by the fact that he had come to tell his wife something he ought to have told her before they married. Not such a bad story, compared with those that other husbands have had to confess to their wives. Many years before, he had fled to the USA leaving a pregnant girlfriend in Britain. His family had helped the young woman, a student, and her daughter, when she was born. At that time Gott had been a student himself – had not even met his wife. He knew this was a common enough tale. The worst part of it was that he had never told his wife, during thirty years of marriage, that he had another child. Or perhaps the worst part was that he was only doing so now because the Prime Minister had threatened to leak the tale to the press.

The couple had dined alone and, after his wife had left him at the table, Gott had had a couple of brandies to steel himself. When he joined her she was sitting at her small desk in the corner of the drawing room, writing a letter. At his request, she joined him at the fire. 'I have something to tell you – something I should have told you long ago,' he began. She looked at him from the other side of the fireplace and said, 'This sounds grave, Edward.' Her face had no expression, but he had not expected her to react otherwise – this was a woman who had borne six sons, at home in her own bed, and never uttered a cry. And so he said, 'I'm afraid this may hurt you. Unfortunately I have made some enemies and they are trying to damage me. I didn't want you to read it in the papers.' And he had told her about his former girlfriend, a fellow student, his graceless disappearance and the birth of a daughter. 'Margot,' he had said, 'I am so sorry. I should have told you before we married. I was so afraid that I would lose you.' There were tears in his eyes when he finished speaking and Lady Margot's face had still not altered. After a silence she said, 'Yes, you should have told me, Edward. At some time during the years we've spent together.'

'I was ashamed,' he told her.

'So you should be.'

'What do you *think*?' he exclaimed, meaning, of course, that he wanted to know what she felt.

But Lady Margot seldom spoke of her feelings and, when she did, usually in connection with her children. She said only that she very much wished he had seen fit to tell her of this earlier. She wondered that he had so little confidence in her. Gott knew his wife to be a resolute woman, a worthy descendant of Fergus the Redhanded and Donald Skullcracker and whatever other member of her bloodstained family it was who had lit a fire under a cauldron and boiled an enemy alive. Nevertheless, he found this aristocratic restraint unnerving. He heard himself say, 'At least it's kept me straight over the years – knowing what I did, what I was capable of.'

He was immediately ashamed of this outburst. He did not actually see Lady Margot smile, but just had the impression she was, although her face had not moved. 'That's a blessing,' she said, and stood up. 'Well, Edward. You've given me a lot to think about. You'll be here for breakfast?'

And Gott said he would be, but thought it unlikely that this question meant that his wife would be ready for a discussion at breakfast the next day, or at any other time. He drank another brandy and went to bed, but not in the matrimonial bed.

And, as he had expected, Lady Margot did not refer to his revelation the previous evening. Instead, she referred to the kipper he was eating, the rebuilding of the north wall of the estate and a very nasty quarrel over a will in the family of one of their daughters-in-law.

It was only after taking off in the helicopter in even thicker fog – 'Clearer south of the Border' the pilot said – that, somewhere over Birmingham, it dawned on Lord Gott that his wife almost certainly knew the story of the woman and the child. He was not sure why he thought this. It might have been that, having been married to Lady Margot for thirty years, her reactions told him. She had not been deceitful enough to pretend to be shocked or surprised, or untruthful enough to say that she was. Equally, she had not let him off the hook by telling him she already knew about the woman and her child, because that would have made things easier for him, and she wanted to punish him as, he had to admit, he fully deserved.

Who had told her? One of his sons, who knew all about their half-sister and met her from time to time? On balance, he thought not. So who else would have told her? And suddenly he knew exactly who had told Lady Margot about his illegitimate child. It had been his mother. Perhaps even his father? He discarded the thought – no, it would have been his mother. And that meant, since Gott's mother had been dead for twenty years, his wife had known his sordid little secret for at least twenty years, perhaps longer. She had known it while she was bearing and rearing at least some, perhaps all, of their sons. Gott was startled. He thought of himself as a clever and competent man but it seemed he had not known what was going on under his nose. His wife and his mother had deceived him. Of course, his mother had thought it right to let his wife know. Of course, Lady Margot had been too well-mannered to bring it up. That would have been against her code. But she would – who would not – have wanted him to tell her the truth. And he had not.

Gott was sobered. And he was not proud of the fact that he also felt relieved. At least, he thought, if his wife had known the story for so long, she was not going to divorce him now. Sadder, wiser and considerably less anxious, Gott landed in London and began to go about his other business.

He had received a surprise invitation from the French Embassy so he rang a senior official at the Foreign Office, to be offered, not just an informative chat but a meeting with a bright young man from the European department.

At lunchtime he arrived in a Whitehall pub to find Wilkes, a weary-looking man in his thirties, sitting in front of a pint and a sandwich he had barely touched.

'Another?' Gott glanced at Wilkes' near-empty glass.

'If only,' Wilkes said sadly. 'I've got to keep a clear head. It'll be FO sandwiches and coffee into the small hours again, I imagine.' Gott barely knew Wilkes and saw in him that slightly camp Old Etonian manner, which, as a Scot and outside this exclusive club, he mistrusted.

'I hear you've got a new daughter,' Gott said. 'Congratulations.'

'Not that I see much of her' Wilkes said. 'My wife could do with me at night, too.'

'Get a nanny,' said Gott, unsympathetically.

'We had one, but she's gone back to Croatia. Scared,' said Wilkes.

'That makes you think,' Gott said. 'Well, not to waste your time – I'd appreciate your advice. Four days ago – short notice, I thought – an invitation comes to me from the French Ambassador to a small, informal dinner at the Embassy. Not a big, public affair, you see, and I don't know anyone at the Embassy – or not on that basis.'

Wilkes nodded.

'In short, I was surprised. I accepted on the principle that the secret of life is being there. Now I want to know why you think I might have been invited – is there anything I ought to know – is there anything I know that I shouldn't say?'

'Are you sure there isn't anything involving the bank?'

'I've tried to find that kind of connection. There isn't one,' said Gott. 'Now I'm going to sit down at a dinner table with a lot of Frenchmen so sharp they'll cut themselves and I don't know the agenda. There must be one.'

'They're pretty upset about this rapprochement with the US,' Wilkes said.

'Rapprochement. We've been up their arses since 1945. But what's that got to do with the price of fish?' said Gott, who, confronted by someone like Wilkes, could not resist coarsening his tone.

Wilkes did not flinch. He said, reluctantly, 'I don't suppose there's any harm in telling you. There's a lot of EU talk about imposing sanctions on Britain if we don't stop aiding and abetting the US. And they're particularly worried about a reinvasion of Iraq. The French are the chief instigators, because of their traditional feeling that they're entitled to mess about in Middle East politics but no one else is. Nevertheless, other countries are supportive. It would be hard to think of any who positively oppose the French stance.'

Gott had not expected this. 'Sanctions? They'll never go through with it.'

Wilkes said, 'Obviously, they've been worried for years about this closeness between Britain and the US. The proposed sale of the bases has exacerbated it. And their clever thinkers have been thinking ahead, imagining an ever-closer relationship with the US, economic as well as military. My guess is your invitation comes from the fact that you're about to begin an assault on the sale of the bases. If what I hear is true.'

He looked at Gott enquiringly. Gott didn't say anything.

'Exactly how far are you going with this?' Wilkes enquired.

The Foreign Office was trying to work out whether he was a thorn in the flesh or a serious problem. The FO believed first and foremost in stability. Not change, not improvement, whatever that might be, just stability. Put the whole of the FO in hell and they'd start a dialogue with Satan, aimed at achieving greater stability in the Underworld. Which was probably why they didn't trust or respect the creators of instability – politicians – and let it show, in their Etonian way.

'I'm planning to oppose the third reading and stop the sale of the bases,' Gott said, steadily. 'I think you know that.'

'Then the French and their allies in Europe will see you as an ally, of a sort. My enemy's enemies are my friends. I should watch your step. They may hope you'll win the vote and then go further, try to get Parliament to vote to take the bases back under British control. We're supposed to be contributing to the EU Defence Force.'

There was a silent question here but Gott did not take the bait. 'What will they want?'

'Information about your plans I should think. They won't press you. This will be to start a relationship with you which might prove helpful later. That's my guess. As I say, be careful.'

'I really can't believe in the prospect of EU sanctions,' Gott declared.

Wilkes said nothing, ignoring Gott's implied question.

'Thanks, anyway,' said Gott. 'It's been enlightening.' He stood up, 'You're busy – I'll let you go.'

Wilkes also stood. 'It would be pointless to say more – it's early days . . .'

'I understand,' said Gott.

About to leave, Wilkes said, 'Perhaps you could spare a moment tomorrow to let me know your impressions. I'm sure Sir Joe would appreciate it.'

'Will do,' said Gott, shaking hands. Then he sat down, stared into his pint and tried to assess the information Wilkes had given him, and not given him. *They couldn't be serious, the Euro finance ministers. They couldn't be going to put brakes on trade with Britain. Or could they?* He stood up, telling himself he was the man who didn't even know what his own mother had said to his wife about him, or when. Bearing that in mind, was he fit to make a judgement on this issue, or any other? Probably not, but he knew he must.

The evening at the French Embassy had been pleasant – and interesting. There had been only eight of them in a small dining room, well-appointed in early-nineteenth-century French style. The hosts were the Ambassador and his wife, the guests a distinguished French writer and his beautiful actress wife, a senior man from the British Treasury and his Arabic wife and an attractive Frenchwoman of about forty from the cultural side of the Embassy, invited, Gott surmised, to be his partner for the evening. For all he knew, she was a spy.

Gott was still wondering why he was there, and had even begun to suspect he had been invited on a linguistic basis. The Treasury man spoke fluent French, as did his wife, and Gott's good Scottish parents, understanding that like many Scots he might have to seek his fortune abroad, had been careful to make sure he was competent in French and German. The conversation during the first part of the meal was general, the food and wines good, as was only to be expected, and the film star was not just beautiful but intelligent and witty. Seated next to him, his companion, Madame Duhamel, was sympathetic and entertaining. She was bringing the Comédie Française to Britain next month and offered him tickets.

It was with the arrival of the excellent beef that the pace hotted up, when the eminent writer, Jacques Laclos, leaned towards Gott, sitting opposite, and asked, smiling, 'And so – what would you say in Britain if we in Europe cut you loose?' The French ambassador's wife had, before dinner, described Laclos to Gott in that experienced undertone audible only to one hearer in a crowded room. 'A distinguished political writer, left of centre.' That was when Gott recalled the name as being that of a man who had recently achieved notoriety for advocating the repatriation of all French citizens of Algerian origin, or their internment. This caused him to wonder what 'left of centre' meant in these circles. He also noted that now the Treasury man was leaning forward a little to hear his reply. 'Cut loose in what way?'

'Intellectually, economically, morally,' responded Laclos.

Gott, taking it that in this instance the 'Europe' to which Laclos referred actually meant 'France', and understanding why it was the French who had coined the term agent provocateur, said blandly, 'We have tried to distance ourselves over the centuries in many ways. By "we" I mean chiefly England. I think it's fair to say the Scots are different. However hard Britain has tried, the attempt has always failed. Unless we distance ourselves geographically, which is impossible, I don't think the effort could ever be successful.' Gott was rather proud of this polished response. He felt a Foreign Office Etonian could hardly have done better. Nevertheless, he felt obliged to push on in a less diplomatic way. 'Did you put your question just as an interesting hypothesis, or do you see a split as a real possibility?'

'I am a theorist, not a politician,' said Laclos. 'Although I must say your plan for an actual geographical separation is interesting. I feel sure that if Britain could pull up its anchor and set sail for America, it would do so.'

'Would you break champagne over the bows? Would you be happy see us set sail, leaving Europe behind?'

Laclos smiled, gave a small shrug and said, 'It would not be my decision.' He was angry, Gott saw. This issue was plainly serious and he wondered why he had not focused on it before. Perhaps he'd been too preoccupied by the campaign against the MoD Lands Sale Bill. Insular. But not even Jeremy, whose sharp instincts Gott normally trusted implicitly, had raised the question. Unless he had, and Gott had ignored him. Still, the blinkers had fallen from his eyes now – no wonder Wilkes had found time to meet him and be evasive.

Madame Laclos smiled with great charm at Gott and said, 'I some-times feel the relationship between Great Britain and Europe is like a bad marriage. One loves the other – the other has fallen out of love. The second lover begins to love again – the first has cooled. One decides to leave for good, gets in the car and drives to Rome – or takes a plane to New York – the other begins to weep and cry out "Come back."'

'Perhaps in the end the lovers will realize they're better off together,' was Gott's inadequate reply. The moment passed, the conversation resumed its even, amusing tenor, the Treasury man gave everyone advice, 'Don't touch the dollar, even if it means buying the *baht* or the *sucre*,' Madame Laclos told a terrible story of filming the latest *Frankenstein* in Prague. After dinner she, who apparently had some reputation as a singer of songs of the thirties and forties, agreed to perform. As the music continued, the Ambassador sat down next to Gott and said in English, 'So – what do you think of our Jacques Laclos?'

'A very interesting man,' said Gott. 'I found his views interesting. We've irritated our European neighbours for years, playing in the middle of two great powers, the USA and the European Union. Monsieur Laclos seems to think those days are over. I wonder if his views are widely shared in Europe.'

'Certainly among the older members of the Union,' the Ambassador said.

'Well then, Ambassador,' said Gott, 'I suppose the question is, what are we all going to do about this?'

'There's talk of EU sanctions against the UK,' said the Ambassador.

'So I've heard,' said Gott. 'But is that practical? A great deal of trade would be lost on all sides.'

'That is one side of the argument,' said the Ambassador. 'The anxiety is that America is wounded, but, like a wounded animal, struggling to survive. Those struggles make it unpredictable, a great threat to stability in the world. And the thinking is that perhaps the UK, by using its bases in support of American foreign policy, is colluding in that.'

'Any measures taken against Britain by the EU would be seen by the US as hostility. Do the governments of Europe really want to declare war on the US?'

'Of course not,' said the Ambassador, and led the applause for Madame Laclos. He stood up and said to her, 'Madame – a last request – the song that was playing when my wife did me the honour of saying she would become my wife – "Plaisir D'Amour".'

And Madame Laclos agreed Shortly afterwards, the party broke up. On the pavement the man from the Treasury said quietly, 'You seemed to be having a chat with the Ambassador. Can I give you a ring about it tomorrow?'

'I'm reporting back to Sir Joe Camden at the FO.'

'Put me on the list.'

In spite of the fact that it was late, Gott had been drawn, as if by a magnet, back to his office. Seated at his desk, he thought. The basic question was whether the EU was bluffing and the Ambassador, at the intimate dinner to which he had invited Gott and the Treasury man, was doing what all good diplomats are supposed to do, lying for his country. Intimate dinners, private words and the rest could sometimes make things change.

But, he declared to himself, his own business, his proper trade, was money. So what was he going to do?

His first act was to brace himself for another brush with the past. He had a long list of people to ring and decided to bite the bullet and first call Gerard Dorfmann, a director of the Crédit Lyonnaise in Paris, at a phone number he knew too well. Gott had been involved in a love affair with Dorfmann's wife Helene for five years. They met when they could; they loved each other. Dorfmann, said Helene, knew about the affair but tolerated it, as he had his own little entanglements. Edward Gott and Helene did not want to divorce their spouses. But Edward Gott and Helene Dorfmann wanted to live together. And this question was still unresolved when Helene was diagnosed with an aggressive form of cancer. She was dead six months later. Gott had taken the blow and endured it, though now, two years after Helene's death, he knew he would never be the same again. A young man will be hit, will mourn, may contemplate suicide and then there will be another girl, another job, another country, perhaps. Gott knew he no longer had that resilience. He had barely thought of another woman since Helene's death. The only person he had told about it was an obscure solicitor who lived with her doctor husband on the borders of Kensal Green and Willesden.

Now he decided he had to ring Dorfmann, the man he had cuckolded, because he needed him. It was risky. Dorfmann might resent him. He might even pretend to help, while secretly taking revenge. But he and Dorfmann knew each other. Dorfmann would be able to assess the information he was providing. His voice would be useful where it mattered. Uncertain of the response, Gott picked up the phone.

At least Dorfmann was awake, when summoned to the phone. He was wearing a jacket and tie and looked as immaculate as ever.

'Edward,' he said in English. He appeared businesslike, mildly surprised and nothing else. Gott outlined his problem. Dorfmann said, 'I hardly need to tell you what the European money markets are making of all this. There are the ugly rumours about a British election bought with dollars. Can you confirm or deny?'

Gott took a deep breath and told Dorfmann, 'I would not care to deny them.'

Dorfmann's pale, clear-cut face was grave. 'Then I would advise your countrymen to take immediate measures to detach itself from the US. Otherwise, you not only become a puppet state, but destabilize the European Union.'

'Will the EU act if we do not?' asked Gott.

'Almost undoubtedly. You may know there is talk of a preferential trade agreement between your country and the US. A transatlantic free trade area.'

Whatever talk there had been, Gott had not heard it. It might be gossip. But it made him think – the move to push down tax barriers and quotas between the two countries would be logical, given what he understood Petherbridge to be doing. And would sour the relationship between Britain and the countries of Europe to the point where Britain might withdraw from the EU. Or be asked to leave. It would be a trade earthquake. Gott disguised his shock and said only, 'Thank you, Gerard. This has been most helpful.'

'Thank you for your very sympathetic letter concerning the death of my wife.'

'I miss her greatly,' said Edward Gott.

'I, too,' said Gerard Dorfmann. 'I take it you will not object to my informing my colleagues of your call.'

'The reverse,' he said.

Edward Gott sat with his head in his hands for almost a minute. But his screen was still flashing numbers at him. He drank a glass of water and called Rod Field, the newspaper editor, who, he guessed, would probably be in his office.

Gott asked, 'What do you know about a French initiative to apply sanctions against the UK?'

'What do you know?' was the predictable reply.

'Nods and winks,' said Gott, cagily.

This reply was plainly not good enough for Field. He said, in a busy man's voice. 'There was a meeting of the French and German Finance Ministers today.

'Embargoes were said to have been discussed. No confirmation. Do you want to have a word with our chief political correspondent, George Lamb?'

And so Gott rang Lamb, a tired-looking man in his thirties, standing in the hall, apparently arguing with the nanny, Katrin, who was apparently arguing with a child. 'Not at all, Lord Gott. We're all still up, as you can hear.' A woman called out something in a foreign accent. A child in tears yelled back.

'I can't give you a clear answer, Lord Gott. There've been whispers of sanctions for about ten days, now. But I don't think anyone would commit to saying it's serious. On the face of it, there are no obvious advantages to the EU doing whatever they're planning to do. They lose trade and money, make their own electorates angry and gain nothing. But what I've heard said seriously, by the political correspondent of *Le Matin* and someone on the *Berliner Zeitung*, is that, taking the long view, they see Britain coming under the effective control of the US politically. You've seen the books, Lord Gott, so you'll know the strength of the rumour that the Prime Minister won the election with American dollars. I won't even ask—' He broke off as the screams of the child grew louder. 'Excuse me,' he said. 'Katrin! Give her the dummy.' The woman shouted back. 'Never mind!' cried Lamb. 'I'll explain it to Mrs Lamb. That I have ordered you to give Tabitha the dummy.'

There was silence now and Lamb breathed out heavily as he said, 'The joys of family life. I'm sorry, Lord Gott.'

'I have six sons,' Gott said. 'Now – I don't want to take up too much of your time but – you were telling me what the arguments seemed to be for sanctions.'

'Yes – well, it's journalists' talk only but, crudely put, some of the EU ministers see Britain as having a pro-US, bought government in place. What they foresee is economics following politics, the US using Britain as a base just off Continental Europe, flooding them with cheap American goods, Britain making use of its European membership to get advantages for American trade. With a British–American free trade area thrown in, if the rumours are correct.' Another man who'd heard about this, Gott thought. Where had he been, behind a pillar, when the gossip was circulating? He must be losing his touch. But Lamb was continuing to speak.

'They see the Bank of England and the Federal Reserve getting together, hooking up the dollar and the pound and turning the joint currency into a rival to the Euro. That way there'd be three main currencies in competition, the yuan, the euro and the dollar/pound. Could be a fantasy, a Euro-nightmare. I can't judge; I'm not a banker or an economist. I only know there are important people in Europe who are spooked. Tell me, Lord Gott, in view of all this, what would you do with your money?'

'If I believed it, I'd buy candles, firewood and a bicycle,' Gott told him. 'I'm much obliged to you, Mr Lamb. Please ring me if there's anything I can do for you.'

'Thank you, Lord Gott.'

'If I were you,' Gott advised, 'I would go upstairs and extract the dummy from your daughter's mouth before your wife comes home.'

Gott then rang a sleeping banker in Zurich and a wide-awake one at the Federal Reserve in Washington. From Zurich he heard that the Swiss banks were taking the threat of embargoes against Britain seriously. From Washington he heard another voice. Leo Radetsky said, 'It won't happen. Can you see the French wilfully stopping their farmers from exporting to Britain, or anywhere? They wouldn't dare. What would Germany and France do to persuade their industrialists they had to take a cut? What about the newer Euro states? They're bluffing, Edward.'

'I don't know,' said Gott.

'Maybe I shouldn't say this, but your Prime Minister, Alan Petherbridge, says they're bluffing.'

'Does he?' said Gott. 'I didn't know that.'

With the screen of share prices still blinking in front of him, Gott thought. Hard-headed men in Europe knew about the bought election, connected it with the sale of the airbases and were drawing conclusions. They were now envisaging Britain as a vassal state of the US, Britain as the bridgehead for sales of US goods in Europe and, finally, the linkage of the dollar and sterling and the final battle, the mother of all currency wars, the battle between the combined forces of the dollar and the pound against the euro, with the yuan looking on and watching the struggle.

There was the sound of a loud explosion, perhaps a quarter of a mile away, which made Gott, shaking his head, begin to make his moves. He knew it was a bomb, he'd heard them often enough before. He didn't know what kind of a bomb it was, precisely where it had struck – in the financial areas close to the river, he thought – or who it might have killed. Nor did he particularly care. Except that if it was not a bombing by Jihad, or a similar group, it would be attributed to them. A politically motivated bombing in the City was always bad news for the nervy international markets. The explosion, coming at that moment, seemed like an omen of coming disaster. He turned to his computer screen.

In his professional career, when uncertain, Gott, father of six, was inclined to ask himself a basic question – what would he do if the problem concerned his own money, not someone else's? Asking the question and answering it, he sold all his currency holdings in sterling, the dollar and the euro. He bought Chinese yuan. He got out of oil, tourism and airlines. He got into insurance, mining, telecommunications, food and drink, chemicals and pharmaceuticals. He bought into land. He bought a failing British hotel chain. He bought into the British Investment Bank, so widely known for money-laundering that it was called, in the City, the Launderette.

As Gott worked, he heard, through his thick windows, the sound of emergency vehicles speeding to where the bomb had gone off. Surveying his newly constructed portfolio, he felt satisfied that although the yield would be poorer, the investments were safer than they had been half an hour earlier. He then did almost exactly the same thing for his clients and drafted a memorandum to the bank, explaining what he'd done and why, and recommending the bank to consider, at speed, revising all its loans and investments in the light of his thinking.

He suspected his fellow directors would not back his judgement, would probably say secretly that he'd gone mad. They might even form an alliance to eject him from the board. His clients might be furious and go elsewhere. If that was the case, thought Gott, so be it. He had formed a judgement and acted on it. This was the way he had always operated, usually successfully. Which was no guarantee that this time he was not making a grave, possibly a fatal, mistake.

But Gott, when it came to the point, liked risk. He felt quite lighthearted as he finished his work. He reminded himself that he was putting everything on the line these days — his job, his political reputation and, had it not been for the early domestic conspiracy against him, he might have been risking his marriage also. The only sign of nerves he experienced was a raging thirst. He drank two more glasses of water and went downstairs.

In the ornate lobby with its atrium of tropical trees, the night guard said to him, 'Hear the bang, sir?'

'Yes,' said Gott, putting on his gloves. 'Sounded like a bomb. Is that smoke I'm smelling?' A reek was permeating the huge area of marble.

'The explosion was at the Canfield Building down on Upper Thames Street. I suppose the wind's blowing it this way.'

'Any casualties?'

'Not so far,' the guard said. 'Too soon to know, really.'

'Are they saying who did it?'

'An anarchist group says they did it. But their leader has denied it. You don't know what to think.'

'No,' said Gott. 'You don't.'

'The drivers can't get out of the garage because of the police cordons down there,' said the guard. 'Shall I get you a taxi, sir?'

'No, thanks,' said Gott. 'I'll walk.'

'Are you sure, sir? Another one could go off.'

'Might just as easily get blown up in the taxi,' said Gott. 'It's all a matter of luck.'

He walked the three miles back to his flat, suspecting that after what he had done he would be too agitated to sleep. He was wrong. Almost as soon as his head touched the pillow, he fell asleep.

Nine

The House of Commons, London SW1. February 24th 2016. 6 p.m.

Joshua Crane stood alone on the terrace of the Houses of Commons. Even from where he stood, overlooking the Thames, the shouts of the huge crowd assembled in Parliament Square and all the way up Whitehall as far as Trafalgar Square could be heard. 'Take back the bases!' 'Take back the bases!' The bridge beside Parliament was thick with marchers, holding banners reading, NO TO US IMPERIALISM, HANDS OFF BRITISH BASES, NO TO THE HANDOVER and REMEMBER KIM DURHAM. Many of the banners showed young Rory Durham at the soldier's feet.

On the other side of the Thames there were more people, people Joshua could scarcely see but whose voices travelled over the water. Over two million people – approximately one in every twenty British adults – had come to London to demonstrate. The police had powers to turn the demonstrators back from Parliament, but had told the Home Secretary that the numbers made this impossible without the Army. And so the marchers had come – and come and come.

That morning's papers had been an almost incomprehensible patchwork of agendas. PETHERBRIDGE STANDS FIRM, had declared the largest, right-wing broadsheet paper (owned by an Australian with US nationality). THE BASES ARE BRITISH was the entire front page of the largest right-wing tabloid (now owned in Hong Kong) and PETHERBRIDGE MUST GO, the largest left-wing tabloid had said (the owner Canadian). If the question of the bases had divided the press along unusual lines, the same was true of the country. Those opposed to the sale of the bases ranged from the reddest-faced Colonel Blimps in their manor houses, to the most wasted anarchists in their Hackney squats. Nevertheless, in spite of the Home Counties brushing shoulders with the inner city, Muslims with Quakers and the home-grown with young foreign demonstrators from Italy, Germany and France, the opinion polls said that the public were evenly divided. On the side of selling the bases to the US were those who had accepted the argument that this was the only way of separating Britain from US war aims, who saw the sale as acknowledging an accomplished fact or believed the sale was necessary to secure continuing protection by the world's greatest military power. Others, including many in the House of Commons, were simply not prepared to challenge and perhaps overturn an elected government over anything but a matter of life and death. Not if the result were to be another election five months after the last.

For the past three weeks, Joshua and the other dissident MPs had been campaigning up and down the country, making speeches in town halls and conference centres. He had written letters late into the night. He had encouraged the waverers and heartened his supporters. Meanwhile, the Prime Minister had piled on the pressure until there were men who, seeing a Party Whip come into the tea room, would simply get up and leave.

Joshua's wife had rung from Yorkshire, offering to come with Joshua on the speaking dates and sit by him loyally on the platform. After the experience of the general election, and knowing that this time Beth dreaded and disapproved of what he was doing, Joshua had found it easy to refuse his wife's offer. Nevertheless, Beth had wished him well, though she could not resist adding, 'And I hope when this is over your good friend Lord Gott will have a job lined up for you.' Joshua felt he could hardly blame her for the comment. His meetings were packed with supporters and his mailbag was 90 per cent in support of him, but the truth was that if the MoD Lands Sale Bill became law his career would probably end, together with the careers of his supporters. Their punishment at the Prime Minister's hands would be swift and terrible. His fate was in the hands of the Labour MPs in the House.

Carl Chatterton and his party had been sitting on the fence. The Labour Party had voted with the Government at the first two readings of the bill, though not without an internal revolt led by Mark Moreno, a charismatic left-winger, formerly a trades union leader, now the MP for Rudgwick in Cumbria and tipped to be the next Labour leader when the party's impatience with Chatterton reached boiling point. Labour's National Executive had declared in favour of Moreno. Chatterton's pitiful agony was that of a man afraid of his own party. In the end he did what his closest colleagues guessed he would. He declared a free vote for his party, which meant that from now until the count no one knew what the outcome would be.

Joshua had spoken well in a House so packed that members had to stand against the walls and in the entrances. He had been praised for his speech. He was, as he stood there on the terrace, the man of the moment. But, if his side lost the vote, in an hour's time he would be finished – a loser, a man who had earned the implacable hatred of the Prime Minister, a man others of his party would hardly dare to be seen with. If they won, of course, it would be a different story. It was not impossible that at some point he would become Prime Minister.

'There are your supporters,' said Julia Baskerville, who had come up behind him. Joshua was feeling the power and weight of the crowd. Like

any politician suddenly experiencing the rapid emotional highs and lows
of triumph, and the possibility of great office, he began, almost, to fear
it. There was the crowd, huddled in their coats and woolly hats, blocking
the bridge and a mile of streets round Parliament – two million of them,
shouting their support.

'How much weight have you lost?'

'About ten pounds,' said Joshua, who had been forced to rush out that
afternoon and buy a new suit, off the peg, so as not to make a major
speech looking like a scarecrow. He said, 'It must have been a relief to
you when Chatterton gave the party a free vote ' He thought Julia didn't
look very well herself. She, too, seemed to have lost weight and she was
very pale. Perhaps she had a cold.

'A relief for me – but not as big a relief as it was for you,' she told
him.

'It keeps the excitement at full pitch.' She worked very hard, Joshua
thought. Her constituency made big demands. 'You OK, Julia?'

A hired steamer had been going up and down the river from Greenwich
to Westminster, banners stretched along each side reading, VOTE NO
TO AMERICAN BASES ON BRITISH SOIL. Now, a light mounted on
the deck raked the side of the House of Commons, picked out the figures
of Joshua and Julia and a voice boomed out, 'Thanks, Joshua – No Yank
bases on British soil.' Joshua caught in the light, was recognized by the
crowds jammed on the bridge. As Julia stepped out of the light, people
began to shout 'Crane! Crane! Crane!' Joshua, surprised, recovered
himself, waved and smiled and then, miming a need to go elsewhere and
do something else, grabbed Julia's arm and retreated from the terrace.
Julia smiled. 'Not since the Nuremberg rallies,' she said.

'You didn't have to say that.'

'I couldn't resist it.'

Then Joshua was claimed by a group of men who had been looking
for him. 'House is about to divide,' one said urgently. They ran inside,
to vote.

7 Adam Street, Shepherd's Bush, London W12. February 24th, 2016. 9 p.m.

William, Lucy and Joe were sitting quietly in the sitting room while Marie lay on the pull-out bed, asleep, under heavy medication. Her husband slumped in an easy chair, looking ten years older than he had that morning.

Somehow, at the time of the Hamscott Common invasion, they had managed to prevent Marie from leaving the hospital, but the problem had not gone away. It had become plain that Marie would never be able to return to the Sutcliffes' house in Yorkshire. It would be sold and the Sutcliffes would move to London. William did not like this idea but consoled himself with the thought that his in-laws, who had no taste for the inner city, would end up living in a pleasant suburb at least ten miles away. At the moment it was not that prospect which troubled him. It was the immediate future.

He was not prepared to spend months, or even weeks, living in the flat with his in-laws while they sold their house and found somewhere else to live. Before the Sutcliffes had got back from the hospital he and Lucy had had a row. When he said he was not prepared to have her parents in the flat while they house-hunted, Lucy suggested that they find another flat and live in it for the duration. William began to shout. He would not pay hundreds of pounds a week to rent a flat while a house Marie could tolerate was found. He'd had enough. He never wanted to see Lucy's parents again. If they moved back into the flat, he ranted, he would seriously consider packing in his job and moving to Spain. Lucy knew he had a long-standing job offer from Felix Arnold, a friend of his parents, in Villalba.

Lucy had stood, silent and appalled, staring at the shouting William. Then the doorbell had rung. The Sutcliffes were back. A grim silence had fallen between the couple.

Lucy now looked at her father and said, 'You'd better get to bed, Dad. William – do you want to come out for a walk with me?'

In the street she said, 'God, William. Do you mean it about Spain? You'd really leave me?'

'Lucy,' he said. 'Lucy . . . You know I . . . Oh, fuck! I don't know what I mean. Let's go and get a drink.'

They headed silently for the local pub on Shepherd's Bush Green. William wondered whether he could really leave his wife and head for

Spain. No, he couldn't, he decided. He could not take up Felix Arnold's offer to help him with the expansion of his hotel unless Lucy came, too. But, he thought, he could sure as hell pack in his job and go there until the Sutcliffes were out of the way. He was wondering how to put his decision to Lucy when, rounding a corner, they saw police vehicles and lights on the Green and police officers and Auxiliaries clustered on the pavement opposite. They stopped, 'Not again,' said William. 'Looks like a quiet drink round here is out of the question. I can't face the flat again.'

They walked through quiet streets, though still hearing sirens and spotting police at intersections. 'I didn't mean what I said about clearing out for good,' William told Lucy. 'But I can't hang about while your parents go through all the business of a sale and buying a new place. Can you imagine your mother while all that's going on? I couldn't take it. I'm serious, Lucy. I will go. But what I've been thinking is this – this place is shite. Look at what we've just seen – cops all over the place, bombs – maybe Mo had the right idea when he got out. Agreed, he and his family were under more pressure – but the pressure's getting worse for all of us. What is this stuff about air force bases – fucked if I know? And all these rumours about the Prime Minister buying an election. And then there's going to be another war in Iraq. What I'm saying is, maybe this business with your parents is a wake-up call. Look at our lives, working all hours to save for a small flat so we can have a baby and then keep on working all hours so we can bring him up – and look what we're having to live through just to get that – bombs and terrorism, the lot. At least we've got a choice. We could go to Spain together. It's a plan, Lucy. Thousands are doing it.'

'Yes,' said Lucy slowly. 'We've got a choice.'

William suddenly wanted it settled quickly. He told Lucy, 'I don't want to wait any longer. I don't want a lot of discussion about what Joe and Marie are going to do. We've got to decide soon.'

'Give me a day or two to think,' she said.

'OK. But don't take any longer.'

Lucy didn't like this. 'Don't bully me,' she said.

They were walking up an avenue of houses. On the pavement outside one of them there were concrete crash barriers. A policeman was on duty in the porch.

'Wonder who that is?' said Lucy.

'Whoever he is, he's better defended than we are. Your parents are mad to move here – this place is a mess.'

Their mood had changed since they left the house. 'Let's forget the pub,' she said. 'I'm on duty at seven.'

* * *

When they returned, Joe was chatting to a thin young man who was sitting on the couch. 'You weren't long,' Joe said amiably. 'In the meantime, your friend dropped in.'

The young man looked up and said, 'Hello, William.'

At first, William didn't recognize Jemal Al Fasi, Mo's brother, although he did recognize the T-shirt and jeans Jemal was wearing. They were his own. Jemal's hair was wet. He must have had a shower. Once he realized who Jemal was, and had got over the fact that Jemal was wearing his clothes, he was even more surprised, simply to find Jemal in his flat. He thought the whole family was in Morocco. He hardly knew Jemal. What was he doing here?

He took in Jemal's face, tired and keyed up, then looked down at the boy's feet. He was wearing his own trainers, which were battered and smeared with mud that had not been properly washed off. There was a big tear on the side of one shoe. William suddenly felt worried.

'Hullo, Jemal,' he said carefully. 'How's the family?'

Grosvenor Cavendish Hotel, Knightsbridge, London SW1. February 24th, 2016. 10 p.m.

Edward Gott had decided that even if the vote were lost he'd throw a big party that night in the best public rooms in the smartest hotel in London. The dissident Conservative MPs, the press, the TV cameras and anyone else he could lay hands on would all be there. When he made the booking ten days earlier he did it with his party against him and his job on the line. It was pure bravado – the desire, if he was going to go down, to go down with a bang. But the vote had not been lost. The three huge interconnecting rooms of the hotel were crammed, the band was playing and the champagne was flowing. In addition, even before the vote had been taken, Gott's career had been salvaged by an age-old enemy.

A few weeks before the vote, the day after the dinner at the French Embassy and his late night at the bank, Gott had arrived early to discover what the first repercussions of his buys and sells on behalf of his clients would be. It was no surprise that what he had done had much the same impact as the bomb on Upper Thames Street the night before. The latter had taken off the side of the Baltic League Bank right up to the third floor, though, by a miracle, only the suicide bombers inside the truck driven into the building had died. No one had admitted responsibility; the assumption was that, being a suicide bomb it was probably the work of Muslim fundamentalist terrorists. But the business of the City of London – money – went on.

At Clough Whitney Credit and Commerce the majority view was that Gott had conducted his own act of terrorism. Gott had needed to summon up his nerve to walk in that morning and, as soon as he did, the problems began. He was called to an immediate meeting with the Clough Whitney CEO, Sir Basil Whitehouse, to explain his dawn raid on his clients' accounts. His boss sat stonily silent as he explained his reasons. The meeting concluded with nothing but, 'You'll be hearing more from me later in the day.' Which Gott assumed meant that Sir Basil was waiting for the CEO of the bank's American side to call. He did not need to ask if he was still being considered as his boss's successor. Sir Basil was due to retire in a year.

That morning, Gott lost one third of his clients. Charlotte Harker, one of the bank's other directors and herself in line for Sir Basil's job, urged the calling of an extraordinary meeting of the bank's directors to discuss Gott's activities. This was rapidly arranged and would take place in three days. Charlotte Harker would now be lobbying for votes against him.

Meanwhile, the bank was besieged by other clients, not Gott's, who had got wind of his extraordinary decisions and were anxious that the same policy, liquidation of lucrative stocks and reliable currency, and investment in less well-yielding stocks, should not be applied to their own accounts. By lunchtime the bank's traders, probably working on hints from Charlotte Harker, were beginning to say that Gott's preoccupation with politics had unhinged him, that he was no longer reliable. They asked for a same-day meeting. Gott, who was due to take a train north for a rally in York with Joshua and other MPs, agreed, and cancelled the trip.

That meeting, with the deputation of Clough Whitney traders, was less difficult than Gott had anticipated. Two of the seven traders had decided not to turn up and, of the remaining five, two – the best of the bunch – were prepared to take seriously what he told them. They might not follow him in his risky decisions, but they could see his logic and would keep an eye on events so that if there were signs he was right, they could move fast. The other three were Charlotte Harker's allies. If there had been a vote, Gott would have lost 3-2, with two abstentions. Not a terrible result. But the meeting with the traders was a minor one – the real challenge would come at the directors' meeting. Meanwhile, he was blocking calls from the *Financial Times* and from the financial editors of the other serious newspapers.

That afternoon, Gott found out, the American CEO rang Sir Basil. His next call was to Gott himself. For the third time that day Gott explained an investment strategy based on guarding his clients' money against EU sanctions and a possible split from the EU by Britain. The US CEO was incredulous. 'That's not an investment policy, Gott – it's a movie scenario,' he said. The call ended with the American, an irate and busy man, saying with barely concealed anger that he would fly to London to attend the emergency directors' meeting.

Even Lady Margot rang from Scotland saying that 'the boys' – the oldest was thirty-two – were concerned about the rumours involving their father's movement of money, including his own – money which would eventually, be theirs. She said they were pestering her, which Gott knew probably meant four or five phone calls. One would have been from Jamie, whose analyst wife might be suggesting that her father-in-law had become unbalanced due to the stress of his recent political involvements. Gott's wife ended her call by telling him, 'I told them, don't you be so sure. Your father's an old fox who has survived many a hunt.' Gott had been touched by this unexpected support from his wife, especially considering his recent admission to her.

Gott's day did not improve. Before he left the office the calls from the financial editors were still continuing unanswered. Jasmine Dottrell put her head round his door. One glance at her face told Gott he was in trouble. 'It's the *Sun*,' she said.

Gott spoke to the editor of the *Sun*. The Downing Street Press Office had released the story of Gott's illegitimate child, exclusively, to the paper. The story would be published next day and the editor asked for Gott's comments. Gott told him, 'It's old news. My family knows about it. And you know this is Alan Petherbridge's revenge.'

'Revenge for the vote against his bill in Parliament, but also to show he means business if you start trying to kick the Yanks off those bases. Any comment on that one, by the way?'

'Just stick to scandal,' Gott advised. 'And, Darren, this isn't earth-shattering. Are you doing it as a favour?'

Obviously Downing Street was giving every help. Gott's daughter, Chloe, her husband and their boy were being stalked in Brighton by reporters. Photographs had been taken outside the primary school where Chloe worked. The headmistress was very angry. Gott's daughter said she loved her father. Chloe's mother, a London solicitor, said she had a friendly relationship with him. Lady Margot told journalists she had known of the matter for many years. Gott knew she would have made this statement anyway, out of loyalty to him – and he would probably never find out if it were true.

Gott called Jeremy in to deal with the fallout. He had other work to do and would not be able to leave Clough Whitney until very late that night. Jeremy took over a small connecting office next to Gott's. This contained a sofa, a coffee table and little else and was normally used in an emergency when it was important to keep two visitors to the office apart.

'Tory Party Treasurer in Thirty-year-old Love Tangle,' Jeremy said when he walked in.

Jasmine said, 'He ran away, that's what the story says.'

Gott defended himself. 'I came back.'

'Not soon enough,' Jasmine said.

'Just get on with your work,' her employer told her.

It wasn't news by tabloid standards. Gott understood that. But even if those involved in his unsensational little tale were all helping to kill it for lack of oxygen, the story could not have come at a worse time. With his professional judgement heavily questioned and his job on the line, the real story was whether a man who had been proved unreliable in his private life would be the same in his public life. As no doubt the Prime Minister had known when he lit the fuse.

The Clough Whitney directors' meeting was as bad as Gott had expected, if not worse. He was given a month to put his clients' affairs on a suitable basis. Then there would be a review. He knew he would be expected to resign before the results of the review were announced. For the next two weeks Gott did almost nothing. He was still backing his own judgement over his clients' money, but after the first rush to get out, the seepage of clients continued. He lived in a limbo of declining influence, not handing in his resignation only because he was too obstinate.

Two weeks into this nightmare of meetings to which he was not invited and conversations which ended abruptly as he approached, Jeremy Saunders called him at his office, where he was tying up loose ends in anticipation of the day when he would pass through Clough Whitney's door for the last time, broken and unemployable. Jeremy told Gott that Lord Haver's private secretary had rung and asked, could Lord Gott spare the time to have lunch with Lord Haver that day? 'He's got something big to tell you, I'm sure of it,' Jeremy told Gott.

After the Haver House treachery Gott had no reason to like or trust Haver, or want ever to meet him again if he could help it. But he trusted Jeremy's instincts enough to agree to the meeting.

Haver was wheeled into the old-fashioned fish restaurant he favoured. The muscly attendant disappeared after settling him at the table. Gott looked across at the lined face and steely blue eyes of his host and wondered if Haver had anything useful to say. Possibly, because Haver was a profoundly vindictive man, he had arranged the meeting only to crow over him or to ram the knife deeper into his already-bleeding back. Well, Gott thought, he could always leave. With this in mind, although he seldom drank at lunchtime on a working day, he agreed when Haver suggested wine. Haver ordered and, unusually for him, took a glass himself. The meal seemed to be almost cordial, Gott thought, and reminded himself to watch his step.

Haver said, 'I don't know about you, but I always discuss business over food.'

'So do I,' replied Gott. 'Though I've known it to give me indigestion.' He looked at Haver, challenging him to try.

A platter of oysters arrived. The two men started to swallow them.

'Always put heart in you,' observed Haver, taking another. 'I gather you've been making a lot of changes in your investment policies recently.'

Gott took an oyster. He suddenly knew Haver would not let him have six of the dozen on the table, that Haver must and would have seven, and that if he took his share Haver was prepared to order and pay for another dozen, just to make sure of the lion's share.

'I have made changes,' Gott agreed. Unprepared to embark on an eating competition with Haver, he took the fifth oyster, swallowed it, ate some bread and butter, sipped a little of his wine and leaned back. 'That's it,' he said. 'Delicious. I hope you can manage the rest. Yes, well – I can't tell you everyone's pleased with my decisions.' He wasn't telling Haver anything – news of the director's meeting, and his own imminent departure, was all round the City.

Haver then surprised him greatly. 'If you'll have me, I'd like to come in behind you. There's a Greatorex meeting this afternoon. I'm Chairman, as you know. I'm going to try to persuade the Board to switch twenty-five per cent of our investments to Clough Whitney. Under your personal supervision, of course.'

Greatorex was the second largest pension fund in the UK. The value of a quarter of its funds to Gott's bank was enormous.

Gott said, evenly, 'That's very good news, Lord Haver.'

'I can't guarantee I'll swing it. What I'll be telling them is that I'm moving some of my personal money to you. Which is the other thing – I want you to take charge of some of my holdings.' Haver's personal fortune was estimated at four billion.

Gott was even more amazed, victory bells ringing distantly in his mind. He asked, 'You want me to invest for you on the same basis I'm using for my other clients?'

'Those who are left,' Haver said. 'Have you followed the policy with regard to your own money?' As is well known, the last taboo is one man asking another about his private funds. Moreover, Gott was still very wary of Haver. He looked straight into his hard, narrow eyes and remembered that this man was capable of almost anything. He answered, 'I never recommend my clients or my bank to do anything I wouldn't do myself.'

'That's probably as close to integrity as a banker can get,' Haver said.

Gott almost smiled, hearing the word integrity coming from Haver's mouth. 'I'm surprised. What makes you think I'm right in doing what I'm doing? Not everybody feels the same.'

He thought Haver might know something he did not. But if he did, he wouldn't tell.

Haver said, looking at the menu, 'Scallops look good – are they fresh?'

'Of course, sir,' the waiter replied.

'He would say that, wouldn't he?' Haver said to Gott. 'Well, all right then, I'll have them anyway. What about you, Gott?'

'Salmon,' Gott said.

Haver gave the order and asked, 'Where were we – yes – why? Why indeed. Well, I was in Moscow last week talking to the Finance Minister there and he told me they were quietly dumping their dollars. They're brooding about fixing the rouble to the euro. Fat chance, but – straws in the wind, Gott. Straws in the wind. The last great takeovers, eh? The dollar absorbs the pound, the yuan absorbs the yen, the euro hooks up with the rouble. Yesterday, I was told by a very serious individual that another government, more important than Russia, was going to dump its dollar holdings. Meanwhile, there's you – I'm guessing you've looked into the UK's future and seen a picture, not a pretty one. Am I right?'

Gott did not answer but responded, 'I'm pleased you're planning a move to Clough Whitney, of course. That goes without saying. But we're a small bank and I'm curious about why you aren't going to your own bankers.'

'I've had a word,' said Lord Haver. 'But they don't understand. They'll follow instructions, but they'll drag their feet, they'll show no enthusiasm and they won't understand the principles. Part of it's that their own percentages will drop. Anyway, I've no desire to talk to my bank and know they think they're dealing with a madman. It's the sanctions, isn't it, Gott? You think the Europeans will go ahead and cut off our oil supplies?'

'I think they might. And even the possibility is enough for me to want to restructure investments.' He paused. 'But an American I spoke to told me Petherbridge thinks the European Finance Ministers are bluffing.'

'Maybe he's bluffing,' said Haver. 'A politician'll say anything because he's nothing to lose. You and I are talking money. That's serious. This bill – are you going to win?'

Gott shook his head. 'I don't know. There's a good chance, no better.'

'Out on a limb, aren't you?' asked Haver, enjoying it. 'Several, in fact.'

'A bit of risk never hurts,' Gott said. 'Life's a risk.'

'Very true,' said Haver. 'I only ask about the bill because it'll have a bearing on everything else. Trouble is, Gott, as a banker you're judging the situation – as a politician, you're influencing it. We don't really want a war with the US, do we? Terrible for business.'

'It's not a challenge, just a return to the status quo,' Gott said defensively.

'That's what you think and that's what I think, but what will they think? Proud and touchy folk, the Americans. Still, there are situations and reactions you can't predict.'

Gott put down his knife and fork. 'Indigestion?' Haver questioned with a tight smile. He finished his own food and looked round immediately for the waiter.

'Oh,' he said. 'I'd like to insist on one thing. Nothing about these transactions – if I can get the board to agree to them. It'll get known soon enough but I'd be pretty unhappy to see this in tomorrow's papers.' Gott, who had been contacted by the press, refused to give interviews and had been subsequently criticized if not mocked by them, would have preferred to leak the news of Lord Haver's support immediately. But the important thing was that his own board should know.

Haver, menu in hand, looked up at the waiter by his side and said, 'Bread and butter – sticky toffee – cheesecake, what the hell is that? – don't they ever change the menu here?'

The waiter made a suggestion.

'Don't be foolish, man,' Haver said. 'Ice cream? In February? I'm not a child.' 'Never mind,' he said to Gott. 'Let's try the cheese. Might as well,' he urged. 'If the Frogs put on these sanctions we'll be reduced to smuggling in Camembert.'

He put more wine in Gott's glass. 'No more for me, with Greatorex to face,' he told Gott. 'I'll call you after the meeting. They're never long. Should be around four.' He paused. 'You know what,' he said, 'I think we're heading for the hell of a mess. No knowing how bad it's going to get.'

Haver's attendant came through the restaurant and he looked up. 'I'm sorry,' he said. 'I must go – I'll have to leave you to enjoy your cheese in peace.'

Gott was pleased to be relieved of Haver's difficult presence. He was now half-convinced that Haver's offers were sincere. But only half. Nevertheless, at 3:45 p.m. Jasmine Dottrell put Lord Haver through. The Greatorex board had agreed to put a quarter of its funds in Gott's hands. Haver's personal bankers would be in touch tomorrow. Gott's career was saved.

And now he, or his group, had won the vote.

Standing by the laden buffet, he said to Joshua, 'Funny about how things can turn around in one day.' Joshua agreed, though he imagined Gott was only referring to the vote. Gott made way for Amelia Strange, who said, 'Congratulations, Lord Gott. Radio car outside your house tomorrow, eight a.m.'

'Tell the driver I'll be the man on the pavement in pyjamas,' Gott said jovially. To Joshua he said, 'Another splash of champagne?'

'Not really,' Joshua said. 'I've just had a text from the PM – "See me, 9.00 p.m. tomorrow."'

'It'll be nasty,' said Gott. 'But you won, he lost, them's the facts.'

'He won't go,' Joshua said. It was not a question.

'No. He won't go. He'll stay and make your life a misery, as much as he can. But I'll tell you what I think. He won't back the US in the Iraq War because he can't now. But he's going to have to explain this to the President and I'm guessing that won't be the end of it. There'll be a plan. I just don't know what it is. But one thing's certain, we can't retreat now. We have to get those bases back under exclusively British control.'

He turned to a man behind him who had overheard him and said, 'I never said that, Jake.'

'Course you didn't,' said the other, and drifted away.

'It's a big one, though,' said Joshua. 'There'd be hell to pay.'

'There already is,' said Gott. Briefly, he told Joshua about the prospect of European trade sanctions against the UK. 'If that happens it would be devastating. It can only be prevented by cutting some ties with our old friends. And those bases are the biggest ties – ties or shackles, I don't know which. I wish to God I knew what Petherbridge was planning.'

Joshua looked wary, 'OK. But not here, Edward. Let's talk about it later.'

'I didn't want to spoil your party, but you had to know,' Gott told him.

At the thought of the next day's meeting, Joshua's face stiffened. Gott clapped him on the shoulder. 'Don't worry – he daren't do anything to you straight away.'

He was seized by one of Graham Barnsbury's pretty daughters who said, 'Lord Gott – someone told me you're a dancing man. All the other men here seem to have two left feet.'

'That's the best offer I'll get tonight,' Gott said and led her to the dance floor.

In a small room leading from the main reception room Julia Baskerville and Mark Moreno were alone. Above the sound of the band playing Julia said to Mark, tall and handsome in a black suit and red tie, 'You're ready to go for it, then?'

'This is the time,' he said. 'With the Lands Sale Bill lost we have to strike hard now, while public feeling is with us. We must get those bases back before Petherbridge obeys American orders, commits us to this re-invasion of Iraq and starts using the bases to ferry troops and materiel out, and suspected terrorists in—' He broke off as a couple came in, he in a dinner jacket, she in a tiny gold dress, and went, entwined, to the window. Moreno said, in a lower voice, 'I've had a tip-off from the Treasury that they're working night and day on this Transatlantic Trade Agreement. It's more than a rumour. If Petherbridge pulls that off the European Union will come down hard on us. Trade sanctions could be the least of it.' He looked sideways, following Julia's eyes, to where the couple embraced. The woman was leaning against a wall, the man pressed hard against her. Moreno continued. 'The EU could kick us out. Even if they don't we'll be pariahs – any power and influence we might have in Europe will be gone. Petherbridge is acting fast – we've got to act faster to stop him.'

'It means getting rid of Chatterton—'

'That's long overdue, Julia. He'd do too little, too late. The delay would give Petherbridge the victory.'

The woman's straps were now off her shoulders. One of her legs was hooked round the man's. Julia smiled. 'I'm with you,' she said. 'But I think we have to get out of here. You first.'

Moreno left. Julia followed on a little later. Re-entering the crowded room she realized suddenly that Moreno had been taking almost no notice of the amorous couple. He had been too fixed on his planned coup. You had to be like that to be a successful politician – oblivious to the outside world.

Up came Joshua, grinning, a drink in his hand. 'All these years together,' he said, 'and I still don't know if you can do the tango?'

'Try me,' she countered. Joshua put his drink down and they tangoed off together, under the chandeliers.

The White House, Washington DC, USA. February 24th, 2016. 3 p.m. (EST)

Ray Hollander was spared the sight of his President's furious face that afternoon. Instead, as he listened to her enraged voice on the phone he found himself staring at the long, calm face of George Washington, in a portrait which hung on the wall of her private sitting room. The voice was enough, though. 'Great!' she said. 'Petherbridge defeated, the airbases lost and millions of people in that miserable little island out on the streets yelling opposition like some mob in Baghdad or Beirut.'

'We knew this could happen, Madam President,' Hollander said carefully. 'We planned accordingly.'

'Let's hope the plans work better than the first ones,' she told him.

'There's no doubt—'

'Who's this Lord Gott?' she interrupted.

'A disappointed man, a lightweight, backed by a few disgruntled Conservative MPs and a rabble of liberals,' Hollander told her. 'It's not a tough opposition.'

'I think you'd better talk to Drew Caldicott,' she told him, and cut the connection.

Hollander breathed in and rang Drew Caldicott, the CIA chief, a man said to frighten everybody, including his wife, his children and his dog. Hollander looked into the terrifying eyes and forced himself to be calm. 'This is a setback, Drew,' he said. 'It's not a defeat. This can be resolved. But there are a couple of problems you can help with.'

'Tell me what you need,' said Caldicott.

7 Adam Street, Shepherd's Bush, London W12. February 24th, 2016. 11.55 p.m.

'So, Jemal, how's the family?' William had weakly enquired on finding Jemal Al Fasi on his couch, wearing his clothes.

'Fine,' said Jemal.

'Back from Morocco?' William persisted.

'I never went. I'm going tomorrow,' Jemal said.

Alarms were still going off in William's head. Jemal had never visited him at home before. They weren't on those terms. So what was he doing here now? William was anxious. Although his father-in-law's main concern at the moment was Marie, lying spark-out on the sofa bed, Joe Sutcliffe had spent his working life as a policeman. He still had the instincts. If there was something wrong about Jemal, it might not be too long before Joe sensed it.

'Jemal,' said William. 'You know a bit about central heating, don't you? I'm looking after the bloke downstairs's flat while he's away and it seems a bit cold – he's got all these fish in a tank and . . .' He tailed off, hoping Jemal had the sense to pick up what he was saying, and glanced at Lucy, who was staring at him, knowing Bob Wood had not gone away. And then Joe was looking hard at both of them.

William was relieved when Jemal got to his feet. 'I'll take a look at it,' he said.

William overdid it. 'He's been saving for this trip for a year. Be a shame if he came back and found his fish dead.'

William let himself into the downstairs flat, hoping that Bob would be at his girlfriend's as he normally was on this day of the week. In the neat, red-carpeted hall he turned to Jemal, who, no longer needing to keep up a front, looked worn and shrunken. 'Is something going on?' asked William.

'I don't like to ask – can you put me up till tomorrow morning?'

Jemal's eyes were wide and unblinking. William knew Jemal would never normally have asked him for shelter. Even with his family away there would be other Moroccans he could go to. Unless he couldn't. Unless he'd done something to one of them – stolen something, assaulted a girl . . .

'Jemal – what's happening? Come on, mate, level with me.'

'I just need a bed for the night,' Jemal told him. 'I've got some friends who are going to pick me up tomorrow morning,' he added.

William knew it all now. The friends were going to get him away. Jemal was on the run.

William caught Jemal's eye and detected a flicker of something there – not guilt or shame, not appeal, fear or defiance, as he might have expected, but something else. Jemal was down because he was on the run. But he wasn't ashamed of what he'd done, or because he'd nearly been caught or because he was begging help from someone who didn't want to give it. Not ashamed, because he was in the right. As a teenager William had started a fight with a Salvation Army officer in a pub – he remembered the look on the Salvationist's face just before William's fist hit his nose.

He groaned aloud. 'Oh, Jesus Christ, Jemal – you got mixed up with one of these groups, didn't you? You're on the run. You thought you'd be safer here, with English people. They wouldn't look for you—' He paused, then burst out, 'Shit, Jemal. Were you in on that air force base thing?' He stared at Jemal and saw the admission in his eyes. William grabbed him by the shoulder. 'You cunt! My wife's upstairs. What kind of a way is this to treat your brother's mate? Mo would go mad if he knew.'

Jemal said, 'Maybe I shouldn't . . .'

'There's armed police all over the streets,' shouted William. 'I don't fucking want them here.' Jemal just stared at him. William pulled himself together and said, 'I've got seventy pounds upstairs. I'll get it. You take it and go. There's a phone over there. See if you can find someone else to help you.'

He turned, and as he opened the door Jemal said, 'Don't turn me in.'

'It's a temptation,' said William and ran upstairs. He burst into his own flat, grabbed his wallet, saying, 'Need some cash—' and ran downstairs.

Jemal's piety had turned political. If he'd been in that fight at Hamscott Common he might have killed somebody. They were looking high and low for him and he was here, in William's house. He had to get rid of him.

Rushing into the downstairs flat he found Jemal still in the hall. He looked pathetically thin and was as bent as a man twice, three times, his age. William thrust the money into Jemal's hand and said, 'Come on, mate – out.'

He walked out of the flat and downstairs to the ground floor with Jemal behind him. In the hall, he went to the front door and put his hand on the latch. The latch shook. The whole front door was shaking as the heavy thuds of something like a battering ram hit it. William leapt back, staring. Almost immediately the whole door fell in and helmeted policeman carrying semi-automatics ran over the fallen door and into the hall.

'Police! Put your hands up!' voices yelled. William did.

A lightning vision hit him, showing Jemal retreating up the stairs, firing at the police, the police firing back and him, William, caught in the cross-fire. But there was no gunfire. A foot tripped him, he fell back across the stairs and was hauled immediately to his feet and handcuffed. Heavy hands searched him for weapons. He heard crashes and shouts from the landing upstairs, men swearing, a cry of pain and then found himself being dragged, half-walking, across the carpet, over the front door and out into the street. Two men threw him into the back of a vehicle, which took off rapidly. He lay on the floor of the van, half-stunned, all the wind knocked out of him.

The whole episode had taken half a minute.

Moments later he realized he was in bad trouble. He lifted his head up towards the gun barrel pointing at him. 'Where are you taking me?'

'You'll find out,' said a man's voice.

'My wife . . .?'

'Never mind about your wife. You won't be seeing her for a bit.'

Ten

106 St George's Square, London SW1. February 25th, 2016. 00:45 a.m.

After the party Gott and a few friends stopped for a nightcap at his flat, and it was only after they left that the ever-diligent Jeremy, who had gone up to his own flat, rang downstairs. 'I've sent you an email you might want to see, boss,' he said. 'Is it too late?'

'Come down,' said Gott, yawning. When Jeremy came in he said, 'Read it out to me. I need to sort out my own laundry. Mrs MacEvoy's had an operation.' It was true, Jeremy thought, that the flat looked dusty and a little neglected. As Gott threw starched shirts, white shirts and striped shirts, making a large pile on the carpet, Jeremy, raising his voice slightly, read:

> Dear Jeremy,
>   I don't know if you will remember me – Debby Carshaw, from Kirkby Rodney. I thought you would want to hear about Alan Petherbridge's father, Robert Wallace.

Edward Gott came to the bedroom door, holding a shirt in his hand. 'Fuck,' he said. His expression was keen and malignant. Jeremy read on doggedly:

> As I told you, I'm in the habit of visiting Mr Wallace at Christmas at Fairlawns, the retirement home where he lived. But does no longer. When I arrived for my usual visit, expecting his usual cordial welcome (!), I found that he was suffering from what he described as a bad cold, although it was obvious to me his condition was far worse than that. When I spoke to a member of staff I was told Mr Wallace had refused to see a doctor. I then saw the manager and said, in no uncertain terms, that she must call a doctor to Mr Wallace. This put her in something of a panic, I think, bearing in mind that Mr Wallace's stepson is the Prime Minister. So, to cut a long story short, not long after my visit Mr Wallace was admitted to hospital with pneumonia.
>   I enquired about him at Fairlawns Retirement Home after the New Year. The manager told me he was back, having

discharged himself from hospital some days earlier, even though the doctor in charge believed he was not yet fit to go. The hospital is probably not to blame, since Mr Wallace was an obstinate old man, as I expect you found out for yourself. Sadly, it was only a matter of weeks until he was back in hospital. The manager of Fairlawns rang to tell me. There was no need for her to do this, as I never had any relationship worth the name with Mr Wallace. I think she was afraid of seeming negligent, bearing in mind Mr Wallace's stepson's eminence.

Mr Wallace died on the 14th. I only discovered this a week later because I was visiting the hospital to see a friend there and thought to ask after him. I feel sorry now I had not taken the trouble to visit him. I'm sure he would have been just as unpleasant to me as he always was during my Christmas visits, but it upset me to discover from the sister in charge (an old pupil of mine, incidentally) that the poor man not only died alone but that there had been not one visitor to see him during his stay in hospital.

Apparently he had not listed anyone as next of kin. When the sister in charge saw the way things were going she rang the manager at Fairlawns and was given an emergency telephone number supplied by Alan Petherbridge's office. She rang that number, a machine answered and she left a message saying that Robert Wallace was seriously ill in hospital. After several days there had been no response and by that time she was fairly sure Mr Wallace would not live. She rang the number again but again no one answered the phone. She left another message. After Mr Wallace's death she left a third message and called 10 Downing Street as well. But there was no one at the funeral but me and the manager of Fairlawns. I attended without much emotion, I have to admit, but it was depressing to find so few mourners. There was a very large wreath of flowers on the coffin which, I imagine, had been sent from London by the Prime Minister. I thought you might want to know all this.

I was pleased to notice the defeat of the Ministry of Defence Lands Sale Bill in my newspaper. I believe Lord Gott was concerned with this, so please pass on my congratulations.

With regards to yourself and a pat to Finn.

Debby Carshaw

Gott dropped the shirt he had been holding on to the pile he had created. 'So the poor old bugger died alone in a Yorkshire hospital,' he said.

'He was a terrible old man,' Jeremy told him.

'He was an old man, and he died alone,' Gott said grimly.

'What are you going to do?' asked Jeremy, anxious in case, after Petherbridge's leak about Gott's daughter, his employer was going to lose his head and take an unwise revenge.

'I'm not going to do anything *now*,' said Gott, 'but it could be useful later.' He stood for a moment, gloating. Then his expression altered and he said, 'Thanks, Jeremy. Get off to bed now. It's late.' As Jeremy left the room he added as an afterthought, 'Find out if he was buried in a pauper's grave.'

Part Two

Eleven

May 2017

That party of Gott's at the end of February started a new and violent cycle in what now looks like the occupation of Britain. It's not called that, of course.

It's called American Assistance. That's why there are American Assistants who sit in at all Cabinet meetings and on all Cabinet committees. There are Intelligence Assistants (the CIA) well-embedded at MI5 and MI6. There are Military Assistants at the MoD, Security Assistants at the Home Office and, of course, Foreign Assistants at the Foreign Office. The 80,000 US soldiers and pilots stationed in Britain are also Assistants. We are a well-assisted nation. The trouble is, it does not feel like assistance at all.

It feels like an occupation. 'A thousand years of freedom gone,' says the opposition, although any history student knows that for much of those thousand years freedom was limited, if not almost non-existent, for vast swathes of the population. But something has gone – and we know it.

I'm sitting in my garden again – under the same budding tree – some leaves are unfurled now – the sun is warm on my back. I've reached the point in my story where I became a participant, instead of a pair of eyes and ears. My involvement with William Frith was the reason.

Immediately after William Frith and Jemal Al Fasi were dragged out of the house in Shepherd's Bush, Lucy, who had heard the crashing in of the door and the sound of men shouting and feet thudding downstairs, headed for the front door of the flat. Her father grabbed her arm as she reached for the latch. He held her back. Joe had been a policeman for thirty-five years. Although he'd served in an area very different from Shepherd's Bush, he still saw events as a policeman will. Initially he'd accepted the arrival of a dirty and gaunt Jemal at the flat as just another undesirable aspect of the Friths' London life. He was chiefly concerned with Marie. But he'd picked up on William's wary reaction to him and went on to full alert when both men retreated so quickly downstairs to the allegedly empty flat. After William dashed in for his wallet Joe knew something was wrong. He was at the window when the street filled with police vans and cars. When he heard the front door crash in he came quickly to a conclusion – Jemal was a fugitive and his son-in-law was helping him.

Holding his daughter's arm he said, 'Let me handle this.'

Lucy obeyed. Joe went downstairs alone. It was only when she looked out and saw two police vans speeding away from the house and squealing round the corner at the end of the street that she wrenched open the door of the flat and ran off downstairs, crying out, 'William! William!' As she ran down she was passed by two men in jeans and anoraks racing up. They barged past her.

In the hall the front door still lay flat on the carpet. The small area was full of men in uniform and out of it. By the gaping entrance to the street Joe was talking to a large man in a tweed coat. Standing five stairs up, Lucy cried out, 'Where's my husband?' and a man below her looked up at her slyly and said, 'We want to ask you about that.'

It was the first time in her life Lucy had ever fainted. The sly man caught her and, coming round after no more than a few seconds, she found herself in her father's arms.

As she looked into his concerned face she heard him murmur, 'Don't say anything, Lucy.'

Joe supported her upstairs, trailed by the large man he'd been talking to. Inside, the sounds of heavy searching could be heard from the bedroom and the kitchen. In the sitting room was Marie, in her nightdress, on her knees by the TV in front of a pile of DVDs heaped on the floor. She looked up brightly when she saw her husband and daughter. 'Here it is!' she said brightly, '*Puss in Boots*! We thought we'd lost it.' And as Joe and Lucy came in, followed by the man in the tweed coat, she said, 'I'll put it on.' Then came a loud noise from the bedroom as the wardrobe was pulled away from the wall. And the sound of music from the set, as brightly coloured images began to flit across the screen.

'I'll need a list of what you're taking,' Joe said to the tweed-coated officer.

'You'll get one within three working days,' said the man, without interest. 'In the meanwhile, we need to ask you some questions.'

'My wife's ill,' said Joe, 'and my daughter's in no fit state to be questioned.'

A small young man, in jeans and wearing gold-rimmed glasses, appeared in the door of the kitchen. He shook his head at the tweed-coated man and returned to the kitchen.

'Where's William?' Lucy demanded. She was ignored. 'None of you have any choice, Mr Sutcliffe,' said the policeman. 'We need to question you and we need to do it now. We have full powers.' From the kitchen came a crash of shattered glass.

'What are your names? What unit do you belong to?' asked Joe.

'You'll have to come with us to Paddington Green,' said the big man.

Marie turned, 'It's too late to go out. We're watching a DVD.'

'We'll look after your wife.'

What followed would have broken a weaker woman than twenty-six-year-old Lucy Frith. She was thirty-six hours in custody, alone in a cell, or under questioning in a very clean, windowless interrogation room. She could not sleep. She spoke to no one but her captors and was racked with anxiety about her husband. She worried, too, about her father, presumably in isolation in another part of the huge police station and her mother, probably alone in a mental hospital.

No one would answer her questions about William. She asked to see her father and a solicitor and got the answer given by officials and parents, 'All in good time.' She answered the same questions over and over, having decided that the truth would benefit William more than silence. The questioning was subtle but not subtle enough to conceal from her the fact that her interrogators thought Jemal had been involved in terrorist activities and that William had been giving him information harvested at Sugden's. It had a frightening plausibility – the theory that William had eavesdropped on the conversations of the politicians and senior civil servants who frequented the restaurant, then passed the information on to Jemal and his group.

And, finally, Lucy and her father were released. As they stood on the steps of the police station with the traffic crawling past them, Lucy was alarmed by her father's appearance. He was unshaven, his shoulders were bent and he was plainly exhausted. They called a taxi and went back to Shepherd's Bush, saying little. Lucy asked if Joe had been told anything about William, and he said he had not. At one point he muttered, 'They have to do their job, I suppose.' Approaching the grim modern fortress of Paddington Green Police Station, she had half expected to be beaten up during the questioning. As they got nearer to home she squeezed her father's hand gently and said, 'I don't think Mum will be there when we get home. She may be in hospital.'

He said, 'I know, love, and I wouldn't get your hopes up about finding William there, either.'

'I'm not, really,' she said, though she had.

When they let themselves into the flat it was empty and still strewn with all their possessions. In the kitchen, every packet and jar had been emptied into the sink. Joe rang the local police and was told his wife was again in the psychiatric wing at St Mary's Hospital. They would not give him any information about William.

For three frantic days Lucy and Joe did all they could to find William – the police would offer them no information except that he was being held under the Prevention of Terrorism Act; their MP could not or would not do anything to help, and the solicitor they employed was discouraging. Lucy said she thought that he, too, was afraid of getting involved on the wrong, the dangerous, side.

Then the Friths arrived in London. A week later, incidentally, the Sutcliffes returned to their Yorkshire village. By now, Marie saw leaving London as a way of getting out of hospital and back into her husband's care. Her ambition for them all to die together seemed to have been relegated to another part of her mind.

Joe was horribly torn. He knew the danger to his wife's precarious mental health if she was dragged into the terrifying business of William's disappearance. But he wanted to stay and help his daughter. This was when Lucy told him frankly that she was too upset herself to deal with Marie's mental health problems and Joe reluctantly agreed to take Marie back to Yorkshire.

The Friths were staying with old friends, former teaching colleagues of Charlie's, in Hammersmith. They embarked on the same futile enquiries Joe and Lucy had made, with the same results. Grace Frith borrowed her hostess's bicycle and rode round the back streets to deliver a letter, addressed to the Al Fasis' friends, at the house where William and Lucy had once rented the flat. They wanted information about Jemal and what trouble he was in and had decided a woman on a bicycle, if spotted, would look less suspicious. The people in the house never got in touch, understandably enough. They didn't know who Grace was. They might have suspected her story was some complicated Special Branch trick, designed to trap them.

Grace rang me. Why me? The answer's simple enough.

On the Mediterranean coast, in the small village of Villalba, my father, Felix Arnold, a retired civil servant, runs a small hotel, seven bedrooms, bar and restaurant. He's been there for twenty years. The Friths live just outside the village. Villalba is an ex-pat colony but ex-pat communities turn in on themselves, read the British papers and denounce the place they came from – which can be trying for an open-minded man like my father, especially in winter when there are no tourists. But the Friths and Dad got along well and this was how I came to meet William, not long after the Friths had moved in and when William was about nineteen. I was a bit of a wreck at that time. I'd been working for fifteen years at the eminent legal firm of Jeffries and Bridges, which specialized in championing people, or their relatives, in cases of official injustice – illegal imprisonments, police corruption, mistrials, deaths in custody. During that short holiday in Spain I suddenly realized exactly how burned out I was. I was thirty-six. I'd brought up my daughter as a single parent, much of that time spent in the legal pressure cooker at J and B. I had no private life. Now I realized I couldn't go on any longer. I went back to London and resigned from J and B and took a job with a firm of solicitors in north-west London.

The next time I met William in Villalba he was married to Lucy and I was a high street solicitor and married to my husband, Sam, a doctor.

But Grace and Charlie knew I'd done fifteen years of investigating unexplained deaths and disappearances, beatings by the Auxiliary Police, constant abuse of power by men and women who had been given it and were under little restraint. It only takes a few.

It's not difficult to get yourself into trouble, something I've often had to point out to clients. It's usually a matter of saying yes instead of no. I said yes when the Friths came to me for help. I knew that at best it would make life hard and at worst, I'd be under surveillance, pressure would be applied to me and, as I told Sam, 'I shouldn't be surprised if I don't have a traffic accident in a tunnel.' It was only half a joke. But I knew William was as likely to get involved in a terrorist plot as fly to the moon. And Lucy and the Friths – Joe, too – were desperate. Like any white, middle-class people, however liberal, deep down inside they'd thought the anti-terrorist legislation would never apply to them, that it was legislation aimed at the Muslim community. Perhaps would be used unjustly. That was wrong and should be put right. But the one thing they did not think was that it would ever affect them. That was what they believed and, like so many after them, they found out they were wrong.

I didn't realize it then, but when I agreed to represent William I joined the opposition, an opposition I didn't know existed. Perhaps it didn't exist then – it just grew, as events progressed. Even Gott, who in a different way accidentally joined the opposition, didn't know what things would come to. But that was in the future.

I started work, initially going to my old firm, Jeffries and Bridges, to see if George Jeffries, who made these decisions, would take on the Frith case. I spoke first to Jacey Smith, with whom I'd worked closely in the past. He told me that George was unlikely to agree to represent the Friths, but he said he'd talk to him and later a meeting was arranged for me with him. George offered what he could. The firm could not officially represent the Friths, but, if I decided to do so, he told me, he had no objection to Jacey's helping me. This was something, though not much, and dependent on the overworked Jacey's goodwill. But Jacey generously offered to give me some of his time.

I asked my own firm to allow me to work a four-day week, with consequent reduction of pay, and they agreed, partly because, as we all know, that arrangement normally means doing five days' work in four. But I also guessed if things turned sour in the Frith case the firm might find me an embarrassment and ask me to go.

I set up a small office in the back bedroom of our house. And started trying to find William. I was rebuffed every time. Under the law, as it stood, no one had the right to know where William was or why he'd been arrested. He had no right to legal representation – that was at the discretion of the police and the Home Office, and they declined to exercise that discretion. Bluntly, we were stymied.

One bright note was struck by Jack Prentiss, about ten days after I'd started work on the case. William's ex-boss, who had heard about the affair through Gott – who else? – rang up to offer me a retainer to represent William. He liked William, of course, though self-interest may have played a part – having a former manager among the 'disappeared' and likely to be charged, eventually, with terrorism wouldn't help him or his business. Nevertheless, the money was a help. So, using Prentiss's money, George Jeffries' facilities and Jacey's expertise – and occasionally, taking the name of Jeffries and Bridges in vain, because it was a name which caused tremors in cases where the authorities were, or thought they might be, in a dubious legal position – I soldiered on.

A second good thing was that I had, for reasons too lengthy to go into, an MI5 officer in my debt. Let's call him X. The day after Jack Prentiss rang I contacted this Mr X. He told me the security people were convinced that Jemal Al Fasi had been among the attackers of Hamscott Common. He had belonged to a small group of Islamic fundamentalists, mostly young British men, who had resolved on direct action because of the terror laws, the increasing use of stop and search and the unexpected raids on offices and houses, because of their expectation that Britain troops would soon be at full strength in Iraq and, perhaps most important of all, because they knew that whatever was available to others in Britain would not, in the current climate, ever be available to them.

X said that formerly, under British law, Jemal would have been charged with an armed raid on a military base and probably murder or attempted murder. Convicted, he would not have seen daylight for at least twenty years. But nowadays, my informant told me during a furtive meeting at the Ritz, Jemal would not get an open trial, and probably not a closed one – three judges pronouncing sentence, no appeals permitted. Because the US was insisting on extradition to America for all those involved. Some of the Hamscott Common captives had already been deported. If caught, Jemal would be handed over to be questioned there and serve time in an American prison, perhaps even face execution. 'Forty- or fifty-year sentences have been given in other cases,' he told me unsentimentally. 'And the questioning's not funny, either. The Yanks don't mess about. And whatever applies to Al Fasi will apply to your bloke, William Frith. They're worried about him because of his job. He could have passed on a lot of sensitive information he picked up at Sugden's.' This was not exactly news to me. 'Your problem is, the more fuss you make, the harder they may come down on your client,' he told me.

The following day I filed suit with the European Courts of Justice on behalf of William Frith, although that put my client in a queue of two thousand similar complainants, after which the European court would hand down a verdict, of which Britain would take no notice. And by that time William might have disappeared irretrievably into the American justice system.

A month went by – we still didn't know where William was, officially, though unofficially I'd learned he was in Belmarsh Prison. But none of us were allowed to contact him in any way.

Then, one day, Lucy rang me from her ward in the hospital. She'd gone back to work because staying at home alone worrying was destroying her and, in any case, she needed the money. She'd been approached that morning at work by a well-dressed man in dark glasses. She recognized William's friend, Jemal's brother, Mohammed. Wisely, he'd come from Morocco on someone else's passport, knowing the name Al Fasi would be flagged up at immigration. He told her he was very sorry about what had happened and asked her to contact me.

I met him in a café round the corner from the hospital. He offered me a lot of money to represent his brother. I refused. I had to tell him there seemed little doubt his brother was guilty – he didn't deny it – and that my client, William, was innocent. I hadn't the time or resources to represent a guilty client. Mo took this well. He told me the whole family had been doubtful about Jemal and his associates for years. Even before they left London there had been arguments in the family about the people he was associating with, threats that he was going to get into trouble and bring trouble to his family. Jemal had countered by calling them cowards and unfaithful Muslims. He told them that unless the faithful joined forces and struck out, they would be crushed. This was why he had stayed behind when the rest of the family went back to Morocco. And now, Mohammed told me, his parents and brothers were blaming him, Mohammed, for orchestrating the move, saying that if they'd stayed behind they might have restrained Jemal, or at least have been there.

All I could do was give him the names of other solicitors likely to be sympathetic and advise him to leave Britain as fast as he could. He was in danger. I also knew my own client's interests could be badly affected by being linked with Jemal.

I was being watched now. A sequence of cars parked outside my house at erratic hours during the day and night, cars which were never interfered with by police and traffic wardens, and from which men and women blatantly photographed the comings and goings to my house. Only a few days after my meeting with Mohammed the house at the back of my own was sold and I heard from neighbours that a group of youngish men and women, too old and well-dressed to be students, had begun to live there. They came and went at varying hours. They had moved in with little furniture. The postman had said they received no post. It seemed fairly obvious that the security services were keeping my house under surveillance from the back. I assumed my phones were tapped and my correspondence and emails read. I don't know what they think I know, or am about to go and do. It may be my connection with Edward Gott that concerns them.

I was contacted by John Stafford, recovering after a liver transplant. He was still worried about the British soldiers, Bob Carter in particular, who were in custody. Like everyone else he saw their eventual fate as extradition to the US to face the American legal system. I had to turn him down because, as with Mohammed Al Fasi, I felt I could not have my innocent client associated with men who had obviously been involved in the seizing of Hamscott Common.

By now I was in touch with the Muslim Council of Britain, all the civil liberties groups, EU lawyers and a cluster of MPs of all parties who were opposed to the summary nature of the wave of arrests. My workload was heavy. And I was even worried about the effect on our marriage. Sam was a childless widower, my only daughter Chloe was married and a mother herself, so we had busy lives, but we were able to live quietly and contentedly, in a unit of two. Now I was always tired, there was an office in our house, the phone never stopped ringing and Special Branch was taking photos of the laundry on the washing line. But Sam was staunch and, in any case, by summer, when people were getting hungry, tired and ill because of the hardships, he was working under pressure himself. We were both in harness and pulling heavy loads.

To be frank, some parts of this disaster were of benefit to me. A few months into the Frith case, and I knew the pressures were beginning to affect my bread-and-butter work at Jellicoe and Ogunbaye. A few months more, and just as I was thinking I might have to resign before they fired me, routine work at the firm was drying up. By this time fuel, food, jobs and money were all in short supply. Conveyancing was down and people for some reason were less keen to divorce. The bread-and-butter work was in decline. But then the terror really kicked in with a rise in summary arrests, raids, disappearances, deportations and police brutality (the dreaded Auxiliaries were frequently responsible). These measures began to affect our ordinary clients – in other words, people were generally staying in the same houses and flats and not falling out with their marriage partners, but random arrests and forced entries into houses began to affect them, the ordinary clients whose houses we had conveyed, whose wills we had drawn up, whose children we had represented on shoplifting charges. Slowly, in our neck of the woods at any rate, families who had been living in the country for two and three generations were being caught in the huge net being spread by the government. Our clients – shopkeepers, local businessmen, plumbers, electricians, employees of the local council, of banks and building societies – were coming to us with tales of summary arrests and disappearances, of doors being kicked in and searches made. Our clients now needed representation by someone with my kind of experience. This saved my job at Jellicoe and Ogunbaye.

It was in August, six months after I'd begun to make a noise about William Frith's detention – and up to that point noise was all it had been, that I got a call from the Home Office at six in the evening and was curtly informed that William would be released from a London jail the following morning. When I asked if the charges had been dropped, the woman at the other end of the line was, she said, unable to tell me. The call was a courtesy, so that I or my client's friends would be able to meet him outside the prison when he was released. I thought it wiser not to question this. William had been arbitrarily taken and was being arbitrarily released – better to get hold of him first and ask questions later. But to date none of the questions about William's legal situation have been answered and I doubt if they ever will be. But we got him back and in the circumstances that was all that mattered. The Home Office woman said that if William had anywhere outside the country to go to, it might be a good idea for him to leave. They would have known about the Friths' home in Spain.

The situation was hard to decode. There must have been massive pressure from the State Department to give them suspects in the Hamscott Common raid. They saw us as a back door for terrorists to infiltrate the States. They had to kick ass. I had expected no mercy for William Frith. Yet now they were releasing him.

On the other side, though, there must have been a different story. William's job made him a suspect at first, but in the end, I think, could have protected him. William had been the manager at Sugden's. William had been in a position to eavesdrop on important private conversations held by people at the heart of government. If William stayed in custody or, even worse, was charged with harbouring or assisting an extremist who had been part of a force which took over an air force base, what would British security look like to the Americans?

It's possible that without the barrage we kept up it might have been easy for the authorities to put William's name down on the extradition papers and get rid of him quietly. But I think at some point strings started being pulled. It helped that by then those concerned must have known

William wasn't involved in anything. William Frith had never even bothered to vote in an election. At all events, he was released.

I remember him coming through the prison gates at eight on an August morning, staggering, throwing his arm up over his eyes and falling over. It could have been comic, though it wasn't. It was the opposite. Luckily, Lucy, who had been getting out of the car, quickly saw what was the matter. It was a sunny day and William hadn't seen natural light since he'd been incarcerated. It had blinded him. She ran to him, pulled him up, dragged off his coat and threw it over his head. Then she and his parents stood round him in a little protective circle, talking quietly to him while under the coat. Grace Frith told me later that William began to weep, almost as if in shame. We took him straight to my husband's surgery, which was when he was weighed and found to be seven stone – he had lost just over a third of his normal body weight in custody. And it wasn't only what had happened to his body – it was what had happened to his mind. He spent a fortnight lying in a darkened room, not speaking. William's mother said that she thought they might never get him back, not in any real sense. It seemed important to act on the tip from the Home Office and a week later the Friths and Lucy got him on a plane. They all went to Spain.

Lucy is running a beach bar. William has been helping her more and more. One day they may become part-proprietors of an expanded Hotel Rimbaud – my father's an incorrigible romantic – but it won't be soon.

Jemal and the other fourteen men captured after Hamscott Common have disappeared into the American justice system without trace. They were extradited to the USA. Lawyers, friends and relatives still do not know where they are. John Stafford and many others are still fighting for them, but the US authorities are obdurate. The European courts have declared all the processes illegal. Gott told me that when the judgement was announced the Home Secretary said, 'Who gives a stuff?' The issue is before the Supreme Court now but no one is hopeful about the outcome. Those men will sit and rot for a long time, maybe for ever. The thought is sickening, humiliating – how, why, have we ceded rights to our own detainees? – but it's still at a distance. You don't see the figures huddled in cells in Texas and Louisiana. I only saw William, coming like a skeleton out into the daylight after six months in Belmarsh. I don't think I'll ever forget it.

And while I was concentrating on the fate of just one man, in the wider world events were going into free fall. As I was talking to the police, the judiciary and the European courts about William, and as the security services were setting up their arrangements to track me wherever I went and whatever I did, Edward Gott and his allies were putting together the case for taking the seven air force bases into British hands. Petherbridge had not resigned after the defeat of the Ministry of Defence Lands Sale Bill. Of course, he's still Prime Minister, now known sneeringly as the Senator for England. Ultimately, the plan which Gott, Joshua Crane and others started in March – to take back the British bases, including the nuclear submarine base – collapsed in July, because Petherbridge and his allies had out-thought the opposition.

After the defeat of his bill – with hindsight, his US paymasters' way of making sure he could deliver and secondly, knew who was boss – Petherbridge had to go into overdrive. He'd lost the confidence of his backers; he had to get the next bit of the programme right. We didn't know – almost no one did – that from November 2015, immediately after the election of the Conservative government under Petherbridge, and before Gott's opposition to the MoD Lands Sale Bill was much more than a twinkle in his eye, land was being slowly bought up by the government and various complicit companies. Many thought the plan had been hatched at Camp David in August, when Petherbridge made his secret visit there. With the defeat of the bill, this land acquisition accelerated.

Look round your own neighbourhood and you'll be surprised by how much property is in state or council hands, from an old closed school here and some playing fields there to the old wing of a hospital under reconstruction. On a larger scale there is Ministry of Defence land. There are factories which owed their survival to government contracts, which can be, and were, sold up when the contracts were cancelled. The property, land and equipment then fell, one way or another, into government hands. Often, the mere threat of lost contracts was enough to persuade the management to sell. Then there were the private sales of land in key parts of the country to various purchasers. It was carefully done. Sometimes the land would be taken by a government department or a local council for a proposed development, sometimes bought by a holding company based offshore, its ownership untraceable. All this was handled discreetly over six months by a small and diligent unit working from Downing Street. By spring 2016, just after the MoD Lands Sale Bill was overturned, four thousand square miles of land in city and countryside was directly in the hands of the government or its corporate agents. It was done quietly and quickly. The only warnings came from the Internet and were ignored as the ravings of conspiracy theorists and nutters.

Just as this was beginning, in dead earnest and at speed, over ten days in March the London Underground and Canary Wharf were bombed, and buses and public buildings in Manchester and Glasgow were attacked. The Scottish Parliament building was damaged in a massive bombing campaign. Over 100 people were killed and 200 injured, 150 seriously.

During the week after the bombings my husband's surgery bulged with people who just couldn't cope – couldn't sleep, couldn't get to work, couldn't get out of bed, couldn't look after their children.

For Petherbridge and his Washington allies – masters – this bombing campaign could not have come at a better time. The usual nutters and conspiracy theorists say Petherbridge and America were responsible. They planned it and carried it out themselves. I find that hard to believe. For an ordinary person from what's called a 'stable democracy' this idea is too awful to accept.

Two days after the bombings, in an atmosphere of shock, grief and fear of further attacks, the Prime Minister announced to the House of Commons that the US had offered aid to Britain and that there had been a Cabinet decision to accept the help of American Assistants. One of the results was a flood of intelligence agents from the US, the other, more visible one was the arrival of 3,000 US Marines and the setting up of camps on secretly purchased or commandeered land. There were large bases on the South Downs, outside Cambridge and Glasgow and in the Kings Cross area of London. Planning permission for the new barrage in the Thames Estuary had been pushed through by the Independent Planning Authority, which had been packed for years by whatever government was in power at the time. The contract had gone to a friend of the President of the USA. And as the barrage was built, a long overdue development many thought, a base and military airfield were being built on the drained land nearby.

There were challenges to all this on many fronts, but in British law there were no recent precedents, except in time of war. It was simply outside the rules. And it happened fast, while many people were so shocked by the attacks that the measures seemed nothing but a way of avoiding more deaths.

At the same time, heavy fortification of the airbases began. The defeat of the bill had changed nothing. Petherbridge said that at a time of acute national crisis the rule book had to be temporarily abandoned. The bases remained, as they always had been, jointly controlled, under a less-than-opaque system, by the RAF and USAF. Huge modern castles dominating the skylines were created, patrolled by heavily armed men and swept over, night and day, by helicopters.

And so, by August 2016 – just as William Frith was released – there were ten thousand American troops in Great Britain. The principal US Army bases were in Glasgow, Cardiff, Edinburgh, Sheffield, Birmingham and London. The inhabitants of the cities grew accustomed to the sight of US military vehicles and armed US servicemen in their streets. The servicemen were quiet and polite. They assisted good causes in their spare time. Children and teenagers were excited by the presence of these heroes. Others were less happy, especially as by this stage the US Assistants had begun to arrive and occupy the corridors of power in Whitehall and at Westminster. Gott, like many others, had to recognize that between them the British government and the Pentagon had changed the rules of the game. Gott and others had parliament and the law, but no constitution to which to appeal. And the Americans had the guns. And they were here. Here to 'assist'.

In retrospect, it seems obvious that something like this must and would happen. What else did we expect? The US administration had always suspected Britain of laxity in rooting out its terrorists and clinging to outmoded concepts governing the collection of evidence, the amount of time to be spent in custody before being charged, and the trials themselves. A lot of these rights had been modified or even cancelled by riders added to existing legislation but even those changes were being appealed. Britain, it must have seemed from across the Atlantic, was suffering from libertarianism-as-disease, giving free reign to nests of terrorists ready to take planes across the Atlantic to continue their attacks on American soil. The British parliament had given the US military a bloody nose over the sale of the bases. Encouraged by this, a movement was growing to take them back altogether. There were huge crowds at Holy Loch shouting exactly that. Was the USA prepared to tolerate being deprived of the bases it considered necessary for control of Europe and the Middle East (not to mention Russia)? Accept a huge strategic reverse, an insult, a threat? And a big encouragement to any other nation with US bases to do the same (they had already lost their five bases in Iraq, when the new government took over)? And so the Military Assistants arrived, to be followed by many other kinds of Assistant. How stupid we were, even the clever ones. It had been planned in advance, but we hadn't suspected a thing.

And we didn't know, then, that in April Humphrey Starke, Petherbridge's Chancellor of the Exchequer, made a secret visit to Washington. He went to discuss the prospect of Britain joining the North Atlantic Trade Agreement, initially a consortium of nations with which the US shared borders – Mexico and Canada – and then, later, under the Latin American Plan, including several countries in Latin America. The trade alliance was controlled, of course, by the country with the most economic clout, the United States.

The news of the Chancellor's visit to Washington finally leaked, in Berlin, a month later. The EU Finance Ministers had been anticipating something like this. For how long no one could guess. Certainly by February, when Gott had dined at the French Embassy, the British Foreign Office already knew, or guessed, something of the sort. The Council of Finance Ministers demanded an assurance that Britain was not planning to break all its treaties with the EU and join something which did not yet exist, but could rapidly be created – a Transatlantic Free Trade Area. They said that if Britain joined a free trade area with the US, it was probable the country would have to leave the EU. The Foreign Office had always taken the line that the nations of Europe would never abandon their trade with a nation of sixty million people. Whether they fully believed this or not, it was what they told the Prime Minister, who wanted to believe it and wanted the public to believe it. The government and the Bank of England promptly denied there was any plan for a trade alliance between Britain and the other countries of the Transatlantic Trade Agreement.

A further leak claimed that the Chancellor had held discussions with officials at the Federal Reserve and a consortium of US bankers. It was plain the matter had been under discussion for months. Perhaps since Petherbridge's bought government had been elected. Or even before, when he met the President to discuss the forthcoming British election and its funding from US sources. These strategies are like Jaws, barely rippling the water but getting closer and closer until suddenly – there he is with all his teeth pointing at you.

The EU struck with astonishing speed. They dragged up a maritime report produced in 2010, a report no one had paid attention to at the time, probably because it was against everyone's interests. The report said that the English Channel and North Sea between Britain and Holland were the most congested waterways in the world, and were now so overcrowded as to constitute a grave danger to shipping. There was particular concern about the oil tankers coming from Rotterdam and the likelihood of serious collisions and consequent ecological disaster. In June the EU imposed a shipping ban on traffic between Britain and the Continent. This meant the end of a quarter of the trade between Britain and Europe. Medicines and medical supplies were unaffected. Fruit and vegetables were allowed in, no doubt as a sop to French, Italian and Spanish farmers. But there were shortages, the worst and most immediate being oil. The US tried to compensate but the cost of the oil tankered from the States was prohibitive and the quantities insufficient.

Their worst nightmare was that Britain, still half in the EU because of previous binding agreements and also tied in with the US, would become a conduit into Europe for cheap goods. And then – the most frightening part of the nightmare – Britain would agree to link sterling with the dollar, creating a hybrid dollar/pound to compete with the euro, already under attack, in the fight with the Chinese yuan.

The sanctions were just a way of telling Britain to back off, stop flirting with the Yanks, and come home to where it belonged.

There came the drip, drip, drip of planted, pro-American, anti-Europe publicity. The 'special relationship', the need to have the military protection of America, the urgency of parting with Europe, bloodsucking, tax-consuming, unaccountable Europe with its petty rules and regulations. For public consumption the Downing Street publicity machine tried to produce an image of Bryan de Crespigny, the French Foreign Minister and his puppet, the EU Minister, Henri Laforge, egging on the EU to spite Britain, for whom the French, since Napoleon, had a long-standing hatred. They went back to the days of the Second World War when the continent of Europe had been under German control and Britain had stood alone under its great wartime leader. But, as the great wartime leader once said, you can't lie to all of the people all of the time. People no longer believed what they were told – anything they were told.

And then, in August 2016, the deed was done. The Transatlantic Trade Agreement was created. Britain joined the existing consortium. The Stock Exchange plunged. It was August – the parliamentarians were on holiday. There were demands, of course, for the recall of Parliament. The Chancellor, the Prime Minister, and, later, the Chairman of the Bank of England, described the treaty as a normal trade treaty made between trading nations; there was no requirement to recall Parliament and, therefore, Parliament was not recalled.

If the EU had acted quickly in June, now it moved faster. It doubled the sanctions. The chicken-and-egg argument goes on to this day. Apologists for the government say the earlier sanctions forced Britain into the Transatlantic Trade Agreement – defence against the arrogant and overbearing states of Europe. The opposition claims the EU is protecting itself against a sinister US–UK alliance. Each side, in other words, maintains it's acted only to defend itself against the other. Who will ever know the truth? Is there one big truth behind this whole sorry affair? Gott claims there is – that this had been planned in outline between Alan Petherbridge and the President of the USA in August 2015, and thereafter he and his advisors used every move, whether made by terrorist bombers or the EU, to take Britain in the direction agreed during that summer of 2015 at Camp David.

Meanwhile, whatever the reasons, we began to suffer. Shortages became dearth. After August, petrol rationing was imposed. Manufacturing jobs went. Shops closed. Tourism collapsed. Fuel cards were issued and slowly, as stocks depleted, electricity was also rationed. The price of everything shot up. Price rises and unemployment meant that people who would previously have thought it inconceivable were standing in Salvation Army queues for meals. Another card was issued, allowing people to buy staple foods at low prices. The very old said it reminded them of the war. My husband said people with roots in poorer countries on the whole fared better, because the experience of producing nutritious food from practically nothing was closer.

Capital haemorrhaged from the country, meaning more lost jobs. A once-prosperous country was living now with unemployment, shortages, lack of money, fuel rationing and electricity cuts. Many with roots abroad left for their countries of origin, or of their parents' or grandparents' origins. The population emigrated if they could. Half a million had gone or applied to go to Canada, New Zealand and Australia. The US made special arrangements for skilled British people to go to the States.

Because of the benefits of the Transatlantic Trade Agreement, and with an educated and docile workforce, the US began to buy in heavily to British firms, or even take them over completely. Gott's firm Citycars was targeted, but he wouldn't budge. Gott had predicted that if the American consortium bidding for Citycars had got hold of it, they would have moved the R and D staff they wanted to the States, then shut down the plant and relocated it in a country with cheaper labour costs.

Europeans were sorry for ordinary people in Britain. That September, Sam and I were staying with my father in Spain, while the Friths, just along the coast, tried to put William together again. 'You 'ave been sold,' said someone, a Spaniard next to me at the bar. He was instantly contradicted by one of the expats, whose income had soared because of the level of business – buying, selling and takeovers – on the Stock Exchange. 'Best thing possible,' said this unrepentant exile in a European country. 'Free trade – fellowship of the English-speaking world – get rid of all the rules and regulations.' I knew it was a rummage sale and once it was over the ex-pat's yield would drop but I wasn't about to start a row in a hotel my father ran. I just said to the Spaniard that I thought the EU would kick us out. 'Damn good thing, too,' said the expat.

In September the European Parliament met, voted and declared that the price of restoring normal trade relations with Britain was for Britain to get out of the treaty with the US and subscribe, heavily, to the European Dream. Half of Britain's armed services must be put under European control in the new European Defence Force. And Britain must join the euro. Petherbridge defied them. The two World Wars were invoked as usual. 'We stood alone then,' Petherbridge declared, 'and we will do so again. We will never surrender.'

A lot of dollars were pumped into the system. Bought-up firms expanded and in blighted areas new branches of US firms – car factories, food processors, small engineering works – opened up. The British government was funding big new projects – the contracts and ownership went to US firms but the jobs to the Brits.

The Thames Gateway project, a new city planned to run east from London to the coast, much revised, cancelled, downsized, upsized, planned again and restarted, would now be built, once the Thames Estuary barrage was constructed. They would build 300,000 houses and bring in 40,000 jobs. New giant National Health clinics and mega-hospitals would bring more work. Shallow, localized, instant prosperity, which wouldn't last, Gott predicted. Taxpayers' money being sucked into US firms. But Gott was a wealthy man. He could afford to take the long view.

The grass roots of the Labour Party saw the new jobs – even the detested airbases were a source of employment – but still voted Carl Chatterton out in September and installed the anti-American Mark Moreno. He began a vigorous assault on the government. He questioned the legality of the new US bases. He challenged the sell-up of British firms. He was launching a bill proposing that Britain should comply with the EU's demands. He even went to Edward Gott and proposed that if Gott would supply details about the sources of the funding for the last election, he would impeach Alan Petherbridge, the Prime Minister. Gott told him he would collaborate on this, but not now. It was, he said, too soon. 'Soon,' Moreno exploded. 'If anything, it's too late. When do you think *soon* will be over. How long? What more do you need, Gott?'

That winter was very hard. Public finances were so depleted that state benefits had to be cut by one third. Domestic use of electricity was rationed to keep factories, offices and hospitals open. No aspect of everyday life was unaffected. You have to imagine households where one partner is unemployed, that have electricity only four hours a day, so that laundry, bathing and cooking have to be squeezed into that time, that have only basic foodstuffs and where all forms of entertainment relying on electricity have gone by 8 p.m. Cars could only be used when absolutely essential.

People were bemused at first as they struggled to cope with life starved of electricity, petrol and, very often, money. They had no real feelings about joining a US-headed trade agreement any more than they had ever been enthusiastic about joining Europe. But forced to choose, this time they picked Europe. The siege had demonstrated the extent to which Britain and the Continent of Europe were now interdependent. And it certainly looked like the quickest way to get their old lives back – paint the house, drive the children to school, find a job, warm up the house.

Public order was hard to maintain. Strong measures were taken – there were the stop-and-searches involving police violence (the Auxiliaries became more out of control.) There were summary arrests, and unaccountable disappearances.

The Scots and Welsh demanded in their Parliaments that Britain should get out of the Transatlantic Trade Agreement and start negotiations with the EU. There was an attack on the base at Holy Loch and it was defended, with the help of a police force committed to public order. A man was shot. There was no apology. The US base on the East Kilbride estate outside Glasgow was stormed by young men – another was killed. Again, there was no apology. There were attacks on US servicemen and US personnel were obliged to stay on their bases, or at least go out in large groups. It was plain that Petherbridge had lost any control over his masters, if he had ever had any – if he had ever expected to have any.

But he intended to keep control over his own country and put in force the Civil Contingencies Act of 2004, which gave the government almost dictatorial powers. By autumn, Petherbridge was certainly the most unpopular man in the country. The public ached to topple him – but the only way of doing so, short of revolution, would come with the next general election, three years away.

Twelve

That summer, Gott was very depressed. He'd been outmanoeuvred by Petherbridge. The land for military camps had been secretly bought, there was a huge US military presence in the country, and the bases he'd risked so much to keep out of US hands were now, effectively, American fortresses. He abandoned altogether any effort to put together an alliance to get the matter of continued US control of the airbases discussed in Parliament. It was too late, he said; it was a *fait accompli*; possession was nine tenths of the law; he had lost; Petherbridge and Washington had won. He took it all as a personal failure, assuming too much blame for not preventing moves which had been well planned by many powerful men and women. When Julia Baskerville tried to tell him this, he said, 'If I go back to all that, then I, or Joshua Crane, or somebody else is going to have a nasty accident.'

He said, 'The Emperor Diocletian abdicated and went back to where he had been born, a slave, to farm. Several years later his co-Emperor asked him to return and resume power. He'd retired to the country and he replied, "If you could see my cabbages, you would not ask me that." I'm with Diocletian.'

In actual fact, Gott grew no cabbages. He was just depressed. Although he'd never been a drinker, he drank more, worked less and often spent all day at his flat in pyjamas. After some months of this, Jeremy was worried enough to ring Lady Margot, who produced a sensible doctor and all Gott's sons. Whether it was the doctor or the concerted attack on him by his children, Gott had to yield and, sulking, get back to work. We thought the constant visits from his son Robin's wife and her children, who had never been checked or reproved in any way, had done the trick. The message was, pull yourself together or Celia, with little Harry and Martha, will come round every week and tear the flat to pieces.

By September Gott was more or less back on his feet again. In fact, he had no financial reasons for gloom. His nightmare was becoming real but he had taken precautions months earlier to protect himself. However, being right is no pleasure when what you're right about is something so terribly wrong.

With work on the new Thames Estuary barrage only just begun, the Thames flooded in September, putting 250 metres of central London beside it under water. Sewers broke, power lines became useless. The City of London was plunged into darkness for three days and the Stock

Exchange had to close. The flooding of the fifty square miles was a disaster.

Parliament itself was under a metre of water on the ground floor. Sewage pipes had burst, the floor of the House was full of stinking water in which unmentionable things floated. Nicely symbolic, said Joshua Crane, who had been nominated by Petherbridge to be part of the inspection team, though you didn't appreciate the symbolism when you were standing in your wellingtons in cold, dirty water in which turds and used condoms floated – and saw, over by the Speaker's Chair, the swirl of water which had to be the wake of a swimming rat.

The Houses of Commons and Lords had to meet somewhere else. There was no chance the great and good would go north, to York, for example. They relocated to the New Crystal Palace in South London. Each morning, a convoy of private cars, official vehicles, police vehicles and outriders swept through the drab streets of South London and up to the new Xanadu at Crystal Palace, watched apathetically by people on the pavements.

It was outside Lambeth Public Library that, Joshua Crane said, he saw the start of the Point and Laugh Campaign. He saw, he claims, a small child in his mother's arms, watching the convoy. The child pointed and laughed at the spectacle. The mother, mimicking the child, pointed and laughed as well. Beside her, a man copied her and the child, though perhaps less innocently. And soon a crowd of about twenty citizens, all standing watching their legislators sweeping through their streets, began pointing and laughing. Joshua was in a car with his friend Douglas Clare, a man from the Ministry of Education due to appear at a Select Committee and Tobias Kerr, right hand man to one of Alan Petherbridge's right hand men. The need to get to Crystal Palace sometimes made for strange travelling companions. He said Kerr was disconcerted by the pointing and laughing. So were many others in the convoy, which probably explains why pointing and laughing caught on – pointing and laughing at US patrols, pointing and laughing at the Mayor and at the man coming down the street to bang on doors and check the IDs of the people in each house. The public was ground down, civil liberties a joke, but you can't arrest someone for pointing and laughing. Petherbridge put together a secret committee of lawyers to see if legislation could be introduced to do exactly that, but word got out that he was trying to make laws to stop people from pointing and laughing – so people laughed their unamused laughs even more.

At this stage Petherbridge was probably hated more by his own party than by the Opposition, the other parties in the House or the country at large. The Conservatives knew he had bought their own successful election. Gott was still refusing to provide the damning evidence but, as the facts mounted up – B53s flying missions at random over cities, troops in the streets, the ever-present American at House committee meetings, the Watchers in the public gallery of the House of Commons – Gott's testimony was hardly necessary. The party was ashamed. Naturally, it had its pro-Americans, too. There are always those who make a profit in hard times. There are always those who will support the strongest side of the argument because they are afraid to do otherwise.

If conditions were hard, the system was awash with money for those who knew how to grab it. 'Bribes have been taken and jobs handed out,' said Gott to Joshua. He mentioned many names – this MP on the board of an oil company, that MP sucking up contracts in the Lebanon, a third who had just been offered a lucrative directorship of an American-owned company. 'A lot of noses in the trough,' he said. 'Then there are the threats – exposure of that schoolboy affair with another boy, now a High Court judge; old Wigston is effectively a bigamist, after a ceremony on a beach in Thailand; Hamish Smith is on the verge of bankruptcy. And Franks can't protest because the US base in his constituency is the only source of jobs and businesses there. Even the MPs who aren't on the take and can't be threatened are doubtful – they've looked into the future and believe it's American, whether they like it or not. They have to ask themselves whether maybe America is the bulwark against chaos and terrorism.

'So,' said Gott, 'Petherbridge is the *capo de capi* of the Tory Party now. Sinister. It's only a matter of time before the mysterious deaths begin. Don't look so sceptical, Joshua. Wait and see. Of course, the party won't be supine for ever. There'll be a leadership contest soon.'

In November a leadership campaign was mounted. Joshua Crane was urged to stand, and agreed to do so although Lord Gott advised him against it. He added up the numbers for Joshua, who refused to be persuaded.

In the end the respected Edmund Thorsen, who had lost the leadership campaign to Frederick Muldoon in 2012, decided to stand. It was obvious that he was the stronger candidate and that Joshua's candidacy would only split the anti-Petherbridge vote. Joshua, disappointed, withdrew. 'Best day's work you ever did,' Gott told him unsympathetically. 'And in any case, what do you think Petherbridge would make of your present domestic arrangements? He'd crucify you before the vote.' Joshua believed no one knew – how could they? He blustered. Gott cut him down. 'We're all under surveillance twenty-four hours a day. Our phones are tapped and our mail is read. Don't be stupid, Joshua.'

'You may be prepared to sit down under this!' Joshua had exclaimed. 'I'm not.' Thorsen was defeated by a narrow margin. The hardship went on.

Joshua had a secret. His secret was Julia – Julia's secret was Joshua.

Agreed, party barriers matter less in these times – the occupation has set the agenda, making alliances between former enemies, enemies of former friends. Nevertheless, there are still protocols; you may vote with MPs from other parties but it's doubtful if it's all right to sleep with them.

The semi-detached marriage between Julia and her surgeon husband in Houston had collapsed, just as Mr Zulfeikar Zulani, butcher of East London, had predicted to his own wife at home. Julia's sister and her husband had taken their children away for a holiday in Florida in the New Year of 2016. They decided to change their flight to look in on Julia's husband, Nathaniel, on their way home. They all had a pleasant dinner together, parted and all would have been well if the Desmond family's flight had not been delayed. Or if they had stayed overnight at the hotel provided, instead of electing to spend the night at Nat's so that the children could see a little more of their uncle. Once there, signs of a hasty, not-quite-efficient-enough clear-up manifested themselves. In the middle of the night Julia's sister awoke, nudged her husband awake and asked, 'Do you think Nat's having an affair?' Her husband said, 'Yes. Go back to sleep.' Julia's sister had found a tube of make-up at the back of a bathroom cupboard. Her husband had looked into the eyes of a man with something to hide. Both concluded that Julia's husband had another woman.

They jointly agreed not to tell Julia. In February, shortly before the vote on the Ministry of Defence's Lands Sale Bill, Julia's sister broke the pact and told her. At first, Julia angrily derided any suggestion that her husband was unfaithful to her. Then, over successive nights, she pieced together the evidence collected over what had seemed to her to have been a very happy Christmas – the hang-ups on the phone, the lost scrunchy in a corner explained as belonging to the short-haired cleaning woman, the occasional faraway look in Nat's eyes. And then events took place as they so often do. Many sleepless night later, she asked her husband over the phone if he was seeing another woman. He said he was not. In June, he rang and asked for a divorce.

This was on the same day that the EU had announced its early sanctions, also the day *Westminster Unplugged* was due to go out live on air. Because of the political crisis, the producer of the show had called an emergency meeting with the director, the presenter and the popular political duo, Joshua and Julia, at his house in Notting Hill. Julia arrived in dark glasses, which she did not take off during the meeting. She did her best to contribute, but everybody there could see something was wrong. Afterwards, Joshua grabbed her and made her come round the corner with him to a pub. No stranger to messy affairs of the heart and being in agreement with Zulfeikar Zulani, though he didn't know it, about the prospects of the survival of a marriage between a young and good-looking doctor and a young and good-looking MP, over five thousand miles apart, he spared her by simply pushing a brandy into her hand and telling her what the problem was. 'He's leaving you,' he stated. And Julia nodded.

It's only fair to say that at this point Joshua was not on the make. He was disinterestedly fond of Julia. He gallantly hauled Julia through the evening's show. Viewer complaints came in later, protesting about how he'd hogged the time and the camera. However, as time went on, Joshua being Joshua, things changed. He began to woo Julia, who rejected him at first, but then Christmas approached, with its silent shout about love, friendship and family. Julia was facing the holiday in the middle of a divorce, with a bewildered child and no husband. Joshua was looking at the ordeal of ten days in Yorkshire with a wife who didn't like him, and showed no sign of returning to live with him in the near future. He would be with children he seldom saw and who were gradually becoming strangers to him. There was every chance that on his arrival he would be faced with the retired, widowed lecturer who had been courting his wife, who might by now have caught her and who would doubtless be in for mulled wine and mince pies on Christmas Eve wearing his old-friend-of-the-family face.

That evening at Julia's house, Joshua had heard Millie on the stairs going up to bed, ask her mother, 'Will we ever see Daddy again?' Having put her daughter to bed, which took a long time, Julia came red-eyed down the stairs and offered Joshua a meal of rice and mushrooms, which was all there was. Then Julia and Joshua had looked at each other and fallen into each other's empty arms.

At least they're happy, and these days it's wise to take happiness where you find it. There's not so much of it about, after all, and the worry that if it's here now, it may be gone tomorrow.

Thirteen

Only last week I went to a dinner party – at Sugden's, of course. It was Edward Gott's 56th birthday, and where else would he celebrate? Joshua and Julia were guests and the ever-present Jeremy and old friends of Gott's, Joe Macready and Thomas Wickham and his wife, Annette. Then there were four of Gott's sons and two of their wives – and me, of course, and my daughter, Chloe. Fifteen of us in all, a vast number of guests in such times – a banquet. Lady Gott was not present but was busy organizing a party for Gott in Scotland. Of course, if Lady Gott had been present I would not have been, and nor would my daughter. It will be plain by now that Chloe is my daughter and Edward Gott's. It's hardly a secret since Petherbridge leaked the story to his favourite tabloid over a year ago.

It's not an unusual story. Almost thirty years ago I was a student at Oxford reading archaeology, when I met Edward Gott. We fell in love, I conceived and Gott – who was graduating just as I found out I was pregnant – ran away. He actually put his pen down in the examination hall having finished his last exam paper and disappeared without a word to the USA, where he had a postgraduate course at Yale lined up.

I'd had irregular periods before exams, which was why I had not realized sooner that I was pregnant – but there was still just time for an abortion. Having a baby at the start of your second year at university is not to be recommended. I didn't go home at the start of the summer vacation but hid in London with a friend, working as a waitress and trying to decide what to do. After several late-night discussions I'd finally made an appointment at a clinic to discuss a late termination and it was the following morning that Edward's mother, Elspeth Gott, tracked me down in the scruffy London flat I was sharing.

Gott (as I suppose I will go on calling him in this narrative) had evaporated to the USA without even going back to Scotland to say hello to his parents. Elspeth knew there was something wrong, called him and badgered the truth out of him. She gave him hell, got on a train immediately, went to my parents and got my address from them without telling them what was going on.

She turned up at the flat without warning and told me, 'It's late but not too late for an abortion. But if you want to have the child, we'll help. But you'd better find another course to follow. Edward can't help you financially and nor, alas, can we. So if you plan to rear a child alone, you'd

better get a degree in something that will help you earn a living.' Bang
went the dream of digging the ruins of Babylon (not too much of them
left now in everyday Baghdad, I suppose) but Elspeth somehow managed
to give me back my cocky sense of being able to do anything I put my
mind to. I got myself on to a law course. Elspeth and Jack Gott and my
parents helped with my daughter, Chloe, and gradually, over time, Gott
and I came together as friends – and parents of course. Gott paid what
he could – very little as he established his career and then more as he was
able to do so. But it was doughty Elspeth and her no-less doughty husband
who played the biggest part in pulling us, Chloe and me, through.

Gott can be very stupid for such a clever man, but then, cleverness
of that kind doesn't guarantee being sensible. So, of course, he never
found the right time to tell his wife. His six sons and their four wives
agreed to keep his secret and, miraculously, did so. But I'm not surprised
he thinks Elspeth told his wife early on about me and Chloe. That would
have been typical of Elspeth Gott. All his 'secret' did was give Petherbridge
leverage over him, with his threats to leak the story to the papers; it also
marked the moment when Gott began to hate him.

So I, and Chloe of course, went to the party to celebrate his birthday.
The restaurant was more than half full. I spotted a party of MPs and a famous
society girl with an American general. There was a TV journalist in a corner
with a soap star and at another table, four men I felt fairly sure were CIA
and Secret Service. I knew enough by now to recognize them. At another
table was a group of three men with the look of successful drug dealers.
Drug dealers were thriving. Their livelihoods had always depended on smuggling. They knew the dodges and they knew the routes. I even had a client
who had given up dealing in drugs and started bringing in petrol. He'd been
caught coming up from the south coast in, believe it or not, a stolen petrol
tanker. He was very indignant. His view was that he'd given up the drugs
trade to deal in a legal commodity – and now, for the first time, he'd been
arrested.

Everyone in the restaurant looked as if they were doing all right. I felt
uneasy about sitting among these powerful, wealthy people. They weren't
suffering; they were the kind who never will. But the rest of us were.
My husband Sam and I were buying vitamin pills with our own money
to hand out to his patients and their children. I learned there and then
that however bad things are there are always smart, expensive restaurants
and people with the money to enjoy them.

The restaurant's owner, Jack Prentiss, was in charge, working with the
manager, the old man who must have been William Frith's predecessor,
now called back into service. The Miss Bonners had gone, retired it was
said, and in their place were some delightful, glossy-haired, straight-
toothed young American women, generally believed to be spies. I had

spoken several times to Harry but I'd never actually met him. He was
grey-faced and worn-looking. Running a restaurant in these hard times
must have been no joke. Presumably this was another area where the
drug-dealers – or former drug-dealers – came in. On the supply side.

Harry came over, wished Gott a happy birthday, and introductions
were made. Hearing my name, he asked me if I'd had any news about
William. I said that Lucy had sent me a postcard about a fortnight ago.

'He's getting better,' I told Harry. 'And thanks for what you did.'

'Thanks for what *you* did,' he replied. But I was never sure what I'd done
or not done in that awful affair. And I was still haunted by the fate of Jemal.

'Tell William if he ever comes back he can have his job back.'

'I don't think they'll ever come back,' I told Harry.

'Never say never,' he said, and wishing Gott happy birthday again he
went off.

'You know William Frith?' said Thomas Wickham, the man sitting next
to me. He looked a little surprised. I am a woman in my fifties and had
been thickening round the waist until the food shortages kicked in; I wash
my hair with whatever I can get – my hands are rough because the hot
water is normally cold. I look tired. I don't look important. He was probably wondering why I was there at all. I knew, though, that Wickham was
a high up at the Ministry of Fear, as we learnt to call the Home Office.
A lot of people – and I'm one of them – wouldn't have invited him to
any party, let alone their birthday party, but he and Gott had grown up
together and perhaps that was the reason. I suppose, like many a func-
tionary before him, he was a good husband and kind to his dog. He may
even have been one of the good guys, working within the system to miti-
gate its horrors. But, alas, how quickly these days one of the good guys
can become one of the bad guys. I couldn't help wondering what he'd
been doing that afternoon – signing an extradition order, viewing video
tapes made inside some unsuspecting person's house, assessing evidence
obtained by torture or sending someone to appear before the three judges
who preside over the more sensitive of our trials these days. And such
judges. Well, I didn't know Wickham but I had to assume he and I were
natural enemies. He either hadn't caught my name when we were introduced or hadn't made the connection when he heard it. I was burning
with rage. I was remembering the skeletal William Frith, weeping outside
Belmarsh, sitting mute on the verandah of his parents' house in Spain for
three months.

OK, no doubt a few years ago Gott's old friend, Thomas Wickham,
was going quietly about his business at the Home Office, trying to make
ID cards work efficiently or writing a paper on the rehabilitation of
offenders in prison. But now he was probably covering up torture in the
same prisons and arming the Auxiliary Police. He had ended up as part

of the civil wing of an oppressive government and I had ended up fighting it. Yet if you'd asked either of us two years before whether that was what we wanted, we would both, I'm sure, have said no. That is what decisions by the powerful and unrestrained really mean – that ordinary people are swept away by the currents and end up where they don't want to be. But however easy it was to go along with orders from on high, and however hard it might have been to refuse, there was Amina Sharif, for example, who had given birth to a dead baby on the floor of a cell while in police custody after the whole family were scooped up in a police raid – and Nasruddin Faisal whose only crime appeared to be that he was a sixteen-year-old down by the canal on a bike at one thirty in the morning. But whatever he'd been doing there, no one knew where he was now, or if he was dead or alive.

John Stafford is still fighting for his soldiers who, along with Jemal and the other men captured after Hamscott Common, have disappeared into the American justice system without trace. Lawyers, friends and family are struggling to get them back, but the fight is hard and the outcome uncertain.

The man I was talking to, Thomas Wickham, was part of all that. Just another example of how life distorts under occupation.

So, 'You know William Frith?' he asked.

I wasn't going to cause a problem at Gott's birthday party. 'My father runs a small hotel in the small town where William Frith's parents live,' I said carefully. 'William and his wife went over there when he was released from prison.' My father was still hoping William would go in with him and help him expand the hotel, but he told me he didn't think that would happen soon, if at all. Even now, William was fragile. I never found out exactly what they did to him in prison. Perhaps Lucy knew.

'Father in Spain,' said Wickham alertly. 'So I suppose you can get over there from time to time.'

Because of the shortage of diesel fuel, foreign travel was confined to business people and, on compassionate grounds, to those with relatives abroad. Medical certificates or letters from religious leaders were required for these trips – astonishing, my husband said, how many people he got in his surgery with urgent family reasons for visiting relatives in Australia, Grenada or Italy. Always somewhere warm, Sam said. Never have so many relatives abroad suffered so many serious illnesses and mental breakdowns.

I agreed with Wickham that my position was useful although actually I was luckier than that. If I wanted to go to Spain I wrote to the Home Office and said I had to see my client, William Frith; a fiction, really, for he no longer needed representation. They never dared refuse me.

Looking at the menu the waiter had handed me, I was excited. Soup (unspecified) it said. Cod with herb sauce. Ragout of lamb. Sorbet. Four courses! And, triumphantly at the bottom – cake! The soup arrived and it was good. Chloe was giggling with one of Gott's sons. Julia and Joshua, though talking to others, Julia to Gott and Joshua to Macready, were holding hands under the table.

Wickham was looking at me steadily now and then said suddenly, 'You were the lawyer responsible for William Frith's defence.' His tone was hard and I was frightened. As my defence of William went on, and the surveillance on me had increased, I had become more and more afraid of being killed by one of those cliché-figures, some 'rogue element in the security services'. Or of ending up in a women's prison in Texas. The fear now returned, just because of sitting at a table with Wickham, hearing his voice, seeing the look in his eyes.

I nodded and agreed, 'Yes, I was.' He dropped his eyes and said no more. The Frith case was a sore point, evidently, but I didn't know why. Didn't want to.

Macready stood up to propose a toast and we all cheered. Wickham and I didn't speak from then on. We ate our meal, and during it many people came up with congratulations. Gott was popular. And finally we cut the cake, had a glass of champagne each, and then most of us – the Wickhams, mercifully, left after the meal – went back to Gott's house. His chauffeur drove quietly through dark and silent streets. Because of the oil shortage Gott was doing pretty well out of his fuel cell car business. He'd put everything he had and some of Haver's money into a new plant and started a twenty-four-hour-a-day production line. That and his investment switches had bought him a very big house in Upper Berkeley Street, once the property of a big supermarket baron whose firm was on the brink of bankruptcy as a result of the food shortages caused by European sanctions. Gott's neighbours were, on one side, the Commission for European Security and Democracy, which was bankrolled from the US, and on the other a wealthy Syrian in exile who was believed to be the US nominee for Syrian President, when and if Syria fell under American control. Inside the ring of steel extending for half a mile around the US Embassy in Grosvenor Square, the neighbourhood where Gott lived was an American enclave. His neighbours can't have wanted him there but, as he said, they would be watching him anyway, so why not make it easier for them – though if he had a lawn someone would no doubt have burnt a fiery cross on it. Anyway, inside the cordon, Gott lived in (comparative) luxury.

We had to be admitted to the area by armed soldiers at the check-point in Park Lane. But even Gott could not override the electricity cuts – we settled in his drawing room, close to a bright fire. Two branched candelabra, perched at either end of a marble fireplace, provided light. We sat in peaceful silence while below, in the street, there was little sound. A car passed. There was the sound of marching feet – patrolling soldiers. Then silence again until, from somewhere in the distance, a piano began to play – Bach, perhaps. But this far-off sound was drowned out by the noise of a surveillance helicopter overhead. A great shaft of light startled us when its beam came, full on, into the windows of the room, then moved on. With that reminder of who we were and where we were, we began to talk. Gott produced a bottle of Courvoisier and we congratulated him as if he'd scored a winning goal in the last minute of a World Cup match.

Chloe played the piano. That evening we had light, warmth and music and were happy. I didn't join in the conversation, just let the voices wash over me, listened to Chloe's music and thought long thoughts. Only two years earlier we had been able to wake up looking forward to more of the same – another hung Parliament, another bit of DIY on the bathroom, another trip to the supermarket, another commute to work – and now we were cold, hungry and poor, trapped in the confines of our small island, pitied by our neighbours and occupied by our ally, the one with whom we had that 'special relationship'. Even the rich who had stayed were poor now. Of course, they could buy scarce commodities one way or the other and pay doctors to provide them with the documentation to take a holiday in France or Italy but this only alleviated a basic state of deprivation.

What was happening in people's minds I don't know. We can't judge the collective mind – there isn't one. What we can see is what is happening to people and, more particularly, the people we know – William, slowly recovering from harsh imprisonment; Chloe, bringing up her child in Brighton while his father is in jail. (Keith was a travel agent and when travel became out of the question he turned his experience and contacts to good use, got involved in smuggling and was caught.) People were certainly waiting for the next election, in three years' time, when they would get their chance to throw out Alan Petherbridge. No donations to the Conservative Party would save him this time. The Labour Party, with Mark Moreno as leader, would have one object, to get the Yanks out. They'd even promised a Constitution. Even the Queen was said to be in favour.

Looking round the circle of faces, on which the firelight flickered, I saw the toll the past two years had taken. And wondered how many of us, like me, were asking that question, that serious question, the question we ask when shattered and bewildered by events – how did we get from a place of safety to here? And will we ever be able to go back?

Gott said comfortably, 'Well – we don't want them to be here – and God knows, the Yanks don't want to be any more either. They need their army for the war in Iraq. They're shocked by the hostility against their troops here. Their men don't like firing on people who look and sound like them. They're plundering the public funds as much as they can, but their bases here are costing them money, they're using contractors to fight in Iraq, and that's costing them, too. With the sanctions, no one is making any money. The Chinese don't like the prospect of a dollar–sterling alliance, so they're making noises about the US repaying its debts to them, which will put America close to bankruptcy. America has done what businesses do when it's expand or go under, but it's not working out that well. Most things,' said Gott the banker, 'come down to money in the end.'

'What do they want with a small, pointless island far from home? Which is what a lot of them are already thinking. Their liberals don't like occupying a friendly democracy. And their conservatives have found out they're paying for what remains of our welfare system, including a free health system they haven't got themselves – and abortions. Our only asset is military and as an aid in waging the unclear "war on terror".'

'Most of us don't want them here and most of them don't want us, but they're afraid to let us go.' There was a silence. Everyone knew Gott's words would be overheard. The long-range listening devices can cover half a mile and there are few places in cities where anyone feels safe to speak.

'There has to be an election in three years,' said Julia. 'It'll be us, under Moreno. No question.' And this was true. Moreno would lead his party towards a victory in the next election and then begin his opposition to the occupation. We should have felt like prisoners with a release date in sight but, and I don't know about the others, I didn't.

'If the Yanks don't want an election, there won't be an election,' Chloe said with certainty.

'I wouldn't put it exactly like that, myself,' her father said. 'It's just that if there's an election, they'll want it to give them what they want.'

There was a riot that night. We had just gone back through the checkpoint when the barrier across the street was flung open and soldiers began to clatter through. A tank followed after. We could hear the firing a quarter of a mile off. Hear screaming and shouts above the clatter of the helicopters ordered up and now driving like mad, giant bees in the direction of Trafalgar Square.

'That's the evening wrecked,' Chloe observed. I was too unhappy to speak. And, next day, it was announced that Mark Moreno was dead.

The future Labour leader had been found on a pavement in a narrow street near King's Cross Station. He had been stabbed several times. Reporting the crime, the police added that Mark Moreno had two previous warnings for kerb crawling in the area, always notorious for its on-the-street prostitutes. Moreno's wife denied this. She claimed that he had been assassinated.

The following day, before it was light, Joshua Crane and Edward Gott met by the lake in Victoria Park, Hackney. I had picked them up in Sam's car. We had not detected any following vehicles on the near-empty roads from central London at dawn. We hoped we hadn't been seen and weren't now being overheard. But we couldn't be sure. Gott and Joshua stood looking out over the water at the lawns and trees beyond. Birds were loud, sweet and busy.

'Do you believe this kerb-crawling story?' Gott said.

'Of course not,' Joshua said. 'That's not the question. The question is, who did it?'

'A consortium of people who want to maintain the occupation,' Gott said. 'I've heard rumours there's evidence Moreno was killed elsewhere and his body dumped where it was found. I've had Jeremy out since 4 a.m. talking to the whores, pimps, pushers and users in the area, lucky boy.'

'Let's hope he finds some public-spirited low-life who's prepared to come forward and say what they saw. This is bad, Edward. Very bad. It's an assassination and who's next?'

'Moreno came to me in January, wanting information to use to impeach Petherbridge. I pushed him off. I told him it was too soon.'

'How could you have guessed . . .?'

'Perhaps I should have guessed,' Gott said. 'But there's a harmless man dead now and we can't turn back the clock. I don't think we can wait for some sodding election now, as if we were back in the 1980s. Do that, and either you and I are dead, or we'll all end up serfs, or there'll be a bloody revolution. Or all three.'

A slender strip of red was showing all along the eastern horizon. Two ducks landed, *splock*, on the lake.

'A lot of Americans want to get out,' Gott added.

'And a lot want to stay. Mark Moreno's widow'll confirm that.'

'We impeach Petherbridge now,' declared Gott.

'That's what I've been thinking,' Joshua said. 'Is it allowed under the Civil Contingencies Act?'

'Only because they didn't think of it,' Gott told him. 'But we have to do it fast.'

'A tribute to Moreno. He was a pain in the arse, but I liked him,' Crane said.

'Well let's act, or they'll be saying that about you. We can't wait for the election. We have to impeach Petherbridge. And succeed.' Gott began to count on his fingers. 'There's the money he took to buy the election. I've got all the details on record. Maybe we'll be able to turn up something about Moreno's death. It was a mistake to dump him so close to an American base, in an area where there are eyes and ears open day and night. Then I'm going to reveal the existence of the stolen tactical nuclear weapon from Hamscott Common.'

'The what?' Joshua exclaimed.

'Later,' said Gott. 'On top of that, I know some very nasty things about Petherbridge's childhood. That'll come in handy now. We'll combine an impeccable legal position with dirty details. Impeach him – get him – then a vote of no confidence. We *will* win. We have to – there's no choice.'

I know what they said, because they told me afterwards. I'd picked them up outside Victoria Station earlier, when it was still dark, and driven them here in my own car. This was an attempt, probably futile, to evade the omnipresent surveillance.

I leaned against a tree, watching the menfolk conferring on serious matters of state – I was tired and afraid. My own name was on a list somewhere, low down, below the fold in the paper. And who could tell, with the US armoured trucks in the streets, constant overflying by planes and helicopters, armed bases everywhere – who could tell if this could be solved by meetings, speeches, declarations, Acts of Parliament, legal judgements from the bench – who could tell if in the end it wouldn't come down to blood, not words?

Some were getting jobs and money from the occupation, some wanted to resist. A guerilla war is all too often a civil war. If it came, it would be an urban war, fought in streets, not through fields or mountains. It would split families and fill hospitals. The country would be torn, anguished, and men, women and children would die indiscriminately.

I saw a police car parked behind my vehicle now and walked over the grass to tell Joshua and Gott that it was there. I'd overheard the last part of the conversation and I said, 'What if Petherbridge won't let you impeach him? He's got an army now.'

There was a silence. 'We can't stop now. It's do or die,' said Joshua. There was another pause.

'Who could ask for anything better?' said Lord Gott.

Then we all walked, not unobserved, over the grass as the sky lightened.